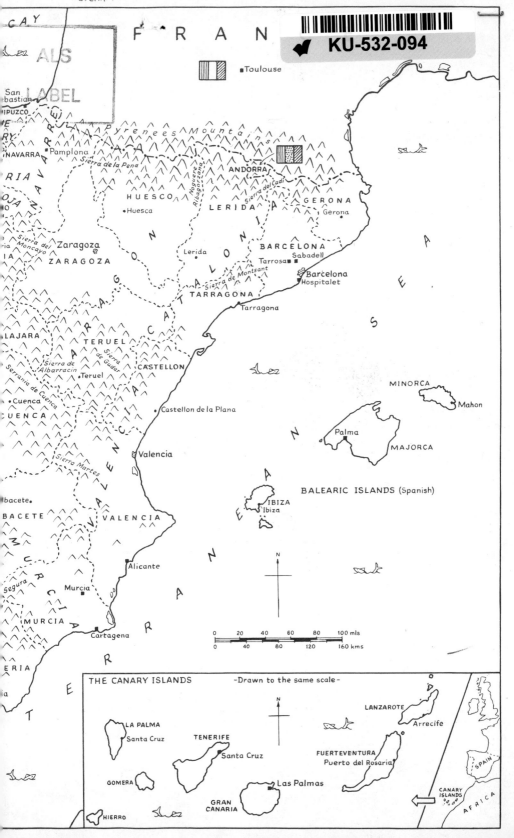

-O.JAN

F R A N C E

CAY

ALS

LABEL

San Sebastian

IPUZCO

NAVARRA   Pamplona

Sierra de la Peña

Pyrenees Mountains

Toulouse

ANDORRA

HUESCO

Noguera Ribagorzona

LERIDA

Sierra del Cadí

GERONA

Huesca

Lerida

Gerona

Sierra del Moncayo

Zaragoza

ZARAGOZA

CATALONIA

BARCELONA

Tarrosa   Sabadell

Sierra de Montsant

Barcelona
Hospitalet

TARRAGONA

Tarragona

A   R   A   G   O   N

LAJARA

TERUEL

Sierra de Guadar

Sierra de Albarracin

Serrania de Cuenca

Cuenca

CUENCA

Teruel

CASTELLON

Castellon de la Plana

VALENCIA

Sierra Martes

Valencia

S   E   A

MINORCA

Mahon

Palma

MAJORCA

BALEARIC ISLANDS (Spanish)

IBIZA
Ibiza

bacete

BACETE

VALENCIA

N

MURCIA

Segura

Murcia

Alicante

MURCIA

Cartagena

ERIA

M   E   D   I   T   E   R   R   A   N   E   A   N

N

0   20   40   60   80   100 mls
0   40   80   120   160 kms

THE CANARY ISLANDS   -Drawn to the same scale-

N

LA PALMA
Santa Cruz

TENERIFE

Santa Cruz

GOMERA

HIERRO

GRAN
CANARIA

Las Palmas

LANZAROTE

Arrecife

FUERTEVENTURA
Puerto del Rosaria

SPAIN

CANARY
ISLANDS

AFRICA

SPAIN
Change of a Nation

Also by Robert Graham
Iran: Illusion of Power

SPAIN
Change of a Nation

ROBERT GRAHAM

MICHAEL JOSEPH

For Chloe

First published in Great Britain by Michael Joseph Ltd
44 Bedford Square, London WC1
1984

© Robert Graham 1984

British Library Cataloguing in Publication Data

Graham, Robert, *1942-*
  Spain
  1. Spain — Handbooks, manuals, etc.
  I. Title
  914.6'0483   DP17

  ISBN 0 7181 2359 X

Typeset by Alacrity Phototypesetters, Banwell Castle, Avon.
Printed and bound in Great Britain by
Billing and Sons Ltd, Worcester

The publishers would like to thank André Deutsch Ltd for
permission to reproduce an extract from *As I walked out one
midsummer's morning* by Laurie Lee, and Cambridge
University Press for an extract from *The Literature of the
Spanish People* by Gerald Brenan.

Contents

CONTENTS

Foreword

This book is the fruit of having lived and worked in Spain for over five years as correspondent of the *Financial Times*. It is an attempt to answer some of the many questions I found myself asking on arrival in 1977. I knew little about the country other than what had happened in the Civil War and the dominance of Franco ever since. Searching around for literature, I discovered there were essentially two categories of books: a wealth of publications on the Civil War in all its minutiae and a second collection dealing with folklore and travel. The long period of Franco's rule was virtually ignored as if an embarrassment — while the folkloric image of Spain persisted despite the profound social and economic changes that had occurred from the mid-fifties onwards. This period, culminating in the remarkable metamorphosis from Francoism to democracy, will prove, I am convinced, a key era in Spain's long history.

In no sense is this book intended as a history of the period. Rather, it is a commentary and an analysis, seeking to explain the evolution of modern Spanish society. Spaniards are not given to writing memoirs and they have a deep-rooted fear of baring the truth. Since 1980, books have begun to emerge on this period, mostly written by Spaniards, which too often are self-seeking and partial. I have relied on published information, my own interviews and access to private archives whose owners still prefer to remain anonymous. I may be guilty of errors of judgement but I hope that even these will stimulate a better understanding of a much misunderstood nation which has lived far too long on the margin of Europe.

Of all the countries in which I have worked as a correspondent, I have never been treated so correctly or encountered such genuine warmth as in Spain. One could ask no more of a host country. I would prefer to thank collectively all those who have helped form my views and provide information rather than indulge in the invidious task of naming names. But I owe a special debt to Jose Antonio Martinez Soler for offering so many provocative ideas, and to Tom Burns for constantly being so enthusiastic about this project. I would also like to thank the *Financial Times*, and in particular Geoff Owen, for providing me with a sabbatical to write this book.

Deya
July 1983

Introduction

To an outsider, the spectacle smacked of comic opera: a man with a bushy moustache wearing the quaint three-cornered hat of the Guardia Civil brandishing a pistol from the speaker's podium in the Spanish parliament. But for Spaniards on the night of 23 February 1981 it was a chilling reminder of the fragility of their democratic system, little more than five years old at the time.

The man in the three-cornered hat was Colonel Antonio Tejero, a garrulous bigot who believed that the old order was being betrayed and that Spain, since the death of Generalissimo Francisco Franco in 1975, had gone to the dogs. Just before 6.30 pm, Tejero with a small group of the paramilitary Guardia Civil burst boldly in on an astonished parliament in full session. Firing intimidating rounds that ripped into the ceiling and visitors' gallery, Tejero quickly had the entire government and opposition at his mercy. Most of the deputies had ducked for safety below their seats. Courageously, the Deputy Prime Minister, Manuel Gutierrez Mellado, got up to challenge the rebels; but this veteran general, hated by the right for trying to modernise the armed forces, was ignominiously man-handled back to his seat. Parliament was held hostage at gun-point. Tejero settled down to wait, confident that Spain would soon be governed by a military junta.

Parliament had been voting on a confidence motion and the session was being broadcast on radio. The whole incident had been heard live and caught on camera. Within an hour Madrid's normally busy streets were nearly deserted. People hurried home to tune into the radio and television. An apprehensive silence engulfed the capital and all the major cities, as memories of the Civil War revived. Union leaders and left-wing activists began to consider safe houses. In the Basque country a steady stream of cars began to cross the frontier into France. Over 25,000 cars left Spain that night, cleaning out the petrol stations of their supplies and exhausting all the bank cashpoints in the border area.

The government was taken over by an emergency cabinet of senior civil servants, co-ordinating with the loyal joint chiefs of staff of the armed forces. But it was King Juan Carlos who took command. When parliament was seized he was dressed in a track-suit, just having returned from exercise. He quickly changed into the blue uniform of Captain General of the armed

1

forces, and began an urgent series of calls to check on the loyalty of his soldiers. His lonely vigil lasted nearly until dawn.

In Valencia, headquarters of the third military region, its commander, General Jaime Milans del Bosch, ordered tanks onto the streets and proclaimed martial law. Milans del Bosch, one of the most highly decorated officers in the Army, had 3,500 men under his command. Counting on his prestige and friendship with the other eight regional military commanders, Milans del Bosch expected the armed forces to rally round him and install a government of national reconciliation which would save Spain from the decadence of democracy. His ally in Madrid was a mild-mannered aristocrat, General Alfonso Armada, who had long nursed ambitions of heading such a government. Armada was to be the acceptable face of the coup. He had been head of the royal military household, and was a godson of Alfonso XIII, the King's grandfather. Armada was expected to persuade the King to back the rebels.

The King's position was like being on the losing side in a disastrous game of chess. The rebels (black) had taken all the pieces save the King and a few pawns. He won out by insisting that either the game be stopped or they wipe him off the board. Several key army commanders wavered in their support but, in the end, none save Milans del Bosch were prepared to play for stakes so high that they risked nothing short of civil war. Armada, when faced with this prospect and the King's round rejection of the use of force, at first vacillated, then tried to conceal his involvement in the coup. The armed forces as a whole rallied behind the King, their captain general. By the early hours of the morning, Tejero's confident expectation of widespread support had evaporated. Milans del Bosch's pleas to his colleagues had fallen on largely deaf ears; he finally conceded the fruitlessness of his enterprise and called his troops back to barracks before dawn. At this turn of events, Tejero put on a truculent face and grandly negotiated his own fate and the release of his parliamentary hostages. All the non-officers who took part in the seizure of parliament were allowed to go free, while he was permitted to leave in a Guardia Civil car without handcuffs. As he left he said nonchalantly: 'I'll get thirty years for this.' And he did.

This account simplifies the highly complex events of the night of 23/24 February, but it is widely agreed that during the course of the coup King Juan Carlos was solitary and desperately exposed. That there was no bloodshed was partly luck, and partly due to the plotters' erroneous belief that the King would not oppose the coup. No previous Spanish monarch had defied rebel officers in this way. Alfonso XIII had, after all, accepted the bloodless uprising in Catalonia of General Miguel Primo de Rivera. The King was no doubt mindful that this helped seal the fate of his grandfather as a constitutional monarch, forced into exile at the onset of the Republic in 1930. More immediately, King Juan Carlos had only to consider the example of his brother-in-law, King Constantine of Greece, ousted from the throne by the military.

2

When parliament met forty-eight hours after the coup to renew the session so rudely interrupted, never had the chamber heard such heartfelt shouts of *Viva el Rey!* King Juan Carlos had won over even the staunchest republicans. Indeed it was ironic that those who congratulated the King most fervently were precisely the same people who had once been most republican. They realised that the King had proved the ultimate guarantor not only of democracy but also of their lives. This was a remarkable personal achievement for King Juan Carlos, in a country with a strong vein of republicanism and where monarchy as an institution had hardly distinguished itself over the centuries.

The 23 February coup was an amalgam of three separate plots being considered in early 1981. Tejero planned a hardline approach in the style of the Turkish generals, and, if necessary, expected that junior officers would go against their natural commanders to install a military junta. Given the rigid adherence of the Spanish armed forces to the chain of command, this risked opening up dangerous divisions in the military. A second plot, favoured by Milans del Bosch envisaged a military government under the aegis of the King, to give it legitimacy. The third plot centred round Armada and aimed for a government of national salvation that contained civilian and military figures, again backed by the King.

These separate initiatives coalesced — though why they should have done is still far from clear. Impatience played an important part. Tejero, in particular, could not be restrained, and rather than let him go it alone, and perhaps spoil the chances of others, they all threw in their lot. This meant that the coup was improvised, and that the three principal protagonists — Armada, Milans del Bosch and Tejero — continued to have differing aims. The disparate nature of the coup was one of the reasons for its failure. Tejero admitted disarmingly at his trial that he originally planned to seize parliament on a Friday but could not guarantee rounding up enough friends and recruits because they went away at the week-end. Happily, in Spain holidays take precedence over coups.

But the most important reason for the coup's failure was that the plotters' miscalculated the extent of their support within the armed forces and the firmness of the King's opposition. They assumed that disaffection with democracy among the military — caused by squabbling within the government, terrorist violence, and what they regarded as the looser morality of democratic Spain — could be converted into support for the overthrow of a legally constituted government. Carried away by their own rectitude and crusading zeal, they failed to see that their friends and potential sympathizers might not agree. Sufficient senior officers either endorsed democracy or were unwilling to risk opposing King and constitution. At a more human level, a number of generals got cold feet at the last moment when faced with the consequences of supporting the coup. Tejero was not entirely wrong when at the end of his court martial he said in an angry aside that many in the armed forces were cowards, lacking the courage of their convictions.

Complacent of their success the plotters had no fall-back position or alternative strategy. When the King refused to support the coup and told Milans del Bosch to withdraw his troops from the streets of Valencia, there was only one alternative — get rid of the King. Milans del Bosch either never contemplated such a possibility or was unwilling to carry it out. Besides, by the time the plotters realised that the King would not support them, it was too late to consider other options.

The plotters showed a cavalier disregard for the importance of the media in a democratic system. Thanks to the presence of radio reporters, cameramen, and TV crews in parliament when it was seized, public opinion was immediately informed and could make up its own mind about the events that were taking place. Radio, in particular, helped to decide public opinion against the rebels.

When the thirty-two principal plotters were brought before a court martial in 1982 they emerged as an unimpressive bunch, despite the fact that several had illustrious military careers. Behind the ringing phrases were not the saviours of Spain but a group of vain, arrogant improvisors incapable of running the country and unafraid to lie to prove their innocence. The most implausible untruth came from Colonel Antonio Machado, in charge of the Guardia Civil traffic depot in Madrid where Tejero recruited the troops to storm parliament. He insisted he knew nothing of Tejero's plans. When summoned to explain himself by the head of the Guardia Civil just after parliament had been seized, he said he was late arriving because of the traffic and his strict observance of traffic signals! This prompted the comment that in order to prevent another coup, it was only necessary to turn the traffic lights red.

In the end the most significant aspect of the coup was not that it happened, but that it failed. Spaniards may have been embarrassed by the banana-republic image of a pistol-waving Tejero in parliament that flashed round the world, but the trauma of the coup also shocked them into realizing the benefits of the democratic system they were trying to build. Moreover, Spanish society of the eighties was in no mood for military government. Spain had changed profoundly during the long years of Franco's authoritarian rule. Those who wished to turn the clock back were a nostalgic minority.

Part One

FRANCO AND THE NATURE OF SPAIN

1 Metamorphosis of Francoism

The coup of 23 February was carried out by men whose attitudes and sense of their own importance was very much a throwback to the days of Franco, when the military were a pillar of state, and accountable to no-one but the Caudillo himself. But even before the death of Franco, the people of Spain had begun to outgrow, both politically and economically, the regime of the old dictator. By the end, the regime was out of touch with the exigencies of modern Spain and incapable of competent government.

Bad news under the Franco regime was either suppressed or dressed up in the most anodyne form for popular consumption. On the morning of 20 December 1973, the authorities were hard pressed to cope: the Prime Minister, Admiral Luis Carrero Blanco, Franco's closest collaborator for thirty-two years, had been assassinated in the centre of Madrid.

'This morning there was a big explosion in the Salamanca area of Madrid which caused various personal injuries. The cause of the explosion is not yet known ... ' Thus began, three hours after the event, the laconic first official recognition of the incident.[1] Carrero Blanco had just attended morning mass and was on his way to his office when a massive explosive charge placed beneath the road was detonated. The blast blew the Prime Minister's specially armour-plated Dodge fifteen metres in the air; the Dodge clipped a parapet of the church of San Francisco de Borja and landed in a courtyard. The chauffeur and bodyguard were killed instantly. Carrero Blanco was dead on arrival at hospital. The explosion was so powerful that it ripped a hole in the street, Claudio Coello, ten metres by seven. Water from the burst mains which gradually filled this crater was symbolic of the tide closing in on the end of an era.

The assassination had been carried out by a commando of the militant Basque separatist organization, Euskadi Ta Askatasuna, (ETA). The commando group, codenamed 'Txikia', had spent more than six months preparing for the attack. Originally, the plan had been to kidnap Carrero Blanco and bargain for the release of Basque prisoners. However, it had changed in June, when Carrero Blanco was appointed Prime Minister and his bodyguard strengthened.[2]

Not since the end of the Civil War in 1939 had there been such a bold attack successfully aimed at the very heart of the Franco regime. Overtaken by sheer age rather than ill-health, Generalissimo Francisco Franco had delegated the daily business of government more and more to his faithful aide. By separating the roles of head of state and head of government in 1973, devolving the latter on Carrero Blanco, Franco had entrusted the fate of the nation to the man most likely to keep Spain on the path of unity, adherence to Catholic values and respect for the inheritance of the nationalist 'victory' in the Civil War. Carrero Blanco, though himself aged seventy, stood as guarantor of all this. He would also guide the young Crown Prince, Don Juan Carlos, Franco's designated heir. Carrero Blanco had played an important co-ordinating role in the long years of discussions between Franco and the Prince's father, Don Juan Borbon, exiled in Estoril in Portugal. The law laying down the rules of succession had been drawn up by Carrero Blanco. But the admiral envisaged the monarchy as ruling over a Spain that was 'Catholic, anti-communist, anti-liberal and free of all foreign tutelage in domestic and foreign affairs'.[3] This undemocratic view of monarchy was in total contrast to what subsequently emerged.

It is academic to speculate now what would have happened if Carrero Blanco had survived. But undoubtedly this act of political violence helped push Spain's future away from continued authoritarianism towards democracy. Ironically, ETA, the organization responsible, derived little benefit. Their action then, and subsequently, has been based on the strategy of provoking the authorities into repressive action to sustain support among the Basque people. Encouraging a democracy was the last thing ETA wanted.[4]

SEEDS OF CHANGE

The evolution of Spanish democracy has been given the shorthand term 'transition'. For some, this transition began with the death of Franco on 20 November 1975 and ended with the promulgation of the nationally endorsed constitution in December 1978 and the ensuing general election in March 1979, complemented by municipal elections a month later. A more clear-cut end was the landslide victory of the Socialist Party under Felipe Gonzalez in the October 1982 election — permitting the first government of the left since the outbreak of the Civil War in 1936.

Yet in many respects the constituent process of democracy continues; and equally the transition did not really begin with Franco's death. Indeed, it is only possible to understand this process if it is defined as the metamorphosis of Francoism: the gradual transformation of an authoritarian regime into a parliamentary democracy.

The seeds of change were sown in the late fifties and early sixties. The vital period was 1956-62, when the regime was obliged to come to terms with a fundamental conflict in the nature and aims of government. How could a

8

repressive political system with a rigid hierarchy of command, obsessed by stability, promote rapid economic development and increased material well-being without being influenced by closer contact with the democracies of western Europe?

In one sense, the answer provided itself. The immediate post-Civil War years had been ones of great hardship and hunger. By the mid-fifties, Franco had fully established his authority and his credibility depended in good measure on being able to improve living standards. This could not be done by continuing the creaking policies of tight economic control and blanket protectionism. The way pointed to a liberalization of the economy, an opening-up to attract foreign capital and technology. With the opposition disunited the regime was confident enough to do this. The diplomatic isolation which the Franco dictatorship had forced on Spain was broken.

The change in approach was evident in the cabinet reshuffle of 1957, with the introduction of technocrats to run the key economic portfolios which had previously been run by ageing and incompetent ministers. The Stabilization Plan of 1959 formalized this change, setting Spain almost irreversibly on the path of a modern market-orientated economy that provided the basis for unprecedented material well-being. The making of Spain's long-absent middle class had begun. Accompanying economic and social change was a slight lifting of the lid on political attitudes, with greater tolerance of non-establishment and nationalist views. Serious efforts were made to attract Spanish exiles to return. Few policies were well planned or clearly defined. For the most part, the regime adapted to circumstance.

A brief survey of some of the events of this period puts in context the trends set in motion. The generation of students who went up to university in 1956 had no direct memory of the Civil War. They were the first to begin serious mobilization against the regime, laying the groundwork for the universities to become one of the principal bases of anti-Franco activity. The student activists of 1956 were to be the political protagonists of democracy twenty years later.[5] The frustrations of low wages among the same generation in the workforce led to the formation of the first new illegal trades union movement — the Workers Commissions — in the Asturian coalmine of La Camocha in 1958. One of the subsequent leading trades union figures, Marcelino Camacho of the Workers Commissions, had been given a passport to return from political exile in 1957.

The same stirrings were evident in the Basque nationalist movement. In 1959, a radical group within the Basque Nationalist Party, rejecting the latter's conservatism, broke away to form ETA — pledged to declare war on the Spanish state to achieve independence for their region.

In the arts, the pessimism that had characterized the post-Civil War years gave way to a bitter realism. A breakthrough occurred in 1955, when Juan Bardem's film *Muerte de un Ciclista*, got past the censors. The film shows the huge divide between the corrupt world of the new rich and the sufferings of the impoverished working class. A poor cyclist is killed in a car accident by a wealthy industrialist's wife and her university-teacher lover. The accident forces the teacher to open his eyes to the real state of Spain, represented by the world of the cyclist. In another development, the authorities, though totally hostile to Picasso's communism, nevertheless sent a delegation to seek a reconciliation with the painter in 1956. The mission failed, but the gesture was the first attempt to end Spain's international cultural isolation.

The Church hierarchy did not make significant moves until after the Vatican Council II in 1962. But well before that parish priests had begun to preach the voice of change. Worker priests were important in the clandestine trades union movement. At the same time, Catholicism was the cover under which the first reforming movement in the armed forces had operated. The movement, Forja, was banned in 1958, but in 1972 some of its principal adherents founded the Democratic Officers Movement (UMD).

It was during this period that the principal companies and banks that now dominate Spain began to grow and develop. For instance, the department-store group El Corte Ingles expanded out of Madrid, catering to the nascent provincial bourgeoisie. Spain's youth took to jeans, establishing the success of one of Spain's most prosperous entrepreneurs, Joaquin Saez Merino.

All these advances were capped by the advent of the most powerful of all media — the television. The introduction of the state-run television service in 1956 was a revolutionary opening of horizons for most Spaniards — even if the quality of programmes and the medium's political control left much to be desired.

REARGUARD ACTION

Together these developments and trends established a momentum of social and economic change which no one person, or group of persons, could control. When it felt threatened or confused, the regime reacted with bouts of repression; but the momentum was only obstructed or slowed — never halted. Those reactionary to change, the *imovilistas*, failed to hold their ground. Their unity was based entirely on a common agreement about what they did not want. They had no formula to offer a fast-evolving society, and could mobilize no wide popular support because they were swimming against the tide.

In addition their leader, Franco, was grounded in common sense. He had no wish to identify openly with one particular group in the ruling elite. Franco was credited with having two big files on his desk, one labelled 'problems solved with time', the other 'problems which time will solve'. In later years, he was reluctant to take decisions or even take the lead. His assertions of authority became increasingly spasmodic. Thus, while the reactionary

10

elements still held all key positions in the armed forces, the intelligence services, and the security forces, and had a blocking position inside the Movimiento — the political and ideological apparatus of Francoism — their power was more apparent than real.

Those who resisted even minimal liberalization nevertheless acquiesced in Franco's decision to formalize the succession of the Borbon dynasty in the person of Prince Juan Carlos. Even the anti-monarchist element among Franco's supporters were appeased by the docility of the young Prince's acceptance of the tenets of the regime. In retrospect, the belief that the monarchy would follow faithfully in Franco's footsteps was remarkably short-sighted. The only way the monarchy could establish its legitimacy was through reconciliation with republican elements of the population oppressed by Franco. The divisions created by the nationalist Civil War victory, the cornerstone of Franco's authority, had to disappear.

A landmark demonstrating the weakening grip of the old guard came in December 1970. Franco decided to commute the death sentences on six members of ETA who had been put on trial in Burgos with twelve others for belonging to the illegal organization. The trial had been conducted by the military amidst unprecedented international publicity. Franco bowed to pressure not only from one of his traditional pillars of support, the Church, but also from the international community — to say nothing of his divided cabinet. In the forties and fifties Franco had been immune to such pressure when far greater repression was being practised against his political opponents. For instance, in 1963, he had refused to listen to international pleas to commute the death sentence on a prominent communist militant, Julian Grimau.

The Burgos trials did not mark an end to repression. If anything, there was an intensification of opposition to Basque separatist violence, which itself became more virulent. Between 1973 and 1975, over 6,300 Basques were arrested.[6] This repression reflected insecurity rather than confidence. It was also a measure of the regime's weakness that, in 1974, a Marxist-inspired urban-guerilla movement began to emerge, the Revolutionary Anti-Fascist Patriotic Front (FRAP). Until this time, with the notable exception of the Basques, there had been no upsurge in guerilla activity since 1950, and what there was had been mostly restricted to rural areas. The regime carried out only one last act of defiance against enemies that sought to overthrow it by violence. Two months before his death, Franco ordered the execution by firing squad of two members of ETA and three belonging to FRAP. The executions provoked the temporary withdrawal of most western ambassadors from Madrid.

In the last five years of the Franco regime, attention was so keenly focussed on domestic issues that there was insufficient will to maintain the remnants of Spanish colonialism in North Africa — or to organize a considered withdrawal from the Spanish Sahara. The Spanish presence in North Africa,

11

which had once been the pride of the army, had been due in no small part to Franco's soldiering as a young man. While Franco agonized on his deathbed, the cabinet agreed to a hasty pull-out from the colony, leaving the contested ground to Morocco and the Polisario guerilla movement.

There was a curious paradox between the increasing weakness of a regime fumbling more and more with the problems that beset it, and the fact that the regime's principal architect and leader was able to die peacefully in his bed.

FRANCO AND FRANCOISM

Franco died at the ripe old age of eighty-four. To the last, he showed amazing physical stamina, surviving in the five final weeks of illness three major heart operations before succumbing to peritonitis.[7] Longevity ran in the family — his father had lived to the age of ninety-two. Unlike most of his fellow Spaniards, Franco was abstemious with drink and abhorred smoking.

The future Caudillo was born shortly after midnight on 4 December 1892 at El Ferrol in Galicia. El Ferrol was one of Spain's three principal naval bases, and for over 150 years his forbears on both sides had been connected with the administration of this base — the men were officers in the naval administrative corps and the women the wives and daughters of such officers. Franco's father, Nicolas, was a paymaster lieutenant (*contador de navio*) at the time of his marriage; while his mother, Maria del Pilar Teresa Baamonde, was the daughter of a commander in charge of naval equipment. The town, which had some 20,000 inhabitants, was sustained exclusively by the naval base and dockyard. From all accounts, it was a closed society with clear divisions between the civilian and the military at one level, and on another separated by the subtle grades of class within the military establishment itself that discriminated in particular between officers on active service and the onshore administrative corps, who were considered inferior. Franco's family enjoyed respectability and a modicum of small-town prosperity; but Franco's father was constantly causing embarrassment because of his rakish escapades with women and his virtual separation from his wife. Franco's mother, on the other hand, was deeply pious and concerned with social welfare; she was undoubtedly the stronger influence on the young Franco — and was later portrayed in Franco's autobiographical film script, *Raza* (Race), as the virtuous essence of long-suffering Spanish womanhood. The strong streak of puritanism in Franco was probably a reaction to his father's behaviour.[8]

Franco's hopes of joining the navy were dashed first by the closure of the school in El Ferrol for administrative officers and then by tighter entry requirements for naval cadetship. He was obliged to turn to the army. At the age of fifteen he enrolled in the Toledo Military Academy. This was the normal age for a future officer to embark on a professional army career, but it

12

must have had a marked effect on all the young recruits. Separated so early from civilian life, they were insulated by the deeply inculcated credo of service to God and the motherland.

Franco ceased to be an active military commander after the Civil War, but for the remainder of his life his approach to government and to life in general was that of a soldier. He insisted on using military terms to refer to his use of power — *mando* or the command — and to his position as head of state — *capitaneria*. (*Capitaneria* means more than mere captaincy since it also refers to the post of captain-general of the armed forces.) Franco's brother-in-law, Serrano Suner, observed that he had always given orders and had never had an adversary approach like that of a lawyer or a politician.[9] Incidentally, Serrano Suner, who served variously as Foreign Minister and Minister of the Interior during the immediate years after the Civil War, was one of the only people ever to exercise a strong influence over Franco. And this influence was of short duration.

Franco once said of soldiering, 'Being a soldier is the easiest of professions — one only has to learn to think with the same calmness as drinking a cup of coffee while bullets are flying about you.'[10] Behind what might appear bravado lies an important key to Franco's character. He achieved his mastery of circumstance through self-discipline. On the battlefield as a young officer in Morocco, Franco showed remarkable courage and bravery; and his reputation was such as to boost the morale of any garrison he came to relieve from the fierce Rif tribesmen. His record suggests that his was not the blind battlefield instinct which overtakes heroes; rather, it was the courage of someone who had mastered fear, who could judge events coldly and who believed firmly in the cause for which he was fighting.

Morocco at the turn of the century was the scene of Spain's last attempt to play an imperial role. The hope of diverting domestic opinion away from national politics, the lure of profitable mining concessions in the Rif mountains, and above all the need to restore some of Spain's shattered ego after the loss in 1898 of its prized colonies — Cuba and the Philippines — lay behind the Moroccan venture. Such a confusion of motives was to lead to military disaster on several occasions. The military either underestimated their formidable opponent, the rebel leader Abdel Krim, were poorly supplied, or were launched into battle to satisfy ignorant political leaders. One of the worst disasters occurred in 1920, when the Spanish army lost 14,700 dead and missing in a twelve-day battle against Abdel Krim's forces. Despite the problems of the campaign in Africa, for an unknown and poorly connected young officer, Morocco presented the best chance for quick promotion and recognition by his peers.

The disastrous loss of Cuba in 1898, deeply felt in Franco's native El Ferrol where many families with a naval background were directly affected, imbued the young soldier with a special passion. Empire in Africa offered the chance of national regeneration. Even after Spain had established control over northern Morocco in the late twenties, Franco still harboured dreams of a greater territory in North Africa. (When Franco was considering entering the Second World War on the side of the Axis powers, one of his demands from Hitler was for the right to a greater empire in North Africa.)

Franco's ambition to succeed as a soldier was probably spurred by his diminutive size. While at Toledo he had been bullied and antagonized for his smallness; he was dubbed 'Franquito'.[11] Immediately on passing out from Toledo, he had volunteered for service in Morocco. However, he had had to wait almost two frustrating years, until 1912, before he was finally allowed to go. After one year's service, he was seriously wounded in the abdomen; when first treated, he was given little chance of recovery.

Franco's courage and leadership abilities were soon noticed and promotion was rapid. Within six years he reached the rank of major. In 1920, he was selected by the then Colonel Jose Millan Astray to help form a new corps to fight in Morocco, inspired by the French Foreign Legion. It was called The Legion, and rapidly became the most efficient fighting unit of the Spanish army in Morocco. Its formidable battle-cry of 'Long live death!' ('*Viva la muerte!*') soon became both famous and feared. Franco later used this volunteer professional force to quash the revolutionary uprising in Asturias in 1934, and again to deadly effect in the Civil War. His days with The Legion were among his happiest. Indeed, during the last eighteen months of his life his doctor used the sentimental recollection of his days in The Legion to boost his morale. The doctor experimented one day by playing a tape of Legion songs. Franco, who was at the time very demoralized and suffering from phlebitis, immediately perked up and proceeded to march round his study, aided by the doctor, singing the songs. This became a frequent therapy.[12]

When the 1930 municipal elections brought in the Republicans, Franco refused to be drawn into backing monarchist officers in the army. The mood of the country, especially in the cities, was against the monarchy, and Franco supported the new republican order, albeit with caution and a certain amount of ambiguity.

However, after they had seen his brutal quelling of the revolt in Asturias spearheaded by revolutionary miners, the Republicans had no illusions about the potential danger of Franco to their cause. As a precaution, the government removed him from his post of army chief of staff to command the far-away Canaries. Franco was probably the only general capable of unifying the army against the Republic. Although pinpointed as a threat to the Republic, Franco continued to be noncommital. Serrano Suner, reflecting years later, maintained that the catalyst in Franco's decision to join the 1936 nationalist rebellion was the assassination of the monarchist Finance Minister, Jose Calvo Sotelo. Suner conjectured that, had the assassination not occurred, there would have been no uprising. As it turned out, Franco's support was vital.[13]

The nationalist uprising was planned to begin in Morocco on 17 July 1936 and to embrace the mainland the following day. Calvo Sotelo's assassination occurred on 13 July. Franco was always cautious, a winner not a gambler. On 17 July, from Tenerife in the Canaries, he issued his first manifesto, calling upon Spaniards with a 'holy love of Spain' to unite and defend her against her enemies till death. Franco then rushed in an aircraft chartered from England to join the army in Morocco. Once his troops were across the Straits of Gibraltar, he conducted a slow and deliberate campaign that culminated in his forces entering Madrid on 29 March 1939.[14] During the course of the fighting he had been appointed supreme commander — Generalissimo — and head of the nationalist state, with the title of 'Caudillo'.

THE CORPORATIST STATE

Chance had played its part in raising Franco to these exalted heights. Two days after the rebellion had begun, General Jose Sanjurjo, who was due to assume the nationalist leadership, crashed to his death in a plane carrying him to Spain from Portugal. General Emilio Mola, a key co-ordinator in the nationalist plot, also died in a plane crash — in June 1937, while going to a meeting with Franco. These deaths removed two important rivals, provoking reports, in the case of Mola, of Franco's direct responsibility. The reports were never substantiated.

Franco's position was further consolidated by the Republicans' execution of Jose Antonio Primo de Rivera, the charismatic son of the former dictator. Jose Antonio, as he was popularly known, had founded the Falange movement. His death removed a man capable of assuming the political leadership of the nationalist cause and of limiting Franco's accumulation of power.[15]

Because he was a contemporary of Hitler and Mussolini and in basic sympathy with the Axis powers' political and strategic aims, Franco has often been equated with the two dictators. Yet he differed from them in several significant ways. Hitler and Mussolini began life as 'outsiders': a driving force for both was the desire to get even with society. Franco, on the other hand, was the product of a caste.[16] His ambition was to excel as a soldier in the service of the motherland, and he came to political leadership almost, if not wholly, by chance. Hitler and Mussolini were political in their ambitions from the start.

By the time he came to power, Franco's basic philosophy was formed. On assuming the nationalist leadership in Burgos in 1937, he declared that the future state would be based on 'a broad totalitarian conception'. Its structure would be hierarchical and corporatist, allowing individuals to enjoy 'the greatest freedom within the framework of the sovereign interests of the state'.[17] It was his prerogative to determine what those sovereign interests were. Hardened by the violence and disorder of the Republic, which he

15

blamed entirely on the 'Reds', he had little doubt about the need for authoritarian rule. During the Republic's ninety-sixth-month existence, there had been thirty-three ministries, and its 11,000-word constitution had been superseded for eighty-six months by a law of public safety which abrogated personal liberties.

For him, disorder destroyed liberty; thus, order itself was a basis from which to enjoy liberty. The framework for liberty was the narrow confines of a Catholic, anti-communist, centralist state, intolerant of, and antagonistic towards, all those who supported the socialist republican experiment. The social aims of this state were uninspiringly petit bourgeois and were well articulated by Jose Antonio Giron, an early member of the fascist National Syndicalist Action Juntas (JONS) and Minister of Labour from 1941 to 1957: 'to enlarge as much as possible the middle class, to establish links between classes so as to achieve a conservative Spain with a nation of small owners, of free men who would have sufficient incentive to preserve the fruits of their endeavours'.[18]

Franco saw himself as a benevolent despot. Sir Samuel Hoare, the first British ambassador to the Franco regime, was reminded on meeting the Generalissimo of a doctor with a good bedside manner, a doctor 'with a big family practice and an assured income'.[19]

The regime established its identity early on. The democratic institutions of the Republic were abolished. The only political groupings tolerated were those that sided with the uprising — the Falange, the JONS, and the Communion of Traditionalists who were essentially conservative monarchists. These groups were husbanded into the Movimiento Nacional, which became part political organization, part ideological guardian of the regime. The Movimiento had its blue-shirt uniform, rallied to the fascist salute and used as its symbol the bunch of arrows, also identified with fascism. There was a brutal settling of accounts with those who had been even remotely connected with the republican experiment. Executions were a daily occurrence and the jails were swollen with political prisoners. Thousands died in the wave of repression that lasted for almost ten years after the end of the Civil War. The press was censored and subservient. Many aspects of life were militarized, and military justice dealt with a wide range of crimes against the regime. Power lay firmly in the hands of one person: Franco. The Spain of these early years was a fascist dictatorship.

By 1950, the worst of the repression had passed. The enemies of the regime had been physically eliminated, cowed into silence or left to the lonely hope of exile. What emerged was an authoritarian, conservative, Catholic regime, sensitive to the rivalries within the ruling elite and responsive to pressures from the opposition.[20] It had ceased to be a classic dictatorship. The regime drew its principal support from the armed forces, the Church hierarchy and the groups within the Movimiento.

The competing interests of these support groups were carefully balanced, particularly inside the cabinet. The service ministries were always occupied by the military; labour and social affairs tended to be in the hands of the Falange or JONS; foreign affairs was more often than not under the control of Catholic traditionalists; education was usually left to the Catholics. Later, when issues became more complex, Franco was pragmatic enough to introduce technocrats to his cabinet. The divide and rule policy was effective in subordinating ministers, but it meant that cabinets were never strong in themselves. Ministers were unwilling to back colleagues over policies which might incur the Caudillo's disapproval. Often, Franco's will was interpreted more zealously than he himself might have desired.

The majority of the ministers throughout Franco's thirty-six-year regime were of mediocre capacity, more concerned with the privileges of office and petty patronage than affairs of state. Franco treated them as disposable commodities, scapegoats to prevent him ever being directly associated with errors of policy. At cabinet meetings his interests were internal order, labour relations, the press, the Church and foreign affairs. Economic matters were of little interest to him, probably because he did not understand them. He was generally taciturn and a good listener. But those ministers who were inveterate smokers were unnerved by his dislike of tobacco. (The weekly cabinet-meeting table had four plates of sweets and smokers were obliged to go out into the corridor!)[21]

Franco liked to say that governing Spain was easy. Certainly he acted as if that were so at times. In winter he always took time off to indulge in his favourite pastime of shooting (also his favourite topic of conversation). His cousin General Francisco Franco Salgado-Araujo, who was his head of military household, complained frequently in his diary of the amount of time wasted in this way. During the season, Franco devoted three days a week to shooting on the estates of the aristocracy or those of the new magnates whom his regime had enriched.[22] In the summer he would travel up to San Sebastian and spend a good six weeks between there, his yacht *Azor*, and the country house publicly donated to him near El Ferrol, the Pazo de Meires.[23] Compared with the hectic pace of modern government, Franco's timetable was most unhurried.

ACCEPTANCE AND RESISTANCE

The ultimate strength of the Franco regime stemmed from the weakness of its opponents. The political class on the republican side had been driven into exile and its support base decimated through executions, arrests or discrimination. Yet, instead of uniting, the Republicans allowed the frictions that had divided them before and during the Civil War to persist afterwards. The Communists were viewed with extreme suspicion because of their dependence on Moscow. Moreover, their record of systematic determination to assert hegemony over the revolutionary transformation of Spain, by fair means or foul, scarcely endeared them to their countrymen. The Anarchists in particular had borne the brunt of their persecution and double dealing. The Socialists were dispersed and demoralized. In general, the pre-war politicians were dispersed to Buenos Aires and Mexico in Latin America; Paris and London in northern Europe; and in Moscow to the east. It was not until 1945 that the various logistical and political hurdles were overcome to allow the formation of a republican government-in-exile in Mexico. Perhaps it was not surprising that the three main groups who had formed the base of the Republic — the Anarchists, Communists, and Socialists — should be disunited in exile when their visions of society were so disparate. This lack of unity was a feature of the opposition until little more than three years before Franco's death.

The opposition seriously misjudged the durability of Franco. The regime was dismissed too simplistically as a fascist dictatorship. Basing their hopes on the success of the Allies in the Second World War and the inherent contradictions of the dictatorship, the opposition believed Franco's collapse was imminent. Such an analysis ignored the reluctance of the Allied powers to support a new destabilization of Spain, underestimated the capacity of the regime to evolve, and failed to take account of the effects of economic development in creating both a measure of prosperity and popular tolerance of the status quo.

The extent of this miscalculation was demonstrated by the abortive incursion of September 1944 into the valley of Aran in northern Catalonia by some 12000 Spanish partisans. With Germany on the verge of defeat, the opposition hoped the Allies would turn to the liberation of Spain. The partisans, many of whom had fought in the French resistance, crossed over the Pyrenees from France with the aim of occupying a slice of Spanish territory, and set off a chain of popular uprising. However, the area chosen was far too easily isolated by Franco's troops and possessed insufficient local population to provide support. The partisan force was obliged to retreat, leaving some 1,400 prisoners and provoking scarcely a whimper of international interest.[24]

The Communists had been the main promoters of this venture, and the party persisted in the tactic of fomenting guerilla activity inside Spain in the belief that this would weaken the regime and encourage popular support for a general uprising. The guerillas operated in the northern republican stronghold of Asturias, in Aragon and Catalonia and, to a lesser extent, in the sierra of Andalusia. These guerillas led a Robin Hood-style existence and succeeded in pinning down a large segment of the paramilitary Guardia Civil. At times even the road from Madrid to Escorial was considered unsafe to travel. However, the guerillas were cut off from their leadership in exile and operated in rural areas, and the general public was kept ignorant of their activity through press censorship. The local population had little incentive to provide positive support, absorbed as they were in the more essential business of daily survival.

The guerilla struggle was abandoned in 1950 – an implicit admission that the regime would not fall by force of arms. Yet it took another decade for the opposition to bury the idea of revolutionary change and seek reconciliation and reform from within. This strategy was slow to mature because of differences between the internal and external opposition. Those on the inside were more realistic, faced with the need for secrecy and the problems of politicizing a nation which the authorities sought to manipulate through apathy. The sole region of Spain never to be fully pacified was the Basque country. Between 1939 and 1975, the authorities were obliged to impose no less than six states of emergency in the two provinces of Guipuzcoa and Vizcaya.[25] The most tangible general evidence of disaffection in later years came from the illegal trades unions and the students. But political divisions still prevented effective unity and lessened the impact of their struggle.

The former Republicans were further hampered by their lack of acceptability among groups such as the monarchists who tolerated Franco but were unenthusiastic about him. The monarchists toyed with pacts but were reluctant to become allied with any group associated with the Republic. The Republicans for their part found it unpalatable to consider a pact with the monarchy after having shed so much blood for the republican ideal. The Borbon dynasty, besides, had given them little to trust in or admire.

Franco, on the other hand, played the monarchist card with great astuteness. He encouraged Don Juan to believe in his chances of acceding to the throne — facing him with the choice of burning his bridges with Franco by becoming allied with the opposition or vice versa. Despite flirtations with the opposition, Don Juan preferred to keep his lines open with Franco; and, once his son had been named heir in 1969, he could not easily undermine his own flesh and blood without also undermining the institution of monarchy.

Franco's ascendancy in the aftermath of the Civil War was aided by the international situation. The Second World War absorbed the attention of those powers who might have been disposed to exert pressure on Franco to be more democratic. Spain was kept out of the war less by design than by chance. On several occasions, Franco came close to openly siding with Hitler; but at a crucial moment Hitler was diverted by the opening-up of the Russian front and he baulked at Franco's demands for a share of empire in Africa and the prospect of major economic and military aid to Spain. Spain's professed neutrality exasperated the Allies since Spanish territory was used by German U-boats, aircraft and an extensive intelligence network. In addition, Franco permitted a volunteer force, the famous Blue Division (*Division Azul*), to be dispatched to the Russian front, and he supplied large quantities of the strategic mineral wolfram to German munitions factories. But Spain managed to stay out of the war, permitting Franco to consolidate his hold at home — and allowing a well-fuelled myth to emerge that all this was due to his skill. At best, it was another example of his innate caution and reluctance to take a decision.[26]

Tarred with the fascist brush and linked to the defeated Axis powers, Spain was cold-shouldered by the international community in the wake of the war. But isolation did Spain and Franco far less damage than intended. It was short-lived and mostly half-hearted, and permitted Franco to stoke up an exaggerated feeling of nationalism. A sustained anti-Spain campaign might have had more effect had not the Cold War overtaken Europe. Western realpolitik made it hard to exclude anti-communist Spain in the line-up against Moscow. It was not long before Spain came under the US diplomatic and defence umbrella, and the all-important acceptance of the Vatican quickly followed. Spain was finally admitted to the UN in 1955.

BALANCE OF THE FRANCO REGIME

Franco's survival cannot be attributed solely to the failure of the opposition and the unwillingness of the international community to overthrow him. The regime enjoyed a far greater degree of acceptance than that with which it has often been credited. Franco's promise of restoring order was welcomed by the Spanish people out of sheer exhaustion, mass poverty and fear of renewed conflict. The reforms which the Republic had sought to introduce had been given little time to work or were abandoned half realized: a shake-up of education, the elimination of a confessional state, the encouragement of popular participation, the recognition of regional autonomy, the reorganization of agriculture and land tenure and social changes such as the permitting of divorce were much to digest for a country where over 40% of the population still lived in rural poverty. The Republic had not even a decade to see through these changes. As a result, it was relatively easy for people to accept, if not welcome, Franco's return to traditional values. Franco touched a raw nerve of national pride by promising the regeneration of Spain — a nationalism reinforced by the fostering of the belief that the rest of the world was against Spain.

The corporatist state, though it lacked any democratic institutions, bound a large proportion of the population with a direct or indirect stake in the status quo. Even at the lowest level, people such as lottery-ticket distributors, taxi drivers, concierges who owed their jobs to being war veterans or their widows, depended on the regime for their livelihoods. School-teachers and doctors were vetted for their loyalty; mayors and local councillors were members of the Movimiento.

The burgeoning bureaucracy in Madrid and the provinces owed its existence to Franco and the victorious side in the Civil War. In addition, a new merchant class had grown rich supporting the nationalist cause. The armed forces were a central pillar of the new state. They were the guarantors of Franco's power and as a result were allowed to share generously in the spoils of victory. Apart from securing posts in the cabinet and higher administration, the military were co-opted onto state and private company boards and allowed to indulge their business interests freely.

Those excluded from this system or who rebelled against it were made fully aware of the harsh penalties they risked. Thus, many tolerated the regime out of fear — a fear cushioned by the benefits of greater material prosperity and the pseudo-liberalism that evolved from the mid-sixties onwards.

An important, and often forgotten, safety valve lay in emigration. A huge wave of discontented and potentially disruptive labour was released via emigration to the booming economies of northern Europe. From 1950 to 1975, over 1·5 million Spaniards emigrated to northern Europe alone. Labour had proved the least docile group and the one that most unnerved the authorities.

The keynote, therefore, to an acceptance of the regime was apathy and inertia. Franco was never loved by the majority of his subjects. At best, he was respected. He lasted so long and Spain changed so much during his lifetime, economically and socially, that he became like a piece of antique furniture in a new room. Spain outgrew him. The country functioned in spite of him, not because of him.

Franco should have released the reins of power long before his death. For the last five years of his life he was too old in body and mind to face up to necessary decisions. But the long wait for him to die at least had the benefit of conditioning Spaniards to think of the post-Franco era. Thus, on his death, it was only a reactionary minority who opposed a democratic solution. (In the first elections, in June 1977, the extreme right won less than 1% of the vote.)

It is interesting to compare reactions to the deaths of Franco and Marshal Tito of Yugoslavia. Both leaders had led struggles to rebuild their nations but with diametrically opposed ideologies. Both survived their contemporaries to become historical monuments. Tito's funeral was attended by world leaders, communist and anti-communist, because of his role in international politics; his record of domestic repression was ignored. Almost no international figures attended Franco's funeral. He had still not been forgiven for presiding over a divided country, for his association with Hitler and Mussolini and for the brutal aftermath of the Civil War. Yet no one expected Yugoslavia to carry out a fundamental change in policy. In the case of Spain such a change was expected because the international and domestic climate was in favour of democracy. There are several specific points to be made here.

First, in 1975, the United States, Spain's most important ally, was about to conclude a new bi-lateral defence treaty. The Carter administration, with its emphasis on human rights, would almost certainly have exerted pressure on Spain if a democratic solution had not been forthcoming.

Second, the Portuguese revolution in April 1974 had demonstrated that

21

the Iberian peninsula would not be allowed to become a Soviet sphere of influence. The Soviet intention in the Portuguese revolution had been to gain access to the latter's colonies of Angola and Mozambique. Once it had obtained this objective, the Soviet Union took its distance from Portugal. More generally, it was in no western country's interests to see Spain destabilized in the wake of the shock created by the 1973 oil price rises; and the Portuguese experience served as a lesson of the dangers inherent in a military revolution. In Spain, this would have been violent, as it had not been in Portugal.

Third, Spain's expanding economy had become inextricably linked with that of Europe. The European Economic Community still denied Spain's request for membership on the grounds that it was not a democratic country; but nevertheless, in 1970, the Community had been prepared to sign a new trade agreement with Spain that sharply increased Spanish exports. Over 40% of Spain's exports went to the EEC, while the latter provided 34% of Spain's imports. This increased trade reflected growing international investment in Spain's automotive sector, chemicals, mining, and agribusiness. Investment by multinational concerns was made on the assumption that there would be a stable transfer of authority in the post-Franco era.

Fourth, the attitude of the Roman Catholic Church in the wake of the Vatican Council II underwent an important change. The Vatican began to take its distance from the Franco regime and encourage liberalism in Spain. This undermined the position of the conservative bishops and also weakened Franco's own hand in dealing with the Church.

Finally, the left was profoundly influenced by the overthrow of President Allende in Chile, in September 1973, and the installation of the Pinochet dictatorship. The Chilean experience made the left conscious of the dangers of provoking the military, and as a result both the Communists and Socialists were more conciliatory towards the idea of gradual change.

Inside Spain, a democratic solution was facilitated by the structure of Francoism. The Movimiento was no real party — rather, it was the guardian of a set of ideals which were so out of step with modern Spain that they easily withered. The military could have taken the initiative but it had become flabby after years of having things its own way. The opposition, meanwhile, did not possess the credentials to promote a clean break with the past. The regime had not been defeated. Haunting everyone was the spectre of another civil war if passions were not controlled. This was almost sufficient in itself to instil caution, and so permit a complete metamorphosis of Francoism, rather than an abrupt reaction to it.

The key to this metamorphosis was the role of the monarchy as a symbol of national unity. Juan Carlos set out to prove that he was King of all Spaniards with a success and flair that surprised even his detractors.

Omnipresent portraits of the Caudillo have now been replaced by those of King Juan Carlos and Queen Sophia. Franco's name has been removed from the main streets of Spain's principal towns and the long years of his rule are being quietly forgotten. But Franco cannot be wiped from the history books like a statue removed from a pedestal.

He presided unimaginatively over a period of repressive stability in which Spain became the western world's tenth industrial power. He had the pragmatism to bend with the times. His patriotism was never in question nor was his sense of self-sacrifice. On account of a combination of domestic and international circumstances, rather than his own actions, he was able to leave a stable succession. Few authoritarian rulers have done this.

But Franco cannot escape the damning criticism that he showed absolutely no magnanimity in victory and consciously ruled over a divided country. The stability he provided was at a high cost in political, social and economic terms. The political life of Spain was suffocated. A system that rewards loyalty above initiative and that prizes conformity above individuality fosters a numbing mediocrity. Mediocrity was the stamp of the Franco era.

Franco failed to tackle many contentious issues: the relationship between central authority and regional autonomy, between civilian and military authority, and between Church and state; the extent to which society should determine its own development; the distribution of wealth; and the system of justice. Spain's European neighbours had been confronting these issues for two hundred years. The Republic, albeit incompetently and incompletely, had tried to do likewise. Franco merely put the clock back and then bequeathed Spain's long-established problems to his successors. This was his real legacy.

2 Scars of the Civil War

Franco never made any attempt to heal the deep scars caused by the bloody Civil War and this was potentially the most dangerous of all the problems he bequeathed to Spain. He persecuted his republican opponents and outlawed all that they stood for. The memory of the Civil War was consciously fostered as a means of reinforcing the regime. Thus, right up to Franco's death, the propaganda of a victorious nationalist crusade triumphing over the evil 'red' enemies of Spain persisted. Even now the traumatic events of the conflict are a highly sensitive issue.

A full forty-two years passed after the end of hostilities before the first official move was made to present an acceptably neutral view of the Spanish Civil War. Under the patronage of the Ministry of Culture, a Civil War exhibition opened in Madrid in October 1981, almost six years after Franco's death. Fittingly, the exhibition was staged in the Palacio de Cristal — the elegant glass structure in the Retiro Park in Madrid where Manuel Azana was elected President of the Republic in May 1936, just two months before the outbreak of the war.

To avoid argument, the exhibition was less didactic than nostalgic. Its aim was to eliminate entrenched prejudices by arousing curiosity for a bygone era, and to promote the idea that the Civil War, for better or worse, was now an integral part of Spanish history. The catalogue even suggested that most visitors would be unable to distinguish between Republicans and Nationalists in the photographs.[7] Over 300,000 saw the exhibition in Madrid before it toured the major provincial cities, where it attracted a further 400,000 visitors. Despite such public interest, there is no sign of any willingness to tackle a more informative project such as a TV documentary on the nature, causes and consequences of the Civil War. The scars are still too raw.

The Civil War has ceased to be taboo. Yet this savage conflict which engulfed Spain from 1936 to 1939 remains an extraordinarily sensitive issue — even though the majority of Spain's present population was born after the war's end. Fewer than 20% of the nation alive today had direct experience of the hostilities.

So long as Franco was alive and ruling Spain, rational discussion of the issue was impossible. Franco and his supporters even refused to admit that the fighting had been a civil war. To the end, Franco chose to see his own role,

24

and that of the Nationalists, as a glorious national crusade against the forces of evil and the enemies of Spain — Communists, freemasons and libertarians. Convinced of the rectitude of his cause, Franco never bothered with the impartiality of historical judgement. The official view was unashamedly selective and partisan, reinforced by rigorous censorship and the reluctance of survivors to discuss what happened. Surprisingly few of the leading participants on either side have put their experiences into print.

At a more mundane level, it is common to find parents admitting they have never discussed their Civil War experiences with their children. Such silence cannot be blamed wholly on the overall blanket of censorship and censoriousness that has surrounded the darker aspects of the war. (For instance, there is still, in 1983, no policy on access to the military archives of the Civil War, the most important of which are still withheld from public view.) Nor can the silence be wholly blamed on the triumphalism of Franco. Few are willing to rake over the coals of an unpleasant experience of which many are secretly ashamed. There persists a feeling that Spain is not ready to face the truth. The communist leader, Santiago Carrillo, when questioned in 1982 by the Irish Hispanicist Ian Gibson about Civil War atrocities gave a reply which could have come from either side in the conflict: 'In this country, one has to do this one day [investigate atrocities] but this must be left to history and at the present moment we have to ensure that the scars of the war do not reopen.'[2] Children, too, tend to have complexes about the role of their parents in the strife. With the advent of democracy, many are anxious not to associate their parents with nationalist repression.

Balzac, that astute commentator on human weakness who grew up in the wake of the French Revolution, observed that traumatic national events produce a form of amnesia: 'Those who today read the history of the French Revolution will never know what vast intervals popular opinion then interposed between the closely succeeding events of the time. The general craving for peace and quiet after a period of violent commotion engendered complete forgetfulness of the gravest recent occurrences.'[3]

This sort of attitude, though wholly understandable, has prevented a healthy dissection of the Civil War memory. The restoration of democracy on Franco's death in 1975 came too late to serve this purpose properly.

On the night of 23 February 1981, when the Cortes was seized by elements of Guardia Civil and the Valencia military region placed under martial law in an attempt to overthrow the democratic government, war memories were revived. People who were too young to have experienced the Civil War nevertheless admitted to reacting as if they *had* — instinctively or ideologically they identified with one of the Civil War sides. General Jaime Milans del Bosch, commander of the Valencia military regime, deliberately referred back to the nationalist uprising. The proclamation of martial law in Valencia employed almost identical language to General Mola's declaration of nationalist aims and orders on 18 July 1936.[4]

SAVAGERY AND VIOLENCE

The deepest scars were caused by the sheer scale of the conflict's violence — scars which were exacerbated by Franco's persistent refusal to offer any reconciliation to the defeated. The conflict and its aftermath was so divisive that it was not until June 1962, almost twenty-five years after its end, that any serious effort at reconciliation between Nationalists and Republicans was attempted. The exiled historian Salvador de Madariaga initiated a congress of notables in Munich. Of the 118 attending the congress, eighty, mostly monarchists, came from inside Spain. Madariaga declared in the closing session, 'The Civil War which began in Spain on July 18, 1936, and which the regime has artificially maintained via censorship, a monopoly of the Press and the Radio and Victory parades, ended the day before yesterday in Munich, on June 6, 1962.'[5] Unfortunately, his words were premature. Several of those attending the congress from Spain were subsequently imprisoned or sent to the Canaries in internal exile. Jose Maria Gil Robles, the conservative Christian Democrat leader who attended the congress, wrote to the disillusioned Falangist Dionisio Ridruejo saying, 'For Franco there is no greater danger than the erosion of the memory of the Civil War.'[6] The first balanced general history of the Civil War appeared one year before the Munich congress, by the British historian Hugh Thomas. Only a foreigner could break through the silence, taboo and inhibitions.[7] The book was long banned inside Spain. Reconciliation had to wait until after Franco's death.

The appalling loss of life during the Civil War and in its aftermath has never been accurately detailed. The toll will probably never be known. Unreliable statistics, fragmentary evidence and the dispersed nature of the conflict impede reliable estimates of casualties. Moreover, the figures themselves convey nothing of the human drama behind each individual loss of life. As late as 1980, it was still possible to come across newspaper advertisements trying to locate parents or relatives lost during the war.

Initially, the casualty figure was put at one million dead and missing on both sides. However, this round figure was more an emotive commentary on the savagery of the fighting than a statement of fact. Hugh Thomas scaled the casualty level down to 500,000, including all causes of death during and after the fighting. Disregarding precise figures, it is now reasonably clear that most of the deaths did not arise from front-line battle. More people died as a result of executions, maltreatment and murder during and after the war than in any other way. Roughly 45% of all deaths could be called reprisals. In these reprisals as many, if not more, died after rather than during the fighting; it is concerning this period that discrepancies are greatest. Some claim that, between 1939 and 1950, up to 300,000 died. Those sympathetic to the Nationalists put the dead as low as 50,000. The toll was swelled to shameful numbers by countless acts of blind revenge: killings carried out after unrecorded trials or trips to the outskirts of town in anonymous trucks.[8]

The Italian Foreign Minister, Count Galeazzo Ciano, who visited Spain in July 1939, observed that executions in Madrid alone were proceeding at the rate of 200 to 250 a day.[9] This widely quoted observation was probably based on hearsay, though it is obvious that the civilizing hand of restraint was wholly lacking. Trades unionists, teachers, minor republican officials and any people remotely connected with the principal left-wing groupings were fair game for the firing squad or the cramped insanitary internment camps. In small villages and towns victims were selected often for no better reason than personal spite — creating divisions in these communities which last even to the present day. It scarcely needed the all-embracing law on political responsibilities, passed in February 1939, to provide a legal framework for the killings. This law gave special tribunals *carte blanche* to deal with anyone connected with a political party of the left during the Republic or anyone who had failed to support the Nationalists. Many victims of these tribunals ended up in forced-labour camps, working in the coal mines, or on the railways and roads.

Persecution of the defeated without any sense of magnanimity destroyed the prospect of early reconciliation and widened the divisions created by the hostilities. During the Civil War, atrocities had been committed with equal abandon by the Nationalists and Republicans, but the scale of suffering imposed by the Nationalists on the Republicans once fighting ended gave rise to one of the blackest periods in Spanish history and placed an indelible stain on the Franco regime.

EFFECTS OF PROPAGANDA

During the Civil War, both sides painted the issues in broad propagandist strokes. The battle was one of diametric opposites: *good* versus *evil*; *left* versus *right*; *black* versus *red*. The options were between revolution or reaction; anarchism or authoritarianism; socialism or fascism.

The polarization was poignantly depicted by the English poet and novelist Laurie Lee, who found himself caught in a small Andalusian village near Malaga at the outbreak of the Civil War:[10]

> The split village now emerged in clearer focus and its two factions declared themselves, confronting each other at last in black and white — labelled for convenience, 'Fascist' or 'Communist'! The 'Fascists' seemed ready to accept the name, this being frankly what they aspired to, with the Falange already organised as a fighting group, a swaggering spearhead of upper class vengeance, whose crude fascist symbols, Italian-inspired, were now appearing on walls and doorways.
>
> The 'Communist' label, on the other hand, was too rough and ready, a clumsy

reach-me-down which properly fitted no one. The farm labourers, fishermen, and a handful of industrial workers all had local but separate interests. Each considered his struggle to be older than Communism, to be something exclusively Spanish; part of the social perversion which he alone could put right by reason of his roots in this particular landscape.

The labels in this conflict were often profoundly misleading. The Fascists were just one element of the forces that supported the military uprising in July 1936 led by General Emilio Mola. Apart from the Falange, there were monarchists and their dissident and fanatical branch, the Carlists, making up what Franco and his supporters called the nationalist side. Equally, all those on the republican side could not be lumped together as 'Reds' (*Rojos*). The military uprising converted the republican government into a popular front. This included bourgeois parties such as Union Republicana and Izquierda Republicana, alongside an orthodox Communist Party and a Socialist Party split between left and right wings, as well as a revolutionary marxist grouping, the POUM. Meanwhile, the powerful Anarchists stood back from government altogether.

Many Spaniards found themselves forced to back whichever side controlled the zone where they lived. Even so, the conflict tended to divide the nation along class lines, so helping the propagandist labels to stick. The landowners, the financial oligarchy and industrialists sided with the Nationalists, who had the backing of the Church. A portion of the middle class and the conservative rural peasantry also threw in their lot with the Nationalists.

Republican support came from the professional classes, intellectuals, the urban proletariat and radical sectors of the countryside. In crude terms, the Civil War ranged *old* against *new*. Conservative, Catholic, centralist Spain was fighting to hold down industrial, progressive, socialist, regional Spain. It was Spain of the 'Black Legend' (*leyenda negra*) and the Inquisition against enlightenment. Such a simplistic image was reinforced by the way in which the anti-clericalism of the Republicans forged a specifically Catholic unity among the Nationalists. In turn, this added weight to Franco's evocation of the language of the reconquest of Moorish Spain by the Catholic Kings. The Nationalist cause was a new crusade against a new infidel. The Church encouraged the idea of crusade, aware that it risked losing permanent influence in Spain should the Republicans triumph. Pope Pius XII in a congratulatory telegram to Franco at the end of the war, thanked the Caudillo for the 'victory of Catholic Spain'.

It is unlikely that the Civil War could have been avoided. The Republic had politicized the working class, suddenly raising their level of expectation, yet it was incapable of satisfying hopes of greater social justice, reforming agriculture, and liberating Spaniards from the grip of the Church. Time was against it; and the country's slim economic resources were under threat from international depression. The politicians were hopelessly divided.

Meanwhile, the opponents of the left — the landowners, the financial oligarchy, the Church, and the military — were appalled at what the Republic was offering. The Republic threatened their very existence.

Added to these opposing interests were the unpredictable desperation of the rural peasantry and urban proletariat; the rise of fascist violence amidst a progressive breakdown of law and order; the anti-clerical sentiment of the Republic; the international climate of political polarization caused by the rise of Hitler and Mussolini; the demands for regional autonomy from a weak but centralized administration; and, finally, a military establishment demoralized by abortive colonial ventures. The insurgents had hoped for a quick coup, an uprising supported by military units countrywide. The failure of the generals to gain immediate control could have proved disastrous for them but for the ditherings of the Republicans, which allowed time for the generals to regroup, transforming an abortive coup into a protracted military campaign.

INTERNATIONAL INTERVENTION

Divisions might have been less pronounced if the Civil War had remained a purely Spanish affair. But the intervention of Hitler and Mussolini on the side of the Nationalists, matched unevenly by the support of the Soviet Union and the volunteer international brigades for the Republicans, widened the significance of the conflict. Against a background of political polarization in Europe and fears about the spread of fascism, the Spanish Civil War acquired a special importance. Quickly it caught the imagination of the thirties' intellectuals as a classic model of the struggle between left and right. 'Spain was not so much a *place* as the name of a cause, and the war being fought there was the Good War, a crusade in which the issues were unambiguous.'[11] Spain also became an experimental ground for new warfare techniques and the future Axis powers' ambitions of international domination.

On the republican side, what foreign governments failed to offer in material support was compensated for by the moral commitment of the international left. Spain became a test of commitment to the ideas of revolutionary struggle that the left had been impatient to put into action and had almost despaired of doing. Foreign left-wing thinkers supported the actions of the Anarchists and libertarians, seeing them in charmingly romantic terms, instead of as people motivated by hunger, desperation, and centuries of repression. The romanticization of battle obscured the causes of conflict and stereotyped the combatants. More good English language poetry, fiction and prose was inspired by the Spanish Civil War than by the Second World War, mostly about the Republicans. Spain was easier to write about; it was basically a distant place and the outcome represented the death of an ideal rather than the loss of a country or political system. 'On that arid square, that fragment nipped off from hot Africa soldered so crudely to inventive Europe . . .' as Auden's famous poem on Spain begins. Poets such as Auden and Spender, writers such as George Orwell (*Homage to Catalonia*) Ernest Hemingway (*For Whom the Bell Tolls*) and André Malraux (*L'Espoir*), and painters such as Picasso (*Guernica*) immortalized the Republicans. Their views were frozen in time by the advent of the Second World War and were seldom updated.

The Civil War ended only five months before Britain and France declared war on Germany. Franco's brother-in-law, Serrano Suner, who favoured a direct military alliance with Hitler, invented the fiction that there were two wars being waged in Europe: one was the struggle of Christianity against the spread of communism; the other was the battle by the Axis powers for supremacy within Europe. Spain was only involved in the former war, which was a logical continuation of the Civil War.[12] A volunteer force was organized, recruited mainly from the Falange with a smattering of pro-fessional officers. It was baptised the Blue Division (*Division Azul*), after the colour of the Falange shirt and was reminiscent of the Italian Black Arrows who came to fight in the Civil War. Consistent with the crusade against communism, the 19,000 strong Blue Division was dispatched to the Russian front, where other Spaniards had incorporated into the Red Army and Air Force. The Blue Division fought for two years on the Russian front until the end of 1943 when it was disbanded under international pressure. Some hardline members insisted on fighting on and a small reformed unit, the Blue Legion, survived up until the fall of the Third Reich.

The Blue Division, with its strong Falangist component, was to be a powerful brotherhood within the armed forces. Some of its members, such as Dionisio Ridruejo, returned to civilian life and gradually distanced them-selves from its fascist fanaticism. But in general the Blue Division came to symbolize the essence of the hardline within the military who had turned their back on any form of reconciliation with their opponents. It was no coincidence that two of the leading figures in the events of 23 February 1981, General Milans del Bosch and General Alfonso Armada, were members of the Blue Division.

Republicans joined the Allied forces or the French resistance for both ideological and tactical reasons. The Soviet Union took in some 2,000 Communist Party cadres, most of whom continued their struggle against fascism with an eye on future infiltration into Spain. Three Spaniards rose to the rank of general in the Red Army, the best known being General Enrique Lister. Most of those who fought for the Allies joined the French Free Fighters. They hoped that Spain would be drawn into the war and in this way the Allies would support a restoration of the Republic and democracy in Spain. They saw themselves as the *avant-garde* of the forces that would liberate Spain from the Franco yoke. Republican casualties fighting for the Allies have been estimated at 25,000, an attrition rate of about a quarter of all those who participated. Blue Division casualties in the bitter warfare on the Russian front were equally high — about 5,000 died.

In addition to those Republicans that fought, a group suffered virtually unnoticed and without the fury of arms. Of the thousands who crossed into France after the Civil War a good 30,000 made the grim graduation from French internment camps to Nazi concentration camps, where some 10,000 Spaniards eventually died. The republican socialist leader, Francisco Largo Caballero died in Paris in 1946 broken by his experiences in Oranienburg camp. In Spain the Nazi holocaust was ignored and Hitler's death in the officially controlled media was greeted with eulogies describing the Fuhrer as a 'son of the catholic church'. Formal recognition that Spaniards had died in Nazi concentration camps did not come until 1978, when King Juan Carlos visited Austria and laid a wreath in their honour.[13]

REMEMBERING THE DEAD

One year after the end of the Civil War, work began on a massive war memorial. The entire side of a mountain near El Escorial, north of Madrid, was reworked. Using forced labour drawn from the ranks of defeated Republicans, an enormous underground crypt and basilica was carved out of the mountains above which a concrete cross 150 metres high and weighing 200,000 tons was erected. This pharaonic monument was finally inaugurated on the twentieth anniversary of Franco's victory. The monument was dedicated neutrally to 'the fallen' (los caidos), and was called the Valley of the Fallen. However, there was little doubt as to who was being remembered. Every night at ten o'clock during the nineteen years that the monument was being built radio stations broadcast a salute to those who had fallen 'for God and Spain' (caidos por dios y España). Republicans were not deemed to have fallen either for God or Spain since according to official propaganda they were anti-Christ and anti-Spain. This revamped vision of Valhalla was denied them as were war pensions for republican disabled and widows.

The Valley of the Fallen is a tasteless reminder of all that was, and still is, most divisive in the Civil War. That Franco requested to be laid beside the nationalist hero Jose Antonio in this mausoleum convincingly proves that to the end he never believed in reconciliation. It is also a revealing commentary on the monument that it should now be expropriated by the fascist fringe for their nostalgic devotionary rites honouring the past. To this day in Spain no monument exists offering mutual respect to the dead of both sides.

Instead of having the anonymous and symbolic tribute to the unknown soldier, Franco opted for the more exploitable myth of the martyrdom of Jose Antonio, whose grave has pride of place in the Basilica. Jose Antonio was ill advisedly shot by the Republicans on 20 November 1936 in Alicante. That day thereafter became a day of national remembrance marked by the spirit of Franco's famous declaration: 'May God grant thee eternal rest, and to us may he grant none till we have harvested for Spain the seed sown by thy death.' Every city and small town in Spain proceeded to name one of its main streets after Jose Antonio, and parents baptised their sons after him. There was also many an idolatrous dedication to Franco, usually a street called General-issimo. Generals like Mola and subsidiary martyrs like the monarchist minister, Jose Calvo Sotelo, assassinated just before the outbreak of the Civil War, also got their share. This one-sided view of history was rectified only after the democratic municipal elections of 1979 when these street names were altered, as in Madrid where Jose Antonio became the Gran Via and Generalissimo, the Castellana.

Other nationalist heroes were men like General Jose Moscardo who held out against all odds and in terrible conditions in the beseiged Alcazar fortress of Toledo during the summer of 1936. At one stage during the seige, the Republicans captured Moscardo's twenty-four-year-old son, Luis, who was then put on the telephone to implore his father to surrender. The ensuing conversation — apocryphal or true — became part of nationalist folklore: the son said he would be shot if the Alcazar did not surrender. Moscardo replied: 'If that is so, commend your soul to God, shout Viva España! and die like a hero.' The son was subsequently shot. When finally relieved, Moscardo's first words were the studied 'nothing to report' (*sin novedad*), the password of the uprising.[14]

Accompanying the mythology of the new heroes was a demonology of the 'Reds'. The Republicans were accused of barbarism and cruelty, and unfortunately for them this reputation was not difficult to exploit. A partic-ularly shameful episode occurred towards the end of 1936 when the seige round Madrid tightened and the more important nationalist prisoners in the capital's jails were moved. Starting on 7 November for over a month some 2,400 prisoners were systematically taken from prison and shot just outside Madrid at Paracuellos del Jarama. Even now the precise number killed is disputed, with some Nationalists claiming the number murdered in cold-blood was nearly 10,000. Responsibility for the massacre is also hard to place, but the blame seems to lie with communist officials in charge of the capital's security, including Carrillo — then aged twenty-one and in charge of public order in the defence junta.[15] Paracuellos became shorthand for barbarous republican revenge, and synonymous with communist behaviour.

The Republicans also played into nationalist hands by their wanton anti-clericalism in the early days of the conflict. Attacks on churches and the murder of priests, well documented by the international press, were easily exaggerated and accepted without question; they struck an emotive chord in Spain's Catholic conscience. The charge that Republicans were viciously and viscerally anti-clerical became general and stuck, with lasting effect.

The politicians of the left were branded with an image of total irresponsibility for their conduct during the Republic. Such propaganda was essential to prove the benefits of the new regime and there was plenty of mud to fling. During the Franco years, the word Republic was understood to mean political irresponsibility and a state of general anarchy.

Finally, the Republicans were accused of selling out the nation's wealth to Moscow, by letting the Soviet Union expropriate the gold reserves in the Bank of Spain, shipped to Moscow for safe keeping. This myth was allowed to persist until two years after Franco's death even though since 1956 the government had documentary evidence accounting for the use of this gold.[16]

Despite these attempts to discredit the Republican cause, the battle for hearts and minds was far from one-sided and if anything the Republicans fared best. After the conflict, the Republicans lost out at home though continued, perhaps more strongly, to win the propaganda war abroad. Shorthand for nationalist barbarism was the death of the poet and playwright, Federico Garcia Lorca. His ill-explained death in Granada came to symbolize something much deeper — the killing of a cultural rennaissance in Spain under the Republic which had put Spanish artists in the European *avant-garde*. Being an exotic figure, Garcia Lorca's death appeared like that of Rupert Brooke during the First World War: the flower of a generation nipped in the bud. His death was ably exploited by the Republicans and their sympathizers.[17]

The other symbol of nationalist barbarism was the bombing of the Basque town of Guernica. Guernica, a small town near Bilbao, was the focal point of Basque culture and kings of Spain traditionally took the allegiance of the Basque people before an ancient oak tree; in return the Basques were given certain privileges. On 26 April 1937, a market day when the town was crowded with refugees, Guernica was bombed and strafed by German aircraft. Guernica had no air defences and was not a strategic target. Its destruction was presented as an error of war by the Nationalists, but it subsequently emerged that saturation bombing techniques were employed for the first time, with the specific aim of demoralizing the population. The incident was immortalized by Picasso's sketches and his major painting *Guernica* for the republican pavilion in the 1937 Paris Exhibition. *Guernica* became synonymous with nationalist savagery and the horrors of war. Under the Franco regime possession of a print of *Guernica* came to be a form of protest.

Republican exiles were too complacent about the rectitude of their cause and failed to appreciate the insidious dangers of nationalist propaganda until it was too late. Thus, even when official propaganda lost its virulence, it was sufficiently rooted to last. This had important consequences in the wake of Franco's death. For instance, legalization of the Communist Party was the most sensitive issue in the process of political normalization after 1975. The issue was sensitive precisely because important sectors of the establishment, especially in the Church hierarchy and among the armed forces, associated the Communist Party exclusively with the 'Reds' of the Republic and the Civil War: the church-burners, the men of uncontrolled liberty and of Paracuellos. The attitude of this sector of the community to the Communist Party was so firmly established that they could neither accept reconciliation, nor even allow the Communists to evolve unhindered. The strength of accumulated anti-communist feeling ensured that the Party could only be legalized after all the other main political groupings; it was only through a bold initiative by the Prime Minister Adolfo Suarez in April 1977 that the Party was legalized in time for the first democratic elections. Though the armed forces acquiesced in legalization, the collective memory of the 'Reds' has not been expunged. This was evident in the trial of those accused for the abortive coup of 23 February. For them there was no way a Communist could be a good, patriotic Spaniard. Equally the stigma of Paracuellos still clings to Carrillo. Even in the democratically elected Cortes he was once reviled with shouts of 'Paracuellos', and a picture of Paracuellos remains the centre piece in a room on the Civil War in the Army Museum in Madrid. If there were any balance, a similar picture should hang of the massacre in Badajoz bull-ring of countless Republicans by the nationalist general Juan de Yague, in August 1936.[18]

Similar considerations, but on a different scale, applied to the political respectability of the Socialist Party. The party was dogged by a forty-year-old image painted by Francoist propaganda. At the time of the first free elections since the Civil War in June 1977, it was common talk that Spain was not 'ready' for a socialist government. The Socialists themselves were concerned by the prospect of being voted in when such an image had not yet been dispelled. Not being 'ready' had little to do with the Socialists' lack of administrative experience: it referred to the residual memory implanted by Francoism of disorderly, libertarian government that threatened the unity of Spain and traditional Spanish values.

To break with this image the Socialist Party was obliged to present itself to the electorate with almost exaggerated moderation. References to marxism were expunged from the Party's ideology and the concept of nationalization all but disappeared. Residual fears about the Socialists played an important part in holding them back from winning the first two elections and forming a government. Furthermore, on the basis of these fears, the newly formed centre grouping, many of whose members had Francoist pasts, acquired greater credibility than it deserved. The historic nature of the socialist victory in the October 1982 elections lay precisely in the way the electorate demonstrated that the negative Francoist propaganda against the left had been buried. Even so on the night of the elections, some owners of houses in the wealthy Madrid suburb of La Moraleja hired extra security guards for fear that 'Red' hordes might sack their properties.

EXILES

Between 350,000 and 400,000 people fled from Spain in 1939, mostly across the border to France, a few by crossing to French North Africa or by boat direct to Latin America. These numbers are only approximations, like all the others relating to the Civil War. Half, or rather more than half, filtered back within the first year — trusting in fair treatment or unable to sustain themselves abroad with the onset of the Second World War. However, at least 150,000 went into longer term or permanent exile. All were crucial members of a modern democratic state: academics, artists, liberal members of the professions, politicians, teachers and trades unionists. The exodus was a serious drain on Spain's human resources. (If the number of exiles is added to the loss of life as a result of the Civil War, then Spain's 1936 population of twenty-six million suffered a decline of over 3%.)

A diaspora was created that stretched from Argentina through Uruguay, Venezuela, and Mexico, up to the US and across to France, Britain, and the Soviet Union. Roughly one third of all exiles went to Central and South America, and Spain's loss was Latin America's gain. Most never dreamed that exile would be long or permanent, believing that international pressure and internal contradictions would topple the Franco regime. Such optimism helped delay the formation of a government-in-exile until 1945, six years after the republican military defeat. The ideological and personal rivalries, which characterized the left during the Republic and the Civil War, sadly persisted. In particular the Communists' ill-concealed desire for hegemony earned them universal mistrust.

As an opposition force, the government-in-exile and the republican figures that surrounded it witnessed a rapid decline after the early fifties. The main value of the exiled government was as a reminder to Spaniards and the international community that the Franco regime lacked popular legitimacy. Yet Franco survived so long that by the time he died most republican personalities had also passed away. Only three republican figures played a role in the establishment of democracy in the wake of Franco's death — Josep Tarradellas, the veteran Catalan leader heading the Catalan government-in-exile based in Perpignan; Jesus Maria Leizaola, head of the Basque government-in-exile since 1960; and the communist leader, Santiago Carrillo.

Some of the exiles began to return after 1945, more after 1950 when internal repression subsided. Many like the essayist and philosopher, Jose Ortega y Gasset, opposed Franco and sided with the Republic but found the deprivations of exile too much. Ortega returned in 1945. Though criticized for being used by the regime, he managed to keep his distance. When he died in 1955 his funeral provided the focus for an important student demonstration against the regime. Less tainted by the internal squabbles of republican politicians, cultural figures in exile often acquired more prestige. Outside Spain were the poets Juan Ramon Jimenez and Ramon Sender; the film-maker Bunuel; the powerful graphic artist Josep Renau (whose posters had galvanized the Republic); the architect Josep Sert; the historians Salvador de Madariaga, Americo Castro and Claudio Sanchez Albornoz; the cellist Pablo Casals and, most significant of all, Picasso.

In view of Picasso's world-wide renown, his refusal to recognise the Spain of Franco carried considerable impact in Spain and abroad. It was a continuing reminder that Spain's greatest living artist, whose work represented a priceless national heritage, was withholding the imprimateur of his approval. A delegation attempted in 1956 to arrange a reconciliation between the regime and Picasso but this came to nothing. On his own, and as a gesture towards Catalonia he agreed to the foundation of a Picasso museum in Barcelona in 1959. However, his views remained clearly underlined by his will concerning the fate of *Guernica*. He stipulated that the canvas should not leave its temporary home in New York's Museum of Modern Art until democracy — and the Republic — be restored in Spain. *Guernica* eventually returned to Spain in October 1981 after complex legal bargaining, Picasso's heirs agreeing to waive the stipulation about Spain being a republic. The possession of *Guernica* closed a chapter in the Civil War.

DIPLOMATIC ISOLATION

Having overtly sympathized with the discredited, and defeated, fascist regimes of Hitler and Mussolini, Franco continued to be anti-democratic and as a result became the pariah of Europe. Diplomatic rejection was an easy way of satisfying the troubled consciences of many European governments over their unwillingness to topple Franco. The Salazar dictatorship in Portugal was treated much more kindly, largely because Portugal had proved friendly to the Allies during the Second World War. The first British ambassador to the Franco regime, Sir Samuel Hoare, set the tone with a visceral dislike and contempt for Franco. 'When therefore I reflect upon our present and future relations with Spain, I cannot avoid the conviction that they will never be satisfactory as long as Franco is in power, and that the sooner he and his Falange machine disappear, the better it will be, not only for ourselves, but for the whole of Europe'.[19] This attitude was reflected in the Potsdam conference communique of 1945 in which the Soviet Union, the US, and the UK declared they would not favour any application put forward by Spain under Franco for UN membership since it was founded with the support of the Axis powers.

Spain's diplomatic isolation was broken, but never completely, while Franco survived. The US was prepared to ignore the anti-democratic nature of the regime and use anti-communist Spain in its Cold War strategy of global containment of the Soviet Union. A bilateral defence treaty was signed in 1952 with the US. The Atlantic Alliance however, refused to entertain the idea of Spanish membership, although it would provide a backdoor means of ensuring that Spanish territory could be brought into service with NATO. Once the USA had accepted Franco the Vatican quickly followed suit, preferring to take advantage of the Church's privileged position in Franco's Spain through a Concordat rather than dwelling on moral indignation over the dictatorship. The rest of the international community was less forthcoming (with the exception of Argentina which provided generous food and financial aid). The republican government-in-exile was recognized by democratic governments in Latin America — Guatemala, Mexico, Panama, and Venezuela — and most of the communist block — Bulgaria, Czechoslovakia, Hungary, Poland, Rumania, and Yugoslavia. This helped sustain the international blackballing of Spain. Not until December 1955 was Spain admitted into the United Nations. Once a UN member Spain was able, three years later, to be admitted to the IMF, the IBRD, and the OEEC, so becoming privy to the principal bodies of western capitalism.

Spain had been excluded from playing any role in shaping post-1945 Europe. Barred from the western multi-lateral military alliance, all the Franco regime's overtures to the European Economic Community were also rejected. Spain first sought to join the EEC in 1962, but was rejected because she lacked democratic credentials. A second application for membership was turned down four years later. In 1970 membership was rejected again, although Spain's increasing trade links with the EEC were recognised by a new preferential agreement. The next application was not made until two years after Franco's death and negotiations were accepted because of the changed political status. Had Spain been a democracy the very first application in 1962 would have been hard to refuse, even though it would have involved a major readjustment for the Community.

The existence of the Franco regime and the divisive heritage of the Civil War therefore ensured that Spain was contained behind the Pyrenees. This had a number of important consequences. By being absent from the main decision-making institutions of western Europe, Spain not only lacked influence but also lacked information on which to base foreign policy. For instance, Spain alone of the major industrial countries failed to understand the true nature of the tripling of oil prices in 1973 (see chapter four). This failure was a direct result of a complacent inward-looking mentality induced by international isolation.

A second consequence was the lop-sided nature of Spain's international relations. Franco's uncompromising anti-communism made normal relations with Eastern Europe and China impossible. Besides, since Moscow was seen to be the controller of the illegal Communist Party the Franco regime developed an exaggerated estimate of the strength of the Party, misjudging its later ambitions. Talks were begun in Paris in 1962 in order to re-establish diplomatic relations with the Soviet Union, but foundered because Franco went ahead with the execution of a prominent communist militant, Julian Grimau, against the pleas of, among others, the Soviet leader, Nikita Khruschev. Grimau had been the commander of a Cheka unit during the Civil War, and he was executed for crimes he had allegedly committed almost twenty-five years previously. Diplomatic relations with the Soviet Union were not re-established fully until 1977. International isolation also affected the liberalization of economic policy. Spain's rejection by the European Community encouraged protectionist attitudes to prevail much longer than was healthy for the economy.

Beyond such purely practical consequences, international ostracism affected Spaniards at the psychological level. It reinforced the sensation that Spain was 'different'. Indeed, by insisting that Spain was different from the rest of Europe — unique and morally superior — Franco sought to counter the campaign against his regime. In this he was more than partially successful. He reawakened a chauvinistic nationalism designed to convince Spaniards that they were right and the rest of the world wrong. Xenophobia was a natural product of this environment. Foreign habits and fashions were looked down upon as liable to pollute Spanishness. Side by side with this xenophobia, a sense of inferiority reappeared, that the Republic had started to cure: Spain and Spaniards were backward, somehow missing out on things.

REWRITING HISTORY

With almost two thirds of all university staff either purged or in exile, as a result of the Civil War, the universities ceased to be impartial centres of learning. Teachers, seen as the chief purveyors of atheistic libertarian ideas, were heavily purged. In some regions, such as Asturias, 50% of the teachers were shot by the Nationalists.[20] The symbol of the new order in the classroom was the crucifix. The secularization of education initiated during the Republic was abruptly halted and the Church's hold over education was, once again, almost total. Education was subordinated to the needs of the regime: loyal christian pupils were preferred to independent, inquisitive minds.

With education in the hands of Catholic groups and the state run by a man inspired by the Catholic Kings, history was corrupted to suit the new masters. A flavour of what Spaniards in primary schools were told about themselves and their country can be had from a book called *This Is Spain* (*España Es Asi*). This prize-winning book was written by a primary school inspector, Augustin Serrano de Haro and appeared in 1946, expressly recommended by the Church. The book presents a numbingly chauvinistic, and at times racist view of Spanish history. Accompanied by constant exhortations to pupils to recite *'España Grande y Libre'* (Spain Great and Free) the author races through the

38

history. The book's message was simple: Spain had been Catholic since 589 and was eternally so despite the republican experience. The Arab conquest was possible only because the Moors were aided by Jews and traitors. The failure to expel the Arabs (for almost 800 years) was due to internal divisions. The moral is that all Spain's ills have stemmed from lack of unity. But for the zeal and patriotism of the Catholic Kings, Spain would never have emerged from the dark days of anarchy; order is solely possible under authoritarian rule. Military defeats suffered by Spain are omitted or brushed aside — the defeat of the Armada, for instance, was due to bad weather. Spain meanwhile saved the (christian) world from the Turkish infidel at Lepanto. The 'Black Legend' surrounding Spain and the period of the Inquisition grew up, the author assures his students, because 'Spain always had many enemies — enemies outside, foreigners, and enemies within, the bad Spaniards'. The Inquisition itself was a model of advanced jurisprudence, and during the same period England, it is claimed, executed 264,000 persons. The Borbon monarchs let the rot set in because they were foreign. The first Republic in 1873 was a failure. Here the teacher is exhorted to draw his pupils' attention to 'the bitterness of the Republican experience'. Alfonso XIII is portrayed as a decent but ineffectual monarch who left Spain to avoid internal strife. The dictator Primo de Rivera was a flawed man redeemed by his patriotism. As for the second Republic, this was greeted with fear by 'sane opinion'. Its breakup was caused primarily by freemasons, and Spain was then saved by the Caudillo.[21]

With such limited cultural baggage, it was not long before the regime sought to reinstate some of the fallen idols. The process began with Ortega whose writing and reputation was most readily serviceable to Francoism. By the sixties, Juan Ramon Jimenez and Sender had come within the net of nationalist cultural respectability. Censorship eased, and gradually even the works of Marx found themselves onto the bookstalls. But the official attitude was paternalistic and operated on the basis that the individual needed to be directed. Academic standards suffered on a diet of neutered courses and selective ideas. No nation's culture could honestly live with itself when so many of its prestigious names were in exile. Meanwhile the state educational system was subordinated to the interests of state-subsidized and mostly Church-run private schools. The cultural bias and educational mediocrity arising from Franco's Civil War victory was arguably the most lasting and damaging scar left by the conflict. There was a fear of criticism, because criticism was deemed to be, per se, hostile to Spain.

The stimulus of ideas was further deadened by the puritan hand of the censor in the arts and media. Some of Spain's best known artists, such as Juan Miro and Antoni Tapies, were denied recognition because they refused to let their reputations be exploited by the regime; neither could use their Catalan first names (Joan and Anton), and the first retrospective of Miro was not held until 1979 when the latter was close to ninety. The works of Garcia Lorca were banned from shops and stage. Jose Camilo Cela's penetrating study of the miserable post-war years, *La Colmena* (The Beehive), had to be published in Buenos Aires. The corrupting influence of Hollywood sex was gagged and the dubbed dialogue, as well as titles, altered. Films by Buñuel could not be imported and masterpieces like Eisenstein's *Battleship Potemkin*, were not shown simply because the director was Soviet and the message could be construed as revolutionary. Curiously enough the Spanish film-makers managed to get away with greater freedom, the censors overlooking the parabolic anti-regime nature of many scripts — perhaps because censorship is geared to control the written word or the pornographic image. Television on the other hand, first fully networked in 1956, was carefully manipulated and controlled, and the practice continued after Franco's death. Journalists had to be products of the official School of Journalism, created in 1941 under the auspices of the Falange. Journalists were sworn to serve the unity and greatness of the motherland. Press censorship was eased in 1966 as a result of new legislation but the media were dominated by the state-owned Movimiento press and radio networks plus the television. The first truly independent newspaper since the outbreak of the Civil War was *El Pais*, founded in 1976. Prior to this date it was difficult to question the conflict, its causes and consequences.

Part and parcel of the desecularization of the state was the revised status of the family and women. Under the 1944 Fuero de los Españoles (National Charter), marriage once again returned to being an indissoluble institution. All divorces that occurred during the Republic were denied validity and annulled. The libertarian image of the woman fighting alongside her male comrades with a gun was dropped. The woman's place was in the home: her role to suckle a child from an ample breast. The temptations of the flesh were reduced to a minimum to protect the purity of the Spanish maidens. In places of dangerous physical contact or visual excitement like beaches and swimming pools, morality was strictly enforced. In the forties, beach guards imposed fines for improper dress and swimming pools had separate hours for men and women. What a sudden reversal! Only in 1936 the Catalan Parliament had, for instance, approved legislation legalizing abortion that was among the most advanced in Europe.

The advanced social legislation of the Republic was not considered again until the advent of democracy. Even then four decades of accumulated conservatism profoundly influenced the shape of such legislation as was finally introduced.

THE REGIONS

The nationalist victory exacerbated the long-running and destabilizing problem of regional autonomy. The treatment accorded the two regions with the most powerful historical demands for autonomy, the Basque country and Catalonia, was vindictive and profoundly damaging. Repressed demands for autonomy from these two regions became the most serious problem of state once democracy was restored.

In response to vocal and vigorous demands for autonomy — a demand that cut across class — Catalonia was given a special status almost immediately the Republic began. The Catalan autonomy statute, endorsed overwhelmingly in 1932, gave the region a government (the Generalitat), conceded bilingualism and devolved a series of administrative functions while the central government retained control over defence, foreign affairs and internal security.

The Republic was slower in acceding to Basque autonomy demands, and the Basque country's autonomy statute was only approved by a rump parliament in Madrid three months after the outbreak of the Civil War. The Basque Nationalist Party (PNV) won this concession basically as a reward for agreeing to support the Republicans. This support was a tactical decision because the Basque Nationalists were basically conservative and deeply suspicious of the Popular Front's ideology.

In Catalonia the Republic was supported with more general intellectual and political conviction. Galicia also supported the Republic in the same way but the Civil War interrupted Galicia's hopes of obtaining autonomy.

Franco believed autonomy weakened the unity of Spain, and was incompatible with a strong central state. This ideological justification was fuelled by a good deal of pure old-fashioned revenge. Franco never forgave the Basque Government's support of the Republic. In June 1937, two months after Bilbao fell to the Nationalists, a decree was promulgated ending the system of ancient economic privileges — known as *Fueros* — accorded the two coastal and economically most advanced Basque Provinces of Guipuzcoa and Vizcaya. The spirit of vindictiveness extended to such acts as the confiscation of the huge assets of the Basque shipping magnate Ramon de la Sota even though he died just after the outbreak of the Civil War. No similar retaliatory measures were taken against other provinces in Spain that rallied to the republican cause. Furthermore, once the Nationalists had overrun the Basque country many Basques volunteered to fight for them.[22] Discrimination against these two provinces appeared the greater since Navarre, the home of the Carlists, was rewarded by being allowed to retain its own *Fueros*. Navarre was the only region in Spain allowed to have a separate fiscal status. Not only were the regional autonomy statutes revoked but a conscious campaign was directed at removing the traces of regional identity. Basque flags were

41

removed and Spanish speaking enforced in schools and public places. The same applied to Catalonia. The Basques however reacted more violently, spurred by the memory of Guernica. During the Franco regime there were no less than six states of emergency declared in the provinces of Guipuzcoa and Vizcaya. Basques formed the highest proportion of the regime's political prisoners.

SOBERING EXPERIENCE

Out of the dreadful experience of the Civil War some good has eventually been fashioned. The spectre of this conflict, and the fear of a repeat performance, conditioned the attitude of the main opposition — and illegal — parties in the twilight years of the Franco regime. The concept of *Ruptura*, a clean break with the past, on the Caudillo's death was rejected by the opposition because it threatened to revive destabilizing Civil War divisions. Such moderation meant that the democratic process was grafted onto the decaying Francoist system without revenge or vindictiveness. The Communist and Socialist Parties went as far as accepting the flag of the winning side in the Civil War in the new democratic order and gave up their espousal of republican ideology to accept the figure of the monarch. Rejection of republicanism was essential for the restoration of democracy since the monarchy was the only institution capable of unifying the two sides in the conflict.

The losing side, or its heirs, was willing to make concessions to play a part once again in national life. The same cannot be said of the winners. The armed forces, as the protagonists of victory, were also allowed to be its chief heirs and guardians. The existence of the military as guardians of the Francoist victory, in the end, intimidated the opposition into moderation. No one was willing to confront the military head-on, so an exaggerated fear of their power inhibited the development of democracy. Three years after Franco's death the constitution was approved, and the military were accorded a special role — guardians of national sovereignty and constitutional order. This role could be interpreted as giving the armed forces a constitutional right to intervene. That there should have been one abortive coup, two attempts foiled, and at least three other instances of disaffected officers discussing coups in under eight years of democracy is eloquent testimony of at least some officers' views of their role as guardians of the victory.

3 The Nature of Spain

The Civil War and the international isolation of the Franco regime that ensued helped prolong the traditional view of Spain. Essentially this was a romantic vision of a pre-industrial society, highly coloured by the exotic oriental influence of the Arab conquest and the prejudices of the Inquisition. Spain was somehow different from the rest of Europe. However, the economic and social changes that overtook the nation in the fifties fundamentally altered both the nature of Spain and of Spanish society, even if in cultural terms a more extravagant image persists.

No moment in Spanish history is better caught by the painter's brush than Goya's *Executions of May 3, 1808.* The populace of Madrid had risen heroically against the Napoleonic army the day before. Though crushed, the uprising led to what became Spain's War of Independence. Goya portrays the brutal aftermath by focussing on the victim of a firing squad in the fraction of a second before execution. The victim is already on his knees. But his trunk is erect, his arms splayed wide above his head. Is he triumphantly baring his breast before his executioners? Or is he merely afraid and confused as to how to die? Two details emphasise the imminence of his fate. The corpses of those already executed are close by, and the muskets of the execution squad are levelled anew, their bayonets almost touching the victim. The drama is heightened by the use of light. The huge canvas is oppressively coloured, save for a lantern on the ground which throws a brilliant light on the man about to die, who is wearing yellow breeches and a white shirt. The whiteness of the shirt highlights the wantonness of the killing, while the background of night stresses the murkiness of the act — an impression reinforced by the anonymity of the executioners, whose faces are turned slightly away, and whose lethal weapons appear almost as an extension of their bodies. Goya is unsparingly direct.

Spanish painters, and not just Goya, are notable for their vivid portrayal of man's inhumanity to man. Sometimes they have focussed on a specific event like the *Executions* or Picasso's *Guernica.* On other occasions the agonised body of Christ has served as a bloody symbol. What other nation's painters have depicted such deadly thorns in the crown of Christ! Walking round the Prado Museum, more dead bodies and violent scenes confront the visitor than in any other major picture gallery. (This, incidentally, includes a collection of non-Spanish paintings, especially Hieronimous Bosch.)

Is this the result of a particular Spanish predilection for violence and cruelty, an obsession with death? Is it more than a reflection of a violent history — one that includes the tortures of the Inquisition, repression in the Low Countries, subjugation of the natives in the New World, two civil wars in the nineteenth century and another this century? Bound up with an image of cruelty and violence is the label of fanaticism, which invariably has religious connotations. The Catholic struggle to expel the Moors, the crusading zeal behind the colonization of the Americas, the inflexibility of the Inquisition, the rigid adherence of the Carlists to their values of Church and Crown, the campaign of the Falange to rid Spain of the 'Red' menace during the last Civil War — all may be cited as examples of this fanaticism.

Spain is the country of black and white. Of all or nothing, *todo o nada*. There is belief without doubt, action without compromise. The image is so all-pervading that it sustains itself. The title of a book on Spain written in the early fifties by the British novelist and essayist, V.S. Pritchett, is symptomatic — *The Spanish Temper*. The dust jacket promised the reader would be taken to the heart of the most 'foreign' of European countries. Spain is different.[1]

Spanish history is full of contradictions and paradoxes, and Spain has undeniably run counter to the mainstream of European history. No other European nation has had its territory three-quarters overrun by the Arabs in an occupation which lasted eight centuries. The Arab conquest, combined with a strong Jewish presence has given Spain a unique semitic influence. Although Spain was the first country in Europe to enjoy a unified state, it has been bedevilled by demands for regional autonomy and remains confused about its own nationhood. In less than a century Spain built an empire in Europe and the Americas equal to none at the time; but the empire began collapsing in the sixteenth century almost as soon as it had reached its zenith, eclipsed by the protestant nations of northern Europe.

Spain defiantly rejected the puritan capitalist ethic, and the wealth from the American colonies was frittered away with little or no concern to generate new resources and capabilities. The great period of international commercial expansion from the late seventeenth century onwards was largely ignored as Spain turned in on itself. While the rest of Europe embraced the age of reason, the main university at Salamanca was still conducting theology classes that included discussion of what language the angels spoke, or whether the sky was made of bell metal or a wine-like liquid.

Spaniards, meanwhile, have been endowed with an unshakeable set of national traits. The deluded Castilian knight, Don Quixote, and the exuberant Andalusian lover, Don Juan, walk across the pages of literature leaving behind them a trail of stereotypes and conditioning an entire aesthetic of the Spaniard. Don Quixote incarnates the spirit of non-compromise, so inflexible as to tilt against his own self-interest and against reality; his hopelessness and failure are forgotten beside his nobility of purpose. The quintessential virtues of the Spanish male are bravery, honour, and pride in the conquest of arms or love. The women have been rather left out, relegated to the condition of dusky-eyed maidens coquettish behind fans, or voluptuous gipsies dancing flamenco.

The image of Spain being 'different' was given an artificial stimulus by the Franco regime. At the time of the Republic, traditional Spain was made to change and began to change. But Franco dusted off the image of the ideal Spaniard and traditional Spain. He exploited this in nationalistic, quasi-racial and chauvinistic terms to counter Spain's international isolation. It also suited the newly-found industry of tourism to promote the folklore of Spain. A promotion campaign even carried the slogan 'Spain is different'. As much as anything this was a smokescreen for Spain's failure to win international respectability; yet it obscured the changes taking place in Spain and Spanish society, especially from the sixties onwards.

A FLAWED VIEW

The basic fault in the traditional view of Spain — both by foreigners and by Spaniards themselves — is the lack of differentiation between what is particular to Spain and what are generalised phenomena of particular stages of economic, political and social development. Spain was much slower in embracing modernism and much later in experiencing sustained economic development than its European neighbours. Thus what has often been considered as 'Spanish' was no more than a reflection of a rural, pre-industrial society. The Spanish virtues were those of medieval chivalry, shared across Europe.

The conditioning factors that furnished this society with its 'Spanishness' were the domination by a ruling class that clung to Catholic military ideals; the poverty produced by a harsh climate and lack of resources; and the insecurity arising from this poverty and usually incompetent domination.

Gerald Brenan in his *History of Spanish Literature* comments:

> It is thus the literature of a people who have scarcely ever known security or comfort. As one reads it one cannot fail to be struck by the fact that from the Middle Ages to the eighteenth century the note of hunger runs persistently through the novels, or that such a large number of Spanish writers have either spent part of their lives in prison or else have been exiles. These things account for the tautness and alertness that characterise so much Spanish literature and for the background of melancholy and nostalgia (soledad) out of which even the gayest passages — and much Spanish literature is gay — have sprung. They also account for the realism.[2]

Once the structure of the economy changes, social mobility increases, the model of society alters and the power of the old ruling class is eroded, and

45

fundamentally new influences come into play. This has happened to Spain over the last thirty years and with far greater momentum and dimension since Franco's death. Spain has ceased to be so different.

SEARCHING FOR THE SOUL

Spain was never part of the European Grand Tour — travel was too uncomfortable to be fashionable. The roads were bad and made dangerous by bandits; the accommodation was rough, and the weather and cuisine were only for tough constitutions. Also the intellectual curiosity shown by northern Europe towards Italy was seldom shown towards Spain. Cervantes' reputation abroad was an exception. Indeed there was a huge gap between the interest of twelfth century scholars such as Adelard of Bath, who went to Spain to study Arabic texts (frequently as a means of rediscovering the Greek classics) and that of the Hispanicists who emerged in the nineteenth century.

Modern European interest in Spain was stimulated by the War of Independence, 1808-14. The names given to this war were symptomatic of prevailing attitudes. For the Spanish, it was a struggle to rid foreigners from their soil and little credit was given to British troops under Wellington for expelling the French. For the British it was the Peninsular War — the Iberian Peninsula being just one place where Anglo-French rivalry was played out. Whatever the national interests at stake, some 200 books appeared in England as a result of the campaign and Goya painted a portrait of Wellington, the first prominent English sitter for a Spanish painter. Meanwhile, large-scale looting of Spanish art treasures by discerning French officers led to the first real dissemination of Spanish art beyond the Pyrenees. Until then the only painter who was widely appreciated was Murillo, because his style and colours were closest to the Italians.

Hardy and curious travellers began to appear in the 1830s; their views were to have a profound effect in conditioning the attitudes of foreigners and Spaniards alike. The most influential were the French writers, Theophile Gautier and Prosper Merime; the English traveller Richard Ford and the scholar sent to sell bibles, George Burrow; and the American writers Washington Irving and George Ticknor.[3] These men offered a wealth of detail and insight into Spain. Their eyes were fresh and excited. But basically they treated Spain as a discovery. On their own European doorstep they had come across a strange and exotic land. Their attention focussed on the most *non-European* aspects of Spain: the South with its magnificent Moorish monuments in Cordoba, Granada and Seville, where the oriental influence so clearly persisted. What in their own societies would have been criticized as egoism was seen in Spain as splendid individualism. Spanish pride was extolled; and few, if any, would have accepted that pride was a reflection of poverty — the sole possession an oppressed peasant could safely retain.

The romantic view passed unchallenged into this century, no doubt aided by the fact that the two regions which looked closest to Europe, the Basque country and Catalonia, were often the first that travellers passed through, and were atypical. The romantic view was still prevalent at the time of the Civil War, and was successfully commercialized by such Hispanophiles as Hemmingway, who popularised Spain at the expense of type-casting the Spanish male as noble, a lover of bull-fights, wine, and hard swearing.

It was the fascination and envy of those who had lost their innocence in an urban, industrialized society and who could afford the luxury of observing what they had lost. Real people still existed in Spain, untainted by the evils of modern civilisation. Even the most politicized of the European left who fought for the Republic frequently gave the impression of secretly wishing to preserve the noble peasant, the valiant Anarchist. After the Civil War the image lingered on.

Side by side with this romantic view of Spain there has been an unmistakable streak of prejudice. Spain's violent rejection of Lutheranism and the Reformation was never comprehended by protestants in northern Europe. Even the seemingly harmless English nursery rhyme — *Mary, Mary, quite contrary/how does your garden grow/with jingle bells and cockle shells . . .* — derives from a caustic anti-Catholic ditty deriding Mary Tudor (the cockle shells were a symbol of the Catholic pilgrimage to Santiago de Compostela). For Europe's Catholics, meanwhile, the teachings and example of figures like Saint John of the Cross, Santa Teresa of Avila and Ignatious of Loyola were a source of admiration and inspiration. Yet many European Catholics found Spain's virulent role as hammer of the heretic both anachronistic and incomprehensible.

The emergence of Hispanicists in the nineteenth century helped spur Spanish intellectuals on to examine the nature of their own country. The moment was ripe for historical introspection. The nineteenth century had seen Spain oscillate between foreign occupation, civil war, democracy and a liberal constitution, a brief republican experiment and Borbon dynastic squabbles to the accompaniment of military coups. The century was completed by the disastrous loss of the two remaining prize colonies — Cuba and the Philippines — to the United States. Spain was put on the couch and the national psyche questioned with a dedication and umbilical absorption only possible in an inward-looking culture. (Spanish writers, incidentally, have shown very little curiosity in writing about other countries.)

All tried to determine what had gone wrong to produce such a decline, such a divergence in progress and ambition from the rest of Europe. It was as though some special hubris existed in the Spanish character. How was it possible that the 'Black Legend' of the evils of the Inquisition still persisted; how was there such an appalling divide between the two Spains, one seeking to enter the modern world, the other viscerally rejecting change? The best known figures to emerge in the course of this national breast-beating were Ortega and Unamuno. They wanted to find out why every Spaniard was attached to Spain but had ceased to be proud of it. Neither were especially original thinkers and the solutions offered were a mixture of national regeneration and moral christian renewal — germs of ideas that came close to those espoused by the Nationalists at the outbreak of the Civil War.[4]

HISTORIOGRAPHY AND AMERICO CASTRO

The most controversial voice among this so-called 'Generation of '98' was Americo Castro, a literary historian and philologist by training. At one stage he had been ambassador of the Republic to Berlin. After the Civil War he became obsessed with the reasons why Spaniards could act so divisively. Spurred on by the Nationalists' exploitation of Spain's Catholic past, he began to re-examine history in a new light. The official concept postulated that an entity called 'Spain' had existed from earliest times — not only before the Arab conquest but before the Goths and Romans had penetrated the peninsula. From the earliest times of christianity Spain had also been Catholic — and was eternally so. Hence the struggle to rid Spain of the Arabs was a re-conquest (*reconquista*) both of territory and faith. Castro saw this as a tailor-made justification for driving the Moors from Spain, expelling the Jews, and the institution of the Inquisition. This also justified subsequent insistence on a highly centralized government which preserved the sacred unity of 'Spain'.

He began by examining the long struggle by the christian states and enclaves against the Arabs. The peninsula contained three distinct castes at this time, consisting of Arabs, Christians, and Jews. During the course of the seven-century struggle (probably less continual and religious in character than depicted) the Castilians, who were the driving force, assimilated several of their adversaries' characteristics, including the theocratic idea of mingling nationhood with religion. With the fall of Granada in 1492, the Moors were run out of Spain and played no further direct part in Spanish history. The case of the other caste, the Jews, was of particular importance. Over 100,000 became converts to protect themselves. These new christians had traditionally been active in finance, administration, intellectual activity, and certain crafts.

The converts and their descendants continued their former activities. Indeed, precisely because the new christians occupied the role of the former Jewish community, the divide in society between the castes was retained and probably deepened. For instance it is now considered likely, and not just by Castro, that some of the foremost figures of the literary Golden Age, Cervantes and Saint Teresa for example, were new christians. (Don Quixote was a parable about the Castilian knight, the pillar of society, viewed with the clarity and distance of an outsider.) The fact that intellectual activity was often associated with caste reinforced the spirit of anti-intellectualism among the old christians and Castilians. This spirit helped to retain the purity of their caste. The racialism inherent in the attitudes of the old christians was evident in the application of tests to check the purity (*limpieza*) of stock for persons applying for jobs or forming merchants' guilds. The inevitable antagonism which ensued contained a class aspect, in that the religious persecution of the Jews via the tool of the Inquisition was also a means of ensuring control over the commercial and administrative activities of the new christians. The disdain for commercial activity by the old christians and Castilians was not a rejection of money; rather it was rejection of identification with a particular class of people. An important reason for the Inquisition lasting 322 years until 1813 was because it served the old christian caste, dominated by Castilians.[5]

Castro perhaps makes Castile too much the villain. But if one accepts his approach certain enigmas of Spain are more easily understood. Certainly it provided Castro with the answer for what troubled him most — the existence of the 'two Spains'. The military class incarnated by Castile was against modernism at all cost, even to the extent of blinding itself to reality. To embrace modernism threatened the purity of the old christians and therefore their domination of Spain.[6]

The essential values of any warrior class are those which ensure survival in a hostile environment — bravery, self-sacrifice, obedience to leaders and a sense of honour. There is a natural contempt for any work that does not demand 'manly' qualities, and a corresponding belief that man's dignity is only preserved by performing specific tasks. In this scale of values trade, commercial activity and administrative jobs are viewed with contempt. Indeed there are striking parallels between it and the ideals of the desert Bedu.

Contempt for commerce on the part of the old christians and their zeal to control the converts to christianity help explain Spain's failure to utilize the immense wealth of the New World. The Catholic crusading colonization of the Americas was conducted by soldiers in search of new soldiering after the expulsion of the Moors. Those who colonized for commercial profit were a minority composed mainly of non-Spaniards, such as the Genoese Columbus, or were Jewish. Those Spaniards who returned enriched from the colonies were indiscriminately labelled Jews; many preferred not to return to avoid this stigma. The wealth of gold and silver received from the Americas was ill spent by the monarchy — eaten up by uncontrolled inflation, or absorbed by the Church on such extravaganzas as the 1,700 kilos of silver used in a ceremonial carriage for Cadiz Cathedral.

Those societies which practice thrift are ones that have earned what they produced through hard work and application of technology. The wealth of the colonies was treated as heaven-sent, proof of God being on the side of — and never deserting — Catholic Spain. Lacking reverence for wealth, the

Spanish beneficiaries of the New World spent without inhibition, and without any thought of redistribution.

Contempt for the accumulation of wealth and development of resources was also evident in the way the new masters in southern Spain showed more concern for exercizing political control over their conquered subjects than for maintaining the potentially rich agricultural system. The destruction and neglect of irrigation systems and cultivated land in the south impoverished Andalusia, and tipped the balance of economic power permanently towards the Mediterranean and the north.

Even the terminology of commerce reflected warrior class contempt. Business was *negocio* — which literally meant 'the negation of leisure'. Furthermore there was, and still is, no word simply describing success in business. The word employed, *triumpho*, is borrowed from the battlefield and the theatre.

With such an attitude towards commercial activity and a permanent fear that the new christians might usurp their privileges, the old christians had a blinkered interest in inhibiting the rise of a middle class. And this they did with remarkable success. A Spanish middle class barely existed until the late 1950s. Previously this class had only emerged in Catalonia and to a lesser extent in the Basque country and the capital. Its absence had major political consequences. It meant that there was no moderating or stabilizing inter-mediary between the peasantry, and latterly the small urban proletariat, and their rulers. On the one hand this encouraged oppression and distance between the two. On the other, it made the peasantry much more prone to explode in acts of disorganized violent protest.

At a more general level, the absence of a well-rooted middle class eliminated a channel through which aristocratic taste could be distilled or primitive popular taste refined and diluted. Life was either rough and crude, or almost decadently refined. Thus Goya could move with apparent ease from painting a sumptuous royal portrait to the horrors of war with complete consistency. Language was direct and without irony — even today irony is not a device frequently used. Spanish evolved a very limited vocabulary to express the tenderness of love because life was fundamentally harsh and insecure. Several commentators have pointed out that Spain is a country where popular arts triumph — ceramics, flamenco, the fiesta, and the bull-fight. Arguably, bull-fighting has survived to this day because there has been no self-righteous middle class to protest at the cruelty. Cruel sports in northern Europe were eliminated not because they ceased to be popular but as a result of middle class propriety. Londoners would have flocked to see heads stuck on London Bridge long after it was stopped. This lack of an intermediary between popular revenge and justice (fairplay) partly explains the ferocity of the Civil War.

50

CASTILE AND CENTRALISM

The unification of Spain was achieved with remarkable rapidity. The fall of Granada occurred twelve years after the two most important Catholic kingdoms in the peninsula had formed a dynastic alliance. Ferdinand of Aragon married Isabel of Castile. They became the 'Catholic Kings' when, in 1492, Pope Alexander VI conferred this title for their services to christendom. The dominant force in this alliance was Castile which now saw itself as both the soul and guardian of Spain.

The basis for unity was allegiance to the monarchy and the Church, who between them had acquired physical and moral control as a result of the *reconquista*. Castilian was the common language, understood if not always spoken. Another factor favouring nationhood was the clear definition of the Iberian Peninsula. The Pyrenees stretching from the Atlantic to the Mediterranean, leaving only narrow gaps at either coast, provided a natural frontier to the north. At the other end, the Straits of Gibraltar separated Spain from North Africa.

The fabric of unity was, however, much weaker than it seemed. Coming from the centre of Spain, the Catholic Kings found themselves incapable of conceiving a form of government other than a highly centralized one. Yet no genuine centrifugal force obliged the people and communities living on the periphery of the Peninsula to look towards the centre. On the contrary, Spain's orography encouraged the identity of small communities and fostered separatism.

If the Pyrenees are included, mainland Spain has twelve ranges of mountains. Their length varies from 150 kilometres to 700 kilometres in the case of the central chain whose main components are the Gredos Mountains and the Guadarrama range. In places these ranges have peaks of nearly 3,500 metres. The centre of Spain is occupied by the vast tableland of the Meseta which stretches unevenly outwards almost to the Pyrenees, to Galicia, east nearly to the Mediterranean, and stopping in the south before the Guadalquivir Valley. The bleak Meseta occupies over 40% of Spain's landmass. Spain averages 600 metres above sea level, the highest country in Europe after Switzerland. Flat plains along the coast are limited and the littoral is sharply divided from the interior. The mountain chains run largely on an east-west axis, none directly north-south.

This rugged terrain has been a formidable barrier to the movement of people, goods and ideas. To establish a highly centralized state would be to defy nature. Any journey from Madrid involved crossing between two and three chains of mountains to reach the populous and more prosperous littoral. Movement was especially difficult on a north-south axis. Communities and regions were thus isolated both from each other and the country as a whole. If self-supporting there was no need for communities to

51

look beyond themselves. Traders like the Catalans, or coastal regions with surplus goods like Valencia, had little interest in turning towards the centre. It was easier to sail a boat to Marseilles, Genoa, Naples and Palermo. It was quicker and safer even in the mid-nineteenth century to go from Barcelona to Cadiz by sea than by land. The same was true of northern ports like Coruña or Bilbao. Those living along the northern coast rarely thought of seeking their fortunes in Madrid, the south of Spain or even Catalonia. Instead they emigrated to Cuba, the Philippines and the Americas. The south was perhaps the closest linked to the centre, because Spaniards of central and northern Spain had moved south during the *reconquista*.

The centre, on the other hand, needed the resources of the periphery, especially after the decline of the mediaeval wool trade. With the centre controlling the purse strings and initially benefitting from the wealth of the colonies, Castile, Extremadura and La Mancha might have generated some self-sustaining economic activity. But the population here was far too small to create an adequate market. Circumstances forced Madrid to look outwards but it did this in a parasitic, quasi-colonial manner. 'Everyone works for Madrid and Madrid works for no one', the saying went.

An effective network of communications would have dramatically altered this state of affairs. But the Catholic Kings and their successors failed to establish one. It is hard to find a rational explanation for such an omission, for the same occurred in the Spanish colonies of America. While the English found or made roads over which they could drag their transport, the Spaniards hauled their goods and belongings on mules without insisting that their settlements had adequate connections by carriage with the outside world. One suggestion is that this attitude to communications and transport was a product of Arab influence. The Arabs in Spain were indifferent to the establishment of roads suited to vehicles with wheels, because of their desert heritage.

This myopia towards communications persisted when the nineteenth-century railway boom occurred in Europe. Spain was not opened up by railways on the same scale as the rest of Europe. (It also opted for a smaller gauge track, which remains to this day.) Furthermore, the railway network followed no rational conception of economic and social development. The network was radial, based on Madrid at a time when Madrid's population was half that of Barcelona. Even today the track between these, Spain's two largest cities, is such that the maximum speed is eighty kilometres per hour.[8]

Even though Franco fervently believed in centralized rule, he ignored the possibilities of a modern network of railways and road. This was a surprising omission in view of the attention to this by his fellow dictators, Hitler and Mussolini. For instance, once Franco had abolished the regional autonomy statutes of the Basque country and Catalonia the logical step would have been to weld them in every way to central government. He ignored communications (save the more glamorous airports) and no major road link was constructed between Madrid and any of the littoral cities. Indeed the largest motorway construction programme, privately run, was in the Basque country and Catalonia connecting these regions not with Madrid but with France — the outside world. The same state of affairs persisted after his death.

Spain's rulers paid more attention to an abstract vision of unified Spain. In the same way the greatest link with the colonies abroad was through 'hispanidad' — a vague concept of the brotherhood of Spanish-speaking communities whose existence was taken for granted, and which therefore need not be preserved by any institutional framework. Establishing Madrid as capital of Spain was a political statement symbolizing this abstract vision of unity. The sole raison d'être for the location was Madrid's geographical position in the centre of Castile; and Castile controlled Spain. Madrid had no resources. It was not until the sixties that the artificiality of Madrid as the centre of Spain began to break down as it generated its own economic activity through the location of factories and offices.

An interesting parallel can be found in Iran and Turkey. In differing eras both Iran and Turkey enjoyed empire, for which the driving force came from people in the dry central plateaux. Both countries ended up with capitals, Tehran and Ankara, in the arid centre as an assertion of centralized authority. Rather than rendering government easier, the artificial capital created a disruptive imbalance.

PROBLEMS OF CENTRALISM

Spain's principal problem since the *reconquista* has revolved round the relationship of central government with the various communities and regions on the periphery of the centre. With rare exceptions, like that of Charles III, the overriding philosophy has been that political control is more important than economic and social development. Political allegiance was preferred above prosperity — a preference which has cost Spain dear. The system was geared to absolutism. The differential lay in the extent to which the rulers were willing and able to wield power.

Ortega makes the point that the unified state of Spain happened early — too early — because the country never evolved a proper feudal system. Spain, he said, lacked the 'robust pluralism' of powerful barons[9]. No Spanish barons read the riot act to the monarch as the English barons did at Runymeade with the Magna Carta. While this helps explain the absence of checks and balances on Spain's rulers, the extraordinary paradox remains. How can Spain have been a unified state for almost 500 years yet still be unable to come to terms with separatist and autonomous demands?

For a start the Kings failed to create an institutional base for the unified state. As a result little attempt was made at the outset to alter historic practices and privileges. Yet language, legal practice, local representation and land tenure were precisely those aspects which helped sustain Spain in a federal or semi-cantonal state. The exception was Catalonia where tension between the crown and the Catalans was almost continuous. Catalonia sought to preserve its commercial privileges against a monarchy jealous of Catalan wealth and wary of its close ties with France. The Basques, up to the middle of the nineteenth century, retained a set of privileges that included the right to mint coinage, hold their own law courts and parliament, and raise a militia. These rights were removed only when the Basques sided with the Carlist pretender in the late nineteenth century. The rise of modern Basque nationalism stems from this. Likewise the rise of modern Catalan nationalism can be traced to the loss in the nineteenth century of their right to use their own commercial law, mint coinage, and conduct education in Catalan.

Significantly, concern for the unity of Spain has been far more acute during periods of authoritarian rule than liberal, republican, or democratic. During the latter periods far greater willingness to accept the regional differences of the nation has been evident. The brief Republic of 1873 resulted in all the major cities in the south save one — from Seville to Valencia — declaring themselves either free ports or independent cantons. The second Republic in the thirties granted autonomy to Catalonia and the Basque country. It was also on the point of conceding a statute to Galicia, and a draft for Andalusia was under consideration. Now, the 1978 constitution has conceded every region the right to autonomy.

Yet under the Republic, and even now, a visceral mistrust persists towards demands for autonomy. The Republic was exceedingly tardy in processing Basque requests for autonomy, and was slower still with Andalusia and Galicia. The 1978 constitution itself when discussing autonomy goes out of its way to first stress 'the indissoluble unity' of the Spanish nation.[10] Since then the attitude in conceding autonomy has been centralist — give an inch and the regions will take a mile. Spain has inherited through the ages a gut fear that federalism will render it ungovernable and weaken the essence of the nation: an essence provided by Castile at the centre.

This point is disputed by Basques and Catalans. Basques, the most radical in their nationalism, do not as a rule deny their Spanishness, but they reject Castile's God-given right to determine what is Spanishness. However, there are Basques, notably ETA and its supporters, who believe that the inclusion of the Basque country in the state of Spain was an accident, and the sooner this is rectified the better.

Even in the case of such extremism the root lies probably far more in a dislike of Madrid and Castile and all it stands for, than in a desire to break up Spain's unity. When the most tangible form of the state was repressive, not surprisingly the family, the village, the city or the region became the natural focus of allegiance and source of identity. Was this why soldiers were exhorted to fight for God first, and then the motherland: not for King and

Spain? The gap between ruler and ruled was exacerbated by Spain's poverty and the uncompromisingly centralist nature of bureaucracy.

Once wealth from the colonies had been dissipated, Spain was thrown back upon its agricultural resources. Its minerals, like copper, so valuable to the Romans, had been exhausted and had to await the turn of the nineteenth century for new foreign technology and capital. Agricultural resources could have been improved, so raising rural living standards to provide an eventual market for industrial goods. But successive governments lacked the will to confront the big landowners and alter the system of tenure. The large estates in the south often had good soil but low rainfall, requiring careful husbandry and irrigation. Unfortunately for Spain, most rain fell in the north, in Galicia, where either the soil was poor and overworked or holdings uneconomically small. Throughout Spain the predominant weather condition was drought. Those regions that managed to move beyond agriculture — the Basque country, parts of Asturias and Catalonia — did so despite the *rentier* approach of governments and almost entirely on their own initiative. But these regions were not interested in financing the well-being of the rest of Spain for whom they showed little respect.

The combination of poverty and an overly-centralized administration was a recipe for corrupt, unresponsive government. Though poorly paid, jobs in the bureaucracy offered the twin attractions of security and peddling influence. The intrigue and the corruption of the administration, boosted by the instability of nineteenth-century Spain, created a huge gulf between what happened in Madrid and the provinces. Civil servants and the new class of politicians had scant interest in matters outside the capital; when dealing with the provinces, they did so via intermediaries who were usually the most unpopular figures — the local boss or *cacique*.

Most Spaniards were, therefore, total bystanders. Denied participation in the functioning of state, there was little incentive to believe in it. Under these circumstances the country was naturally fissiparous.[11] The sense of frustration and exclusion in the provinces produced a groundswell of resentment which, when provoked, burst into violence. Usually it was ill-organized, directionless, and self-defeating — the blind anger of people who feel hopelessly defrauded. Rage was vented on the most obvious symbols of oppression or privilege — the landowners' property or the church. Once these had been burned or damaged there was nothing left to do except await repression. This was the pattern of peasant protest in Andalusia in the nineteenth century and through to the Civil War. No wonder anarchism found followers in rural Spain and among the newly industrialized workers. It had already existed without the label. It was not natural to Spain — as often stated — but natural in this environment.

REGIONAL DIVERSITY

The diversity of climate, historical experience and people make many generalizations about Spain unwise. Yet one fundamental differentiating factor within Spain has been the presence or absence of Arabs. The Arab penetration halted at a rough line running from Galicia through Asturias, Cantabria and the Basque country before running across the southern flank of the Pyrenees to northern Catalonia. Much of the central and northern part of the Meseta was a contested no-man's land. In those regions where the Arabs did not penetrate, the Celtic and Iberian strains (in some instances already mingled with the Goths and Romans) remained intact. The rest of Spain, especially the populous south in what is now Andalusia and Murcia, was heavily intermingled with Arab and Berber blood. Almost eight centuries is a long time for racial and cultural assimilation.[12]

In the south features are largely semitic. In the north people are taller, skins are fairer, in some instances clearly Celtic.[13] In the case of the Basques, racial purity is more refined. Protected by high mountains in small valleys fertile enough to be self-supporting, the Basques have managed to survive as one of Europe's oldest autochthonous races. Their ancient language, Euskerra, loses its roots in the mists of time and scholars still dispute its origin. It is widely accepted as Europe's oldest extant language being distinct from, though similar in construction to, Iberian. Prior to the advent of the Romans and Latin, Iberian was the main indigenous language, probably of North African origin. Spain also housed one other autochthonous race which has now either disappeared or been wholly assimilated — the Guanchos who were the original inhabitants of the Canary Islands, subjugated in the fifteenth century.

Victorious Castile expelled the Arab population and turned its back on the heathen Arab culture. Nevertheless a large number of Arabic loan words found their way into Castilian Spanish. Many words referring to everyday institutions and persons were directly incorporated and remain. For instance, *alcalde* from *al qadi* (mayor); *aduana* from *al diwan* (customs house); *almacen* from *al maxzan* (shop); *albañil* from *al banni* (bricklayer, mason). The same is true of foodstuffs: *arroz* from *al ruzz* (rice); *aceite* from *al zait* (olive oil); *naranja* from *naranj* (orange). In central and southern Spain a high proportion of place names, rivers and mountains retain unaltered Arabic origins. *Medina*, Arabic for town, became a prefix (Medina Sidonia). The Arabic for river — *wadi* — became the prefix *guad*. Hence the biggest river of the south is called Guadalquivir from *wadi al kabir* (the big river).[14]

While Castilian incorporated words without fuss from Arabic, it avoided doing so with Euskerra and Catalan. This is probably because the conquering Castilians had more daily contact with the population in the south than with the Basques, Catalans and Galicians who were already part of 'Spain'. It may also have been because Castile's cultural imperialism was singularly in-effective. To this day these three peoples have retained their language despite attempts of varying vigour to stamp them out and despite the modernization of Spanish communications. These languages persist in regions next to frontiers where the same language is still spoken or understood on both sides. Castilian, Catalan, and Portuguese are all Latin based; the regional context has provided the differentiation. Gallego (Galician) is an adaptation of Portuguese, while Catalan has been influenced by Provençal rather than Castilian.

The largest non-Castilian speaking community has been, and remains, Catalan; the smallest is Basque. Catalan is spoken in differing forms from just inside the French border, along the Mediterranean coast to Valencia and in the Balearic Islands. (The principality of Andorra also uses it as the official language.) Basque, on the other hand, suffered a process of attrition and survived strongest in the interior and in small communities rather than large towns like Bilbao. Throughout the forty years of the Franco regime, public use of the three non-Castilian languages was forbidden; but it is reckoned that six and a half million speak Catalan; a further three million speak Gallego, and 650,000 Euskerra. Just over a quarter of the present population of Spain therefore speak a language other than Castilian for their mother tongue, a high proportion for a centralized state.[15] The constitution describes Castilian as the 'official Spanish language', and ambiguously accepts bilingualism in the regions. The educational effort now being made with these three languages, especially Catalan and Euskerra, will inevitably raise the per-centage of bilingualism.

Those regions with non-Castilian mother tongues have acquired the great-est sense of distinction and historic identity. When it came to discussing autonomy under the new constitution the Basque country, Catalonia and Galicia were accepted as historic regions and treated differently. Andalusia subsequently won similar treatment. Andalusians, draw identity from the most distinctive Castilian accent which reduces all sibilants to a single soft 's' and half the words sound swallowed.

Language must not be seen in isolation. Climate and the level of prosperity vary enormously creating substantial differences. Often it is hard even to find a connecting thread of Spanishness between say the austere granite monastery of El Escorial, the fantasy of a Gaudi building in Barcelona, the soft stone farm houses (*pazos*) in Galicia, the discreet romanesque churches of Asturias, the sugar white villages of southern Andalusia, or the moorish refinement of the grand mosque in Cordoba.

It was natural that those living on the Meseta in Castile, La Mancha, Leon, and Extremadura, should be affected by the bleakness and harshness of their environment. Life was a constant battle against the elements — vicious summer heat, blighting winter winds; poor crops struggling against erosion and drought; sheep constantly herded in search of pasture. The austere spirit that emerged from this struggle to survive, nourished on Catholic belief, was the essence of Castile. The inclement Meseta supported only a limited population in small, widely dispersed communities. Urban civilisation seemed inappropriate to the vast expanses of the tableland.

In contrast, the Mediterranean coastal belt had both the resources and climate to develop urban centres which already existed from Phoenician times. The Phoenician presence extended all the way round the Straits of Gibraltar to Cadiz. Mediterranean agriculture was settled and broken up into small holdings. Round Valencia the irrigation systems initiated by the Romans and developed by the Arabs were preserved after the *reconquista*, as in the plain of Murcia, which helped to assure prosperity from citrus and rice crops. In Catalonia, agriculture was complemented by a nascent textile industry and the growth of Mediterranean trade. The Catalan trading tradition was stimulated by inheritance laws that, unlike the rest of Spain, followed the principle of primogeniture. The eldest son was left the entire property or the best parts of the vineyards, citrus and olives, forcing the younger sons to fend for themselves. From the Catalan involvement with trade comes their attribute of *seny* — canny common sense. Life on the Mediterranean littoral was never harsh. The soft climate generated a gregarious outdoor community whose early prosperity ensured that this was the first place in Spain to embrace bourgeois values.

Parts of Andalusia possess the most fertile soil in Europe, but much of the interior never recovered from the effects of the *reconquista*. Land was redistributed to those whom the Kings felt like rewarding. Large estates were created, with a landowning class that had little interest in agriculture, which in turn created a mass of landless labourers in an already populous region. The decline of Andalusia was obscured while Seville retained the monopoly of trade with the colonies. However, from the eighteenth century onwards, the plight of the landless labourers was dramatic. The image of Andalusian indolence stemmed from the cultivated idleness of the rich and the enforced idleness of the poor, who either had no work or relied exclusively on seasonal employment. No wonder these people were fatalistic and their gaiety a reflection of southern heat and a mask to forget their essential misery.[16]

While the hallmark of Andalusia was the latifundia and landless labourers, Galicia was distinguished by its minifundia — small family holdings. Originally these holdings were rented from the Church which, during the Arab conquest, had become a major landowner with the wealth it derived from the pilgrimage to Santiago de Compostela.[17] These holdings sustained small scale animal husbandry and sufficient crops to keep a household. But pressure on the land, combined with divisions resulting from the system of inheritance, reduced these plots to subsistence level. The peasantry became progressively poorer, and the land was soon unable to support the population. Seafaring and fishing were only partial answers. Galicia, like Andalusia, became a land of exiled emigrants. The Galicians held and still hold a special fascination for other Spaniards with their misty heaths, tales of witchcraft, paleo-christian mysticism and peasant cunning.

Galicia and the north coast have an Atlantic climate with mild humid winters and markedly different seasons. In Asturias, Cantabria and the Basque country rural poverty was less marked, as the land holdings, family owned, were large enough to be economically sound. The communities however were isolated. Urban growth only came in the late nineteenth century with the rise of industry. Iron ore and coal had long been mined but the development of technology had been slow and was brought in from England. With industry came banking. The Basque sense of thrift and hard work, refined from contact with northern Europe, was instrumental in the development of the modern banking system. What could be more different than grimy industrial Bilbao fogged by pollution, and hot coloured Seville basking in the decadence of its Arab and colonial past? The exception to industrial development in the north was the inland province of Navarre. This prosperous rural community was an enclave of conservatism, loyal to the Church and crown.

IMPACT OF CHANGE

The past thirty years has witnessed an irrevocable shift in the nature of employment and the structure of the population. This is the biggest change in Spanish society in the five centuries since the expulsion of the Arabs and Jews. In a very concentrated period of time, Spain has ceased to be the agrarian society of old. The majority of the population no longer lives in — or depends on — the land. Instead most Spaniards live in the cities, especially the big urban centres, and their livelihoods depend upon industry and the service sector. This movement is a direct consequence of the modernisation of the economy and Spain's closer integration with Europe. The pattern of change in Spanish society is similar to that earlier set by Italy.

Just under half of all the forty-nine provinces in Spain have been depopulated in the past thirty years. The provinces that have lost most people are the poorest agricultural ones — basically those covering the Meseta (except Madrid), inland Galicia and the interior of Andalusia. There has been a net shift of population from south to north, with Madrid, the Basque country, parts of Cantabria, Catalonia, and the area round Zaragoza as the main growth areas. Due to the boom in tourism, both the Balearic Islands and the Canaries have witnessed a net inflow from the peninsula. The areas of net immigration are industrial and commercial centres. Nine provinces alone now account for half the total population. The provinces containing Madrid and Barcelona house nearly a quarter of Spain's 37 million inhabitants between them.

Internal migration was accompanied by a major period of emigration abroad, essentially to northern Europe. In the sixties over 1 million persons left to work in northern Europe, for the most part in France and West Germany. Perhaps less than half of this emigration was permanent; but it provided a dual stimulus for change. Remittances from these workers were a vital source of hard currency to finance Spain's growing appetite for imports; while for the workers themselves exposure to foreign cultures was a modernizing influence.

Side by side with the dramatic shift in the population has been a change in the nature of employment. As late as the 1920s, 57% of Spain's active population was employed in agriculture. In the next thirty years this fell by only 10%. But from 1950 onwards it fell by almost 10% every decade, and by 1980 it had dropped to below 18%. In contrast the number of persons employed in industry and the services has nearly doubled since the 1920s. Again the pace of change began to accelerate after 1950. By 1980 almost 37% of the active population was employed in industry and 42% in the services (the administration, banking, commerce etc). This rapid change in the nature of the workforce was evident in the sharp decline of unskilled labourers, and the corresponding increase in skilled labour. For instance between 1965 and 1980 the number of unskilled workers dropped by 52% while the proportion of skilled workers rose by 22%.[18]

It is too soon to describe Spain as a truly urban society. People in the cities still retain family ties with the land. Even those living in towns tend to identify with an area of countryside or a small town. There is constant reference to *mi pueblo*. Such a strong identification with the family roots has undoubtedly helped the rapid assimilation of people into towns. It is only a question of a generation before Spain is a fully urban society. Already the typical problems of urban society are manifest — crime, use of hard drugs and pressure on the unity of the family.

The shift in population and the nature of employment has stimulated new aspirations and new values. The average Spaniard's aspirations for middle-class prosperity and comfort are no different now from any other European. The modernization of the economy has broken the old mould of rulers and ruled. Not only has it created new social distinctions within the working class, it has also amplified into a major social force what was previously a minority — the middle class. Enriched, not always through entrepreneurial initiative but sometimes via corruption, protectionism and monopolies, the middle class is a product of the Franco era.

Another element in the modernization of Spain is the dramatic improvement in the literacy rate. In the 1920s over 60% of the population was illiterate, but this is now down to 8%. This is high by European standards but essentially represents an older generation, now unlikely to learn to read and write.

Poverty, in some cases severe hardship, persists in parts of Andalusia,

Extremadura, Galicia, and La Mancha. But the principle that society should seek to protect those less fortunate and should offer certain basic services (education, health, pensions, unemployment benefit) has been established. Spain is moving towards a form of welfare state in line with the rest of Europe. The traditional Spanish situation of the individual and family against a totally hostile world is no longer the norm. There is even an ombudsman, the *Defensor del Pueblo* (Defender of the People) who takes care of citizens' complaints about the abuses of the state.

The 1978 constitution, the eighth since 1812, enshrines a bourgeois democracy that requires respect and tolerance of opposing views. For the first time in Spanish history this is being generally observed, demonstrating a new level of political maturity. Spaniards are learning to live in a society which gives them obligations *and* rights, not obligations alone. Just take the question of paying taxes. Prior to the advent of democracy, Spaniards either paid no tax at all or sought to avoid paying because they saw no obligation to do so. It was handing over an ill-deserved gift to the state which gave nothing in return. In less than five years the payment of taxes has become a habit, a sign of social responsibility. In 1970, only 303,000 persons paid taxes, one in every twenty-six gainfully employed Spaniards. By 1982 the figure had risen to over 6 million persons.[19] No country in Europe has witnessed such a sudden change in taxation habits.

The national psyche, still painfully analyzed by many a Spaniard (as if Ortega, Unamuno and their disciples did not do enough), will take time to react fully to these profound economic and social changes. There is now, for instance, a much greater and more widespread sense of security and respect for the person. (It is amazing how quickly the slogan, 'under Franco we lived better' has disappeared.) If there is no security, people — and governments — live by improvization, which is how Spain has survived until now.

Of course, the democratic state remains in its infancy. The past is still too close. This is evidenced by the reactionary elements among the military and civilians who wish to turn the clock back. It is the familiar story of the old christians desperately trying to reassert dominance over the new christians. The absence of support for their incoherent nostalgia demonstrates how far these latter-day Quixotes have failed to understand that society has progressed beyond them.

61

Part Two

WEALTH AND
THE RISE OF
THE MIDDLE CLASS

4 Wealth and the Rise of the Middle Class

Incapable of coming to terms with the decline of empire and the loss of wealth from the Americas, Spain was the last major European country to undergo an industrial revolution. The first modern industries grew up in the Basque country and Catalonia, the two regions closest to northern Europe. The Basques concentrated on shipping, steel and mining while the Catalans excelled in textiles, generating wealth that produced a small middle class. But it was not until the boom of the late fifties that wealth began to spread nationwide and a middle class established itself throughout the country.

Spain was slow to latch onto the fashion for jeans, but by 1959 a little known textile and clothes manufacturer in Valencia, Joaquin Saez Merino, judged the market was ready to expand. He began producing jeans under the brand name of 'Dylan'. This nearly ruined him because the jeans sold poorly and the brand name, he discovered, had already been patented by a British company.

Undeterred, he came back with 'Lois' jeans, a name suggested by an office boy. This time he was determined to promote his product properly, and realised that the most effective means was television. Short of funds, he haunted the advertizing agencies until he finally found one that would accept his terms: a bonus payment if the advertisement was successful and, if it failed, delayed payment. The campaign was an immediate success, and since then Saez Merino and 'Lois' jeans have never looked back. By 1980, he controlled over 50% of the domestic market and had established the fourth biggest jeans manufacturing operation in the world with factories in Argentina, France, Ireland, and Portugal.

Saez Merino's story mirrors in many respects the change in Spanish society — how, in a single generation, it has moved from a rural base to an industrial base. He started off his commercial life in 1942 when, at the age of fourteen, he went to work in a small store owned by his parents in Millares near Valencia. The village had 600 inhabitants and a small farming community where the men worked in the fields; the women scraped extra money from a cottage industry of sandal making. Saez Merino was put in the shop because he was considered too weedy to work in the fields.

Because the womenfolk spent their spare time sandal-making, he noticed there was a demand for made-up clothes. He started stocking the store with

65

trousers bought in Valencia. By the age of sixteen he was selling work trousers and shirts from a donkey in neighbouring villages, often getting up at four in the morning and walking for five hours to the nearest village. This was a time of terrible shortages. Unable to rely on suppliers, he decided to buy his own material and have it made up in Millares. In the village there was an under-worked tailor who made up the patterns, and plenty of spare-time labour. The business prospered and in 1948 he was joined by his elder brother, Manuel, who had just finished military service. His main problem was the small size of the textile companies, which obliged him to buy cloth in varying quality and quantity. He took the plunge and decided to manufacture his own cloth.

This has been the basis of his operations ever since. The ultimate secret of his success is that Saez Merino has followed the sociological change in Spanish society. From making good but crude workmen's shirts he moved into jeans which were both work and leisure wear; and recently with the country more conscious of sport and leisure, he has branched into sportswear.[1]

The same transformation of society is underlined by the founding of the department store group, El Corte Ingles. This was the brainchild of Ramon Areces Roderiguez, born in 1904 in a small Asturian village of poor parents. He emigrated to Cuba where he worked in a Havana department store before going on to Canada and the USA. With his savings he returned to Spain just before the Civil War, opening a store in central Madrid. In 1940 the store was established as El Corte Ingles, mainly selling clothing. The name appealed to the bourgeois aspirations of the Madrileños — the snob appeal of quality English cloth. In the hungry post-war years the business moved slowly but Areces cautiously made sure that the store had its own chain of quality suppliers. At the end of the fifties he was ready to expand and in 1962 the first department store was opened outside Madrid, in Barcelona.

Since then El Corte Ingles has established a presence in Spain's major cities, and pioneered modern retailing. The store chain broke the traditional barrier of loyalty to the small shop and also, by being open continuously, prepared the ground for a revolution in shopping habits. The chain's success has stemmed from its imaginative use of advertising (especially city billboards), quality products and an eager market of urban spenders. The goods have been deliberately upmarket and it has become a stamp of middle class membership to visit El Corte Ingles. The group has grown almost exclusively on its own resources, and the Areces family still controls what is arguably the richest and most solid private company in Spain.[2]

POINT OF TAKE-OFF

These two entrepreneurial sagas may be isolated instances, but they have an interesting common element. Both Saez Merino and Areces expanded at a moment when Spaniards began to have more disposable income. They also provided for the aspirations of the consumer starved of choice by rationing and the poverty of the early years under Franco. The point of take-off in both instances was between 1959 and 1962.

It was also during this period that Jose Maria Ruiz-Mateos, a young sherry merchant, began his meteoric accumulation of wealth. He founded Rumasa in 1961 which, at the time of its nationalization in 1983, had become the largest private holding company in Spain embracing banking, construction, drinks, hotels, insurance, and urban and agricultural property. When tax returns were first published in 1978 by the government, Ruiz-Mateos emerged as the richest man in Spain with a personal fortune of 8·9 billion pesetas. Indeed few of those with the greatest declared wealth in this list had inherited it. Instead they were the direct beneficiaries of influence and friendship with the Franco regime, or were entrepreneurs who had exploited the system.

The coincidence in the dates of take-off of these three groups is no accident. Towards the end of the fifties Spain had reached a watershed. The Franco regime had survived for nearly twenty years and consolidated its position. While still internationally isolated, it nevertheless enjoyed the support of the USA and had been finally admitted to such international institutions as the UN and the IMF. Beside this new measure of political consolidation, economic policy was running out of steam and under serious stress. The policy, broadly defined as autarchy, was a rigorous, consciously/chauvinistic attempt at self-sufficiency whose chief characteristic was heavy state intervention and protectionism.

Autarchy served a purpose in the bleak post Civil War years, by cutting back on imports and encouraging domestic production. But with Spain's low level of technology, limited credit and dependence upon imported energy, there were clear limits to the ability of such a system to stimulate rapid economic development. A new economic team was formed in 1957, headed by a trained lawyer and economist, Alberto Ullastres, in the Commerce Ministry, Mariano Navarro Rubio as Finance Minister, and Laureano Lopez Rodo as the chief technocratic co-ordinator. These men believed in a less rigid system that limited state intervention, stimulated competition and opened up Spain both to foreign investment and more imports. All three were members of Opus Dei and there was more than a casual link between their membership and this more 'liberal', market economy philosophy. Opus Dei firmly believed in the morality of making money and the development of a middle class. This was a break with the Falange's corporate view of society in which the classes were vertically linked and the state acted as the prime mover of economic activity.

The change of course was formalized in 1959 in the 'Stabilization Plan' — a national belt-tightening exercise as a prelude to liberalization of the economy and stimulating growth. The regime's propagandists were soon to maintain that the Plan was the sole cause of the subsequent boom and 'economic miracle'. The Plan was undoubtedly a catalyst, but in many respects it did no more than keep pace with the actual state of the nation's economy. The artificially high value of the peseta, sustained for absurd reasons of national pride, was dropped. Autarchy had to disappear if Spain wished to align itself more with Europe, and one year previously in Rome the European ideal had become reality with the formation of the European Economic Community. Ullastres was a fervent European.[3]

The ensuing surge in economic development owed remarkably little to government initiative. For instance, a vital stimulus was the prosperity of northern Europe, whose expanding economies absorbed excess Spanish labour. Remittances from this labour were a vital source of foreign exchange. At the same time the increasingly leisure conscious middle and lower income groups in northern Europe became the core of Spain's tourist industry. In the case of tourism the initiative came as much from the foreign tour operators as from the government. The hard currency generated by tourism and from emigrant remittances underpinned imports of machinery and new technology. In the mid-sixties foreign exchange from these two sources was equivalent to 40% of the import bill.

The government, in its desire to gain credit for the boom, tended to ignore the role played by entrepreneurs, who perforce were grouped into the corporate structure of the vertical syndicates. Their success stories were expropriated by the government's as if its own. Men like Saez Merino and Areces owed little to the government and almost existed in spite of it. Others, however, depended heavily upon the administration to survive, and their skills were sadly exposed when the boom tailed off in the mid-seventies, and political protection evaporated with the advent of democracy.

PERIODS OF GROWTH

To reach this point of take-off almost 100 years passed in desultory and often unco-ordinated attempts at industrialization. The early initiatives in the middle of the nineteenth century were largely a result of local enterprise prodded by aggressive foreign capital. The French were extremely active in financing and developing the railways, the Germans in developing power supplies, while the British showed most interest in developing mining concessions. The foreign presence was facilitated by three important laws passed in the 1850s covering the establishment of finance, mining and railway companies. The law regarding finance companies for instance, approved in

1856, was the first move to create a modern banking law and prompted the creation of companies like Banco de Bilbao and Banco de Santander — 125 years later, two of the country's principal banks. Initially foreign-controlled finance companies were much larger. For instance Sociedad de Credito Mobiliario Español, promoted by the Pereire brothers of Paris, had a paid up capital more than three times that of the Bank of Spain, which had yet to be recognized as the central bank.[4]

The foreign presence was little short of colonial exploitation. Leading local dignitaries, like the Duke of Alba, and prominent politicians were brought in as sleeping partners to provide the necessary political muscle and know-how. Projects were carried out on a concession basis, often with the government not fully understanding the nature of the rights granted, or with only limited study of the national benefit. Few of Spain's politicians were ready to protest over the mortgaging of national resources to foreign interests. Indeed the first challenge to the activities of foreign capital did not come until the 1930s when the Republicans sought to curb the privileges granted to ITT under the telephone monopoly.

Investment, especially in railways, power generation, and mining, was by no means low. However, it failed to provide the motor for a more general industrialization as in northern Europe during the nineteenth century. This was only partially the result of foreign capital not being reinvested and a large amount of equipment being imported rather than manufactured locally. A more basic cause was the gap between these modern industrial sectors and the rest of the 'traditional' agrarian economy. These modern sectors, using foreign technology, were not integrated with the areas in which they operated. The blast furnaces in Vizcaya could absorb only a tenth of all the ore mined in the region.[5] Scarcely any of the minerals mined in southern Spain by the British company, Rio Tinto, were destined for transformation locally. Spain was a producer of raw materials, and left the more advanced nations to get extra profits by transforming them — and selling the finished products back to Spain. The situation is much the same now in developing countries which supply raw materials.

Lacking skilled manpower, technology and finance, and with a population whose income per capita was very low, Spain was in no position to take proper advantage of her resources. In 1885, the first year of an official telephone service in the capital, there were only forty-nine subscribers.[6] In the absence of a middle class, the lead in entrepreneurial activities had to come from the landowning aristocracy and the ruling politicians, who were all too frequently contemptuous of everything to do with commerce except the profit. And if the landowners had been slow to introduce mechanization on the land, how could they be expected to embrace industrialization any quicker? The industrial and financial magnates did not really begin to appear until the 1920s.

Two other factors prevented early industrialization. The coal produced in the mines of Asturias, Santander and, to a lesser extent, Vizcaya was of poor quality. So long as coal was the basis of industrialization this was a hindrance. The country was, in addition, so fragmented by its rugged, inhospitable terrain that it required great foresight and a good deal of public money to provide it with a solid communications infrastructure. As mentioned in the previous chapter, Spain's rulers suffered from myopia over good communications with the effect that it was extremely difficult, right up to the 1960s, to distribute goods produced in the domestic market cheaply and effectively.

Catalonia was more advanced than any other region in the mid-nineteenth century. But it is doubtful whether the opportunities for growth were fully grasped. The vital textile industry was pre-occupied by the advanced production techniques in northern Europe. Agricultural incomes, in what for Spain was essentially a privileged rural community, suffered in the early 1890s as a result of phylloxera which destroyed profitable vines. This disaster was followed by the damaging loss of trade with Cuba and the Philippines in 1898.

BASQUE INITIATIVE

In the end it was the Basques who took most advantage of early attempts to modernize, by pushing aside the pretensions of Malaga and Seville to be industrial centres, and producing cheap iron by using charcoal-fired furnaces. In the north the first modern ironworks were in Asturias, but it was in the province of Vizcaya, especially round the port of Bilbao and the River Nervion, that the industry grew up in the latter quarter of the nineteenth century. Because Basque vessels took ore to Britain, the returning vessels could carry quality British coal to their furnaces at very cheap freight rates. Moreover, the important trade link between the Basques and Britain put them in direct contact with an industrial revolution and provided a model which they eagerly imitated.

Basque businessmen were also the first to appreciate the connection betwen finance and industrial development. What started out as venture capital for industrial development, advanced by a handful of businessmen, burgeoned into consortiums that also conducted commercial banking. The presence of these mixed banks at an early stage in the development of a modern economy shaped the peculiar structure of the Spanish economy — even to the present day. The banks were not simple intermediaries but were both shareholders in and lenders to industry.

The nineteenth-century Basque businessmen were thus both industrialists and financiers. For instance the leading figure behind the foundation of Banco de Bilbao, Pablo de Epalza, was originally a trader with Britain and Cuba. He then moved on to found the first modern iron foundry in Vizcaya with a group of associates many of whom subsequently became the original

70

backers of Banco de Bilbao. The Ybarra family was typical of its kind — heavily involved in mining, they were eventually to bring the Bessemer process from Britain to the iron and steel industry. The bank briefly enjoyed the right to issue notes. But among its first investments was the Bilbao-Tudela railway. The bank was conceived as a tool to promote Basque industry especially in Bilbao.

This has survived and it is remarkable that of the big seven private banks in the 1980s two still retain their headquarters in Bilbao — Banco de Bilbao and Banco de Vizcaya. Both think they would lose something of their character if they were to move to Madrid, even though the use of Bilbao as base entails an element of duplication. One other of the big seven banks was founded largely with Basque capital — Hispano-Americano. Another, Banesto, also has strong Basque links, having evolved from the original Pereire finance company Credito Mobiliario Español.[7]

Another prestigious bank, wholly Basque in origin, was Banco Urquijo, founded in 1870 under the name of Orquijo y Arenzana. This bank, incorporated as Banco Urquijo in 1916, became one of the great promoters of industrial development in Spain; and during the Franco era, under the leadership of Juan Llado, the bank could claim credit for bringing the modern automotive industry to Spain in the form of Seat, the Spanish offshoot of Fiat of Italy.

In contrast to the strong Basque presence in banking, the Catalans failed to show the same financial solidity and dynamism, despite their more ancient trading traditions and better developed industrial base. Indeed the first modern commercial bank in Spain was founded in Catalonia — Banco de Barcelona in 1844. However, this bank was to collapse in 1920, the first serious Spanish banking crisis. All subsequent efforts to build a strong bank with a clear Catalan identity have failed. The most recent and spectacular case was that of Banca Catalana built up in the sixties by the Catalan nationalist Jordi Pujol from the former Banca Dorca. The Catalana group of banks had to be intervened in 1982 with losses outstanding of 138 billion pesetas.[8]

No convincing reason has ever been advanced for this difference between Basques and Catalans; but undoubtedly regional differences have played their part. Basque involvement in both venture capital and industrial development made them more conscious of all aspects of risk and profit, more cautious and thrifty with their money. For instance, the Banco de Bilbao was the first to initiate a savings bank to attract working class savings, making sure that the bank was open on Sundays — the worker's one day off — to encourage them to use the facility. The Basque banks were run on a system of checks and balances on management, with a rotating presidency. In some instances, this system continued through to the 1940s. The Catalans, on the other hand, tended to be more speculative.

On a more practical level, the Basques were fortunate in having a strong growing economy which they could easily monitor. When Basque banks wanted to expand they looked abroad. Banco de Bilbao's first office outside Bilbao was in Paris, then nearby Vitoria, followed by London and only then in Madrid — a telling order of priorities. Perhaps because the Basque country was producing strategic products (iron, steel, minerals, explosives, shipping) it had more contact with Madrid than did Catalonia. The Catalans tended to be more inward looking and content with small scale operations.

BANKS AND UTILITIES

The bulk of what are today Spain's major banks took shape at the turn of the century — Banesto, Hispano-Americano, Vizcaya and then, a little later, Central. One reason for this coincidence was the loss of Cuba and the Philippines in 1898. This provoked a major shake-up in Spanish overseas investment and trade. Many businessmen who had accumulated wealth living in — or trading with — these colonies, were forced to reassess their activities and look anew at the prospects offered by Spain herself. The importance of the loss of these rich colonies has perhaps been underestimated until now by historians.

The case of the foundation of Banco Hispano-Americano graphically illustrates the impact of the loss of Cuba. The leading light behind Hispano was a Basque, Antonio Bassagoiti y Arteta, who had built an important business empire in Mexico that included banking, an iron foundry in Monterey and Tabacalera Mexicana. When war broke out over Cuba he personally sent provisions to the beleaguered Spanish forces and organised a subscription among the Spanish community in Mexico to buy a gunship for the Spanish fleet. In 1900, two years after the loss of Cuba, he proposed to a group of some thirty friends, mostly Basques and Asturians, that they form a bank which would stimulate commercial and industrial ties between Spain and Latin America. The bank, according to its statutes in 1901, confidently predicted it would exist for 'at least fifty years'. Interestingly, it was the first mixed bank to base itself in Madrid and fan out from the centre so that in seven years it had established itself in Barcelona, Malaga, Granada, Zaragoza, Coruña and Seville. It was also the first bank to begin with a wide share base — within a year it had over 2,000 shareholders.[9]

The second reason for the founding of new banks at the turn of the century was the urgent need for development finance, especially to introduce electricity. A good example of the interaction of interests was the founding in 1907 of Hidroelectrica Española (Hidrola). A young Basque engineer, Lucas de Urquijo, fresh from studying in Victorian England, could see the immense future in developing a nationwide electricity supply network. He could rely for finance at least partly on his brother, the second Marques de Urquijo, their uncle having founded the bank of that name and been enobled. He felt the main difficulties were technical: building transmission lines across rugged terrain.

In 1907 he met another young engineer, Juan Urrutia, who was toying with exploring for oil in Mexico or staying and developing electricity in Spain. He had already built a small dam across the Ebro to bring power to Bilbao; and he was persuaded to stay in Spain and attempt a dam across the River Jucar north of Valencia, to provide electricity for both Madrid and Valencia. With their plans ready, Urquijo and Urrutia joined with another Basque group, headed by the president of Banco de Vizcaya, Enrique Ocharan. Hidrola was formed with a capital outlay of 12 million pesetas. The dam across the Jucar was the first big hydro works in Spain and its 250 kilometres of transmission lines to Madrid were the longest then built in Europe. At the time Madrid only had 50,000 electricity subscribers. Hidrola quickly became the chief supplier of electricity to the capital and the second biggest utility in Spain. The names of the founding families even in the 1980s, long after Hidrola had become a public company, remained as closely associated with the board as with the banks.[10]

The ascendancy of Basque capitalism was given an important boost by the First World War. Spain was officially neutral, but its supplies of ore, copper and strategic minerals like mercury and wolfram were at a premium. Even its normally expensive and low quality coal was in demand. Much of this trade went through northern ports. In 1916 there were seventeen Basque shipping companies among the nation's thirty-two leading groups. Basque registered tonnage was 312,000 in ninety vessels. Mines and shipping apart, the modern steel industry was able to lay solid foundations. Temporary recession was compensated for by the protectionism of the Primo de Rivera dictatorship, and the confidence of Basque capitalism was undented.

The crowning symbol of this confidence was the suburb of Neguri which had, and still has, no parallel in the rest of Spain. Neguri was sited away from any sight or smell of the grime of Bilbao, yet close enough to monitor daily how the banks, factories and shipping were performing. The early 1920s mansions, toned down versions of Victorian vulgarity, stand today as a monument to the triumphant affirmation that Basque wealth was on a par with that of the England it admired so much. In the 1920s this wealth was split between no more than thirty families and their offshoots. These families, with their distinctive sounding names (Echevarrieta, Oriol, Orbegozo, Urquijo, Ybarra), were at the core of Spain's modern industrial development.[11]

73

TWO LONE WOLVES

The First World War was a turning point. The ascendancy of the new industrial-financial oligarchy was assured, as was the progressive diminution of the significance of the traditional landed aristocracy. A number of figures with thousands of hectares to their titles, such as the Dukes of Alba, Albaquerque, and Infantado, or the Conde de Romanones, managed to bridge the two worlds. Yet this was less the result of financial entrepreneurial skill, more because of their illustrious titles. The wealth of the new oligarchy, who also acquired titles, was based on banking, heavy industry, mines, and the utilities.

Two figures loomed larger than life — a Basque shipping magnate, Ramon de la Sota, and a Majorcan millionaire, Juan March. Their backgrounds were entirely different. Sota was in the tradition of industrialist and financier, but he was the first magnate to embrace Basque nationalism, and as such was never fully accepted by his own peers. March was the son of a labourer turned small-time pig-breeder who owed his success to quick wits, a natural feel for finance and a total absence of scruples, patriotic or personal.

Sota trained as a lawyer but branched quickly into ship management, then shipping, trading, mining, and finance. His passion was shipping but his main profits came from iron ore mining interests which he was able to acquire when, following the cancellation of the Basque *fueros,* mining rights ceased to be municipal property. He helped found the Banco de Comercio in 1891, a bank which was subsequently taken over by Banco de Bilbao, with Sota as an important Bilbao shareholder.

The base of his empire was a shipping company, formed with his cousin Eduardo Aznar, Sota y Aznar. In 1900, he conceived what was then the bold notion of cutting Basque dependence upon British shipyards and established a major Basque shipyard on the banks of the Nervion. This was the origin of his company, Euskalduna, the most advanced shipyards in Spain, whose first vessel was commissioned in 1905. Traditionally Basque shipping thrived on tramp trading, picking up cargo in one port and taking it to another without a regular line. By the outbreak of the First World War, Sota y Aznar was the largest shipping company in Spain — and it built its own vessels. Although Spain was officially neutral, Sota was a great anglophile and took the studied risk of placing his entire fleet under the British flag. As a result of loss of shipping from German action, freight charges soared and Sota was left a wealthy man.

For taking that risk, King George V awarded him a knighthood in 1921 — the only Spaniard so decorated. He cold-shouldered the offer of a noble title from Alfonso XIII as it did not conform with his Basque nationalist beliefs. He himself was a marquis but never used the title. The combination of his wealth, his Basque nationalism and paternalistic but sincere attempts to humanize labour relations in his business drew envy and suspicion from his fellow Basque capitalists. For instance, the Ybarra family refused to let him take a stake in the main Bilbao steel-works, Altos Hornos de Vizcaya, and his own grandiose scheme for a separate plant in Bilbao foundered. He switched plans and went ahead undaunted with the most ambitious private industrial project of the era — the development of iron ore mines at Ojos Negros in the Sierra Menera near Teruel and the construction of a 200 kilometre railway to Sagunto on the Mediterranean, where the ore fed a steel complex. In the thirties the project was hit by recession and came under the wing of Altos Hornos de Vizcaya, after Banco de Bilbao had called in a credit. Since then Sagunto has been an almost continuous problem for the Spanish steel industry with the polemic of its closure dogging the early months of the socialist administration in 1983.

At the close of the 1920s, Sota's income was reckoned to be as large as the Spanish treasury's tax receipts. He had taken steps to buy out his partners in Sota y Aznar and after a row involving Euskalduna walked out of Banco de Bilbao where he was a board member with 5% of the equity, to join their main rival, Banco de Vizcaya: yet another feud among warring clans of the Basque financial oligarchy. The enmity he aroused cost him and his family dear as result of the Civil War. He died a month after the outbreak of the Civil War; but when the victorious nationalist troops entered Bilbao his goods were all confiscated in retribution for his republican and Basque nationalist sympathies (his ships had been used to evacuate civilians). The courts then drummed up a series of accusations, including the sending of a congratulatory telegram to President Wilson of the US in 1918! Posthumously he was fined a staggering 100 million pesetas and in 1950 his goods were publicly auctioned for 32 million pesetas.

Legal proceedings were also begun to recover the fleet, part of which had been despatched to England. These proceedings eventually succeeded and the Sota empire disappeared in all but name, with the military governor of Bilbao occupying one of his principal residences. Only in 1982 was some measure of legal reparation accorded the heirs, on final settlement of the fine imposed in 1940. It was symptomatic of the divisions caused by the Civil War that his prize vessel had its Basque name removed, and that his portrait was taken down from Bilbao's exclusive yacht club. The conservative Basque oligarchy never forgave his behaving as an outsider; and the moral of Sota's business affairs is that success carries with it a high price in envy and enmity.[12]

Juan March was more fortunate, but he made a business out of being on the right side — although he was only ever on the side of himself. He was Spain's first and only international wheeler-dealer. Despite his peasant origins, his birthplace, Majorca, was an outward-looking community with a tradition of Mediterranean trade and contraband. (In neighbouring Ibiza there is even a statue in the main square erected to a pirate.) March began by dealing in pigs, then quickly moved into buying up estates. These he broke into lots and sold on credit to Majorcan peasants, knowing full well the longing of these people to work their own land. He graduated from this to dealing in tobacco and cigarettes. In 1906 he bought up a tobacco plant in Algiers and five years later had managed to obtain the tobacco monopoly for the Spanish Zone in Morocco. This was no small feat since it broke the whole principle of the Spanish government's tobacco monopoly. That March operated much of the time through contraband was no secret. However, his launches were faster than the Spanish government's and he knew the way to any official's heart.

Just after the outbreak of the First World War, March formed a shipping company, Transmediterranea, which obtained a monopoly of traffic with the mainland, the Baleares, and North Africa. Though ostensibly neutral, March was not averse to helping both the British and Germans with information and by carrying cargo. He was a man that both sides sought to cultivate since an arc of the Mediterranean from Majorca through to Algiers was his empire. He emerged from the war even more powerful and gained a tighter grip on the tobacco business. The Prime Minister, Francisco Cambo, declared a personal war on March labelling him 'the last pirate of the Mediterranean'. Spain's tobacco monopoly income had plunged drastically because March was offering better quality at lower prices! Undaunted by the threat of persecution, March presented himself as a parliamentary candidate for Majorca and in 1923 was resoundingly elected amid much comment about his lavish entertainment of voters.

With the advent of the Primo de Rivera dictatorship he fled briefly to France; but was soon back doing favours for the regime, such as arranging the purchase of a slice of Tangier from a wealthy Jew. By the time of the Republic his activities covered banking, oil brokering, property, utility investments and tobacco. As evidence of his skill, he had managed to set up an oil purchase agreement with the Soviet Union, even though the two countries had no diplomatic relations.

The Republic was at a loss as to how to cope with such a maverick. The left regarded Juan March as the ugly face of ruthless capitalism. Nevertheless, the more moderate members of government realised he had useful contacts with the international banking community and was well known in the corridors of several European chancelleries. March, however, baulked at the idea of bankrolling the Republic, gauging correctly that he would get insufficient favours in return. He decided to flee the country. This time he was picked up on the Basque frontier and brought back to Madrid under arrest. There then followed a bizarre indictment of March in the Cortes. No formal charges were brought but he had to defend the accumulation of his fortune which parliament knew — yet could scarcely prove — came more by foul means than fair. The indictment, though not strictly proven, led March to take up 'residence' in prison (he had his own cook and valet). Here he spent sixteen months before enjoying the unique distinction of being let out of the front gate by the chief warder, who had, for a substantial consideration, taken pity on the man's confinement. March successfully fled, leaving Spain via Gibraltar. He was the Republic's capitalist enemy number one.

March's part in the nationalist uprising has been heavily publicized because he paid for the charter of the aircraft in the UK that took Franco from the Canaries to North Africa. This led to speculation — but no clear proof — that he was bankrolling the nationalist cause. He certainly helped to raise money and allowed his wealth to be used as collateral. But his career consistently showed that he was too cunning to place all his eggs in one basket. The ambiguity of his allegiance was evident in the Second World War when his organization is alleged to have provided intelligence to both the British and the Germans. His most spectacular piece of legerdemain was to wrest control of the shares of the Barcelona utility, Barcelona Traction, from a group of international shareholders between 1948 and 1952. Through a technicality, a court in Catalonia declared the company bankrupt even though financially sound. March, through intermediaries, managed to prevent the company's rightful owners from taking protective legal action. March and his associates ended up with majority control. 'Legalized theft' was how some saw this; others regarded it as March exploiting Franco's debt to him. The legal wrangles that then followed in the International Court of the Hague lasted until 1970 by which time March was dead but the law remained on his side. Barcelona Traction had become Fenosa, the largest utility in Catalonia.

The clamour of the Barcelona Traction case obscured the rest of March's activity in post Civil War Spain. Autarchy, with its tight exchange controls, coupled with the poverty of Spain in those years, made him turn abroad. He spent much of his time in Switzerland where he had residence. One suspects he hedged his bets on the Franco regime and also mistrusted his two sons' use of his assets.

Juan March died in 1962, aged 82, as a result of a car accident near Madrid. As to the sheer scale of his operations and his reported wealth, he bequeathed more mystery than fact. At the time he was considered one of the ten richest men in Europe, a Spanish JP Morgan. But this was wholly unproven. It could be that as a speculator he not only gained but lost as well. The assets he left in Spain were substantial but not on the scale of wealth he was credited with. This scale could exist only if most or a good part were outside Spain — not improbable since he was always dealing in foreign exchange and had the best contacts of any Spaniard in Tangier in the crucial war and post-war period when it was a customs free zone and the main place for the peseta black market.

In Spain Juan March left a medium sized bank bearing the family name; a string of industrial investments in sectors such as cement and construction; island fiefdom in Majorca; and a cultural foundation whose ostentatious marble building in Madrid suggested that the original aim was a form of expiation. The ultimate difference between the likes of March and Sota was a sense of commitment. Sota was deeply interested in industrial development, and without minimizing the profit motive, was committed to modernizing first the Basque country and then Spain as a whole. March was attached to his native Majorca but treated Spain as a table on which to play. He was too cynical to entertain high-minded ideals about the development of Spain. Interestingly for the scale of his operations, the March empire did not take full advantage of the boom of the sixties. Indeed the last five years of March's life, when his health was fading, was the moment when the new money was about to be made. It was only in the late seventies, with a new generation of the family, that the March interests began to play a more active role, investing in Spain and raising the profile of the bank.[13]

Though the circumstances are different, there is a parallel between the fate of Juan March under the Republic and that of his nearest modern equivalent, Jose Maria Ruiz-Mateos, under the socialist government. Both were uncontrollable mavericks. Ruiz-Mateos was the most conspicuous capitalist figure with the advent of democracy. Engaged in a battle with both the Bank of Spain and the tax authorities, the absence of clear cut laws let him run impudent circles round them. Despite warnings to hold back on new investment, the Rumasa group continued to grow, with an increasing tangle of inter-company relations. In the end, the government of Felipe Gonzalez was left with no option but to expropriate the entire Rumasa group in February 1983. This was not an act of normal nationalization. It was a preventive move to discover the state of the group and the extent of its losses in order to shield the financial system from the consequences of its possible collapse. It was the only way of bringing Ruiz-Mateos to heel.

FRIENDS OF THE REGIME

The Nationalists looked upon businessmen, bankers and industrialists as their allies and natural supporters. Several suffered the fate of Ramon de la Sota, having their goods sequestered. In the early years of the Franco regime, some were harassed for their republican sympathies, such as Juan Llado of Banco Urquijo who was briefly imprisoned. Few trod the path of exile. Most tolerated the regime, even if monarchists at heart, because it promised stability. There was scarce a company annual meeting that did not contain fullsome praise for the Caudillo.

In the wake of the Civil War there was still a clear divide in the ownership of the means of production. On the one hand a tightly-knit financial and industrial oligarchy, predominantly northern in origin (especially Basque) controlled the major banks, insurance companies and, through them, key sectors of industry like power generation, mining, ship-building and steel-making. At the other end of the scale was a mass of small traders and businessmen running cottage-style industries and workshops. The gap was wide. Nevertheless the scale of the former's operations were small by the standards of Europe at the time.

The Civil War did create, however, possibilities for unprecedented social mobility. Families had been uprooted from one region to another; everything was in short supply and improvised; and most important of all, the new administration had installed its own personnel from top to bottom in an expanded bureaucracy. For anyone ambitious there were two methods of upwards mobility: through skill, luck and hard work, or by knowing the right people. The Franco era was the triumph of paleo-capitalism — primitive market skills operating in a jungle of bureaucratic regulations, protectionism and peddled influence.

The arch paleo-capitalist was Eduardo Barreiros, who at one stage in the late sixties earned the sobriquet of Spain's Mr Ford. His father owned a small garage in Galicia and he began at the age of twelve working as a mechanic. During the Civil War a bus owned by his father and run on a local route between Orense and Los Peares was requisitioned by the Nationalists. Barreiros became its driver, transporting troops to the front in Oviedo and bringing back wounded. He did well enough for himself to move into second-hand car dealing. Fascinated by engines and conscious of the high cost of petrol he experimented with converting engines to diesel. The experiment worked and in 1947 he was converting engines not only for his own use but also to order.

By 1949 he had taken over a workshop in Madrid and within a decade owned a large scale engine manufacturing plant and a truck assembly line. As a fellow Galician he came to the notice of Franco. Barreiros was able to supply contracts both to the Spanish and Portuguese armies. He bought up a huge estate in Extremadura where Franco stayed as his shooting guest, a sure seal of approval from the Caudillo. His star was set when in 1964 Chrysler agreed to provide him with technology and new capital. The official car of the regime became the Chrysler/Dodge Dart. Barreiros also became one of the few families permitted to set up an international arms dealing business. The glossy magazines filled their pages with the story of Eduardo Barreiros and his four brothers, the stocky Galician who had had his fingers gnarled as a mechanic, now the model new Spaniard.

However, Barreiros was eclipsed by disagreements with Chrysler who gradually assumed control of his truck and car manufacturing operation. The clever untrained mechanic was unable to cope with the problems of scale, new technology, complex finance and greater competition. The name, like a firework, splurged and faded by the end of the seventies.

The shortages and poverty of the forties and early fifties forced people to take the initiative. The incentive to improvise explains the mushrooming of small businesses throughout the country and the advent of a new merchant class. Autarchy was an appallingly inefficient system and the heavy protection through import licences, quotas and currency restrictions was fertile ground for abuse and self-enrichment. Those without initiative wasted their time filling in forms and complying with regulations; those with initiative spent far too much energy trying to evade the same constrictions.

During these years it was arguably the nationwide black market which stimulated a hitherto unknown entrepreneurial spirit. This black market — now politely called the parallel economy — provided the basis for take-off before the Stabilization Plan of 1959. Industrialists, for instance, were desperate for foreign currency to buy machinery and spare parts abroad. In the case of the Catalan-based textile industry, probably the most powerful lobby, a special system was arranged to provide foreign exchange for purchasing cotton and industrial machinery. Others had to use their wits.

No other country in Europe was then surrounded by so many customs free zones. In the north was Andorra, of great benefit to Catalonia; in the south was the British colony of Gibraltar, internationally-administered Tangier, the enclaves of Ceuta and Melilla, and the Canaries. All thrived on the benevolence and corruptibility of Spanish customs officials. The most important were Andorra and Tangier. Until losing its international status at the end of the 1950s, Tangier was a free exchange zone with a sophisticated peseta black market. Andorra was used as a means of smuggling, so streamlined that goods often did not even have to transit the landlocked principality, but were merely billed there before continuing direct to Barcelona. Barcelona's early neon lighting is reputed to have come from Andorra.[14]

The role of entrepreneurial skill in the rise of the merchant class should not be overstated. Corruption and favours played their part. At the local level, mayors and municipal officials were selected for their loyalty to the regime and their own connections with the civil governors and officials of the Movimiento further up the ladder. In the absence of free elections, the mayor and the local head of the Movimiento (sometimes one and the same) were petty deities, often perpetuating dynasties that lasted throughout the regime. These were the men who controlled whether or not rural land could be developed, where the roads would be built and who helped determine the public works contracts. If the authority conceding construction permits is personified in the same man who owns a property company or construction business, it requires little imagination to exploit the possibilities. This happened up and down the countries in towns big and small.

With the tremendous shift in population from rural to urban areas, property sales and property construction became a major source of new wealth. Profits from property dealing and construction certainly helped generate new income. But uncontrolled speculation had a disastrous effect on the physiognomy of Spain, especially the Mediterranean coast. A combination of greed and lack of government control led to the rape of the coast with lasting repercussions.

The Stabilization Plan corrected the worst distortions created by autarchy. But corruption had become so endemic, so much a part of a system which cemented the loyalties of the administration and the business community, that by this stage it was institutionalized and parasitic, and no longer served a dynamic or stimulative function. In this way it differed from the rapid industrialization of Italy a decade earlier. Corruption there was widespread but dynamic, smoothing the wheels of a creaking system. Another difference with Italy concerned money generated in the parallel economy. In Italy this was frequently reinvested in productive processes, whereas in Spain the natural tendency was to channel funds abroad or opt for property speculation. This, in turn, meant that there was less diversification in Spain.

The Stabilization Plan was the first sign of the regime responding to the collective interests of the business community. But in general the interests of the nascent bourgeoisie were complementary to, and compatible with, those of the dictatorship. The latter wanted to make profits, the former was concerned with political respectability and stability. What better for Franco than a boom which highlighted the 'miracle' of modernization and raised living standards? What better for the new money makers than cheap credit, cheap labour, a prohibition on freely organized labour, an expanding market, high tariffs on imports, a rising stock market and soaring property prices? The relationship between the regime and this new class was incestuous rather than symbiotic.

BLURRED DISTINCTIONS

This was most apparent in the blurred distinction between the public and private sector. There were three state monopolies — petroleum distribution (Campsa), telephones (Telefonica) and tobacco (Tabacalera). The capital of these monopolies was mixed but the representatives of the state on the boards were generally passive figures, manipulated by the private shareholders, dominated by the big banks. In the case of Campsa this enabled private refineries to operate with a guaranteed profit margin from Campsa, who purchased their products no matter what price was paid for the crude. Telefonica developed as an efficient modern company with the largest single investment programme in Spain: but the domination of private interests ensured that policy was geared to dividends rather than socio-economic benefit and public service. Thus costly installation of rural telephone lines was delayed or ignored and expensive infrastructure and communications investments, normally carried out by a national telephone company, were left in the hands of the Ministry of Transport.

To promote industrial development and ensure the state presence in strategic sectors, a holding company, Instituto Nacional de Industria (INI) was formed in 1941 based on Mussolini's state holding company, IRI. Policy was haphazard and throughout the Franco era INI never seemed certain of its role. The pattern of its company-ownership and sector control defied economic logic. The intention of being a catalyst for industrial development was consistently tempered by the fear of alienating the main private companies. There was never a guideline for minimum or maximum involvement in any one sector. It was rare that INI owned companies completely, unless it had been obliged to buy loss-making companies from the private sector. Frequently INI was asked to partner private sector companies as a form of semi-state guarantee for borrowing. INI companies had access to specially cheap long-term credit.

By the end of the Franco era, INI was responsible for one sixth of industrial production and its companies accounted for 15% of Spain's exports. INI produced 45% of the nation's coal, 17% of its electricity, 60% of its chemicals and petrochemicals and 33% of the cars. It had a near monopoly on military equipment manufacture and of air transport. Yet for all its weight it was uncoordinated and unwilling to use its authority. INI latterly came under the Ministry of Industry, a ministry with little weight in the administration. Unlike its Italian counterpart, IRI, the holding company was not involved in banking — the private banks did not want the state interfering in this sector. Nor was it the sole state holding company. The powerful Ministry of Finance controlled the Patrimonio Nacional which had shares in such viable operations as Campsa and Telefonica. It was as if INI was deliberately kept weak and malleable.

INI in fact was used as a golden dustbin by the private sector into which loss-making interests were discarded on generous compensation terms from the state. For instance, in 1967 a special coal company was formed by INI, Hunosa, to take over the activities of seven leading mining companies in Asturias. The companies had been suffering chronic losses and had been slowly decapitalized without new investment. Rather than nationalizing all Asturian mining, Hunosa merely comprised the loss-makers whose owners were anxious to divest. The term 'nationalization' was never used. The administration was intimidated by the owners' threat of closing down the mines, for the record of labour militancy in Asturias made closure unacceptable. Thus the owners were favourably compensated for mines producing low quality coal which could no longer be operated profitably. Hunosa was subsequently to prove the biggest loss-maker within INI, requiring a special government subsidy. Five years later INI found itself in the same position with the two biggest private shipyards, which had invested over-optimistically and had been hit by the decline in international shipping.

The confused role of INI was epitomized by the saga of a textile company, Intelhorce, set up in Malaga in 1957 with the aim of promoting industrial employment in southern Spain. Intelhorce, with a 3,500 workforce, became the largest industrial employer in southern Spain outside the shipyards in Cadiz. But after running at a loss, INI decided to sell the company off to private Catalan textile interests, the Castell group. The theoretical logic of the sale was that Intelhorce could be made profitable and that textiles were best left to the private sector. In fact Intelhorce, using sophisticated modern machinery and cheaper southern labour, was undercutting the Catalan textile industries which accounted for 70% of the total Spanish textile business. The sale to the private sector was seen as a means of curbing this competition. Five years after the sale, Intelhorce was offered back to INI because of continued losses. By 1979 the company had accumulated losses of 11·2 billion pesetas. INI refused to absorb the company and finally it was taken over by the Ministry of Finance when its owners, Banco de Madrid and Cadesbank, had to be intervened. The government was then obliged to keep Intelhorce going but was accused by the private sector of price-cutting!

During the Franco regime, INI itself was not necessarily badly run or poorly staffed in its central administration. However, it was constantly deflected from its objectives, and its various companies were used by the regime as a means of patronage to reward or pension off faithful or troublesome servants. There were almost 4,000 board jobs in INI, directly and indirectly controlled, nearly half of which were superfluous sinecures. To cap it all the private sector cynically cultivated INI's image as a deficit-ridden group, eating up state funds; the very reason for much of this deficit was that INI was obliged to assume responsibility for operations that private companies had thrown into its lap. This image persisted into the 1980s, even though the group was radically altered — its energy interests were split into a separate holding, and its functions were rationalized.[15]

The two worlds of administration and business rubbed shoulders so closely that the concept of conflict of interest was unheard of. Spain had to await the advent of the socialist government for a lead in separating the two. This situation was facilitated — and compounded — by the relatively small elite running the administration and the financial oligarchy. Laws were lax and antiquated, and it suited few that this should be otherwise. The Bank of Spain only became a fully publicly-owned central bank in 1962 and there was no pretence of its independence as an institution until 1978 at the earliest.

Franco's apologists insist that he was incorruptible. However, he appears to have been either very blind or very weak in relation to those around him.[16] His brother, Nicolas, was closely linked to the Coca family, small time businessmen and financiers from Salamanca who thanks to the mantle of Francoist protection built up a large banking and property empire. The Castell group which controlled Banco de Madrid, Cadesbank and a string of industrial interests in Catalonia was friendly with the Marques de Villaverde (Franco's son-in-law). The Fierro family, owners of Banco Iberico and of a large industrial empire that spanned tobacco, domestic appliances and car making were the main French industrial representatives. Amongst others, they represented Avions Marcel Dassault which sold the Mirage fighter to the regime.

Like the Shah of Iran, Franco seems to have preferred to turn a blind eye, no doubt believing that a little profiteering bound those with their fingers in the pie to the regime in an oriental system of obligation. Financial scandal, of which there was potentially much, was a forbidden topic in the press as it reflected badly on the regime, as a result of which a false air of public probity pervaded.

The exception was the Matesa affair, which broke in 1969 after a decade of boom. The scandal broke less because of its scale, substantial though it was, but more because of the chronic war within the administration between the liberal technocrats identified with Opus Dei and the hardline Falange who saw their grip loosened by the boom and the emergence of the new consumer society.

Matesa was a Barcelona-based company producing textile machinery which mushroomed in the wake of the Stabilization Plan. Officials lauded the company as the archetypal entrepreneurial success of the 'miracle'. But in 1969, either through chance or acting on a tip-off, customs officials uncovered serious irregularities in Matesa's use of special official credits. On the basis of Matesa's success in selling looms abroad, the company's chief executive, Juan Vila Reyes, and his associates, had set up a series of dummy companies outside Spain. These paper companies then provided export orders to Matesa — orders which enabled Matesa to obtain soft official credit to the tune of 9·8 billion pesetas. This money left the country and even now its fate has not been clarified. The release of this information was the first dirty financial linen exposed to the public. Because of the trauma, Franco soon sought to paper over the cracks.[17]

If undue attention appears to have been devoted to the corrupt nature of Francoist economic development, this is to stress one fundamental point. Most of the wealth of the new middle class and oligarchy was made easily. The boom conditions provided a rapidly expanding but still protected market. Entrepreneurial effort lay in currying favour 'at court', not convincing clients with products. Thus a complacent and untried (in a capitalist sense) class of businessman emerged, who were poorly equipped to deal with the economic crises of the seventies.

MEASURING THE MIRACLE

Spain has never witnessed such spectacular growth as during the sixties — and will probably never do so again. The economy grew on average 7% a year throughout the decade. Real income per capita averaged over 6% a year in growth. This was triple the average for the previous years of the Franco regime; and it was five times greater than that achieved from the turn of the century up to the Republic. The period of highest growth was between 1961 and 1964.[18]

Many parts of Spain during this time seemed like a vast construction site — frontiers were being pushed back. Construction workers were poached overnight by rival firms. Virtually whatever was produced was sold. Seat, thanks to its quasi-monopolistic control of the car market, had queues of people waiting for new cars. In some respects it was like an East European market. There was, for instance, no colour choice for a Seat car. General motors discovered in 1979, when it had decided to invest in Spain, that there had never been a market study on customer colour preferences for cars.

Figures for the purchase of cars, use of telephones, possession of washing machines and TV sets all bear out the rapid rise in countrywide purchasing power. In 1960, there were only 10 cars for every 1,000 inhabitants. By 1969, there were 58 per 1,000 and in 1975, 111 per 1,000. Spain started the decade producing only 2 million tons of steel; by 1970 production had been raised to 7 million tons, most of which was consumed domestically.

This rapid rise in consumption reflected a sustained increase in wages. Industrial wages rose on average 7% in real terms during the sixties, providing a marked improvement in living standards.[19] In the case of the professional classes and salary earners the increase was certainly more substantial and the gap in incomes was not narrowed.

It is far easier to trace the rise in wealth of successful individuals like Areces or Saez Merino than the fate of the many thousands who began to prosper for the first time during the sixties — those who were able to buy cars, the full range of domestic appliances, hire apartments for holidays, spend money on clothes and luxuries. The members of the new middle class did not have names. Only by looking at dry statistics is it possible to see the change. In 1965 white collar workers in industry and the services — civil servants, administrative staff and technicians — accounted for 20% of the active population. By 1980 the percentage had risen to 31%. This is the core of Spain's new middle class but it is still only two thirds of the average size of the middle class in other European countries.

A more general impression of the generation of new wealth can be found in the increase in per capita income. In 1950 per capita income (in current pesetas) was 6,532 pesetas — lower in real terms than at the beginning of the Republic. Ten years later average per capita income was 20,234 pesetas, the level of a country in the first phase of development. By 1970 the average income per capita had almost trebled in current terms to 64,859 pesetas; and by the end of the decade it had increased fivefold in current terms to 349,611 pesetas — bringing Spain close to Italy and above Ireland.[21] A sidelight on disposable income was the growth in money spent on lotteries and forms of gambling. Between 1970 and 1980 average spending by Spaniards over fourteen increased eightfold.[22]

This period witnessed the first considered effort to create some balance in regional development, by encouraging 'poles' around medium-sized provincial towns. Seven such poles were established — in Burgos, Huelva, La

Coruña, Valladolid, Vigo and Zaragoza. The choice of these pole sites was more the result of local lobbying than deliberate planning, and some of the most backward regions were ignored. The experiment was also conducted by a regime that resolutely refused to acknowledge historic regional identities. This inhibited proper use of the poles to stimulate genuine regional development. The policy had a significant impact on the towns themselves — Valladolid perhaps being the most successful and Huelva being the most damaged. Huelva was converted irretrievably into a major chemical, refining and petrochemical centre with wholly inadequate control over pollution. It also meant that the impoverished south, with its surplus labour, had been landed with capital intense investment that generated little employment. Nevertheless the existence of these poles, with their attendant investment and spin-off, fostered a new professional class in these towns.

The boom conditions were intoxicating; and since the 'miracle' was greater than either the administration or society dared believe, the illusion of success was greater too. The high degree of technological dependence, the heavy reliance on (still cheap) imported energy, the high level of protectionism for local industry, the cheap cost of credit, the exploitation of labour and the continued prosperity of north European economies were never seriously considered. Yet these were the pillars on which the miracle rested. Those industries most protected were those employing large amounts of manpower — car and commercial vehicle manufacture, shoes, ship-building, textiles. With hindsight, complacency was inevitable given the paucity of independent views, and the suspicion that all outside opinion was associated with the opposition. A few semi-exiled Spanish economists in the IMF and OECD sounded the alarm bells, but were not taken seriously.

Thus when energy prices tripled in 1973, Spain behaved with blind indifference to the rest of the industrialized world. While Sunday driving was temporarily banned in neighbouring Italy (like Spain, 70% dependent upon imported energy), Spanish industrialists prepared for a new boom. Virtually every key sector invested in expansion during 1973/74 — even sectors requiring high use of energy, such as aluminium which wanted to expand to produce double the nation's needs.

The problems of Spanish industry in the early eighties are in good measure directly attributable to the errors made then. Before these investments began to pay for themselves, recession set in, creating overcapacity. Energy costs put up production and wage costs. To cover these extra charges more money was borrowed at a time when cheap interest rates had evaporated. Industries which had been making steady profits for more than a decade were suddenly overmanned, over-producing, their margins being squeezed into the red by high financial charges. The list was a long one covering the whole steel industry, ship-building (as much as 40% overcapacity), cars and trucks, textiles (with more than a quarter of the 400,000 workforce surplus), domestic appliances, paper, chemicals, and aluminium. Remedial action was

86

exceptionally slow. Although the beginnings of recession were evident in 1975, action did not begin until two years later. The extent and depth of the recession were not fully appreciated until 1979/80. It was only then that a national energy plan which sought to cut dependence upon imported oil was approved.

This complacency in the durability of economic growth was remarkable considering the Franco regime had entered its twilight days. It needed no prophet to foresee that political change of *some* sort was underway. Political uncertainty was only apparent after Franco's death — confirming the maxim that Spaniards react rather than act!

The delay in coming to terms with recession is more understandable and was a consequence of the introduction of democracy. This said, the effects have been dramatic right across the board. As Spain entered the eighties, demand for many key items of consumption, such as steel, tractors, trucks, cars and domestic appliances, fell back to the same level as the end of the sixties. For instance, a new national steel plan drawn up in 1974 envisaged an annual growth rate of 5% and a consumption of 20 million tons. The plan was subsequently scrapped as over-optimistic, and in 1982 consumption was less than half the predicted level at 8 million tons.[23]

This sharp turnaround has exposed the thin framework of the Francoist 'miracle'. Companies and their promoters rose suddenly, spluttered and then fell, sometimes into total oblivion. The Coca family, one of the most prominent financial groups during this period, had its bank absorbed by Banesto — and was never able to occupy the proud glass skyscraper that was to be its headquarters on the Castellana in Madrid. Ignacio Coca was himself involved in a lengthy dispute with the authorities over alleged illegal export of funds and fraudulent revaluation of assets. Coca was one of thirty banks which were absorbed or intervened between 1978 and 1983. A drive up the Castellana in Madrid in 1983 reveals an interesting rule of thumb — the size and ostentation of the buildings are in inverse proportion to the durability of their owners and managers.

The king of property development under the former regime, Jose Banus, has seen his assets whittled away by recession. Banus built the wealthy Madrid suburb of Mierra Sierra, the capital's Barrio de Conception and Pilar, and on the Mediterranean coast, the luxury port development of Puerto Banus. The latter has only been saved by Arab money. The once dynamic electrical equipment manufacturer and batteries producer, Femsa, founded by Italian emigré Mario Caprile after the war — and at one stage Spain's only industrial multi-national — has been sold off amid losses to Germany's Robert Bosch. The textile empire of the Castel group has been seriously compromised by the demise of Banco de Madrid and Cadesbank. The model paper and pulp group, Torras Hostench has gone into temporary receivership while the chief member of the family that promoted the group, Higinio Torras, has fled the country with an arrest warrant out for financial misdealing with the small

Banco de Pirineos. The leading road haulage company, Mateu y Mateu, run by Mariano Mateu — 'the king of transport' — collapsed in 1979 leading to legal action against both him, his brother and his son.

Even the most prestigious banks were not immune to the effects of recession. Banco Urquijo, which had pioneered so much industrial development, had to be taken over by Hispano-Americano in early 1983 to assure its future — while the main private industrial group it promoted, the chemicals conglomerate Union Explosivos Rio Tinto (ERT) found itself in a crisis. ERT was the result of a merger between Union Española de Explosivos and Minas de Rio Tinto, both dating from the early era of industrialization. The former prospered on a near monopoly of the explosives business; the latter grew from mining interests in southern Spain developed by the British.

It is not just the mighty who have fallen. Spain has suffered the most serious recession of any European country since the thirties. In 1973, 120 companies went into temporary receivership with outstanding debts of 3·7 billion pesetas and assets of 6·5 billion pesetas. By the end of 1981 the number of companies affected had risen to 820 with debts of 129 billion pesetas and assets of 215 billion pesetas.[25] Since bankruptcy is a more complex device and used less frequently, the figures for bankruptcies are lower; nevertheless, they tripled during this period.

In general the demise of companies has been due to a mix of malpractice, incompetence and bad luck in misreading the market. But the democratic context has made an important difference and required a substantial adjustment. Democratic government, accountable to parliament, has been less able to support private groups in difficulties with public funds unless such action is proven to be in the public interest. Employers have been obliged to pay taxes under a more progressive fiscal system and they have been obliged to deal with free trades unions. Since 1977, competition has increased as a result of liberalization measures. This, on top of recession, has been a great deal to digest — clearly too much for some.

A QUESTION OF SIZE

Given the size of the Spanish domestic market, it is puzzling why there has been so little concentration of interest outside banking. The scale of operations has remained small.

The stock markets, for instance, contain virtually all the 'large' private or mixed (private and state) companies. Spain's four stock markets in 1983 quoted less than 150 companies and the number has varied minimally in recent years. Most of the companies in Spain are very small. A survey of registered company capital for the year 1977 showed that 66% possessed 10 million pesetas or less; just under 10% had registered capital of between 100 and 250 million pesetas; 2% of the companies accounted for 67% of all capital registered. The bigger companies tended to have foreign minority holdings or control.[26]

The persistence of small-scale operations is most evident in the retail trade which employs over 12% of the workforce. Almost 60% of all shops in 1980 still had a sales area of less than 40 square metres. Those with sales areas of over 400 square metres accounted for only 1%. The economies of scale and the accompanying social consequences have yet to come. The resistance seems to come as much — if not more — from the potential owners and promoters as the public.[27]

There appears to be a basic fear of size — of having to deal with organized labour, of being more exposed to the tax authorities and labour inspection, of losing the paternalistic touch. An essentially local view of the market for goods and products conditions the size of operations: the market is just one town or a region. Ambitions are satisfied by having 'made good' in the eyes of the local community.

Spanish society continues to mistrust wealth, not respect it. History has taught Spaniards the impossibility of gaining wealth from scratch without the direct support of the regime of the day or some godfather within. Windfall profits came with the gold from the Americas and they are still expected in the national obsession with the lottery, especially the huge Christmas hand-out — the richest lottery pay-out in the world. The Spanish language has yet to invent a word for the self-made man: to be self-made by hard work and skill is to defy nature. In the past century a few have shown that this is possible but their reward has usually been the envy of their peers and subordinates.

5 The Power of the Banks

If a broad middle class emerged with the economic 'miracle' of Franco, the banking system had been evolving its own particular character since the turn of the century. The importance of the private banks lay in their combined or 'mixed' role — acting as both traditional commercial banks and as investors in all aspects of the economy. Controlled by a limited oligarchy and owning large slices of the economy, the private banks wield enormous potential power.

Once a month this oligarchy gathers over lunch to discuss their problems and consider the fate of the nation. The luncheon is wholly informal and rarely attended by anyone other than the presidents of Spain's leading banks. This club is self-limiting and has traditionally comprised the seven private banks with the largest assets. The pecking order has been — Banesto, Central, Hispano-Americano, Bilbao, Vizcaya, Santander, and Popular.

The dramatis personae of these gatherings have been almost unchanged for a decade. Nowhere else in Europe have the same figures run key financial institutions for so long, nor is there any other country in Europe where the banks have so much potential weight. These seven banks control directly and indirectly over 80% of commercial bank deposits. They are in a position — if united — to exercise formidable influence over the life of the nation.

The presidents themselves say much about their respective banks and banking. Jose Maria Aguirre Gonzalo, head of Banesto, is the grand old man of Spanish banking, who entered the profession aged forty-four and became chief executive of Banesto in 1970 at the ripe age of seventy-three. An engineer by training, he founded a construction company in 1927, Agroman, which he has run actively for fifty years and is now the second biggest in Spain. He has seen the Republic of Primo de Rivera, the abdication of Alfonso XIII; he negotiated with the anarchist CNT over the introduction of the first modern mechanical construction equipment and he has been through the Civil War, the rise and death of Franco and now the advent of democracy — events which he treats with both humour and sadness, for to him everyone is now a *chico* (boy). His secret is vitamin C and walking a kilometre a day. The bank is marked with his Basque sense of thrift (there are no official cars), which only breaks down at annual meetings when shareholders are handed out expensive boxes of chocolates, chosen especially by him, the size depending on the shareholder's stake.

Alfonso Escamez, head of Banesto's arch rival, Central, is a canny levantine. Escamez has spent over fifty years in the bank. He worked his way up from being a clerk in a local branch office to become president in 1973. Despite a portly frame and soft eyes, he rules his bank with an iron hand. Though the bank's shares are widely distributed, Central is very much moulded in his image. Enormously discreet and reluctant to make public statements, he has been outspoken in accepting democracy and acts as banking advisor to King Juan Carlos.

Behind these patriarchs is a newcomer, Alejandro Albert, who assumed the presidency of Hispano in April 1983 from Luis Usera. The latter had been head of Hispano since 1968, and despite a serious car accident he stuck to the helm; at one stasge he seemed set to groom his son for the succession until this appeared too much like dynasty. Aged seventy-five, he became honorary president, after refusing to endorse his successor. Albert, a trained lawyer who has studied in London and Paris, joined the bank in 1964. He has specialized in international banking and has the clean cut look of the profession. His appointment at the age of forty-eight marks a major generational change.

Banesto, Central and Hispano form the front line of this club because of their size. Hispano now enjoys more muscle following its take-over of Banco Urquijo in 1983, with whom it already had a cross-share relationship. Behind them comes Jose Angel Sanchez Asain — the first instance of an accomplished technocrat from humble origins breaking into the banking oligarchy. Brought up in a poor suburb of Bilbao, Sanchez Asain's career has been split between the research department of the bank, the academic world and the administration. He became president of Banco de Bilbao in 1974 at what was then considered the young age of forty-five. Quiet mannered and with slightly hunched shoulders, he has been instrumental in breaking the predominantly conservative mould of his colleagues. His was the first bank to agree to lend money to the newly legalized Communist Party, despite warnings of massive deposit withdrawals in protest. His decision was vindicated when no withdrawals were made.

The twin Basque bank, Vizcaya, is headed by another engineer, Pedro Galindez, a frail figure of a man who has been one of the pioneers of dam construction in Spain. Galindez has left most of the running of the bank to Pedro Toledo, an aristocratic version of Sanchez Asain. Galindez is more the figurehead for the interests of Basque capital that still dominate the board of the bank. Prepared to delegate responsibility, Galindez has seen his bank become the most aggressively innovative of the seven.

The most distinctive figure gracing these meetings is that of Emilio Botin, chief shareholder and president of the family bank, Santander. Shy, secretive, with a languid Edwardian elegance, he has been running the bank for more than thirty years. Some bankers believe him to be one of the wealthiest men in Europe. In Santander one only has to refer to Don Emilio, for there is none other. His mansion on the headland in Santander is below a monumental twenties-style hotel which he bought to prevent development. In the bank there is also Don Emilio (*hijo*), regarded as a junior though in middle age. Don Emilio holds court in his private residence cum office, the *Palacete* — the last remaining private palace on the Castellana — and his son works in the bank's new skyscraper. A brilliant financier, who has been on the Santander board since 1929, Botin was one of the first to realise the value of cultivating the Spanish emigrant community in Latin America. Don Emilio has the natural contempt for government of a man used to doing things on his own terms.

Though Banco Popular is the smallest, the influence of its president Luis Valls Taberner is far greater than the bank's size would suggest. Valls is a man fascinated by the business of banking, and has a passion for collecting the ties of international banks. He comes from a prominent Catalan business family but his father was an historian and republican member of parliament. He rarely makes public pronouncements but when the politeness of seniority has evaporated, he is often the man who presents the banks' position to the government. Cautious and mandarin-like, he is one of the most prominent members of Opus Dei. He acceded to the presidency of Popular in 1974 aged forty-six.

To some these people are a quaint patriarchal gerontocracy. For others they are a disparate and hopelessly disunited group fumbling towards understanding the changes that have occurred since the early seventies. Yet another view is that, despite their faults, they represent the one sector that has proved most adaptable and resilient to traumatic political and economic change. The prevailing view is both more simplistic and uncharitable. These men and their banks represent a rogues' gallery, plotting the interests of capital and manipulating the state. They owe allegiance to no one and represent self-perpetuating dynasties.

Superficially, there is much to make the latter view stick. For instance, the next person tipped to assume the presidency of Banesto is Pablo Garnica, already in his seventies, whose father once held the same position. Banesto in particular has done little to refurbish its image and has been frequently dubbed 'Bunker Español de Credito'. A glance at its board shows that its members include Jose Maria Oriol y Urquijo, head of the utility Hidrola and related to two of the most powerful industrial and financial families in Spain; Jamie Argulles, former Franco ambassador to Washington; and two former Franco ministers, Federico Silva Muñoz and Gregorio Lopez Bravo. Both Silva and Oriol's names have been linked since Franco's death with allegations of destabilizing democracy. However, to extrapolate from one bank — even though the largest and most conservative — is misleading.

While possessing enormous potential power, these banks have rarely used it. They are torn by rivalry, often of the most infantile sort: the league of who is biggest. In 1979 Escamez organised a triumphal opening of a $200 million pyrite mine complex near Seville, inviting the King, four ministers, and a jumbo load of dignitaries to eclipse Banesto on the very day the latter was holding its annual meeting. Central in 1983 incidentally was trying to sell off this pharaonic investment.

TENTACLES OF INVOLVEMENT

The closest European parallel to the involvement of banks in the economy is that of France and Belgium, but in neither of these two countries has there been such an all-pervasive involvement as in Spain. The previous chapter showed how these banks evolved on the back of, and in tandem with, industrial development. The banks were not simple intermediaries providing a financial service but were also direct participants in economic development. At the same time the essential character of the banks was mixed — there was no specialization. Banks acted both as takers of deposits and short-term commercial lenders, and at the same time provided long-term finance or merchant investment. Because banking evolved slowly there was no real attempt at specialization.

The first serious effort to encourage specialization was made in 1962. Banks were offered the opportunity of defining themselves as purely commercial banks or opting to become industrial banks, specializing in industrial invest-ment with a series of attendant privileges. The purpose of this division, coinciding with the new policy of promoting rapid industrialization, was to ensure that banks would concentrate their skills. Most opted to be styled as commercial banks. At the same time the larger banks either created their own industrial arms or bought themselves into existing industrial banks.

Those banks which opted to become purely industrial built a heavy exposure through loans and equity involvement in industry. While the economy was expanding this entailed no risk but in a deep recession like that since 1977 the effects were disastrous. All the industrial banks have had to be bailed out when not already linked to a big commercial bank. By 1983, none of the original seventeen industrial banks were independent of a large commercial bank.[1] The most serious losses in the banking crisis stemmed from the industrial and property portfolios of these banks.

More generally, the 1962 policy was unfortunate in doing nothing to lessen the direct involvement of the banks in the economy. It was not unusual for a bank to be a shareholder in the consultants planning a new factory, in the company running the factory, in the stockbrokers promoting the company's shares, in the utility providing power to the factory, in the company providing raw materials and equipment to the plant, in the company insuring the

93

operation, in the transport and distribution of the finished goods and their eventual promotion. Obviously the risk was spread and not exclusive, but business was often broken up on the basis of an understanding with other banks.

Take the case of Banesto. This bank possesses its own industrial arm, Bandesco, which holds most of the bank's portfolio. Banesto controls the largest insurance group that covers all aspects of the insurance business, Union y Fenix. The latter in turn is an important shareholder in industry, the utilities and property and generally involved in the same companies in which Banesto itself holds stakes, or against whom it has loans outstanding. Banesto controls one of the four private petroleum refineries, Petromed, and is also the dominant force in the largest electricity producer and supplier in southern and western Spain, Sevillana. Through Agroman it controls over 30% of all major construction work in Spain, and Banesto also controls one of the biggest property development groups, Urbis. Involvement in mining includes the zinc concern, Asturias de Zinc. Among its industrial investments are the special steels company, Acerinox, and Motor Iberica, the commercial vehicle producer. It is present in the drinks trade via a significant minority stake in Pedro Domecq. These are just a few of the more obvious examples. Banco Urquijo, because of its specialization as an industrial bank, had an even more complete portfolio prior to its take-over by Hispano-Americano in early 1983.

Throughout the Franco era the banks were under no pressure to divulge their interests. Indeed, only since 1978 have banks begun to publish accounts that have remotely reflected their patrimony. And even then there has been, with rare exceptions, reluctance to disclose the extent of their equity investments. This air of secrecy has rebounded on the banks, for it has contributed to the impression of occult resources and tentacle-like self-involvement.[2] It is estimated that prior to the recession in 1976/77 the private banks controlled as much as 40% of all Spanish industry. Control was exercised in three principal ways — equity participation and acting as nominees for shareholdings deposited by shareholders; cross board membership between the banks and the companies; and through credit.[3]

PRIVILEGED SYSTEM

The Civil War and its aftermath left banks wary of lending medium and long-term. However, access to such finance was essential for economic development. To meet this need a system evolved which survives today with remarkably little change. The basis was a trade-off between the banks and the state. Banks were obliged to place a portion of their deposits with the Bank of Spain at low interest. At the same time they were obliged to use a further portion of their deposits in officially directed investments. Such investments were primarily cheap loans, or low yielding bonds of specific state or stragegic sector companies. Initially over 30% of all commercial bank deposits were earmarked for use in this way. In the case of the *cajas de ahorro* (non-profit making savings banks), the percentage was over 60%. The funds so used were called 'privileged circuits' because of the privileged rate paid by the recipient for the funds.

The banks complained that the system distorted interest rates, but on balance it was beneficial. The low returns on state-directed investments were compensated by the 'free' funds lent short-term at high rates. Furthermore, the administration made no effort to control operating margins. This meant that bank margins (the difference between the cost of obtaining deposits and lending them) became the highest in Europe. The banks were also in a commanding position to ensure that their own companies received privileged long-term funds. This was especially the case with the electricity utilities which have a particular need for long-term finance.

The existence of this cheap credit acted as a form of disguised subsidy. The private electricity companies were among the chief beneficiaries. So long as imported energy was cheap and their financial charges were low, these electricity companies were literally able to work out their accounts by deciding the level of profits and dividends and arranging the rest of the balance sheet accordingly. The banks connived in this practice as all the major banks were represented on the boards of the private utilities.

Share ownership of the utilities has been diluted but in 1980 it was estimated that the private banks owned 9% of total utility shares, a further 7-8% through their investment companies and another 5% via family interests of bank members. In addition, up to 40% of proxy votes were deposited with the banks.[4] The importance of this relationship stems from the fact that the banks and the electricity companies between them accounted for almost 80% of the capitalization of the stock market. The private utilities produce 80% of Spain's electricity.

The web of inter-connecting relations between the banks and the electricity companies permitted two forms of cartel — over zones of influence and operation, and pricing. Electricity supply was split up on a regional basis, reflecting the original way in which hydro-electricity was developed. In some instances small local fiefdoms grew up, such as Banco Pastor's control of Fenosa in Galicia, and Banco Herrero's (run by the family of that name) of Hidroelectrica de Cantabrico in Asturias. In the case of larger companies with a wider capital base such as Iberduero, there were clear regional limits in the north and west of Spain. In these cases, bank business was traditionally divided on the basis of ancient association, with no attempt at competition.

While zones of influence and 'loyalty' to shareholder banks was understandable, a practice grew up which was nothing less than a form of trust. As the economy evolved, electricity was provided from a mix of conventional coal-fired power stations, fuel oil, nuclear energy and hydro-power. The cheapest form of electricity was that produced by hydro-power, and the most expensive, especially after 1973, was fuel oil. As a result of the carving up of Spain into zones of operation, those companies with the greatest access to hydro-electricity were in the most beneficial position. In a year of good rainfall Iberduero, Spain's largest utility, could produce 70% of its energy needs from its dams. By contrast, Sevillana in the south, with access to far less hydro-power, could only produce half this.

To compensate and even out prices, an informal, sophisticated and highly secretive system of mutual compensation was evolved. Those with the greatest amount of cheap electricity paid in most, and some were not even net contributors. This compensation fund was subject to no public scrutiny or administrative control. Indeed, one of the principal aims of the socialist electoral platform from 1977 onwards in demanding the nationalization of the high tension grid network — their sole nationalization pledge — was to monitor closely the system of pricing and establish how this compensation fund had been operating. One socialist suspicion was that occult funds were being used for political purposes. However, those inside the industry maintained that the purpose of the fund was to dress up the balance sheets of the weaker utilities so that their financial results looked stronger.[5]

One indication of the size of the compensations being paid emerged with Iberduero. Iberduero has amortized all its major hydro-works and has more water stored in its dams than the whole of France. Trying to resolve the future of its controversial nuclear power plant at Lemoniz, seventeen kilometres from Bilbao, Iberduero threatened on several occasions in 1981 and 1982 to write off its investment, worth almost $2 billion, and pull out altogether. Work had been paralyzed since February 1981, when ETA assassinated the chief engineer, Jose Maria Ryan — repeating the process with the poor man's replacement almost a year later. Iberduero could afford to write off this investment without severe financial hardship so long as it withheld its contribution to the compensation fund. By doing this Iberduero could cover its loss with five years of good rainfall. Iberduero alone in Spain could afford such a write off but it would seriously disrupt the system of compensation.[6]

The story of the Lemoniz nuclear power plant is itself indicative of the changing political power of the utilities and their main shareholders. Iberduero decided to construct the Lemoniz power plant in 1972 at a moment when the electricity companies had opted to 'go nuclear' to cover projected energy demand for the eighties. Iberduero's close association with all the key political and economic Francoist figures in the Basque country allowed it to choose the site of its convenience, and it was situated so that transmission costs to Bilbao were negligible. The original plans took little account of its proximity to one of the most densely populated zones of Spain. The heavy-handed approach of Iberduero made it a target first for ecological protest and, subsequently, the violence of ETA, who chose to represent the company as a symbol of capitalist exploitation by the financial oligarchy backed by the central government.

A SENSE OF IDENTITY

With few exceptions banks have been wary of size. The process of concentration, evident elsewhere in Europe, has been relatively slow. When all banks were required to register anew in 1947 there were one hundred and twenty. Between 1947 and 1979, when foreign banks were permitted once again to operate branches, another seventy-three Spanish-owned banks were established. The main periods for the establishment of new banks were 1948-1950 and 1963-73, when the rules on new banks opening were considerably relaxed. Between 1947 and 1981, ninety of all the registered banks disappeared through merger. A further four were struck off the register for malpractice.

The merged banks were in the main bought up either directly or indirectly by the big seven banks, the most acquisitive being Banco Central. All the banks that vanished were small, family-owned banks that scarce extended to more than three branches. This offers yet further evidence of the extraordinary fragmentation of the Spanish economy. The evolution of banking can easily be traced in the nomenclature — from family to local town and then to region. For instance, the small Vigo-based Banco Viñas Aranda changed its name in 1954 to Banco de Vigo Viñas Aranda; three years later it became Banco de Vigo and in 1974 it was re-baptized Banco de Galicia — fully identifying with the region and under the wing of one of the big seven, Banco Popular. A similar trajectory was followed by the bank, Succesores de Clemente Sanchez S.A. in Caceres. In 1965 the name became Sanchez de Caceres and in 1972 transformed into Banco de Extremadura.[7]

Considering the importance of banks within the Spanish economy, it was surprising that regulations on branch expansion were not relaxed during the boom period. Between 1948 and 1968 the number of branches increased by only 1,724 countrywide. To make up for this there was a phenomenal expansion between 1968 and 1980 — out of all proportion to the country's banking needs. The number of branches increased sixfold to over 11,000, making Spain, along with Belgium, the most heavily banked country in Europe. The vast number of bank branches in all major cities, towns and even villages is one of the first things that strikes visitors to modern Spain.

An effort by Central and Hispano-Americano to merge in 1965 never prospered — Franco was firmly opposed. He feared that the merged banking unit would be too powerful to control; and others of the big seven might then merge to form a dangerous monopoly. 'I prefer the nationalization of the banks to these monopolies,' Franco is supposed to have said.[8] This attitude was typical of Franco wanting to keep everything within manageable proportions, and supporting the idea of the small businessmen. The fear of size among businessmen and bankers had its political counterpart in the person of the Caudillo.

The question of size was also related to the perceived psychology of the client, and the image of a small bank giving a personal service was infinitely more appealing. The big banks were always reluctant to change the names and merge most of those institutions they bought out.

Finally, the size of the banks was conditioned by rivalry, a rivalry dominated by frequently puerile yardsticks of success and dominance. The 'league' table was drawn up on the basis of who held the most deposits. Profitability was gauged on sheer size rather than on return on assets or return per employee. Thus there would always be a scramble at the end of the year to boost deposits — paying under the table rates — to show big increases. In the same way, profits were dressed to suit the league position. When in December 1978 Banco Central announced it was buying out the medium-sized bank of the Fierro family, Banco Iberico, this put Central ahead of Banesto. Within a week Banesto announced the takeover of a similarly sized family bank, Banco Coca. Unfortunately for Banesto the move was made with little inspection of the Coca balance sheet; and although it retained its supremacy as the number one bank, it sustained heavy losses.

IMPACT OF CHANGE

Little evidence exists of the banks acting in concert as a lobby to define or alter economic policy under Franco. Individual banks or groups of banks may have exerted pressure on particular issues, such as holding back tax reform, the level of interest rates or whether specific companies fell within the net of the 'privileged circuits', but in general the combination of the Civil War trauma, subsequent poverty, and then the boom of the sixties dissipated the banks' pioneering commitment to economic development. It was replaced by a scramble for profits. This was especially the case among those banks granted licences in the sixties, which were run by *aficionados* of banking — interested but untried amateurs.[9]

Perhaps the greatest political influence exerted by financial institutions during the Franco era was at the local level by the savings banks and rural co-operatives. The *Caja* boards consisted of a mix of local dignitaries and loyalists to the regime, frequently members of local administrations or the Movimiento hierarchy. The 40% of *Caja* funds unaffected by use in the privileged circuits was theoretically intended mainly for housing finance. However, there was enormous discretion and *Caja* funds were often used to aid local businessmen and people connected with the regime. More insidious was the power of veto, which the *Cajas* frequently had over the granting of credit, factory licences and suchlike.

In the Basque country and Catalonia, the *Cajas* helped to sustain a sense of regional identity, particularly in cultural promotion, since a sizeable slice of their annual surpluses was earmarked for cultural activities. It is no accident that in these two regions the savings banks account for 45% of total bank deposits against the national average of 30%.

In the early seventies change began to impose itself on the larger banks. Rapid expansion and the introduction of mechanization required more sophisticated management, while the diversification of the economy required a greater variety of financial products from the banks. In response to this challenge, a generational change occurred in management in Bilbao, Popular, Vizcaya, and to a lesser extent in Hispano. The essential running of these banks was handed over to people who, though in some instances still associated with the old oligarchy, had nevertheless been trained abroad or were thoroughly technocratic. This 'modernist' influence added a further twist to the existing rivalries and differences among the big seven. Therefore, at the time of Franco's death and during the early period of transition, the chances of the banking lobby expressing a unified coherent viewpoint were strictly limited.

Reforms to the financial system in July 1977, instigated by Professor Enrique Fuentes Quintana as Economics Minister, accentuated the divide within the banks. The Fuentes reforms were timid and assumed that Spain's financial system would remain controlled for the foreseeable future. Nevertheless, the measures represented the first real breath of liberalization ever known in Spanish banking and finance. Competition was stimulated between the commercial banks and the *Cajas*. The use of privileged circuit finance was reduced progressively and the number of private and state companies able to use such soft loans was cut. The Bank of Spain acquired a new set of statutes that formally declared the central bank to be an independent institution with the governor chosen by the king for a four-year term of office. Foreign banks were allowed to establish operations, albeit on a limited scale; and new financial instruments were encouraged. Not all these reforms occurred at the same time. The decree on foreign banks was approved in 1978 and foreign banks began operating the following year, but the statutes of the Bank of Spain were not approved until 1980.

The conservatives put up a strong resistance against the advent of foreign banks, but only succeeded in imposing certain limitations.[10] Furthermore their lack of unity and their complacency permitted two ailing local banks to be snapped up by foreign banks. In the case of one, Banco de Valladolid, the big banks never believed the Bank of Spain would dare dictate to a foreign bank. In the other, Banco Lopez Quesada, the big banks were hopelessly divided. Some felt it unnecessary to bid for an ailing bank which someone else valued more highly, while others wanted to buy the bank just to keep it out of foreign hands. The opposition to the foreign presence was led by Banesto and Santander and was motivated almost exclusively by a primitive fear of competition. Increased competition was precisely what resulted.

The presence of foreign banks in Spain, apart from stimulating competition, established the principle of reciprocity. With liberalized laws on foreign investment, this enabled Spanish banks to initiate a significant expansion abroad. The opening up of bank branches in Europe, the US, Central and especially Latin America from 1979 onwards was a major extension of Spain's commercial and financial presence abroad. The motives for such expansion combined a genuine desire for diversification with an element of political caution about Spain herself. With the 'league table' mentality at work, motives of pure prestige also played a part.

These changes occurred when the Spanish economy was in severe recession. Banks suddenly found themselves having to make huge provisions to cover bad and doubtful debts and portfolio write-downs. Between 1977 and 1982 the big seven banks set aside over 700 billion pesetas in such provisions. With varying degrees of speed (most were slow off the mark), the banks sought to reduce their exposure. Loans were cut back, especially in industry, and, where possible, assets sold. Banco de Vizcaya, once so heavily involved in industry, had liquidated all its major industrial investments by 1982, including those in steel, the core of Basque industry. Banco Urquijo, the most prestigious industrial bank, desperately sought to diversify and reduce its industrial involvement in order to survive. Between 1978 and 1981, Banco Urquijo sold off interests in forty-three companies of which thirty were industrial.[12] Often the banks had to accept lower-than-book value for sales. Alternatively, in the absence of any foreign or local buyers, they were obliged to pump in more money in the hope of keeping companies alive for better days. Unofficial estimates in 1983 suggested that the major Spanish banks possessed less than half the industrial equity investment they held at the beginning of the seventies. Furthermore, their loan exposure had been substantially reduced, with foreign banks taking an important share alongside the Official Credit Institute (ICO).

The efforts by the banks to reduce their exposure had an important consequence in those industries that needed restructuring like steel, shipbuilding, copper refining and aluminium. The problems of these troubled sectors were seen more in financial than industrial terms. The problems of production planning, manpower levels, sales or products, and future technology took second place to the demands of the banks to restructure and recover their debts. This was especially evident under the government of UCD, and delayed the process of dealing with the real problems of vital sectors of Spanish industry.[13]

Recession also weakened the private utilities. From 1977, the electricity companies faced several problems: credit became much more expensive to obtain, and this extra financial cost could not be wholly recovered by higher tariffs because the government wanted to hold down inflation; to sustain shareholder and investor confidence, the companies needed to maintain their practice of paying high dividends, and the only way this could be done was by progressive decapitalization. Precisely this happened. Insufficient provision was thus made for amortizations.

In public, the electricity companies retained the image of healthy capitalist enterprises run by a manipulative oligarchy. The reality was very different. Their financial structures were dangerously weak — a weakness further undermined in 1982 by the decline of the peseta which caused substantial foreign exchange losses on their foreign loans. The banks were in no position to offer serious help, nor could the government be of much comfort since the kind of tariff increases required to generate extra cash flow were politically unacceptable. A concentration of the eleven major companies into, say, five with a rationalization of their operations is perhaps the only solution. But this solution has been resisted both because of a fear that such bigger units might be an incitement to nationalize, and because of traditional rivalries.

THE BANKING CRISIS

In January 1978, the Bank of Spain intervened in a small commercial bank, Banco de Navarra, as a result of irregularities and heavy losses in the inter-bank market. This was the beginning of a crisis in Spanish banking which lasted through until 1983, getting bigger each year, and culminating in the expropriation of the Rumasa group. During this period the cost of covering losses and refloating ailing banks totalled a minimum of 400 billion pesetas. The final cost of the crisis will certainly be more and will depend upon the balance of tidying up the eighteen Rumasa banks and their web of inter-company dealings. The losses make this the most costly banking crisis in post-war Europe, far exceeding the so-called 'secondary bank' collapses in the UK in the early seventies.

Recession and liberalization of the banking system accentuated the problems of the badly-managed banks, but the basic causes were deeper. Spanish commercial law was wholly unprepared to cope with a modern financial system — some legal concepts dated back to the early nineteenth century. Glaring gaps existed in the laws covering key aspects of inter-company dealing, holding companies, and loans to directors. At the same time, the powers of the Bank of Spain were limited and timidly used until the crisis broke.

Blame for the crisis can be fairly evenly distributed between the banking system, those who ran it, and the government. But certainly if the UCD government had acted with greater resolve from the start the number of banks affected would have been fewer, for the victims were fundamentally those banks conceded licences in the early sixties.[14] Run by inexperienced management who mixed banking with industrial and real estate ventures, the banks were vehicles to finance group investment, which resulted in a high degree of risk within companies wholly or partially owned by the intervening bank. To compete against the well established banks, these newcomers offered under-the-counter extra interest, which of course made their operations more expensive.

Often there was little to separate bad management from fraud — yet these practices were known about and tolerated. It was common knowledge that the management of the new banks was thoroughly untried, but most had some form of political protection, which was how they obtained licences in the first place. Moreover, rules were flouted because sanctions were derisory or non-existent.

The most dramatic instance in the whole banking crisis concerned the Rumasa group of banks. Banking was only one of the activities of Rumasa, and it was intended to service and fund the rest of Ruiz-Mateos' highly diversified activity. Ruiz-Mateos founded Rumasa with 300,000 pesetas capital; he held 50% of the shares himself and the remainder were distributed in 10% blocks among close members of the family. The original core of his business was the sherry and brandy trade but in the early sixties he bought into a small Cordoba bank with one branch and 5 million pesetas capital. Encouraged by the relaxation of banking laws and on the back of the economic boom, he moved into banking in a big way, but continued to act more as an entrepreneur than a banker — buying up small family banks and then reselling them — essentially trading their licences. As recession hit Spain the buyers for these banks dried up. He was stuck with a string of small banks and perforce had to consolidate the group. He also acquired a flagship, the medium-sized Banco Atlantico, with a majority stake. This made Rumasa the eighth largest banking group in Spain.

Ruiz-Mateos was never accepted by the banking community. His financial legerdemain disturbed the bankers, who also felt threatened by his oft-stated ambition of taking over one of the big banks. His sights were set on Banesto and in 1982 he made serious efforts to sell off his banks in return for becoming the latter's chief shareholder. Similar overtures, with less conviction, were made to Hispano. The moves never prospered since no-one trusted this mercurial Andalusian. He never disclosed any detailed information on Rumasa and refused to publish accounts of the group.

Ruiz-Mateos fought a rearguard action to stave off his difficulties. He delayed inspections, held back on social security payments, quarrelled with tax assessments, created more dummy companies to hide behind; but as fewer and fewer banks did business with Rumasa, risk within the group increased. More and more he was also obliged to resort to paying extra interest. He himself was on the board of none of his banks and confused matters further by utilizing the highly respectable image of Banco Atlantico

— the only one of his banks which did not carry his busy bee symbol.

By 1979, the Rumasa group was the main preoccupation of the Bank of Spain and the banking community. Ruiz-Mateos astutely exploited the fear of a collapse in the banking system, and was allowed to stay afloat, his problems concealed from the public who were lead to believe he was a benign capitalist creating jobs and standing up to the financial oligarchy. He and Rumasa were one of the few household names in Spain. He had acquired the store chain Galerias Preciados, the prestigious leather goods company, Loewe (ignoring Bank of Spain instructions to make no new investment), and was fast coming to dominate the entire wine and sherry business. He was able to spin out an audit imposed upon his group by the banking community, and even had the temerity to threaten to sack the auditors, Arthur Anderson, in order to gain time.

When the socialist government decided to act, the legal mechanism of expropriation was questioned but the need for a form of state intervention was recognized. The banks, normally so afraid of state control, welcomed the move. Emilio Botin went so far as to send a congratulatory note to the Economy Minister, Miguel Boyer (which cost Santander heavily, because Ruiz-Mateos' friends sparked a rumour campaign against the bank leading to deposit withdrawals). The Rumasa group had become like a cancer in the financial system: the body appeared fit but the organs were rotten.

Ruiz-Mateos, prior to the expropriation, claimed the group's assets and reserves were worth 119 billion pesetas. The government scaled this down to 5 billion pesetas, and later announced that preliminary estimates of the difference between assets and potential liabilities was 200 billion pesetas. Tax payments due for 1981 and 1982 totalled 30 billion pesetas alone and in some instances had been transferred to company reserves or treated as extraordinary profits. A parallel and publicly unrecorded company, Rumasa B, had been created to attract unaudited funds. In some instances it was revealed that Rumasa banks held almost 90% of their risk within the group. It also emerged that two other banks, Masaveu and Expansion, were run by Rumasa fronts, and inspectors uncovered almost ninety companies whose existence was previously unknown.

Ruiz-Mateos had survived by exploiting tolerated practices and legal loopholes, and waiving the ultimate blackmail of the banking system's confidence. The expropriation of Rumasa marked a sharp break in the incestuous relationship between the business and banking community, and the government. It ended the blurred community of interest that laid the government open to permanent blackmail. Since 1965, Rumasa banks, as a result of Bank of Spain inspection, had received twenty-seven private warnings, sixteen notes of warning, twenty-three fines totalling 178 million pesetas for failing to comply with banking norms and eighteen sanctions connected with branch expansion.[16] Successive governments had acted in the hope that the problem would disappear; the banking community behaved in the same way. The banks thought it sufficient to give Rumasa a wide berth and pay their contributions to the fund that guaranteed deposits.[17]

If the expropriated Rumasa banks remain in state hands, the state will have an important stake in the banking system. It already controls, with a majority shareholding, Banco Exterior, which acts as both an export finance institution and a commercial bank. Exterior is the same size as the big seven banks and on occasions has been treated as part of the club. The addition of the Rumasa banks gives the state 11% of commercial bank deposits. As a single share this is on a par with Banesto, Central and Hispano. With the state thus involved, banking practice is liable to become more transparent and competition sharper. It could also force the private banks to act much more in concert to defend their interests — which have become separate.

This may prove the catalyst for the beginning of a series of mergers among the big banks themselves. The difficulty now concerns the trades unions, and mechanization. Up to 30% of bank staff were traditionally employed in discounting bills. In most banks this percentage has been sharply reduced; but the banks are still heavily overstaffed. Golden handshakes have been offered as an incentive to early retirement, but Bilbao found this so expensive that the scheme was played down. Employment among the big seven between 1978-81 declined by only 3·8%, mostly natural wasteage.[18] It is hard to see a management that is traditionally weak with unions trying to force through genuine rationalization measures. As it is, the Bankers Association (AEB) has been incapable of extending banking hours into the afternoon.

CHANGING BASIS OF POWER

Greater state intervention in banking, combined with the effects of recession, have made considerable inroads into the traditional position of the private banks. Nevertheless, they represent the biggest single block of economic and financial interests in Spain. Their influence ultimately depends on the will to use it.

The big banks are more heterogenous now than before and are likely to remain so until generational changes in management occur or are completed. There is remarkably little common perception of interest. The banks, for instance, have yet to make up their minds on their own political role. They form part of the Employers Federation (CEOE) but have always kept their distance despite the fact that they add a good deal of muscle to the organization. In 1981, the Employers Federation more or less openly nailed its political colours to Alianza Popular, well before the disappearance of UCD. The more enlightened of the big seven, Bilbao, Hispano, and Vizcaya, dislike such partisan identification and feel that banks should play a more neutral and 'national' role.

In the 1982 general election, none of the big seven backed the idea of a socialist victory. However, it was extremely important that the three banks already mentioned were prepared to offer their co-operation in advance to the socialists if they won. (This was not the case in the first elections of 1977.) Banesto and Santander, meanwhile, have made no bones about their distance from the socialists who nevertheless knew that, in the wake of their victory, they would not face a completely hostile reaction and would enjoy the direct support of some. The implied trade-off is that the banks are not nationalized. The political parties as a whole, short of their own funds, have to rely upon the banks for money, which gives the banks some leverage — especially since such funds can be lent at soft rates of interest, or effectively given, by the simple device of writing off the loan as a bad debt.

The real power of the Spanish banks is their capacity to instil confidence in a government, or withhold it. Suarez for one feels that he was a victim of this withdrawal of confidence in 1980.[19] Yet the banks remain politically muddled, timid and unable to use the power at their disposal. This does not exclude individual bankers and financiers in prominent positions from political activism. In the wake of the abortive coup, several important banking names were mentioned as linked with the extreme right.[20] However, this is hardly convincing evidence of their power.

6 Wages, Workers and Unions

About the same time as the banking elite was beginning to emerge, the miserable condition of much of the rural population led to sporadic outbursts of violence. This was fertile ground upon which to sow the seeds of anarchism at the turn of the century. In the cities, working class consciousness was slow to form, largely because of the backward state of the country's economic development. But by the twenties, Spain had a vigorous, if ideologically divided, trades union movement. This played an important role under the Republic and its traditions survived to be revived with the advent of democracy.

Mention, for instance, the name 'Marcelino' among a group of workers and further identification is unnecessary. Marcelino Camacho Abad, secretary-general of the once banned and now legal Confederation of Workers Commissions (CCOO), is a symbol of those who led the courageous struggle for trades union rights under the Franco regime. This was the most consistent and exposed form of political opposition. His slight, almost frail, figure and mild manner belie his tough ideological formation in the Communist Party and his combative spirit. He has seen the inside of many a prison for his activities; now, the sole trace of these prison years is the self-taught erudition of a lathe operator turned thinker.

The Franco regime meted out double punishment to Camacho: first for his republican affiliations during the Civil War when he was a political organizer for the Communist Party with troops at the front, and later for illegal organization of labour. For fourteen years he was exiled, first in a Tangier labour camp, but in 1943 he escaped to Algeria via French Morocco. When he was able to return to Spain, he plunged straight into trades union activity. Until trades unions were legalized in April 1977, Camacho was hauled before the public order tribunals more than a dozen times and spent six years in different prisons on a variety of charges. But the fruits of his and his colleagues' struggle are apparent. Spain's working class has acquired elemental rights and safeguards long denied, and wage levels have been brought close to the European norm.

It is fitting that such a trade unionist's background should be linked with the rise of industrialization. Both Camacho's father and grandfather were railwaymen on what was then the privately run Madrid-Zaragoza-Alicante line — the line financed by Rothschild capital as a result of the new railways law of the 1850s. Camacho's father was a pointsman and his mother operated the crossing barrier. His father was a member of the socialist General Workers Union (UGT) which had been the first to recruit successfully among the new industrial working class growing up with the railways.

His mother died when he was nine years old, and the local priest was anxious to send him to a seminary (he was an altar boy in church); but his socialist father baulked at the idea of the Church influencing his upbringing and, after finishing primary school, Marcelino joined the railways. At the age of seventeen he was already a member of the UGT and had joined what was then the small Spanish Communist Party. At the outbreak of the Civil War he sabotaged the railway lines at Ariza and escaped to the republican zone. His political activism with the Communists even earned him a brief spell in detention under the Casado Junta — those Republicans who at the end of the war sought to negotiate surrender with Franco behind the back of the Communists.

Camacho never had any doubts about his role as a trades unionist. When working in Algeria as a lathe operator, he was the Communist Party's labour liaison official. At the outbreak of the Algerian independence struggle in 1954, the French authorities first imprisoned him because of his communist affiliations, then expelled him to Morocco; but he was able to return to Algeria. On being given a Spanish passport in 1957 at the beginnings of a more liberal period in Franco's government, he returned. Camacho took a job with Perkins Hispania, later to become Motor Iberica.

In 1964 he helped found the first permanent commission of the CCOO among the engineering and metal workers of Madrid, which became the core of increasingly effective labour pressure on the regime. CCOO's aim was to work from within the official vertical syndicates, placing its own men in key positions. Camacho was one of a group of trades unionists who, in 1966, handed in a petition for better working conditions to the Labour Ministry signed by 30,000 workers. He was arrested, briefly imprisoned, and dismissed from the Perkins works council (*jurado de empresa*). The workers quickly re-elected him but the election was disqualified by the authorities. The following year he was detained for being an organizer of the CCOO as the authorities attempted to crack down on mounting labour unrest. A protest demonstration by 60,000 workers helped secure his release.

From 1967 for six years, he spent all but 105 days in prison — including an initial twenty year sentence for the best known labour trial of the Franco era. This was case number 1001/72 in which nine of the leading figures (mostly communist) behind labour unrest and the formation of CCOO were put on trial and judged, on the same day that Carrero Blanco was assassinated. Though formally pardoned by King Juan Carlos after Franco's death, he was twice detained prior to the legalization of trades unions. In July 1976, at a clandestine meeting in Barcelona, he was elected secretary-general, a post

107

openly confirmed two years later at the first legal congress. Twice elected as PCE deputy to the Cortes, he abandoned his seat in 1981 to devote himself full-time to trades union activity.

Camacho brushes aside the importance of his personal protagonism; and indeed he was just one of many who suffered for what in other industrialized countries at the time was considered normal and legitimate: the right to organize labour. However, his case is illustrative of the way in which CCOO emerged as the dominant trades union force in the twilight of the Franco era, and of the troubled labour period prior to the first democratic elections.[1]

BIRTH OF A UNION

The roots of CCOO date back to 1958 when a group of pit-head miners in the privately owned Asturian coal mine of La Camocha, decided to form themselves into a workers commission. The original meeting was in the colliery washroom. This commission promoted its own members to posts within the officially-sponsored mine works council. The original commission did not last long, but it was the basis for subsequent action in 1962 and the movement spread, especially to Barcelona and Madrid. According to CCOO, these commissions sprung up 'spontaneously', and any formal link between the PCE's Soviet prompted decision to work from within the Franco system, rather than topple it from outside, is denied. The Communists certainly did not officially swing behind the commissions until 1964 when Camacho helped found the first permanent commission in Madrid. Camacho, however, began his policy of infiltration from within as soon as he got his job with Perkins.[2]

The main established trades unions, the UGT and the anarchist CNT, rejected this tactic as being too risky: the leaders could far too easily be identified and organizations could thus be decapitated by detention and imprisonment. The UGT and the CNT, so powerful in the pre-Civil-War period, also firmly rejected any role which might seem collaborationist. They were therefore confined to a clandestine role, and were far less visible than CCOO in the mounting labour unrest that characterized the end of the Franco era.

The establishment of CCOO as a major force in less then twenty years, at a time when free trades unionism was banned, was a remarkable achievement — the first of four major phenomena that have characterized the working class movement over the past century. The second and perhaps most individually Spanish phenomenon has been the rise and fall of anarchist influence in trades unionism. Having attracted a mass following for more than twenty years up to the Civil War, the CNT is now a mere shadow of its former self with limited, if not wholly marginal, influence.

The third phenomenon has been the staying power of the Socialist UGT. Founded in 1888 under the inspiration of Pablo Iglesias, the Madrid print worker and 'grandfather' of Spanish socialism, the UGT has been in the forefront of the working class movement. Yet it has gone through alternate periods of strength and weakness. In the first three years after the death of Franco it looked as though CCOO would exert near total hegemony over the trades union movement. UGT, however, has re-established itself as a leading force, if not the trades union with the largest following. Between them, these two unions account for two thirds of all affiliation, although affiliation is very low.

The fourth characteristic is the lack of basic unity or working class solidarity. Time and again, unity has been compromised by ideological divisions, political mistrust and tactical disagreements. In the early stages of the trades union movement the Socialists and Anarchists were split both on organizational methods and revolutionary aims. Latterly there has been a sharp divide between the UGT and CCOO — reflecting the rivalries and divergencies between the Socialist and Communist Parties. Unity has been best achieved on a regional basis or in specific sectors, such as mining.

THE ANARCHISTS AND UGT

Until the late nineteenth century, the concept of collective action to protect workers' interests and promote changes in work conditions had scarcely penetrated Spain. Given the limited nature of industrialization and the poor state of communications, this was hardly surprising. Only in more industrialized Catalonia were there two organized labour groups; but these were conservative in nature and limited to the cotton and textile industry. Meanwhile, in the countryside, the peasants and labourers were ripe for action but lacked both the means and the leadership to be effective. As a result their protests took the form of inarticulate violent action that was easily repressed. Between 1840 and 1870 at least five peasant revolts occurred in parts of Aragon, Castile and above all in over-populated Andalusia. Protest over work conditions and pay, and, in the case of the peasants, land distribution, was invariably bound up with a more general discontent and frustration at the way the government ignored their interests or local grievances.

Mikhail Bakunin judged Spain to be in a sufficiently primitive stage of pre-industrialization for action and in 1868 despatched his disciple, Guiseppe Fanelli, to spread his own interpretation of the First International's revolutionary philosophy. Fanelli's three month visit to Barcelona and Madrid, expounding ideas of liberty, international brotherhood and direct action that included violent overthrow of capitalism, was the germ of the Spanish anarchist movement.[3]

Though successful in recruitment, there was no formal attempt to organize all the various groups until 1910 when the Anarchist Federation, CNT, was constituted. By the end of the First World War, the CNT claimed a membership of 700,000, five times that of the UGT. Attracted to its ranks were a mixture of self-educated idealists, impoverished traders, criminals, alienated industrial workers, oppressed peasants and a mass of hangers on seduced by the thought of justice and revenge on society.

Any government or employer was bound to react to a group of people mobilizing behind the philosophy: 'all exercise of authority perverts and all submision to authority humiliates'. Whether in town or countryside, the CNT and the employers became locked in a bitter conflict, briefly tranquil under the Primo de Rivera dictatorship when the CNT was banned and forced underground. It bounced back with the advent of the Republic, claiming a membership of one million by the time of the Civil War.

But the Civil War and its aftermath decimated the CNT, and reduced it to a hard core of militants mainly in the Barcelona area. The leadership was forced into exile, from where it backed guerilla action against the Franco regime until 1951. By 1956 the authorities, as a result of a big metal workers strike in Barcelona, had effectively dismantled what organization was left. In exile, the CNT was loosely associated with the UGT, but to no great purpose. By the time trades unions were legalized in 1977 and the CNT had applied to register, it boasted some 40,000 members.[4] The real membership is considered to be below this and the residual strength lies with a few particular sectors — Barcelona transport, bank employees and print workers.

The size of CNT membership has always been elusive. The Anarchists have been accused of grossly inflating their numbers. But this accusation misses the point. The Anarchists were loosely organized on a federal basis, and, rather like a balloon, contracted or expanded, depending on the input of air. In the right circumstances they could call up amazing reserves of manpower (this was evident in their Civil War effort). But equally, the idealism which many brought to their ranks vanished with repression, or with the internecine squabbling that all too frequently pitted rival groups against each other.

The trades unionism of the Ararchists fell permanently into the dilemma of priorities. Through direct action the anarcho-syndicalists aimed to introduce a libertarian millenium in which the means of production were self-managed and society operated through a series of loose federal relationships. But in terms of improving the lot of the working man, they permanently fudged the issue as to whether this meant first fighting to change conditions on the shop floor and in the countryside, or directly overthrowing the state. During the Republic and the Civil War the Anarchists were constantly in conflict with their comrades of the left because they insisted that the republican struggle was merely the first stage in a broader revolution. This made the Anarchists dangerous to everyone. It was no accident that the Communist Party took especial pains during the Civil War to control, and if necessary eliminate

110

them. The Anarchists threatened to outflank the left through their exaggeration and irresponsibility.

In the wake of the Civil War, first in active organization of guerilla activity and then in illegal strikes they were obvious targets for repression and suffered accordingly. But this alone does not explain the decline of anarchism among the working class. The principle explanation was simpler still: in a society exhausted by conflict and violence, the anarchist creed lost its appeal. As the economy developed, employment prospects improved and the regime's attitude towards labour became more paternalistic, the appeal of the CNT further waned.

Anarchism was a product of the pre-industrial society, an almost natural reaction to the primitive class structure and the misery in which so many had lived. Increased affluence, coupled with employment and emigration, removed the previous potential for recruitment. It is arguable that those who support CNT today do so more out of a sense of tradition than real conviction. The only natural heirs of anarchism to be found are the members of the radical peasants organisation in Andalusia, Sindicato Obrero de Campo (SOC), which believes in direct action (though mostly peaceful). The SOC lives off a gut mistrust of authority and the chronically hopeless situation of landless labourers in Andalusia.

The CNT made more noise than anyone else at a moment when working class conditions in Spain were first put under the microscope. But in terms of solid achievements in improving these conditions, it promised more than it was able to deliver — or its achievements were so radical as to be unacceptable and were quickly reversed. By contrast, the UGT was more pedestrian and puritanical. The UGT believed in organization and had its objectives far more clearly defined — and it was prepared to work within a parliamentary context to achieve workers' rights even though its origins were to be found in the ideas of the First International. Therefore the UGT was far more acceptable to employers and governments than the CNT, and was thus able to bring about genuine improvements in working conditions. The UGT also made a far more lasting effort to improve the level of working class culture via the *Casas del Pueblo*, small community centres with libraries, and adult education.

The UGT was constantly pulled in two directions from within. One current of opinion looked to marxist ideas for inspiration, while the other, more dominant current was reformist, moderate, and sought to work with the system. The UGT leader, Francisco Largo Caballero, even took the polemical decision not to oppose the Primo de Rivera dictatorship, thus ensuring that UGT was able to remain a legal entity co-operating with the government. This pragmatism was to emerge again in the 1980s.

The UGT drew its strength from the new centres of industry in the north — in Asturias among the miners and steel workers in the triangle of Aviles, Oviedo and Gijon; and in Vizcaya, principally in the steel and metal-working industry that grew up on the banks of Bilbao's River Nervion. These were industries that either required some skill and apprenticeship or generated a great deal of solidarity among workers. The level of education among UGT was generally higher and its organization certainly better than that of the CNT. The UGT also picked up recruits in Madrid as it began to generate more employment. The strong UGT presence in Asturias led to the union playing a major role in the abortive Asturian revolutionary rising in 1934.

The UGT might have evolved independently from the Socialist Party, but the Civil War and its aftermath made the two mutually dependent. The UGT lost its assets, and its organization on the ground was largely dismantled. The worst incident of repression was the seizure of twenty-two Asturian miners in 1948, who were tortured and dumped in a mine which was then blown up. In exile, the union leadership followed the vicissitudes of the Socialist Party. This meant that the UGT, like the Socialist Party, was badly split first in the forties and then again in the early seventies when those in the interior sought to rejuvenate both the union and the party. One of the main figures pressing for a shake-up during the latter period was Basque-born Nicolas Redondo, elected UGT secretary-general in 1973. Aware that the UGT had lost ground to CCOO, the new leadership nevertheless insisted on continuing as a clandestine movement. Offers to join up and work within the commissions of CCOO were firmly rejected. This decision was polemical at the time, but fully justified with hindsight from the point of view of retaining the union's identity and its socialist orientation.

CATHOLIC GROUPS AND REGIONAL INFLUENCES

Despite the eclipse of the CNT and UGT, there was still fertile ground for a new attempt to organize labour by the end of the fifties. The quickening pace of economic activity, the expansion of the labour market and the chronically low level of wages provoked the rumblings of unrest. Catholic organizations and the new spirit of christian-marxism which attracted many young priests, played an important part in fomenting unofficial trades union activity. At the same time, the Catholic Church hierarchy was willing to permit its own workers organizations to counter the Falange who had monopolized labour policy. The regime itself had no wish for a confrontation with the Church and, in any case, did not really see the move of the Church into labour groups as a threat.

The main Catholic lay groups working among the labour force were the Catholic Workers Brotherhood (HOAC) and the Catholic Youth Workers Movement (JOC). Members from these groups were instrumental in helping to found the first trades union, parallel to the official vertical syndicates. The Workers Union (USO), was founded in 1960 with the moderate aim of improving shop floor conditions and wages. Though active, USO was weakened by its own moderation. It lacked the backing of any of the exiled political parties and the Church hierarchy never considered giving any support. The importance of USO, however, lay in its being considered by the authorities as Catholic and therefore inoffensive and semi-tolerable. This mantle of acceptability also fell upon the nascent Workers Commissions, the authorities taking time to understand the true nature of the latter's aims. Even among priests anxious to support trades unionism, USO lacked militancy. This lead the more dynamic priests to throw in their lot with CCOO.

More generally, priests were prepared to place Church premises at the disposal of the nascent groups for illegal meetings, and the parish was galvanized as an organizational structure. In the original Workers Commission of La Camocha, the local priest was also invited and agreed to be a member.

In the particular context of the Basque country, Church backing lay behind the formation of a regional trades union. ELA/STV was founded in 1911 by Basque Nationalists in close association with the Basque clergy, who regarded trades unionism in Spain as too overtly socialist and anti-church. At times ELA/STV seemed more of a social welfare organization for Basque workers, than a trades union. Not until 1933 was the right to strike taken on board, somewhat timidly. As a result of the Civil War, the union collaborated closely with the Basque Nationalist government-in-exile.

The union was an important force behind the persistent anti-regime industrial action in the Basque country but was divided over its close links with the Basque Nationalist Party and its overtly confessional — and anti-communist — tone. These divisions were eliminated once unions were legalized and ELA/STV now accounts for a quarter of all union representation in the Basque country. It is considered the best organized and most efficiently run of any Spanish union.[5]

Basque nationalism is undoubtedly the major element in the success of ELA/STV; it also contributed to the birth of another more radical union, LAB (Langile Abertzale Batzordeak). The same combination of regionalism and christianity was repeated, but with less success, in Catalonia in 1958 with the formation of a Catalan christian workers organization, SOCC (Solidaritat d'Obrers Catalans Cristians). The latter exercise failed because SOCC lacked the tradition of ELA/STV and came into existence to some extent in competition with the Workers Commissions. With the powerful Catalan Communist Party backing the Commissions, SOCC was an unattractive option.

More success has been evident in Galicia, with an overtly nationalist alliance of union forces, INTG (Intersindical Nacional Gallega). This grouping had the support of various Galician nationalist parties following the legalization of trades unions; but it lacked the moderate Catholic character of SOCC in Catalonia or ELA/STV in the Basque country. In Andalusia, the

113

radical peasants organization, SOC, does admit a christian-marxist element, but also relies on the purely regional nature of its members' demands.

Regionalism has been and still is of enormous importance in understanding both the nature of affiliation and the level of working class militancy. When the UGT began to rebuild its organization in the mid-seventies, its strength came from those areas where it had always been strong — Vizcaya and Asturias. There is no other country in Europe, even one possessing a federal structure, with a union similar to ELA/STV. Furthermore, the combination of nationalism and industrialization in the Basque country ensured that, during the bulk of the Franco era, it was the scene of more conflict than anywhere else. One study showed that between 1963 and 1974 just over 30% of all Spain's labour conflicts occurred in the two most industrialized Basque provinces of Guipuzcoa and Vizcaya, against almost 20% in Barcelona and its surrounds and a further 12% in Asturias. These three areas accounted for 65% of Spain's labour unrest.[6]

THE RISE OF CCOO

Except in the Basque country, CCOO pushed itself to the front of these conflicts. The dismantling of the CNT and UGT allowed the new Workers Commissions to penetrate their former strongholds such as the Asturian mines, once dominated by the special union, SOMA/UGT, and the very symbol of UGT's presence in the working class struggle.

The form of organization and representation offered by CCOO caught the imagination of workers. It was geared to specific demands, like raising wage levels and reducing working hours or altering unacceptable practices. The CCOO leaders were clearly visible, and, unlike the UGT and CNT leadership in exile, were close to the everyday problems of their members. The Commissions were not discriminatory in their recruitment and encouraged the radical Catholics. But early on, communist sympathisers were the main element. The Communists were well organized, their members benefitting from the Communist Party's small size but considerable influence at the time of the Civil War, and its lack of a mass union movement of its own. As such, it was a less obvious target for repression.

Growing on the back of the economic boom, CCOO was able to implant itself across the countryside and to be first on the shop floor when new factories were created, or development spread to the new 'poles' such as Huelva, Valladolid and Zaragoza. Perhaps more significant was the growing industrial and economic importance of Madrid and its suburbs, where the penetration of CCOO had national impact. The union's presence in the capital helped it to be well informed. In the twilight of the Franco era, the CCOO had so successfully penetrated many factory works councils, large and small, that employers were often obliged to negotiate with them alongside the 'official' representatives.

The increased confidence of the illegal labour movement in dealings with management was supported by strike action. Although strikes were illegal, from the mid-sixties onwards the numbers of hours lost through strikes, and the number of workers involved in such actions, grew steadily. Statistics vary, but on one calculation the number of strikes trebled between 1966 and 1970. Between 1970 and 1975, the number of workers involved in strike action rose from 366,000 to 556,000 and the number of hours lost nearly doubled.[7] Despite all its repressive action, the regime failed to prevent labour militancy. By the end of the Franco era, the infiltration of CCOO into the vertical syndicates was nearly complete. Meanwhile, UGT had recovered some of its force. The trades union movement was undoubtedly the most powerful democratic force when the transition to democracy began.

VERTICAL SYNDICATES AND LABOUR CONDITIONS

The essence of the vertical syndicate was to combine management and labour, employers and employees, in a series of corporate units representing different aspects of economic activity. It was a concept borrowed and adapted by the Falange from Mussolini's national socialism. The attraction for its promoters was that it eliminated the (dangerous) marxist view of class struggle. Instead, the worker was incorporated into the state apparatus via the syndical organization, and in return for a series of paternalistic benefits would accept subordination to the employer. The employer, for his part, was then theoretically responsible to the state for operating successfully in the national interest. Affiliation to the syndicates was obligatory, and dues were deducted automatically. Representatives were originally selected entirely from Falange appointees.

The legal framework for these organizations lay in the Labour Charter (Fuero de Trabajo) of 1938, which directly acknowledged the role of the Falange as chief militants within the syndicates. The Labour Charter made it clear that anyone upsetting production was guilty of a crime against the state. Official trades unionism was therefore part of the state apparatus and became an important bureaucratic empire in itself, attached to the Movimiento. Under Article 222, going on strike was formally branded as an act of sedition.

The vertical syndicates proved to be extremely unwieldy and rigidly bureaucratic organizations. The system was tailored to bolster political stability rather than promote economic and social development, even though the more radical members of the Falange genuinely believed that they were promoting greater social justice. In theory, the system suited the employers because labour was subordinated, but as the economy began to expand the inherent strains of a rigid system, especially the regulation of salaries by the Ministry of Labour, became apparent. From 1958 onwards, the principle of collective bargaining was admitted and the official attitude towards strikers was relaxed, effectively conceding the legitimacy of purely economic claims.

As the syndicates evolved, they were blown along by events over which they themselves exercised less and less control. Their stifling, bureaucratic nature and obligatory membership disenchanted the workers, so making them willing converts to the new unions as they emerged.

The Caudillo's own interest in improving the lot of the working class was ambivalent. Like many a Spaniard he clung to the view that the peasant and honest working man was the repository of true Spanish values. This was mixed in with a simplistic and genuine desire to raise living standards. But the stability of the regime was his first priority and he was unwilling to admit or understand the real nature of working class grievances. After the Civil War he met 'model' workers in brand new factories and saw the peasantry at close quarters when he was out shooting. He satisfied his social conscience by insisting on details (obligatory canteens in factories, for example) rather than on broad issues.[8]

The system was not, however, completely loaded in favour of the employer. The worker, in lieu of the right to strike, was given job security — legislation made the sacking of labour both difficult and expensive, which encouraged a civil service 'job-for-life' mentality. Workers could only be easily dismissed for subversive activity.

The corporatist approach of the syndicates also gave the employers a one-sided view of their own interests. Since they felt the state was fundamentally on *their* side, they did not really bother to check whether there was a conflict of interest — nor did they trouble to organize themselves properly. The employers, with the advent of democracy, suddenly had to invent an organization, the Employers Federation (CEOE), to help broaden their approach to the issue of labour relations.

THE ACHIEVEMENT OF ILLEGAL ORGANIZATIONS

The principal achievement of the then illegal trades unions was political. Their protest was a constant reminder, from the late fifties onwards, that working class support could not be taken for granted. Not all protest was successful. For instance efforts by a wide spectrum of the opposition to organize a national strike on 18 June 1959 — the so-called Huelga Nacional Pacifica — was little short of a disaster. The Communists were accused of trying to manipulate the strike to obtain all the credit and the semblance of unity shattered even before the strike was called. From that time, the national strike lay in abeyance as a weapon of protest.

More successful and damaging were regional strikes like those in Vizcaya, or sector strikes like those of the Madrid metal-working industries. The regime always reacted to this sort of pressure with force; and as the illegal organizations grew stronger the regime felt correspondingly more threatened and reacted with even more force. Thus in 1970, two men were killed as police broke up a construction workers strike. The following year a partial state of emergency was imposed as a result of worker protest over the Burgos Trials of ETA militants. The number of politically motivated strikes between 1963-67 was only 4%, while between 1967-74 the percentage rose to 45%. The overall level of worker mobilization in such protest was small compared to the size of the labour force. If one accepts that often the same groups of people were involved in strike action in any one year, probably less than one in twenty wage earners took part. Nevertheless, the impact always seemed to belie this: partly because the authorities invariably overreacted; partly because the action occurred in politicized areas like Madrid, Barcelona, Asturias or the Basque country.

If this was the stick, the carrot consisted of wage increases. Between 1964-75 wages grew in constant terms at an annual average of 8%. In other words, while each year workers obtained on average 17% more pay, inflation only removed 8%.[10] In some instances these increases were the result of labour scarcity, not due to full employment as the authorities pretended but to the regional imbalance in the demand for labour. There was, for instance, a shortage of construction workers in Madrid yet unemployment in Andalusia.

The increase in wages was most notable among unskilled workers and apprentices, a phenomenon of other boom economies. However, union pressure still focussed on improving these pay levels still further. Union pressure in general frightened the employers, and wage increases from the mid-sixties tended to be a barometer of conflict inside a specific sector in the country as a whole.

Wage increase also reflected the changing level of education and skill in the workforce. Between 1963 and 1970 the proportion of unskilled labourers and apprentices among wage earners declined sharply, from 46% to 39%, and by 1976 it had dropped to 33%. By contrast, the number of skilled workers rose modestly, with a much bigger rise in those holding administrative or technical jobs. Those holding administrative jobs, from being only 12% of wage earners had risen to 19% by 1976; while the proportion holding technical qualifications, though small, doubled to 3%. The overall level of education of the workforce during this period also changed dramatically, so that education among workers to secondary school level became common, whereas previously most had only reached primary level, if that. In 1964 only 5% of the active population had secondary education — sixteen years later it was almost 25%.[11]

The practice grew up of providing two extra monthly payments, one to precede the summer holidays in July and the other to coincide with Christmas.

117

A good many companies went so far as to make three extra monthly payments to their employees. In a society hitherto unused to such substantial rises in real earnings, it is easy to understand how high wages distracted attention away from other aspects of work, such as industrial health and safety.

DEMOCRATIC RIGHTS

On 28 April 1977 when the decree legalizing trades unions appeared in the Official Bulletin, six unions applied to register — CCOO, UGT, USO (all of which could be considered national), ELA/STV and the SOCC (both regional), and the merchant seaman's union, SLMM (Sindicato Libre de la Marina Mercante). The intervening period since Franco's death had been tense. The unions were impatient to be formally recognized, but they were given a much lower priority than legalization of the political parties.

It was not easy winding up the huge empire of the vertical syndicates which had a full time staff of over 32,000 and a string of buildings and subsidiary organizations throughout the country. A special organization had to be created, innocuously called the Institutional Administration of Socio-Professional Services (AISSP). All the 32,000 regular syndicate employees were transferred here to be reallocated, though a rump remained, apparently doing nothing.

Frustrated over their semi-tolerated status, the new unions were torn between protesting strongly to underscore their demands and keeping silent to avoid provoking the die-hard conservatives. Tension was frequently high, and reached a black point in March 1976 when five workers were killed during clashes with police in Vitoria. This provoked a massively supported general strike.

Worse was to come in January 1977, when five left wing labour lawyers were brutally assassinated in their Madrid offices. The killings were the work of right wing extremists abetted by members of the near-extinct vertical syndicates in crude retribution for the pending legalization of trades unions. Redondo can say with some justice: 'the trades union movement is the one that has made the most sacrifices for democracy'.[12]

Trades union rights, along with those of the employer, have since been guaranteed in the constitution.[13] However, only the nature of these rights was defined, and it was left to subsequent legislation to define how they should be used. The most important was the Workers Statute which came into force in March 1980. The Statute removed direct state involvement from labour relations, leaving them to be resolved between unions and management. It provided guarantees on minimum wages, access to social security, and covered the contractual nature of wage agreements. Collective bargaining was accepted as a means of wage negotiation and democratically elected

Works Council representatives were recognized as the interlocutors between the workers and management inside companies.

A significant aspect of the previous system remained relatively unaltered — the ability of managements to hire and fire. The concept of temporary work contracts was admitted as was the termination of contracts for 'objective reasons', but the tight job protection of the previous system remained. Another law, passed in October of the same year, was primarily concerned with covering unemployment — the Basic Employment Law. This also covered payment of Social Security quotas by the employers and workers.[14]

This legislation left a number of grey areas which caused unease among the unions. The whole question of the right to organize within the civil service and the police forces was vague on such vital matters as strike action. Also left in the air was the position of civilians working within the military establishment. One of the features of the former regime was the way in which a number of aspects of civilian life were effectively militarized. The merchant navy, for instance, came under the control of the navy and its personnel, though civilian, were treated as military employees. The same applied to civilians working in military factories (the majority) and in administrative jobs, and extended to such areas as air traffic control. A different inter-relation between work and military control existed in the mines: Franco waived military service obligations for those who wished to work in them. All these issues are in the process of resolution; the most delicate one outstanding at the time of the socialist government's advent to power concerned the right to strike of certain categories of public employee.

THE SOCIAL CONTRACT

The principle labour reforms were envisaged in the Moncloa Agreements of October 1977, subscribed to by all the major political parties. However, their realization was extremely slow, and the proper legal framework in which workers could enjoy their rights was not in place until five years after Franco's death. It was not really until 1980 that more attention was focussed on such issues as productivity, work conditions and industrial training; and even then, as a result of the continued economic recession, job security and job creation were the unions' abiding concern. Indeed, Spain's difficult economic situation and the precarious financial state of many companies had resulted in the operation of an implicit, and at times explicit, social contract between the government, employers and trades unions — the unions accepting wage restraint in return for greater protection against unemployment and the prospect of job creation.

A pact between the UGT and the Employers Federation laid the framework for wage agreements in 1980, even though the other main union, CCOO refused to take part. In return for accepting a wage band of 13-16% — just ahead of inflation — the UGT agreed on productivity deals and pledged themselves to curb strike action. The agreement, the AMI (Acuerdo Marco Interconfederal), also referred to the need to reduce the number of working hours, create new jobs and improve working conditions.

It was the first time that a document, jointly subscribed by national management and labour representatives, referred to such issues. Behind the agreement lay a wholly new concept in Spain: that a community of interest existed between management and labour and that differences were best solved by a system of mutual trade-offs. The agreement served as a framework for some 800,000 companies employing 6 million workers — half the active population. The number of hours lost through labour unrest fell by 32% in 1980 as a result. Also built into the agreement was a form of wage indexation already utilized in the Moncloa Agreement. This provided for the topping up of wages if the mid-year inflation rate exceeded the projections on which the original wage increases were based. The agreement was renewable and was followed up in 1981.

A more broad-based social contract was achieved in June 1981 to cover 1982. This was a tripartite agreement between the government, the CEOE and the principal unions — profoundly influenced by the abortive coup of 23 February and the continuing recession. The move to promote agreement was primarily political and the CEOE was reluctant to participate. The government's aim was to demonstrate publicly a sense of national solidarity in the wake of the coup. The unions, in return for accepting a drop in real earnings, were promised improved pensions, greater aid to agricultural workers, better cover of unemployment benefit, and investments to create new jobs. This was a carrot to keep the unions off the streets, and the promise of 350,000 jobs was wildly exaggerated. The unions' leaders only accepted it as a public palliative to demonstrate to any restive rank and file that their interests were being protected.

The commitment on employment was virtually ignored, undermining the real value of the agreement which was unfortunately called the National Employment Agreement. The experience is unlikely to be repeated in the same form. It was in the national interest at the time that such a pact should emerge; but the chief beneficiaries were the employers who were able to plan wage levels well ahead for 1982.

Attention has also been devoted to reducing working hours. The AMI pledged to work towards a cut of 126 hours in three years, to 1,880 hours per year by 1982. However, in 1982 an analysis of wage agreements showed that 30% of the total workforce was still working more than 1,880 hours a year; by contrast, 17% of the workforce was working less than that. The average working week thus remained over forty hours, even after 91% of all the agreements had conceded thirty days of holiday a year.[15] The socialist government is committed to reducing the working week both on philo-sophical grounds and as a way to ease unemployment. The aim is to meet union demands for a thirty-five hour week — a cut of over 12%.

UNION RIVALRY

The two main unions, CCOO and UGT, have enjoyed an uneasy coexistence. Much of the time since the death of Franco they have been locked into an unedifying scramble for hegemony of the trades union movement. This power struggle is perhaps an inevitable result of their sudden emergence into legality, but the working class movement has been split and weakened by it.

The fundamental source of rivalry is the political parties behind them. The CCOO insists that it is not an instrument of the Communist Party and it is true that a significant proportion of its members are not affiliated to the Party. Nevertheless the Communist Party has always sought to control CCOO. After all, the French and Italian Communist Parties openly identify with their own trades unions. When the first legal congress of CCOO was held in 1978, a forty-two man executive was chosen — of these two were indepen-dents, three belonged to fringe parties to the left of the Communists but all the rest were Party members, six of them on the Party executive.[16] The change since then is that the Communist Party itself has been weakened by internal divisions. The distance now observed between CCOO and the Party is tactical. Camacho wants to avoid the deteriorating image of the Communist Party reflecting on CCOO. He also wants to make CCOO more independent so that it can exert greater influence over the Party rather than vice versa. The communist ideological dominance prevails; for instance, it was communist orthodoxy which was largely responsible for the split within CCOO in 1976 that led to the formation of the more radical federation, CSUT (Confeder-acion de Sindicatos Unitarios de Trabajadores). The principal force behind CSUT came from the revolutionary marxist groups, ORT (Organizacion Revolucionario de Trabajo) and PTE (Partido de Trabajo Español).

The UGT, on the other hand, has never pretended to be anything other than the trades union arm of the Socialist Party, acting in a subordinate capacity (unlike the British trades unions' relationship with the Labour Party). The sole instance of the UGT being able to dictate policy to the party is in Asturias where the mining union, SOMA/UGT, controls the local party. According to Felipe Gonzalez: 'Historically, relations between the PSOE and UGT have been fraternal and I think they will continue to be so given the profound harmony between the aspirations of the two organizations. However, rela-tions between UGT and a government formed by the PSOE could be more variable because the government has to take into account the whole nation, not just its own electorate.' This potential conflict, already evident in some of the wage negotiations of 1983, is inevitable; but is unlikely to alter the fundamental identity of interest between UGT and PSOE.[17] To underline this unity of view, Gonzalez addressed a UGT May Day rally in Madrid in 1983. A Spanish premier had not done this since the thirties.

The first union elections held in 1978 gave the CCOO a clear edge over the UGT, although between them the two groups dominated the results. The CCOO picked up 34% of union representation against 20% for UGT. Compared to the socialist vote in the first general elections, this was a poor showing and much worse than expected by the UGT leadership. The CCOO had attracted many Socialists into its ranks as a result of its better organiz- ation and obvious presence on the shop floor. With UGT well beaten into second place, the rivalry increased; and UGT initially made the mistake of trying to outflank the CCOO by being more radical. This led nowhere. Both the Suarez government and the Employers Federation — to say nothing of the Socialist Party and the UGT — saw a danger of a Portuguese-style situation emerging with a single dominant union effectively run by the Communist Party. Initially the Suarez government tried to boost the influence of USO, seeking to make it a sort of christian democrat trades union linked to UCD. But the marriage was incompatible and USO itself had no mass appeal among the workforce.

The only alternative was to build up the UGT as a counter-weight to the CCOO. The opportunity presented itself when the CCOO decided to pull out of preliminary discussions in 1979 for the first social contract agreement, the AMI. The CCOO regarded the proposals put forward by the government and the Employers Federation as going against the interests of the working class. Redondo and the UGT leadership, on the other hand, believed that the mood of trades unionism was fundamentally against the idea of 'class war' and were prepared to trim their sails to be moderate. The UGT agreed to sign the AMI. In doing so, Redondo took the risk of being accused by his own rank and file of selling out to the government and employers. The Deputy Premier, Fernando Abril Martorell, who did most of the negotiating, told Redondo he thought the AMI would never hold. But it did, and the curious situation arose of a centre-right government and a right wing employers organization actively co-operating with a socialist trades union to bolster the latter's power. There was even co-ordination over strikes, with information being passed to UGT over the extent to which employers or the government was prepared to go; strikes were even arranged so that UGT could call them and win them.[18]

This co-operation, combined with Redondo's correct assessment of the mood of the rank and file, permitted the UGT to claw back lost ground. In the 1980 elections, it increased its share of the vote to almost 30%. UGT began to make inroads into CCOO strongholds like the huge Seat workforce in Barcelona. At the same time the UGT attracted support from those who had formerly been involved in smaller unions such as USO. The fruits of the UGT strategy of moderation were more marked in the 1982 union elections. Official figures gave UGT 36% of the vote and CCOO only 33%.

The CCOO complained that the official figures did not include all the election results, in particular those for Catalonia. Justified or not, this complaint cannot conceal the trend in support for the UGT, which has clearly caught the mood of trades union militancy during the recession much better than the CCOO.[19] The sheer size of the support for UGT however, need not necessarily reflect its real influence. The CCOO continues to retain dominance over the construction sector, one of the largest industrial employers, and in the key metal-working sector, as well as possessing more activists. In the 1983 May Day demonstrations, the two unions, for the first time since they were legalized, were unable to agree on a joint programme. The CCOO made a point of demonstrating its power to pull a crowd, and the CCOO demonstration outnumbered the UGT by almost ten to one.

AFFILIATION AND POWER

Despite the high public profile of the unions, affiliation is low. Over half the workforce has no contact with the trades unions and from a high-point after legalization, union membership appears to be declining. Statistics on affiliation are unreliable and the unions themselves are unhelpful. Furthermore, each tends to suspect the other of inflating membership. All too often the unions are happy to include paid-up members, lapsed members, and sympathizers, i.e. those who merely vote for their candidate in union elections.

The most thorough independent survey of union membership to date concluded that total affiliation to all unions in 1981 was no more than 1·8 million — or 20% of the wage earning population of 9 million. This conclusion was reached on the basis of studying the 1980 union election results. A total of 2·7 million votes were cast of which 636,000 went to independent candidates openly identified with a union. Since by no means all these votes were from paid-up, or even lapsed, members, the study revised the level of affiliation further downwards.[20]

The inference is that most workers are willing to draw the benefits from union activity without direct participation. Equally, a low level of affiliation is a natural result of the small scale of Spanish industry where the majority of companies employ less than fifty persons. In such companies, unionization is actively, and often easily, discouraged by the management. By the same token, the levels of membership are most marked in large companies or in sectors where work generates solidarity like mining, or seafaring.

If real membership were as both claimed, then their financial positions would be much stronger — even self-financing. As it is, the unions are probably picking up no more than 60% of their potential dues. Members join and then quickly fall behind with their dues. For instance, the well organized mining section of the CCOO, with 25,000 affiliates, was receiving average monthly dues totalling 204,308 pesetas in 1980. If all had been paying properly, the income should have been 375,000 pesetas, so that only 55% were paying their dues properly.[21] The sole exception to the low level of paid-up membership is ELA/STV in the Basque country.

By European standards contributions are small, averaging 200 pesetas per month in 1982. Here again, ELA/STV stands out — at 475 pesetas, its dues are more than double anyone else's. Perhaps it is no accident that ELA/STV is the only union to offer free individual legal service to its members. Apathy is an important factor in the lack of payment. Under the vertical syndicates, dues deducted directly were accepted almost as a form of tax by the workforce. Legalization of the trades unions left them free to collect dues but they could not use the company to direct debit in their favour. The ANE agreement allowed unions to collect in this way for the first time, but only in companies with 250 workers and more. This underlines the contradiction between workers expecting more privileges yet doing little to achieve them — most cannot be bothered to pay because they feel the advantages from union activity will accrue to them anyway.

With small dues incompletely paid up, the unions are financially very weak. They do not have large pension funds or other assets at their disposal. Instead they are debt-ridden and dependent upon bank loans and, in some instances, support from internationally affiliated bodies. The unions would be in better financial shape if they had been able to retain their historic pre-war assets, whose value is impossible to even guess with accuracy. In some cases the UGT *Casas del Pueblo* were very substantial buildings on prime city sites; these were all taken over. Valuation, apart from legal title, has been made more difficult by changes to these buildings — additions or completely new structures. On one estimate these union assets could currently be worth 200 billion pesetas.[22]

These assets belonged primarily to the UGT and the CNT. Legal title has been complicated by the banning of these unions and the creation of the vertical syndicates. The property used and improved by the vertical syndicates was funded by contributions from all working Spaniards. If one then adds to this legal mess the emergence of one large new trades union, CCOO, how then can the funds — those that can be realized — be shared out? Initially, the UCD government demurred; delay also suited the CCOO because it was given time to prove its strength. Any adjudication that left the UGT and CNT chief beneficiaries was clearly to its disadvantage. UGT, on the other hand, even went so far as to seek foreign credits with these historic assets as collateral.

As part of the National Employment Agreement (ANE) of 1981, the Calvo Sotelo government pledged to provide funds to the unions directly out of the budget. For the period 1982-84 a total of 800 million pesetas per year (at constant rates) was set aside to 'consolidate' the unions. These funds were to be handed out proportionately on the basis of trades union election results.[23] This subsidy did not seek to interfere with legal action to claim the historic assets; instead it sought to right an historic injustice in accordance with present day realities. In 1983, the CNT successfully challenged the subsidy in the courts on the grounds that this was an unfair redistribution of confiscated trades union assets. The Socialist Government disregarded the court's judgement and maintained the subsidies.

The subsidy cannot resolve the long term problem of trades union finance. Dues have to be raised and properly collected. At present the lack of finance makes sustained strike action difficult and unlikely. Strike funds are minimal and extended strikes are only possible in small companies or those places where the local population identify closely with the demands of the strikers. Thus, if one considers that the strike weapon is the main means of pressure on the private employer and the government, the unions are weak. Disruptive action is possible but large scale sustained strikes, such as occur in the UK public sector, would be difficult.

The strike as a political weapon has been employed warily under democracy, always orchestrated from above by the politicians. Such has been the case with protest demonstrations against terrorism or against military intervention in 1981. All the main political parties have shown a notable fear of trades union militancy being exploited for purely political motives. Significantly, on the night of 23 February, the trades union leadership went to great pains to keep people off the streets in order not to antagonise the military. The only union strike action to protest against the events of 23 February was in the mines of Asturias on the following day — and this got no publicity at all.

The ultimate strength of the trades unions thus depends a great deal upon the private employers and the government's perception of their power. The Employers Federation, which represents 1·3 million companies controlling 75% of all jobs in Spain, has been increasingly combative since 1980. The CEOE has judged the unions to be weak in three principal ways — their lack of unity, their lack of funds, and the employment situation caused by recession. This has enabled employers to take a tough line with strikers, especially in small plants. Security forces are frequently called in and workers are often intimidated by privately hired armed security guards. Furthermore, on questions of pollution, factory hygiene, and general working conditions, the employers have been able to exploit the unions lack of resources and so save large sums of money on environmental investment. But in pure wage terms, the CEOE has not imposed its will successfully, and indeed, since the end of the Franco era, has been buying peace on the shop floor with high wages. The first effort at wage discipline came when the AMI fixed wage levels for 1980, and this required government intervention.

The phenomenon of wage levels is to a large extent outside the hands of the employers. Wages are primarily determined by the annual increase accorded the public sector, which is contained in the budget. This has based public sector increases on a combination of political and economic considerations — the need to retain the loyalty of the civil service balanced against inflation levels. The bench-mark has been high; too high in purely economic terms, indicating that the unions' inherent power to mobilize disaffected workers is a constant cause for concern, no matter what the complexion of the government. This view is reinforced by the kid-glove treatment accorded the preservation of jobs in industrial reorganization.

THE WELFARE STATE

The accelerated introduction of a form of welfare state since the mid-seventies has radically changed the condition of the working class. There is greater protection in unemployment, improved access to public health facilities, and a concerted attempt to provide adequate pensions. Although the Franco regime was moving timidly in this direction, it is doubtful whether such advances would have been made without democracy. The previous regime was not geared to thinking in terms of major social expenditures.

Unemployment benefit, for instance, was first introduced in 1961, but on an extremely limited scale. The original benefit was small, restricted in time, and largely ignored the problems of those affected by industrial accidents. Important modifications were made in 1976, when the period of cover was extended from one year to eighteen months, and the situation of those affected by industrial accidents was improved. Subsequent developments came in the Basic Employment Law and the ANE. Only a comparatively small proportion of registered unemployed are covered by benefit, because a different system covers the agricultural unemployed and because first-time job seekers are excluded. If these two categories are removed, then almost 60% of the registered unemployed receive benefit. In a decade, the actual number of persons receiving unemployment benefit has grown more than tenfold to over 750,000.[24]

Construction workers — the sector worst affected by recession and previously among the least socially protected — account for 41% of all those on benefit. The system is far from perfect and is constantly under review, as the number of unemployed increased in 1983 to over 2·2 million. The least protected remain the young, agricultural workers, and women.

The extent of those suffering from lack of social security payments is hard to ascertain. Employers find social security contributions a heavy burden. They have to pay 85·1% of the contribution, the employee 14·9% — the former contribution being double the European average.[25] These payments have been a constant source of friction with the administration and more often than not employers have taken the law into their own hands to avoid the

126

full burden. This has nearly always been to the detriment of the worker. For instance, payments have been held back and workers have found themselves on the streets without access to benefits because their employers' contributions have not been properly paid. With the difficulty of shedding labour and the high costs of dismissal, employers have sought not to register labour, which again leaves them without benefit. This practice has been encouraged by persons holding more than one job, and is of particular importance in the textile and shoe industries, to a lesser extent in construction and some of the service sectors. In the shoe industry, up to 35% of the workers (some 20,000 persons) are reckoned to be improperly employed. They are either working at home, in clandestine workshops, or abusing the social security system. Social security in this industry represents 12% of production costs: not surprisingly if they can be avoided, they are. In the same industry in 1981, when the official number of employed dropped 32%, exports rose by almost 15% in volume! Such a situation could only be explained by the existence of a parallel economy.[26]

Another element obscuring the extent of suffering is the extended family system. This helps to soften the hardship of the first time job seekers in particular, and reduces the overall pressure for state financial assistance. An interesting side-light on the number of young jobless is that once they find jobs they are generally more militant in demanding higher wages.

Unemployment benefit and pensions between them cover the bulk of social security expenditure, accounting for nearly 9% of GDP.[27] The cost of pensions has risen even more rapidly than that of unemployment as more persons have been brought within the net. Over the decade up to 1982, the number of old age pensioners increased on average by 184,000 a year. The total number of pensioners by 1983 was 4.7 million. In Spain, state pensions have a great significance because the number of private pension fund schemes is limited.

All the political parties have stressed the need to increase pensions in their electoral platforms. The main change from the Franco era has been to raise the overall level of pension handouts, and to promise a form of linking income to inflation. This said, the world of pensions is a jungle of special cases and reflects the curious prejudices of the old vertical syndicates as to whom was most deserving in society. The system will be rationalized, but the level of welfare benefits will be conditioned by the exigencies of the budget. Social security expenditure is running at the same level as that of the general state budget, which moved into deficit in 1980.[28]

RURAL POVERTY

Unemployment and pensions are easily identified as emotive issues. So far in the democratic state they have been tackled at the expense of three less obvious, but still significant issues — the level of rural incomes and employment; industrial safety and health; and the role of women in the workforce. The most dramatic is the first, and it is graphically illustrated by the plight of *jornaleros* (day labourers) in Andalusia.

Here, large numbers of landless labourers and their families still survive on a precarious existence of seasonal employment. From November to March there is little work, and mechanization of agricultural production threatens what little there is. They survive off the olive, cotton, and sugar cane harvest. But olive trees are being ploughed up because of surplus production and the cheaper cost of vegetable oils, and the rise in wages has switched production from labour intensive to capital intensive processes. Farmers are given subsidies of up to 40% to buy machinery which can harvest cotton for a quarter the cost of human labour. Some 40,000 families depend directly on the six-week cotton harvest (a period when even the schools are emptied to maximize family earnings). In this climate the *jornaleros* react to the introduction of machinery as if someone has walked into their house and robbed them. In 1982 less than 20% of the cotton picking machines due to be introduced actually operated. Some were withheld by their owners, others were sabotaged in what amounts to latter-day Luddism.[29] Battles over agricultural machinery have been fought elsewhere in Europe, but more often a century ago and at a time of rising alternative employment. In Andalusia there is no alternative employment, and even some of those who emigrated in the sixties have now returned.

The radical peasants organization, SOC, argues that it is not against machines, but against machines replacing people when there is no alternative work in the countryside. The sole current alternative is dehumanizing *empleo comunitario* (public works employment). This takes the form of jobless labourers being hired by the local authorities on a daily basis to do such things as dig ditches. Since the funds are used up primarily on paying wages, there is little left to finance any useful activity. It is seen as a form of institutionalized unemployment and has been the focus of annual protest. After protests in 1983, labourers were guaranteed a four day week and a daily wage of 1,200 pesetas, with a promise of a reform of the system in 1984.

To pick up more money, an important sector of the seasonal labour force in Andalusia goes north to France for the wine harvest: 80,000 Spaniards, the bulk of them from Andalusia, travelled to France for the harvest in 1982. The families of landless labourers live close to the poverty level and on the verge of desperation. Their relationship with the landowners and authority, especially the Guardia Civil, is one of barely concealed hostility. The situation is made

128

worse because there is a feeling that only by desperate or spectacular acts — burning of crops, damaging machinery, occupation of land, and hunger strikes — will anyone pay attention to their plight.[30] The SOC has understood this well, but it is heartily mistrusted by the main unions who regard it as irresponsible. The SOC activist, Paco Ortiz, when hauled before the courts for the ninety-sixth time in eleven years (mainly for illegal occupation of land) had a poem dedicated to him which was posted in a local bar. The Guardia Civil ripped the poem down.

In much of Extremadura the problems are similar but are less noticed because Andalusia is more populous and protest there more virulent. Extremadura has some 90,000 *jornaleros* whose plight was scarcely bettered by the Franco regime's much trumpeted Badajoz Plan. This was an ambitious scheme to bring new land under cultivation using water from the Guadiana River and creating a series of agricultural settlements or colonies. The land was sold to peasants on long mortgages and on condition of their being model citizens. The colonies were seen more as a means of controlling rural discontent than raising agricultural production and improving the nature of land distribution. Much of the land under irrigation reverted to its original owners while rural incomes and living standards did not rise appreciably. At the end of the seventies, only 20% of the houses in the colonies had hot water; in the case of the *jornaleros*, the proportion was under 5%.[31]

Rural poverty is not confined to these two areas; they are merely where it is most evident. For instance, in pure income terms, parts of the interior of Galicia are probably worse off. With land divided into tiny holdings, families survive at subsistence level in an almost closed economy and without assistance from the state. Incomes are so low that farmers refuse to pay their small social security contributions. In 1982, over 30,000 farmers rioted in Lugo during a rally to protest against being forced to pay such contributions.[32] Although the main unions are now rooted in the countryside, the union leadership is more concerned with industrial and political issues. The fate of rural communities depends upon government initiative, or now a combination of this and the new autonomous governments.

INDUSTRIAL SAFETY

It is ironic that Spain should be the first country with a painter who depicted an industrial accident — Goya's *Injured Bricklayer* — yet be among the last to apply proper norms of industrial safety. Industrial growth in the sixties and seventies occurred with a cavalier disregard for safety and health. State owned companies were only marginally more conscientious than private concerns, who short-cut safety measures to maximize profits. The principal attitude to safety and health was not prevention but monetary sanction. In other words, companies preferred either to be fined for polluting or negligence, or to pay money out to victims of industrial accidents. This was always infinitely cheaper than any attempt to right the cause. The labour inspectors were on the side of management; professional illnesses were treated in the statistics as ordinary sickness; thus Spain has the lowest rate of professional illness in Europe.

This primitive state of mind was exemplified by the appallingly bureaucratic way in which victims were compensated. Under decree 1036 published in 1959, a detailed list of cash payments was enumerated. The absurd rigidity of the means of calculation and its unashamed sexual bias is self-evident. Loss of a right finger was compensated by 31,500 pesetas, a left finger by 25,000 pesetas. If a woman lost her sense of smell she was paid 18,000 pesetas but in the case of a man only 8,000 pesetas. A woman's nose was worth 112,000 pesetas against 54,000 pesetas for a man's. A woman's ovary was valued at 40,000 pesetas and a single male testicle 21,000 pesetas! In 1983 this was still the basis for compensation.[33]

In the construction industry in 1981, there was one death for just over every 4,000 workers. The unions maintain the death rate is higher because persons who die off the work site are not included in official statistics. Construction deaths accounted for 20% of the 1,099 fatal accidents in 1981. Laws on controlling manufacture with such substances as asbestos are outdated and well behind those of other industrialized countries. In 1983, exposure to asbestos particles was still governed by a twenty-two-year old regulation which set a limit of 175 particles per square metre. Moves to bring the level down to the European norm of two particles per square metre, proposed in 1982, were being resisted by asbestos users — they pressed for a four year delay in introducing the reductions.[34]

The mortality rate has declined but general conditions, rather than improve, have tended to get worse, especially in small and medium-sized companies. Companies are obliged by law to have a health committee but in 1982 only 60% had them in Madrid: elsewhere it was likely to be a much smaller proportion. No more than 40% of companies actually had a special budget for industrial safety and health. A sample of 226 companies in Madrid employing 165,000 workers showed 60% to be suffering noise levels above the acceptable limit. The same percentage were working with dangerously high levels of pollution. Between 20% and 30% of workers in these factories were suffering from various respiratory complaints.[35]

There is little real pressure on the companies. The unions lack the resources both to finance costly studies and to take legal action. Union members themselves are not sufficiently conscious of the abuses occurring and would still prefer monetary reward, in the form of higher wages, to better working conditions. The change is likely to come less from union pressure than from the general need to conform to international standards, especially those of the EEC.

FEMALE EMPLOYMENT

The Francoist view of society left the sexes strictly partitioned at work. If a woman worked outside the house it was either in the fields, or in some employment related to charity, culture, education and health. This view was perpetrated by the Movimiento which had its own, important women's section, long run by the formidable sister of Jose Antonio, Pilar Primo de Rivera. A woman's role in industrial society was not taken seriously and, initially, if a woman wished to work she had to obtain a certificate from her husband granting his express permission.

Female employment began on a large scale in the sixties, but mainly to save labour costs. Specific industries and certain industrial processes such as textiles, the leather industry, and shoes used much cheap female labour. But equally, in the fast expanding service sector, women began to be employed because they were thought of by employers as cheap and temporary — women would stay up to five years, then leave to marry and have children. When employers discovered that women wished to stay and were serious about their right to return to their jobs after childbirth, female recruitment slowed. From forming only 22% of the active labour force in 1964 the proportion rose to 28% over the next ten years. Since then it has fallen back to 27% as a result of the recession — though interestingly the drop has been much less significant than that of men because of married women rejoining the work force.[36]

The participation of women in the work force is still small compared to other European countries. It is, for instance, half that of the UK; and in a sector like banking, which in Britain absorbs a high proportion of women, in Spain only 10% of the work force is female. The financial pressures on family finances, changing family habits (fewer children), and the feminist movement have begun to have some impact, and there is now a much greater consciousness of the need to rectify the balance. The concept of equal pay without sexual bias has been grudgingly conceded but has yet to take practical form. As with industrial safety, the employers complain that they lack the funds.

Part Three

THE INSTITUTIONS

7 Return of a Borbon

The monarchy was the one institution that emerged relatively unscathed from the divisions of the Civil War. Though wary of monarchists, Franco opted to settle the succession on Juan Carlos, the grandson of Alfonso XIII who was forced to abdicate in 1930. Groomed by Franco, King Juan Carlos confounded his critics by quickly asserting himself and championing democracy: the crown has proved to be the lynchpin of the nation's smooth transfer from dictatorship to democracy. For Juan Carlos, the role has not always been simple to carry out.

Bilbao, 4 February 1981. It is a cold grey morning with a strong breeze blowing off the Atlantic. A fine drizzle mixes with the pollution from the blast furnaces and chemical works so that the grimy industrial skyline along the River Nervion blurs and glistens. In the cinder courtyard of Altos Hornos de Vizcaya, the huge steel-works that has underpinned Basque industry for more than fifty years, a small group of executives and their wives await King Juan Carlos and Queen Sofia. The reception committee seems even smaller beside the massive police presence ringing the perimeter, sharp-shooters manning strategic points, others standing expectantly by rows of their brown vans.

Along the route from the centre of Bilbao, security is the sole evidence of the royal visit: not a flag to cheer, not a patriotic slogan to obscure the violent graffiti on tenement walls that call for an end to the Spanish presence in the Basque country, amnesty for political prisoners, and the removal of all nuclear power stations. A few faces peer curiously from behind windows. Inside the main administrative building of the steel-works, a terse notice announces the royal visit. It was put up only the day before — after much debate over whether it was advisable to announce the royal presence at all — as if the visit were the most discreet, yet casual, occurrence.

This is far from the case. Since Juan Carlos assumed the throne in November 1975 and promised to be king of all Spaniards, he has never visited the Basque country. The political climate has been too tense. Under threat of action by ETA, his security advisers have feared for his safety, and the military have been uneasy about any gesture which might appear like appeasement to the Basques, whose separatist demands threatened the unity of the Spanish state. Never have so many police, Guardia Civil and special

135

units of the armed forces been involved in a royal tour. The King has gone ahead with the visit despite the resignation of the Prime Minister, Adolfo Suarez, six days earlier. It is the most delicate and important royal visit he has undertaken. His own authority and credibility are at stake.

The King arrives with Queen Sofia in one of the royal, blue Mercedes. In a voluminous blue raincoat, he shakes hands and hurries inside. One person starts clapping, then stops, embarrassed by the silence. The King and Queen begin a routine, familiar from the hundreds of industrial operations they have toured: explanations with moquettes and diagrams, signing guest books and then the smiling face with the right questions. But the King quickly breaks the formality with an engaging smile or a hand on the shoulder. A member of his entourage comments that the King is showing remarkably little sign of strain. This is the second and most crucial day of the three day visit. Ahead lies an address to members of parliament and local councillors in the assembly hall of Guernica. The ceremony is to be a symbolic peace-making between the crown and the Basque people. Some incident is expected.

Two hours later, as the King moves to the centre of the historic Basque assembly hall to address the packed audience, the incident occurs. Some thirty members of Herri Batasuna, the radical coalition that acts as the political front for the tough military line of ETA separatism, suddenly rise. Left hands raised in the air, fists clenched they start singing *Eusko Gudariak* (The Basque Soldier), the fighting song of Basque nationalism. For a moment the audience is stupefied. The King holds his ground. Then pandemonium breaks loose as moderate deputies try to shout down the demonstrators with cries of: *Viva el Rey! Fuera, Fuera!* (Long live the King! Out! Out!). After nearly ten confused minutes, plain clothes Basque security men forcibly eject the militants. Some leave protesting violently. Scuffles break out with rival politicians.

All the while the King looks on with utter calm; sometimes he even smiles. Then when all have been ejected, the King resumes his speech with a special addition to his prepared text which brings thunderous applause: 'Despite those who have no qualms about intolerance, who have not the least respect for representative institutions or the most elementary norms of freedom of expression and harmony, I reaffirm my full confidence in the Basque people.'[1]

It was a masterly performance. The serious risks involved in facing such an incident had paid off, even though a number of persons were outraged that the King's person should have been subjected to such treatment.

February 1981 was the most testing month of King Juan Carlos's reign, the month he won his spurs and the affection of his subjects. The Basque tour was a modest baptism of fire compared to what happened on the night of 23 February. The man who many on the left wrote off as inconsequential and a puppet of Franco proved to be the cornerstone for the preservation of democracy. When parliament was siezed and the Valencia military region

136

placed under martial law, King Juan Carlos through vigorous assertion of his authority was largely, if not solely, responsible for averting bloodshed and ensuring the failure of the coup.

THE NEED FOR LEGITIMACY

The restoration of the Borbon dynasty in Spain has no parallel in Europe's recent history. The Greek monarchy was restored in 1935 after an eleven-year republican experiment. But in the case of Spain there was a forty-four-year gap between the exile of Alfonso XIII and the accession of Juan Carlos. In the interval Spain experienced a republic, a civil war, and a dictatorship. Juan Carlos was apprenticed exclusively under the dictatorship and permitted to ascend to the throne through laws promulgated by Franco. Furthermore he became King while his father, Don Juan, had still not renounced his rights to the throne. Don Juan did not cede his rights until 14 May 1977, a full eighteen months after his son had been crowned.

Thus, at the outset, King Juan Carlos lacked the formal blessing of his father and the legitimate order of royal inheritance. Since the Franco regime had been constructed round the victory of the nationalist side in the Civil War, the legitimacy of the laws which established Juan Carlos's right to the throne were also in doubt. This was not an auspicious beginning.

In public, Franco insisted his designation of Juan Carlos was not the 'restoration', but the 'installation' of monarchy. When formally designating Juan Carlos as the future king before the Cortes on 22 July 1969, Franco made it clear that the kingdom of Spain was the fruit of the nationalist uprising of 18 July 1936 and that the monarchy was conditioned by the principles of the Movimiento.[2]

In private, Franco was more ambivalent. He knew Alfonso XIII reasonably well, having accompanied him on a tour of Morocco and enjoying the status of Gentleman of the Royal Bedchamber. His admiration for the achievements of the Catholic Kings made him a monarchist at heart. There is nothing to suggest that he seriously contemplated any solution to the succession other than a monarchy. This was also the view of Admiral Carrero Blanco, whose opinion from an early stage was extremely influential. Nevertheless, Franco was determined to select his successor himself, in his own time, and within a proper juridical framework. The most serious question was whether or not he should hand over power while still alive.

In 1946, Carrero Blanco proposed that the sole solution lay in a monarchy.[3] This recommendation was explicitly endorsed the following year when Franco promulgated his Ley de Sucesion de la Jefatura del Estado (Law of Succession). The law designated Spain as a kingdom and laid down that Franco's heir could enjoy the title of king. There can be few historical

137

precedents for a man who is not a king granting his successor the title of king![4] Even before this, Franco had shown deference to the monarchy by promising, on Alfonso's death, to transfer his remains 'in due course'. In fact Alfonso XIII's remains only returned to Spain in 1979, when they were laid to rest in the Escorial. He was so tall that his legs had to be broken to fit him into the royal catacomb.

Franco was fastidious in legitimizing his self-conferred power of designating the succession. Throughout his forty years' rule there were only two referendums. Both, directly or indirectly, sought popular endorsement for the succession issue. The 1947 Succession Law was subjected to referendum; then in 1966 another referendum was held to approve the Ley Organica de Estado (Basic Law of the State). The voting figures were puffed up — 82% and 85% in favour — and there was no universal suffrage, but the results helped give the appearance of legitimacy. If nothing else, they convinced Franco of his own rectitude.

The other clear sign of Franco's intentions was his desire to see Juan Carlos educated in Spain. Despite considerable reticence, Don Juan agreed to this. In the autumn of 1948, Juan Carlos, aged ten, arrived in Spain with his younger brother Alfonso, and began school in San Sebastian with twelve hand-picked companions. From then onwards, 'Juanito' was educated in the mould dictated by Franco, rather than his father, and groomed to be the future head of state. This included a full course at the Zaragoza Military Academy from 1955-57, training as a pilot, service in the Navy, and passing through various departments of Madrid University. He had no foreign education, despite efforts by his father to let him attend Louvain University. In 1961, Juan Carlos was allowed to take up residence in the Zarzuela Palace, a small country mansion on the outskirts of Madrid near the Pardo Palace were Franco lived. Thus while Don Juan retained his distance in exile in Portugal, his son was intimately involved with every aspect of the Franco regime. On occasion, Franco clearly treated him like the son and heir he always wanted but never had.

The communist leader, Santiago Carrillo, has subsequently regretted what he said less than two years before Juan Carlos ascended the throne. But at the time his words echoed what many felt about the legitimacy and posture of Juan Carlos. He saw Juan Carlos as the man who would continue Francoism. 'He has discredited himself in the eyes of the Spanish people because he has sold his father for a crown, and even the monarchists don't forgive him for that.'[5] In agreeing to be Franco's successor, Juan Carlos swore to uphold the fundamental laws of the regime and the principles of the Movimiento. Monarchism thus seemed an integral part of the Movimiento — a curious development since the original fascist ideals inspiring these principles were strongly republican in tone. Mussolini, after all, had pushed aside King Umberto.[6]

The monarchy's claim to legitimacy lay both in its deep-rooted tradition and in its being a symbol of unity for all Spaniards. It had survived for centuries, with only the briefest republican interlude in 1873-74, through to 1930 despite periods of rule in which kings and queens displayed scant respect for their long-suffering subjects. As a result of the Civil War, the monarchy and its supporters came very close to compromising the institution as a symbol of unity. The monarchists, including members of the royal family, supported the nationalist uprising. Don Juan himself tried his best to enlist in the nationalist ranks, first on the front at Burgos with the army, and then offering himself to Franco to serve as a naval officer in the cruiser, *Baleares*. (Don Juan had trained at Dartmouth Naval Cadet College in the UK.) In a letter to Franco, Don Juan asked to fight the 'war against the foreign enemies'. Franco politely refused, correctly realising that this might encourage a monarchist following and divide the nationalist cause.[7] The *Baleares* was sunk not long after Don Juan made the request.

Franco's refusal was probably decisive in securing the throne for Juan Carlos. Although Don Juan clearly wished to be partisan in the Civil War, he was not allowed to be. By not fighting and being made to leave Spain after an initial trip from France to Burgos, he, and therefore the monarchy, was not tainted by the attrocities of the victorious Nationalists that marked the early forties.

This enabled Don Juan to take his distance from the Franco regime and offer the monarchy as the only viable alternative to the dictatorship. Further-more, by refusing to cede his rights to his son even when it was clear that Franco would never let him return to the throne, Don Juan at least preserved the fiction that the monarchy, as an institution rather than in the person of Juan Carlos, was a symbol of unity.

'It was absolutely essential', wrote Julian Marias, 'that Spain be ruled by someone both outside and above the Civil War, who did not represent any of the two warring sides — not even the sum of the two but rather someone who could enshrine part of the raison d'etre of either.'[8] Despite his association with the Franco regime, Juan Carlos himself was not connected with the Civil War and from the outset this helped the process of legitimizing his authority.

There were five principal stages in this process. The first was King Juan Carlos' speech from the throne after Franco's death in which he clearly measured his distance from the past and promised to heal the scars of the Civil War in a pluralistic society. Next, the framework of the democratic state, with him as its head, and the abolition of the Francoist Cortes was endorsed in the referendum on political reform in December 1976. The third step occurred when his father agreed, one month before the first democratic elections, to cede his rights in his favour. This act was unequivocal in conferring the blessing of the head of the Borbon line on Juan Carlos as rightful monarch. The fourth stage came in June, when the elections were held peacefully and democratically. In the absence of a constitution, they were an implicit confirmation of a parliamentary monarchy. The man selected by the King as

139

Prime Minister, Adolfo Suarez, emerged as victor heading the UCD coalition, and the Communist Party had taken part only two months after being legalized, on the express condition that the monarchy be accepted in a pluralist parliamentary system. The final step in the process of legitimization came with the approval of the constitution in December 1978, which defined Spain as a 'parliamentary monarchy'.[9]

THE ROLE OF DON JUAN

Alfonso XIII abdicated in 1941, one month before his death and after ten years of exile spent mostly in Rome. He abdicated in favour of his third son, Don Juan, then aged twenty-seven. Don Juan had been the heir apparent since February 1933 when his two elder brothers had both renounced their rights. His eldest brother, Don Alfonso, decided to renounce all rights to the throne in order to marry a commoner, a Cuban, Edelmira Sampedro. Within ten days of his renunciation, his elder brother, Don Jaime, followed suit because of physical incapacity. Born dumb and partly deaf, a mastoid operation left him a deaf mute at the age of four.

It was a difficult moment for Don Juan to become the head of the Borbon dynasty. The process of repression, let loose in the wake of the nationalist victory, was still in full flow. Franco was obsessed with securing the new regime and avoiding being sucked into the Second World War. Don Juan, like the rest of the monarchists, having supported the Nationalists, was in one sense on the winning side. He had little sympathy for the Republicans, who had been responsible for his father's exile and abdication, and no love for the Communists, controlled by Moscow and the most organized opposition group. He had even sent a congratulatory telegram to Franco to celebrate the nationalist victory, ending with the fascist slogan: 'Arriba España!'.[11] Initially, Franco did not want Don Juan on Spanish soil because he feared he might become a focus of opposition. This was an obvious point of friction. Don Juan's antagonism towards Franco was not really ideological; simply, the Caudillo stood directly between him and restoration of the monarchy.

Franco had the measure of Don Juan from the outset. He perceived Don Juan's eagerness to regain his father's lost throne and astutely exploited this. He calculated correctly that by dangling the bait of restoration in front of Don Juan, he could prevent him from causing political trouble. Don Juan not only fell for this bait, he failed to appreciate that the weak point of any absolute ruler who comes to power through military conquest is an obsession with legitimacy and succession. Franco was no exception. Franco's cousin, General Francisco Franco Salgado-Araujo, who was his chief of military household, reveals in his diaries that the succession was an almost daily topic of conversation.[12] The legitimacy of the Franco regime and the succession

140

were intimately linked. The Caudillo sought to expropriate Spain's monarchical traditions to his own ends and employ a monarchical solution for his heir. Thus while Don Juan suffered all the difficulties of having to press his case for restoration from outside Spain, Franco nevertheless depended upon his acquiescence, if not his co-operation.

Like the rest of the opposition in exile, Don Juan miscalculated the strength of the Franco regime. There were many monarchist generals on the nationalist side but few were willing to risk going against Franco and openly favour restoration. Those that did were easily neutralized. The British Ambassador, Sir Samual Hoare, wryly observed that when it came to action 'there were many who were only monarchists as long as there was no monarchy.'[13]

Don Juan was also not alone in putting his faith in the Allies to end Franco's dictatorship — although at the outbreak of the Second World War he was judged by some to have pro-German sympathies. In 1945, as the Allies were about to cross the Rhine and victory appeared imminent, he issued a statement from Lausanne in which he called on Franco to accept the failure of his totalitarian experiment and stand down in favour of a restored monarchy.[14] The Allies were scarcely concerned with Don Juan's pretensions and the manifesto was launched in a vacuum: he had made peace with none of the principal exiled opposition movements.

Efforts were made in 1947 to reach an understanding with the Socialists but neither monarchists nor Socialists were really ready for an alliance. Don Juan was more seduced by the idea of some arrangement with Franco, and the first formal meeting between Don Juan and Franco off San Sebastian in the latter's yacht, *Azor*, in 1948, frightened away the Socialists. (During the meeting they called each other Your Royal Highness and Your Excellency respectively.)[15] Following this meeting, Don Juan agreed to let his two sons be educated in Spain.

Though difficult for Don Juan to resist this move, it nevertheless provided Franco with a formidable weapon. He could play son off against father. From then onwards Don Juan was placed in the permanent dilemma of whether he should move into outright opposition to the regime, so risking both his own prospects and those of his son; or whether to play along with Franco in the hope of either himself or his son one day ascending the throne — so alienating the opposition. Don Juan's position oscillated, but he never really broke with the regime. When in June 1962 the first serious attempt at reconciliation between monarchists and moderates on the republican side occured in Munich, Don Juan disowned the communique. Franco once said condescendingly: 'Don Juan is a good man, a gentleman and a patriot; only he suffers the natural vacillations of one who lives in the wilderness.'[16]

Don Juan also suffered from a lack of financial resources. When he moved to Estoril in 1946, Don Juan had very little money and certainly none to finance a political movement to promote the monarchy. Initially his expenses were covered by the Marquises of Pelayo, who also lent him their villa. Then a formal secretariat was set up with a monthly budget of 67,500 escudos. This was paid for by donations from the grandees and nobility of Spain, organized by Pedro Sotomayor. Though he eventually collected a large group of advisers that formed his private cabinet, his household was essentially small and the capacity to organize within Spain limited. The political complexion of those surrounding him was either aristocratic or conservative, or both. He also attracted some disillusioned former collaborators of Franco, the most notable being the first nationalist Minister of Education, Pedro Sainz Rodriguez, and, latterly, the former ambassador in Paris and Washington, Jose Maria de Areilza.

The quality of advice varied and Don Juan was always in the uncomfortable position of having to make decisions about his native country which he barely knew at first hand. His judgement was blurred by the nostalgia of exile, and the offended dignity of someone who had been constantly rejected. Significantly, few of the people directly connected with Don Juan played a prominent part during the transition period, or after democracy was re-established.

In these circumstances it was only to be expected that relations between Don Juan and his son Juan Carlos, would be strained. Juan Carlos was constantly torn between filial loyalty and his duty to Spain. He was also faced with the cold reality of life under the Caudillo's gaze. He was better informed on what was happening, could read Franco's mind better, and could more readily understand the socio-economic changes. He also had to prove himself, as he risked being dubbed either as his father's or Franco's puppet.

As early as 1958 the young prince was fairly confident Franco would eventually designate him as successor over the head of his father. The likelihood increased when Princess Sofia gave birth to a son, Felipe, in January 1968. Don Juan realised this even if he was unwilling to endorse the idea. For someone raised to believe in heredity and his rights to the Spanish crown, it must have been hard to accept — all the more so since restoration of the throne was his sole raison d'etre.

When Franco finally came to a decision on the succession in 1969, it was a bitter blow to Don Juan. He issued a statement from Estoril in which his irritation and pain were self-evident. He complained of being left a mere spectator, accused Franco of failing to consult the Spanish people properly and underlined that the sole way forward was a democratic solution. The statement was not allowed to be published in Spain. The reaction caught the young prince off guard since preliminary soundings indicated that his father would take the news in a more stoical fashion.[17] It would have been natural for Don Juan to suspect his son of being, on occasion, under Franco's thumb. This may have been one of those occasions.

The issue of precedence was sufficiently sensitive to inspire various attempts to mediate between father and son as Franco was overcome by illness and old age in 1974 and 75. For instance, Serrano Suner, by now a

142

convert to the cause of Don Juan, went on his own initiative to see the latter in Switzerland to propose that father and son both appear before the Cortes in a joint session to underscore the continuity and legitimacy of the monarchy. Serrano Suner proposed that Don Juan reign for a symbolic period of two or three months then cede his rights, thus saving the dignity of the institution and demonstrating that it was above the Franco regime. The scheme never prospered.[18]

A little publicized initiative which throws an interesting light on the role and intentions of Don Juan occurred in November 1975. While Franco agonized on his deathbed, the former head of the High Command (Alto Estado Mayor), General Manuel Diez Alegria, was informally approached by leading members of the military establishment and asked to visit Don Juan in the name of the armed forces. Don Juan was at this time in Paris which was also where the bulk of the opposition had gathered, grouped round the coalition, Junta Democratica. The purpose of the visit was to ensure that Don Juan did not come out with any statement on Franco's death that might either inflame the situation or prejudice the vital role his son was about to play. General Diez Alegria accepted the mission on the express condition that Juan Carlos knew and approved. He met Don Juan in Paris and successfully talked him out of making any statement. General Diez Alegria suspected the mission might have been inspired by Juan Carlos but he was personally assured that this was not the case.[19]

Don Juan may have kept silent but he withheld the cessation of his rights for eighteen months. Those who have accused Don Juan of opportunism saw in this delay a deliberate move to test the durability of his son on the throne while he waited in reserve.

RIVAL CLAIMANTS

Once Franco had decided on a monarchical solution, the choice of king was not clear cut between Don Juan and his son. Other contenders lurked in the field. Indeed it is a sad reflection on the Spanish royal family that so many divisions should have existed. These divisions in part dated back to the previous century and concerned the dynastic claims of the Carlists. Others centred round the tragic ill health of Don Jaime, the elder brother of Don Juan. As in every other sphere, Franco was prepared to divide and rule.

Apart from Don Juan, no less than three contenders appeared with claims of varying seriousness. Members of the Franco family also allowed themselves to be carried away by dynastic ambitions for the Caudillo's granddaughter, Maria del Carmen, and married her off to the son of Don Jaime. The claimants were more pathetic than attractive, and, except for the Carlists, lacked any popular base.

The Carlist claim, dating from 1823, was of questionable validity. At the time the church hierarchy and the anti-Liberals rallied to Ferdinand VII's fanatical brother, Carlos, in the belief that this was the best means of preventing the liberalizing influence of France. A brief and unsuccessful uprising in Catalonia was the germ for this fiercely traditional, Catholic movement which was to provoke two civil wars in the nineteenth century.

When Ferdinand VII died, his sole heir was Isabella, and the Carlists maintained that salic law operated, banning the crown from passing to female hands. This was the basis of all subsequent Carlist claims to the Spanish crown. The main support for the Carlist movement was in the Basque country and Navarre among the small but comparatively prosperous yeoman farmers. They were the backbone of the fighters in the Carlist civil wars, and in 1936 they proved an important ingredient in the nationalist uprising. The Carlist movement, grouped into the Comunion Tradicionalista, was, as a result, accepted by the Franco regime as a political entity. Don Juan made several overtures to secure their support and even went so far as to identify with their reactionary and profoundly catholic ideology. But the Carlists kept their distance.

In 1952, the Carlist heir, Javier Borbon-Parma, decided, on his own initiative, to proclaim himself Javier I, the rightful heir to the Spanish throne. The move would have been positively burlesque, but for the weight of the Carlists within the Franco regime and the threat this posed to Don Juan. Javier's move split the Carlists, some of whom went to make public amends with Don Juan in Estoril. It also irritated Franco. In 1957 Javier went on to claim the French throne, while his son, a naturalized Frenchman Carlos-Hugo, further set the cat among the pigeons by declaring himself to be the Prince of Asturias — the traditional title of the crown prince of Spain.

All this rebounded on the unfortunate Juan Carlos. When he was attending classes at Madrid University in 1960 he was barracked by student demonstrators who tormented him with shouts of: *Viva el Rey Javier!* and *Vete a Estoril* (Go to Estoril — Don Juan's place of exile in Portugal). Carlist extremism discredited itself and made it possible for the more moderate elements to come to terms with Don Juan and Juan Carlos. Meanwhile, Carlos-Hugo Borbon Parma married Princess Irene of the Netherlands in 1964, potentially raising his dynastic stature. But his increasingly outspoken socialist views and retention of French nationality led to his expulsion from Spain in 1968. He did not return until after Franco's death and on renunciation of all claim to the throne.[20]

A more curious claimant was Francisco-Jose Carlos Habsburgo-Lorena y de Borbon. His claim was made in 1969, just six months before Franco announced his choice of Juan Carlos. It seemed almost like a job appliction from someone claiming the right qualifications — Spanish, Catholic, male, and of royal lineage. He lived in a rented flat in Vienna and based his claim on his mother being the sister of the Carlist heir, Jaime III, who had died without issue. The Movimiento press gave the claim some play but no-one took it very seriously.

Of greater embarrassment to the destiny of Don Juan and Juan Carlos, was the position of his brother, Don Jaime and his children. Despite being a deaf-mute he married Manuela Dampierre Ruspoli, an Italian. At the time of marriage, Don Jaime once again renounced his rights to the throne. In return he was given the title of Duke of Segovia. He led a disorganized bohemian life, had two sons and was then divorced in Romania. In 1949 he re-married, this time an Austrian singer, Charlotte Tiedman, and decided to try and revive his claim to the throne. He argued that due to the care of an Austrian doctor his physical defects had been overcome and therefore his original renunciation was invalid. He also sought Franco's assistance in recovering a fortune which he maintained his father had left in England. The latter was pure fiction. To what extent he was being unscrupulously manipulated and how much he himself genuinely believed he had a chance was never clear. Both Franco and Don Juan ignored his claims.

Franco was not, however, indifferent to the existence of Don Jaime's two children, Alfonso and Gonzalo. Alfonso, as the eldest grandchild of Alfonso XIII, was technically first in line to the throne, even though his father had renounced all title. Moreover his father promised to be more malleable than Don Juan. Efforts were made to let Don Jaime send his two children at an early age to Spain, but these never materialized.

The issue was kept simmering with the still-unresolved status of Alfonso de Borbon-Dampierre. It came to a head when he married Maria del Carmen Matinez Bordiu, the twenty-year-old daughter of the Marquis of Villaverde and grand-daughter of Franco. There is nothing to suggest that Franco considered this a serious dynastic alternative, although the thought must have crossed his mind. He appeared to see the match as a useful weapon to bring Don Juan into line and keep Juan Carlos at heel, and did not stop members of the government and his own family from giving encouragement to this dynastic option. Although Alfonso has denied that this was an arranged marriage, it was assumed to be the case and certainly the relationship did not last.[21]

The argument arose over suggestions that Alfonso be given the title of prince and be addressed as 'Your Royal Highness'. Both Don Juan and Juan Carlos vigorously opposed this idea which was supported by the Franco family with the endorsement of Franco himself. (The wedding invitations even carried the title.) Eventually a solution was reached after the wedding whereby Alfonso was given one of the Borbon titles, the dukedom of Cadiz. The compromise was Juan Carlos' idea, which he cleared with his father and proposed to Franco in person. He maintained that the existence of two princes in Spain at the very moment when Franco's health was declining and the succession on everybody's minds would create confusion. He arranged that the title of prince should be reserved solely for the heir to the throne. He also said it was a mistake to call Alfonso 'Prince of Borbon' since this had a French flavour — a subtle but important point. There is a residual feeling that the Borbon monarchy is frenchified and devious. One of the hurdles Juan Carlos had to overcome himself was the popular label 'he is a Borbon', meaning not sufficiently Spanish and representative. The solomonic compromise over Alfonso's title cooled the issue. Even so, the Franco family liked to have the new couple called 'Their Royal Highnesses' and curtsies made before Maria del Carmen as if she were royalty. For a while they even lived in the Pardo Palace with the Caudillo.[22]

If Alfonso had been more astute and dynamic, he could have exploited his position. But he had suffered from an unhappy childhood spent in boarding schools, scant parental affection, and he did not master what should have been his native tongue until the age of eighteen, when he came to live in Spain for the first time. Alfonso was merely swept along by events, neither opposing nor openly contesting Franco's designation of his cousin as successor. Now a banker, he is a figure of interest solely to the gossip magazines.

These unseemly dynastic squabbles complicated Juan Carlos' position and did not benefit the monarchist cause. But for press censorship, the institution of monarchy would have suffered in the public eye. The monarchists themselves were divided in their loyalties — unsure whether to continue supporting Don Juan or switch their allegiance to Juan Carlos once it became clear that he was Franco's chosen successor. This dilemma was epitomized by the monarchist newspaper, *ABC*, which had consistently backed Don Juan. Its editor realised that to continue to support Don Juan as against Juan Carlos would increase the danger of a public rift between father and son, damaging the monarchy as a whole. Thus, very painfully, *ABC* threw its weight behind Franco's designated heir.[23]

THE CHALLENGE FOR JUAN CARLOS

The pictures of the Crown Prince being groomed for his future job show an eager but serious face, that seems weighed down by responsibility and desperately anxious to get everything right. It was a tough apprenticeship. Franco liked to trail him by his side and they looked an odd couple. Even when Franco wore thick heels his head scarcely reached Juan Carlos' shoulder, the latter's thin athletic figure towering above the ageing Caudillo. The contrast in age was complete, with forty-six years between them. Franco was at ease, totally in command enjoying his paternalistic role with *his* chosen successor. Juan Carlos was clearly conscious of being scrutinized, yet was unable to display much of a personality in public other than that of the model soldier. His speeches were wooden and unconvincing. It was in good measure this forced public role and almost unreal boy-scout image that made him such an unknown quantity, and subsequently so surprising to his detractors. While Franco was alive, he was given little opportunity to prove his mettle. He was best known for being a yachtsman, judo expert, and radio ham.

From 1969 onwards he led a curious existence. He was right at the centre of power but had no power himself. Carrero Blanco, who was effectively running the country, made sure he did not get in the way. As a result of his long dealings with Don Juan, Carrero Blanco profoundly mistrusted him and was reluctant to pass on confidences to Juan Carlos in case these might reach his father. When Diez Alegria was appointed head of the armed forces High Command in 1970, he discovered that Juan Carlos was not on the list of twenty-five persons with special safe telephone communications. Carrero Blanco protested that this would cost 'at least one million pesetas'. Diez Alegria replied: 'I don't care if it costs five million pesetas.'[24] Even after Carrero Blanco's assassination, Franco did not willingly bring Juan Carlos into the decision-making process. When in the summer of 1974 Franco was incapacitated by phlebitis, Juan Carlos' take-over was temporary and people in the administration were reluctant to push decisions his way.

Of necessity his circle of contacts was limited to those that the regime either approved or tolerated. Contact with the banned political parties and the left in exile was virtually impossible; the most he could get away with was clandestine meetings with members of the Socialist Party from bourgeois backgrounds, such as the Solana brothers. In general he was surrounded by people with military backgrounds and of conservative bent — as he had been all his life. Monarchists prominent in the regime who cultivated him were often from Opus Dei, like Laureano Lopez Rodo, Minister of the Plan and then Foreign Minister.

It was not merely the exiled opposition that was sceptical of Juan Carlos' credentials. Within the Falange there was an important anti-monarchist element. The power of the Falange had been weakened by the ascendency of Opus Dei, but it still held weight inside the Movimiento. The hardline within the Falange regarded hereditary monarchy as a system likely to undermine the corporatist state and impede the path towards national socialism. For them, Spain's last monarch had been no paragon of virtue devoted to social justice and the rejuvenation of Spain; and there was nothing to suggest, despite his grooming, that Juan Carlos would be their ally.

Alfonso XIII left the Spanish monarchy with much to live down. He claimed that he abdicated to avoid bloodshed in a selfless act of patriotic abnegation. But the mood of the country was against him and what he stood for, and he would have risked his life if he had stayed on. Even moderate intellectuals of the stature of Ortega had called for an end to monarchy and the advent of the Republic. A famous article by Ortega in the newspaper *Sol* in 1930 carried the phrase *Delenda est monarchia!*. Alfonso had an arrogant, distant view of his fellow countrymen that only mellowed in exile, and at times he seemed most interested in shooting and the pleasures of female company.

This background was a tremendous toughening process for Juan Carlos. He had to prove himself to his father, to Franco, to his detractors. He had to steer as neutrally as possible between the intrigues of the Franco family and the administration on the one hand, and those of his father in Estoril and the rest of the exiled opposition on the other. Behind him was the example of a grandfather dying in hopeless exile and before him a brother-in-law ignominiously kicked off the throne of Greece by army colonels. In his own family there had been an appalling personal tragedy: his younger brother, Alfonso, killed himself accidentally while playing with a loaded revolver at the family home in Estoril. Juan Carlos was in the same room when the incident happened. He was sixteen at the time.[25]

Above all he had to wait patiently. He was in the frustrating position of seeing Franco's declining health at close quarters, yet being unable to force the Caudillo to step down or relinquish part of his executive authority. On the other hand, this long wait not only prepared him but helped Spaniards adjust to the concept of a restoration of the monarchy. Furthermore, Juan Carlos realized he could take nothing for granted: least of all national acceptance of the monarchy.

THE DEMOCRATIC OPTION

International doubts about the new king were evident at his coronation. Spain's friends and potential allies were reserved. Few heads of state attended the ceremony which, in more normal circumstances, would have been de rigeur. The most prominent were the French and West German Presidents, Valery Giscard D'Estaing and Walter Scheel. Spain had yet to achieve international respectability as a democracy.

However, those that doubted Juan Carlos' commitment to democracy ignored one vital element. The monarchy had no credibility, and was associated with Francoism and nationalist victory in the Civil War. The most permanent future lay in a monarchy endorsed by a properly elected parliament and guaranteed in a popularly approved constitution. This option coincided with the national mood which both favoured and expected change.

Having had very little real experience of authority, Juan Carlos suddenly found himself heading a system that had been fashioned round Franco's personal power. Economically and socially Spain had changed; but in political and institutional terms it had not. The main institutions of Franco — the Council of the Realm, the Cortes, the Council of the Movimiento and the armed forces — were dominated by conservative and reactionary elements identified with the nationalist cause and the Franco era. Juan Carlos' greatest strength was that these elements were far more apprehensive of what might happen than he, and, thus scared, were basically prepared to adopt a wait-and-see attitude. This left the initiative with Juan Carlos.

Valuable time was wasted while he measured his own strength. His caution was evident in his asking Carlos Arias Navarro to stay on as Prime Minister. It was an uninspired choice which almost certainly delayed the implementation of democracy; Arias accepted unenthusiastically. He had been Minister of Government at the time of Carrero Blanco's assassination in 1973. Beneath this ministry's ambiguous title lay responsibility for internal security — a responsibility which in theory covered the task of preventing the unfortunate fate of Franco's closest aide. When offered the job, Arias demurred saying the post was too important. Franco curtly told him: 'Your loyalty will be sufficient.'[26] Loyalty was about his main virtue. He was a dithering administrator, heavily influenced by his background as former director-general of security. His basic experience was in police work and administration, and he carried the additional stigma of a grim repressive record on the nationalist side in Malaga during the Civil War. He was not the best man to encourage a mood of national reconciliation.

Arias was aware that change was afoot but incapable of understanding its real nature and consequences. He clung patriotically first to Franco and then to King Juan Carlos. In February 1974, he had pledged before the Cortes that he would introduce a new law of political association, and made clear the need to incorporate moderate loyal opposition to consolidate Spain's future. His project of political reform prospered neither before Franco's death nor afterwards. Uncertain of the extent of his own authority as premier, his administration got trapped between two competing forces. On one side there was mounting politically motivated labour unrest, a deepening economic crisis, violence in the Basque country, and increasingly open defiance from the outlawed political parties. From another quarter, Arias was forced onto the defensive by the disaffected die-hard supporters of the former regime. The government itself contained figures firmly identified with the former regime, such as Jose Solis of the Movimiento in the Ministry of Labour and General Santiago Diez de Mendevil as Minister of Defence (later to defend strongly those involved in the abortive coup of 23 February). Arias was Prime Minister from December 1974 to June 1976, a crucial period during which the success of the transition to democracy hung delicately in the balance. Luckily for Arias this period has been buried in the overall achievement of democracy.

Eventually the King was forced to sack Arias. Pressure for his dismissal mounted as lack of progress in introducing democratic measures damaged Spain's international image and caused growing frustration inside the country. The King himself risked losing prestige, and survived on the benefit of the doubt and his youthful image that symbolized the change from the Francoist gerontocracy. The sacking of Arias was the King's first assertion of authority.

149

If Juan Carlos erred in his choice of Arias, he was inspired in picking his successor, Adolfo Suarez. The two had first met in 1969 when Suarez was Civil Governor of Segovia. The contact was retained and, on Suarez's part, cultivated. When Suarez was director-general of television he used to send video-tapes of Juan Carlos' public appearances to the Zarzuela Palace. Close in age, they got on well together. Most of the people Juan Carlos had contact with in the administration were of an older generation and he appreciated the views of this young aparatchik. Two years before Franco died he even commissioned Suarez to write a memorandum on what he should do on assuming the throne. Suarez provided him with a three-and-a-half-page assessment which he believes played a part in his selection as premier. The two other factors to which he attributes his choice were his conduct in the Arias Government as Minister of the Movimiento and the patronage of Torcuato Fernandez Miranda.[27]

Fernandez Miranda was head of the Council of the Realm and the most influential person planning the political reforms that lay ahead. The King respected his advice and he strongly backed Suarez as the right man to accelerate the process of political reform, legalize political parties, and prepare the way for general elections. Although Suarez had spent all his life inside the Francoist administration, he was in many ways a neutral figure. Brought up in the small Castillian town of Cerebros near Avila, he came from a modest family. His academic record was indifferent and though qualifying as a lawyer, he was not a member of any key corps within the civil service. He had worked his way to the top through his wits, charm and cold ambition. He knew the administration inside out — from provincial bureaucracy to state companies and government departments.

Groomed in the intricacies of the Francoist power structure (his very means of survival), Suarez was well qualified to understand where and how it was best dismantled. These assets were appreciated by few at the time and it required considerable courage on the part of the King to select Suarez. The new Prime Minister's curriculum vitae completely lacked democratic credentials and the opposition reacted with understandable disappointment and dismay. Ironically those who acquiesced in the appointment with the greatest tranquillity — the military and the Bunker as a whole — were to be the ones most adversely affected.[28]

Within one year Suarez had successfully legalized political parties, including the Communists, presided over the first democratic elections since 1936, and had legalized the trades unions. The crucial breakthrough came in November 1976 over the Law of Political Reform. Meeting from 16-18 November, the Franco Cortez voted to establish a lower house (taking the old name of the Cortes) and an upper house, the Senate, to be elected by universal suffrage. The law abolished the Movimiento's main body, the Council, which had previously sat above the Cortez with effective powers of veto. This spelled the end of the Movimiento itself. Voting was 425 in favour, 59 against, and 13 abstentions. The majority vote for the law did not stem from any belief in democracy — many rallied to support the bill because they either failed to understand its implications or were too complacent to take it seriously. Suarez persuaded the deputies with the argument that the old order would be respected, and most left the Cortes with the impression that the Communist Party would never be legalized.

The vote's importance cannot be overemphasized. Suarez was pledged to hold general elections in early 1977 — a pledge inherited from Arias. If the vote had failed, it would have removed all credibility from the commitment of both government and the King to introduce democracy. Any election held without reform of the law would have been a charade. This, and the separate legalization of the Communist Party, were Suarez's doing.

CONSTITUTIONAL POWERS

The constitution was formally sanctioned by the King before the Cortes on 27 December 1978. For just over three years, the King had been acting as head of state in a legal vacuum — relying on a combination of Francoist laws, temporary adaptations, and common sense and mutual agreement with the politicians. In theory he had enjoyed near absolute authority. In practice he was ruled by his commitment to restore democracy, and from the June 1977 elections played an increasingly less exposed role. Suarez was clearly in control of the executive and the King became arbiter and symbol of national unity. Although Suarez had started off as a direct royal appointee, the elections in which UCD triumphed were a popular endorsement of the appointment.

In the pre-constitutional phase the most important aspect of the King's role was his unequivocal public support for Suarez. This reinforced government policy and also aided consensus politics with the opposition parties. An interesting insight into the royal prerogative concerned the concession to the monarchy in the 1977 elections of a right to nominate forty-one senators. His choice was essentially cautious. The most significant gesture was the nomination of Justino de Azcarate, a republican intellectual closely associated with Ortega who had been exiled in Venezuela. Others included the novelist, Camilo Jose Cela; the head of Banco Urquijo, Jaimie Carvajal, with whom he was at school; his close personal friend, Manuel Prado y Colon de Carvajal, president of Iberia; Guillermo Luca de Tena, a member of his father's private cabinet and the least connected of this family (owners of the paper *ABC*) with the Franco regime; and Miguel Primo de Rivera, grandson of the dictator. While some senators bore the clear stamp of his personal choice others were included after consultation and recommendation from Suarez and Fernandez Miranda (himself a royal senator). For instance, Suarez's closest associate,

Fernando Abril Martorell was made a royal senator as was his Movimiento colleague, Ignacio Garcia Lopez.

The constitutional definition of the monarchy partly reflects the role played by King Juan Carlos from 1975 through to 1978. If he had behaved less responsibly and shown more partiality, it is doubtful whether his powers could have remained so loosely defined, and his potential to act on them, so substantial. This said, some of the monarchists and members of the royal family, pressed for a more important role for the crown. Suarez firmly resisted such pressure. It would probably have been much more difficult to work out the constitutional role of the monarchy had Don Juan succeeded to the throne — if for no other reason than that he was a much older man.

The constitution described the institution of monarchy as the symbol of the state's unity and permanence. The King 'arbitrates and moderates the regular workings of the institutions, assumes the highest representation of the Spanish state in international relations, especially with those nations belonging to the same historic community, and performs the functions expressly conferred on him by the Constitution and the law.'[29] The King's principal domestic role is therefore as referee. His powers regarding the executive and the legislature are, in principle, ones of assent and signature. He summons and dismisses parliament and calls general elections. This can only be done on the recommendation of the Prime Minister with cabinet approval. He proposes the candidate for the premiership and appoints ministers but only after consulting with the leaders of the parties, and the speaker of the Cortes. And as a further safeguard, the candidate has to win a vote of confidence by an absolute majority before the appointment is valid.

There are instances where the constitution authorizes the monarch to 'exercise' power. It is incumbent on the King to exercise supreme command of the armed forces; to exercise the right of pardon in accordance with the law; and to exercise high patronage of the royal academies. It is also incumbent on the King to be informed on affairs of state, entitling him to preside over cabinet meetings if invited by the Prime Minister.

RELATIONS WITH THE MILITARY

The constitution has given the King a wide area of discretionary authority regarding the armed forces. On many occasions he has proved that he is more than a titular head of the military establishment. The most dramatic proof was on the night of the abortive coup when he personally ensured the loyalty of the armed forces to the constitution and the crown. In addressing the nation, the King made a point of wearing the blue uniform of captain-general — symbol of his *ultimate* authority since the armed forces have the role of guardians of the nation's sovereignty. His message to the nation on that night left no doubt that he was in command — it was very brief, and consisted almost entirely of describing the orders he had relayed to the captain-generals of the military regions.[30]

The King has also utilized occasions like the annual Epiphany military celebrations in January to deliver stern lectures on patriotism and observance of the constitution. He has clearly assumed the role of mentor and guide to the armed forces, educating them to accept the new democratic order. This has not always been easy, and is little appreciated by the reactionary extremists among the military. But the task has been smoothed by his own experience as a soldier.

The King devotes one day a week to audiences with members of the military and as much as one third of all his time is taken up with military matters. He makes a point of going on exercises and assisting at military ceremonies. He feels very much at home in the officers' mess, attracted by the camaraderie of military life. In the palace, the majority of the staff posts are held by men with military backgrounds, including the head of the royal household, General Sabino Fernandez Campo. He is on christian name terms with many military commanders, and his own promotion from Zaragoza has taken him to the rank of colonel.

THE POWER TO INFLUENCE

The constitutional limits on the crown belie the real power in the hands of the monarch. It is a subtle power bound up with the capacity to influence people and policy. The extent of such influence depends upon the respective strength or weakness of individual governments and the personality and experience of the monarch. Juan Carlos' singular protagonism has given him a stature that lends weight to any opinion or advice he offers to the government of the day. His weight has increased since the 23 February coup in 1981. Felipe Gonzalez concedes as much: 'His majesty's constitutional role clearly remains the same. The events of February 23 might well have contributed to the King's person being more firmly rooted, if that is possible, among his people.'[31]

The King has employed his prestige and authority in the open on rare occasions. One such occasion was his visit to the Basque country. Less consistent with his constitutional powers was the calling of the leaders of the main political parties to the palace on 24 February 1981. He warned them bluntly that he had been dangerously exposed by the attempted coup and might not be able to succeed in stopping another one. He urged the politicians to stop quibbling and work together for the good of the nation. He further warned against any campaign to denigrate the armed forces. At least one of the political leaders attending this meeting now feels that the King was acting at the limits of his constitutional powers and believes the meeting should have

153

been delayed. Delay would have permitted a calmer review of events and a reconsideration of Tejero's surrender document in parliament which was approved by the King — this exonerated all Guardia Civil below the officer rank who took part in the seizure of parliament. At the time of the meeting the political leaders emerged like chastened prefects from the headmaster's study.

The leaders of the main political parties were also called to a meeting with the King on the eve of the general elections of 28 October 1982. This time the two principal Basque and Catalan nationalist parties were included. The purpose of the meeting was to remind the political parties to respect the result, the reminder being made in case Spain should elect the first government of the left since the Republic. The King was using his powers as national referee to remind the parties of the rules of the democratic game — he was clearly inferring that the crown disapproved of any destabilizing tactics by the opposition.

King Juan Carlos' singular position, which has evolved since 1975, makes a good working relationship between the crown and Prime Minister essential; otherwise there is a risk of constitutional conflict. A custom has grown up for the Prime Minister to go to the King once a week, and the King is kept informed of all major decisions. Compared to other European monarchs, he is brought much more into the decision-making process at all stages. For instance, when he started in office, Felipe Gonzalez was almost deferential in his concern to take the King into his confidence and seek his advice — even on such details as to whether he should turn up at the airport to meet King Hussein on a private visit. The longer the Prime Minister stays in office, the greater his own stature and confidence.

In the case of Suarez, the two began close together but became more distant after the passing of the constitution. There was a good deal of mutual admiration and respect, cemented by an identity of purpose. Yet the relationship was made difficult by Suarez's need to prove he was something other than a royal appointee. He found himself caught between wanting to build up the figure and prestige of the King, yet resenting it when the credit for democracy mostly landed in the King's lap. This led Suarez to define the separation of powers and to inform the King of decisions after rather than before they had been taken. In an assertion of his own authority, Suarez forced Armada from the royal household in June 1977, to be appointed military governor of Lerida. Suarez was convinced that Armada exercised a bad influence on the King, and was incensed when, in the June 1977 elections, he discovered that Armada had been distributing electoral propaganda for Alianza Popular in envelopes posted from the Zarzuela Palace. His suspicions also led Suarez to firmly oppose a move by Armada's sympathizers to appoint him as number two in the Joint Chiefs of Staff (JUJEM). Suarez was still resisting this appointment, which apparently had the King's blessing, at the time of his resignation. A week later the appointment was made.

Towards the end of 1980, as the difficulties of the Suarez government increased and the military began to show signs of restiveness, the Madrid rumour-mill put out word that the King was losing confidence in him. True or false, the rumours had the effect of discrediting Suarez. Close associates maintain that he felt demoralized by this apparent loss of confidence with the King. The King, of course, could not demand his resignation, only hint.[32] Suarez himself insists that this was not a factor in his resignation and that the King asked him to stay on.

Another instance of the King's capacity to influence concerned the 'respectability' of the socialist leader, Felipe Gonzalez. In 1982, with general elections and possible socialist victory in the offing, word spread that the King approved of Gonzalez. The King told conservative and right-wing elements, including members of the armed forces, that they had nothing to fear from Gonzalez. Such an imprimatur of approval did not increase the socialist vote. However, it had an important effect in maintaining tranquillity in the wake of the socialist victory.

The King's influence depends to a great extent on him keeping himself well informed. He operates with a very small permanent staff, whose prime function is protocol. This has sometimes been criticized as inadequate, but if the King were to be seen to possess a large staff whose aim was to make independent assessments of Spain's political, economic and social problems this would immediately undermine the government. So the King relies for his information on independent visitors — he receives at least thirty a week apart from delegations — many of whom he has surprised with the extent of his information. Filtering the visitors is the job of Fernandez Campo, who replaced Armada in 1977. He is the man in closest daily contact with the King and, de facto, his closest advisor. A soldier with a liberal reputation and experience in government (he worked in the Prime Minister's office in the Arias Government and became Under Secretary for Information and Tourism), Fernandez Campo is an extremely influential figure.

Through frequent contact with fellow heads of state, the King has access to privileged information on foreign policy and international relations, especially in the case of some developing countries, such as Saudi Arabia and Morocco, where he has direct personal relations with the rulers. Such relationships have enormous diplomatic potential, yet to be fully exploited. At another level, these contacts have been instrumental in the selection of Marbella as a retreat by Gulf rulers. On occasions it has even been difficult for the King to direct King Hassan of Morocco to deal with the Prime Minister on affairs of state. Sheikh Zaid of Abu Dhabi has been known to telephone the Palace from his Marbella home to complain that the water supply had been cut. The palace promptly called the Marbella municipality to ensure that his water was restored.

The King has proved the most important ambassador for Spain and is an integral part of Spain's international image. Occasionally he has acted on his own initiative: he went ahead with a visit to Argentina despite criticism in parliament; but when he met the military junta, he made a point of wearing a civilian suit. After his departure, the case of some Spanish citizens in Argentinian jails was reconsidered. When visiting Mexico in 1978, he insisted on meeting Azana's widow, a meeting which proved to be the prelude to an emotional reconciliation with the huge exiled republican community in that country. During the Falklands conflict he issued a statement deploring the violence and offering mediation. He also declined an invitation to the wedding of Prince Charles because of the royal couple's intention to begin their honeymoon in Gibraltar.

Through his power to grant titles, the King can also exercise patronage, either on his own initiative, or at the suggestion of the Prime Minister. So far he has made sparing use of this power, honouring prominent cultural figures like the guitarist, Andres Segovia, and occasionally politicians. Following his resignation, Suarez was given a dukedom.

By remaining in the Zarzuela Palace and refusing to move to the more formal and grander Palacio de Oriente in old Madrid, the King and Queen have given royalty a discreet style. The rejection of the Palacio de Oriente for all but limited formal occasions made it clear that the monarchy did not wish to have a court surrounding the royal family. The sole court occasion in which due honour was given to the grandees of Spain (still entitled to diplomatic passports) was the funeral for the remains of Alfonso XIII in 1979. Some nobility feel let down by the King and pour scorn on the royal family for appearing ordinary and middle class. It is not a wealthy monarchy like its European counterparts and is effectively dependent on the annual payments from the state budget. (In 1983 these totalled 300 million pesetas.) The Queen has been seen to wear the same dress more than once.

The King has established himself as a genuinely popular figure with an easy charm, simple tastes, sound common sense, and a dislike of pomp and display. The combined elements of popularity and stature are the core of his legitimacy before his subjects — far more than the nation's monarchic traditions. Many Republicans justify their support of the monarchy by claiming they are *Juancarlists* (supporters of Juan Carlos), so remaining Republicans at heart. In these circumstances only a strong prime minister can go against the wishes of the King, and the King can undermine the authority of the premier by pitting his own prestige against him. The King, however, must remain permanently vigilant that the monarchy retains the respect of the people. The accumulated mistrust of the Borbons has not been dispelled, merely put on one side.

8 The Political Parties

The moderating role of King Juan Carlos was vital in restoring the life of political parties after forty years without free parliamentary elections. The King chose Adolfo Suarez as Prime Minister to steer the country through the transition and establish a constitution. The exiled or underground parties, such as the Communists and Socialists, were able to draw on existing organizations and traditions; but the centre and right had to start in a vacuum since Franco had bequeathed no party. The triumph of Suarez's centre party, UCD, in the first elections was undermined by subsequent personal rivalries, contributing to the major swing to Felipe Gonzalez's Socialist Party in the October 1982 elections. It now forms the first government of the left since the Republic in the thirties, and its success heralds the end of a series of forced coalitions in Spanish politics.

One wing of the white dove was painted green, the other orange. Thus daubed, the unfortunate bird bore the green, white and orange colours of UCD. The dove flapped awkwardly as its handler prepared to launch it — a gimmicky symbol of hope at the end of a special congress to rally what remained of the party in preparation for the October 1982 general election campaign. Weighed down by hastily sprayed paint and bemused by the noise and light in Madrid's Palacio de Congresos, the bird was reluctant to leave its handler. Twice it was thrust in the air, and immediately tumbled to the ground. At the third attempt the bird summoned enough force to flap aloft amid the cheers of the delegates and the flashing of press cameras. It circled the main podium clumsily, nearly bumped into a partition, then flopped to the ground. No one seemed to mind: the bird had finally flown, the gesture had been made.

UCD, weighed down by its own contradictions, had just witnessed its last public act of faith. It was a shadow of the party that won Spain's first two free elections since the Republic. Absent from the congress were an array of notables, headed by the former UCD leader, Adolfo Suarez. He had just formed his own party, Centro Democratico Social (CDS), pretending this preserved the true centre reformist philosophy which UCD had negated. Gone too were the Social Democrats, the Liberals and the bulk of Christian Democrats, who had all once formed the loose coalition of UCD.

Yet delegates left the one day congress in fighting spirit, roused by a speech from Landelino Lavilla who had assumed the party leadership two months earlier. Lavilla, former speaker of the Cortes who had always shown the unease of a senior civil servant in public appearances, suddenly seemed to have surprised himself with his own powers of oratory.

Briefly it seemed that UCD might salvage something from two years of debilitating infighting. But the party was like a man with his leg amputated who still feels the missing limb. The euphoria lasted less than a week. Disagreements re-emerged and more desertions followed. The temptation of an electoral alliance with the right wing Alianza Popular (AP) of Manuel Fraga was spurned, even though he promised to win an important slice of the UCD vote. The party went into the elections convinced of its own suicide.

Having called the elections early because desertions had eroded its working majority in parliament, UCD barely possessed an election manifesto. Lavilla was forced to fight a campaign that did its best to make promises as though the party had not been in government for the past five years. The electorate was not convinced. Having won 6 million votes as late as 1979, UCD ended up in October 1982 with only 1·3 million: a dejected rump who could not face the alternative of the Socialists on the left and AP on the right.

Having dominated Spanish political life since 1977, UCD had virtually disappeared by October 1982. UCD's 166 members of parliament were reduced to twelve. The saga of UCD, born as a ruling party and dying as such, is one of the most remarkable recent political phenomena in a western parliamentary democracy.

Mourned by few, UCD has been fast forgotten — except by the banks to whom it owed money. Despite the brevity of its existence and its spectacular disintegration, UCD served a useful function. It responded to the peculiar circumstances of Spanish political life in the wake of Franco's death. Franco bequeathed no political party. A political grouping needed to be invented to unite those who wanted moderate reform without overly antagonizing Franco's supporters, or identifying too closely with the opposition on the left.

UCD owed its brief success to a cautious electorate testing the inexperienced waters of democracy, and to Suarez's image and skills: it was like that of an insect which gives birth and then dies. The advent of the Socialist Party to power was certainly eased by, and may not have been possible without, the interregnum of UCD. The electorate was able to shed residual fears of the suitability of socialists to govern, and the historic socialist vote was reinforced. After forty years in exile, the PSOE came to dominate both the Cortes, the municipalities, and the majority of the new autonomous governments, within six years of renewed legality.

158

SEEDS OF DESTRUCTION

If UCD had lost the first elections in June 1977, it probably would have broken up. It was formed in May 1977 with the sole purpose of fighting the elections, and was not a party even in the loosest sense. It was a self-interested coalition without any clearly defined ideology. The 'union' provided a broad umbrella under which right wing, centre and reformist would-be politicians could join hands providing the mutual support necessary to ensure they assumed the mantle of power left by Francoism. Initially, fifteen groups or parties formed the coalition, but by the time of the elections the number had been reduced to thirteen. The organization consisted of a three-man electoral committee, run by Leopoldo Calvo Sotelo who had resigned from being Minister of Public Works to organize the coalition's electoral strategy.

There were two vital ingredients in UCD's electoral success. The first was the person and image of Suarez. As Prime Minister he held back from associating himself with a political party, but as the elections drew close he was instrumental in forging the coalition of UCD and became its de facto leader. UCD therefore had at its head a man permanently in the public eye who clearly enjoyed the King's support. Suarez was more palatable to the public than the left realised. His clean youthful looks were in themselves a breath of air after the old men of the Bunker, while his small town Castillian background and his lack of identification with either the aristocracy or the bureaucratic elite were to his advantage. He epitomized the changing face of Spain and the emergence of a new middle class. He represented what many Spaniards aspired to be — a provincial boy made good, with a devout wife and a large happy family. His first interviews were given to the best-selling social magazine, *Hola*.

It did not matter that he had been secretary-general of the Movimiento and worn the fascist blue shirt. His age excused him from involvement in the divisive aspects of the Civil War heritage and the majority of Spaniards — whatever they felt about Franco — had collaborated with the former regime in order to survive. Thus the stigma of association with Franco's government, which might have been attached to Suarez and a good many of his UCD colleagues, did not disturb the electorate. On the contrary, he seemed to suggest a desire shared by all those who had known the previous regime to move on and modernize Spain. Suarez was the symbol of change. His past was no contradiction or political embarrassment.

Significantly, the older generation of politicians associated with Francoism who sought to form parties fared disastrously in the June 1977 elections. Jose Maria Areilza, former Franco ambassador to Paris and Washington and Foreign Minister under Arias, decided to have nothing to do with UCD when it was clear the coalition would not entertain his ambition of being Prime Minister. He, along with Fraga, Alfonso Osorio and other notables such as

Federico Silva Muñoz, failed to disassociate themselves sufficiently from the former regime. At the outset there was little, apart from image, to suggest to the public that Suarez would do better than such figures.

The second ingredient in the success of UCD was the close interconnection between it and the state apparatus. UCD had no organization but it utilized the facilities of the administration. The resources of the civil governors, who controlled the local police and security and therefore had close tabs on the electorate, were tapped unashamedly. Through Suarez's contacts, UCD hired many of the better talents from the Movimiento whom democracy was about to make redundant. Over one third of the UCD deputies elected were to come from this source or the Francoist administration; they were labelled the *azules* (blues), after the blue shirts of the Movimiento.

The other political parties, poorly organized or only recently made legal, could tap no such resources or gain such public exposure. For instance, Suarez did not formally enter the campaign, but the electorate was permanently reminded of his presence and he gave himself the all important right of an eve of election address to the nation.

The odds were further weighted against the left and in favour of UCD by the electoral law, passed by decree in March 1977. The province was chosen as the constituency. There were sound arguments of simplicity for this choice since Spain was administered on a provincial basis. It meant, however, that a small vote in rural areas, traditionally conservative, returned a deputy, whereas it required a very substantial vote in an urban area, more likely to be of the left, to attain that basic level of representation. The minimum number of deputies per province was two. Thus, for instance, Soria with three deputies had one for every 34,000 inhabitants, while Barcelona with thirty-three deputies had one for every 134,000. The effects of this system were highlighted in the election results. On 34% of the vote, UCD obtained 47% of the 350 deputies in the Cortes. The Socialist Party obtained just under 5% fewer votes but obtained only 34% of the seats.

The selection of the de Hondt system of voting favoured large parties at the expense of smaller ones. This was also a factor which made the formation of the UCD coalition so necessary — lone parties like the Liberals or Social Democrats would have stood very little chance. The de Hondt system was adopted specifically to encourage the formation of large parties and prevent a fragmentation of parliament. Voting for the Senate was on a simple majority basis without party lists. This too favoured the traditional conservative vote.

To avoid dependence on financial backers, it was agreed that the state would provide funds on the basis of seats won and votes obtained. While the Suarez government's posture on this and the de Hondt system could be considered altruistic, it was far less so regarding the voting age. This was fixed at twenty-one, on the basis that the youth vote would be radical and anti-centre. In excluding the eighteen-year-olds, Suarez eliminated almost 3 million potential voters from the electorate of 23 million. The constitution reduced the voting age to eighteen in time for the 1979 elections.

These manoeuvres could be called gerrymandering. However, they occurred against a background of constant concern that supporters of Francoism, especially within the armed forces, would react if the left came to power in the first elections. The defeat of Suarez in June 1977 would also have been the rejection of the King's candidate, and by the same token a rejection of the King's aim of modernizing Spain without breaking violently with the past. The victory was not quite as clear cut as he had hoped, but it was a sufficiently popular endorsement to give both him and UCD legitimacy. With 166 seats UCD's nearest rival was the PSOE with 118. Although UCD had been imposed from above the election result immediately gave it political respectability.

After victory, the abiding characteristic of UCD was of a coalition of cynical self-interest *forced* to be a party. It was most united when acting purely as a party of government — introducing the fundamental reforms which any democratic government would have had to have done following Franco's death. Its fissiparous nature became evident once this initial stage had passed and the party needed to take decisions with an ideological content, such as educational reform, where Christian Democrats noisily defended continued Church influence and control.

UCD's success was essentially that of Suarez, and with some justice he could look upon it as *his* party. He was made its provisional president and confirmed in the post by the first congress in October 1978. He set out to dominate the organization with his appointees, converting UCD into a presidential party. This created permanent tension between Suarez and other groups that felt excluded from power.

To hold these groups together Suarez needed to feel confident of his public image and performances, yet the threat of internal revolt always put this confidence at risk. Loyalty from the parliamentary party and members of the government was not, on the whole, personal — it was support for the most powerful person of the moment. Among several influential colleagues Suarez was regarded as a man chosen by the King for a specific task — administering the introduction of democracy. Perhaps it was no accident that internal opposition to Suarez began after the constitution had been approved and he had obtained a second electoral victory in March 1979. He had overstepped his mandate and UCD threatened to become too much a Suarez party.

These tensions and contradictions provided UCD, from its inception, with the capacity to destroy itself. Great selflessness from its constituent parts would be necessary to avoid a break-up. This was never shown.

THE FALL OF SUAREZ

From the 1977 general elections until his resignation in January 1981, Suarez changed his cabinet on five major occasions and resorted to forty-two different ministers. These cabinet reshuffles were rarely due to the failings of individual ministers — few were even given time to get used to their jobs — but almost entirely due to personality clashes and disagreements with the party's power-brokers. In the wake of the March 1979 general elections, Suarez attempted to do without the barons in his cabinet. He calculated that he had been vindicated by the decision to call early elections after the approval of the constitution. These were the first constitutional elections and Suarez headed UCD as the clearly identified leader of a party that had established a national organization. UCD had maintained its share of the vote — no mean achievement for a man who had been running the country almost three years in difficult circumstances.[3] Suarez's experiment of a hand-picked cabinet lasted until September 1980 when, increasingly undermined from within, he was obliged to restore the barons. Back came Cabanillas, Fernandez Ordoñez, and Martin Villa.

Suarez made the basic error of trying to monopolize power. In so doing he alienated his detractors in UCD and exposed himself as the scapegoat for government policy. For instance, the ill-judged switch in policy regarding autonomy for Andalusia in 1980, ceasing to treat it as an 'historic region', rebounded on Suarez and could not be deflected onto anyone else. The Minister for the Regions, Manuel Clavero Arevalo, himself an Andalusian, had already resigned in protest.[4] Suarez's action over Andalusia was one of the principal reasons why Felipe Gonzalez called a parliamentary motion of censure in May 1980. Suarez reacted as though victimized by a denigration campaign orchestrated by the Socialists. But also UCD members such as Rudolfo-Martin Villa sought to get rid of him in the wake of a censure motion that saw the party totally isolated in the Cortes.

The September 1980 cabinet reshuffle produced the best balanced and most experienced of Suarez's governments. Suarez sacrificed his closest personal colleague, Fernando Abril Martorell, who, as deputy premier, had been the most powerful man in the cabinet and acted as a shield for Suarez. He promoted Calvo Sotelo to the deputy premiership, a man acceptable to all the factions within UCD. But the harmony in the government lasted less than fifteen days. Suarez was conscious that a group of up to forty deputies could no longer be relied upon to support him. He therefore could not rely on a working parliamentary majority, especially in the event of a censure motion.

Increasingly paranoid about his position and wounded by the hostility of his critics within the party, he concluded in early January 1981 there were only two solutions. The first was to call fresh general elections to prove that UCD was *his* party by winning, or, through losing, gain the opportunity to mould

UCD into the centre reformist party of his choice. Alternatively, he could resign so that UCD might continue without him as the source of friction. Suarez's own private polls showed that in the event of an election the Socialists would get 34% of the vote, UCD only 26%. Suarez claims he rejected this option not for fear of losing but because at this moment the military would not have accepted a Socialist government. He therefore chose to resign, announcing his move on 29 January, only days before UCD was to begin its second congress in Majorca.[5]

Suarez denies that his decision was influenced by pressure from either the military or the King. The King, he maintains, asked him to rethink his resignation. Yet if this version is taken at face value, it sets an extraordinary precedent — of a Prime Minister throwing in the towel before being defeated and in so doing causing a political vacuum. What he judged a responsible action was an irresponsible betrayal of the voters who had placed their confidence in him.

In his resignation speech, Suarez gave no concrete reason for his departure other than to suggest that he did not wish to be a barrier to the installation of democracy. It sounded like noble, premature retirement. Yet it is hard not to see that, side by side with the wear and tear of five taxing years in office, Suarez was motivated by personal pique. He stepped down to let the next leader appreciate the difficulty of governing Spain and controlling the party. On leaving office the King conferred on him a dukedom: he seemed set to take a back seat.[6] Yet within nine months he could not resist returning to interfere in UCD, and his own attempts to regain control of the party were as disruptive as anything else.

Suarez's resignation as premier and leader of UCD heralded the beginning of the party's end. His departure left a gaping hole in the leadership. His appointees still dominated the party's organization but the parliamentary party was clamouring to make up for their exclusion under his leadership. Suarez designated Calvo Sotelo to be his successor as Prime Minister, and managed to ensure that the UCD leadership fell on one of his faithful, former Defence Minister Augustin Roderiguez Sahagun. A temporary truce was provided by the trauma of the 23 February coup. But soon the power struggle was on in earnest, with the protagonists showing a cavalier neglect for its consequences to government.

The Social Democrats and Liberals complained that UCD was being pulled too much towards the right. The Christian Democrats, headed by Oscar Alzaga and Miguel Herrero de Minon, by now the most numerous and vociferous of the groupings, felt the party had alienated its real electoral support — UCD had to pull away from ill-defined centrism towards an enlightened right wing catholicism. The 'Blue Shirts' (former Movimiento members) hung on, shifting alliances to ensure that UCD stayed together. Suarez threatened to leave the party as the balance of forces swung away from him. Calvo Sotelo replaced Sahagun as party leader, restoring the former presidential style, unifying the premiership and party leadership in one person. This merely made Calvo Sotelo's task in government more difficult. Legislation that might be controversial among UCD factions was held back.

Calvo Sotelo, nephew of the monarchist minister of finance assassinated in 1936, was ambitious but reluctant to face the consequences of his ambition. Fond of music and books, he had a natural distaste for bashing heads together and mud slinging. He stood aloft, giving the impression first of calm then of sheer indecision. With his large glasses and high domed head, he came to look like a sleepy owl worried about falling off his perch.

The first to desert the sinking ship were former finance and justice minister, Fernandez Ordoñez, and his group of Social Democrats, to be followed by a large section of the Christian Democrats, liberals and finally Suarez and his followers. In a last ditch attempt to re-animate UCD, Lavilla, who had the integrity and energy to run the party, took over the leadership in July. He had been the main contender to take over from Suarez in January 1981, and had then been blocked by Suarez himself. But the change occurred too late — Suarez's desertion had been the final straw. No one believed in UCD, and factionalism prevented its ideology from being defined. The raison d'être of UCD — to be a party of government — was fast ceasing to exist. The polls showed electoral preference for the Socialists.

By the time of the elections, UCD's supporters had been reduced to the members of the government. The party had split in four directions. The Christian Democrats formed the Partido Democratico Popular (PDP) and allied with Fraga and AP on the right. The Social Democrats formed Partido de Accion Democratica (PAD) and the Liberals, flirting until the last with UCD, eventually held back altogether. Suarez formed his own centre party, CDS. Calvo Sotelo and Lavilla just managed to get elected as deputies. The bulk of the twelve UCD deputies returned were those from the Movimiento — the 'Blues' who had nowhere else to turn, but who still knew how to operate an electoral machine. Following this defeat, it was just a question of how UCD could be wound up with the least indignity to the reputation of its members.

ASSOCIATIONS AND THE MOVIMIENTO

The rise and fall of UCD explains the continued search to create a large party to pick up the centre and right wing vote that is the natural balance in the parliamentary system to the hegemony acquired by the Socialists in 1982.

The personalities and political groups which briefly coalesced in UCD were the consequence of the timid political liberalization of the Francoist system in the late sixties. The push to liberalize came from two directions. Firstly, there was the purely technical consideration that to govern a complex modern state of over 30 million inhabitants required greater devolution of authority to keep the machinery of government in motion. Secondly, Franco faced more overtly political pressure: to head off political unrest minimal concessions had to be made in broadening the base of participation in government. Since political parties were banned and all political activity had to be channelled through the Movimiento, the conflict between those who favoured liberalization and those who blocked it was played out behind closed doors. It had no institutional framework and was a highly personalized process.

The first small concession to the idea of a plurality of views occurred in December 1968. In approving a statute for the Movimiento, an article was included (number 15), permitting associations. The concession was extraordinarily circumspect since these associations could in no way be construed as political parties. Their existence was possible only within the Movimiento, and as long as they encouraged a 'legitimate exchange of opinions'.

When it came to define article 15 more thoroughly in July 1969, the concession was hedged even further. Apart from being apolitical, the associations required a minimum of 25,000 signatures to be constituted. The concession amounted to nothing more than the expression of a greater diversity of view among the ruling elite. The Movimiento cast a dead hand on those aspiring to create associations. By the end of the sixties, it had lost the virulence of its Falange hallmark, yet was no longer interested in searching for new ideas. Instead it had become a giant bureaucracy for ensuring loyalty to the regime. Since Franco retained his mistrust of politicians and political parties, the Movimiento leadership was reluctant to take the initiative and convert itself into a political party. This made it difficult to conduct meaningful political activity inside the Movimiento.

The move on associations showed that the regime was incapable of coming to terms with the existence of even moderate political parties. The closest it came to a change of heart was in the wake of Carrero Blanco's assassination when Arias was Prime Minister. Arias promised, apparently with genuine good will, to alter the law on political associations, but the law approved by the Cortes in December 1974 was far removed from his earlier pledges. The sole novelty was a public acceptance that associations could be political. Otherwise they remained under the Movimiento. One step forwards, three quarters backwards.

Arias even disappointed those like Manuel Fraga who had championed reform from within. Fraga, ambassador in London since 1973, saw himself as holding centre stage in a party that would bridge the gap between Francoism and democracy — a Spanish version of the right wing of the British Conservative Party. Rather than go along with the idea of political associations, in June 1975 Fraga opted to create two limited companies whose aims were the promotion of political studies. The first, Fedisa, was formed in association with other aspirant post-Franco politicians — like Jose Maria Areilza and the christian democrat, Pio Cabinallas, who as a Minister of Information under Arias pressed hard for a more liberal law and had then been forced to resign in October 1975 because he was considered too progressive. Another member of Fedisa was the social democrat, Francisco Fernandez Ordoñez, who had resigned from his post in the administration at the time of Cabinillas' dismissal. The second company, Godsa, only differed from the first in that it was a vehicle exclusively for Fraga's personal ambitions. These two ventures underlined the desire of those identified with the Franco regime to keep their distance and prepare for a parliamentary democracy.

The same could be seen in individual groups that formed despite the laws against them but were tolerated because the persons involved were known (and half-trusted) members of the administrative elite. This was the case with the right wing christian democrat group known as 'Tacitus' which formed in the early seventies. The nucleus of this group were members of the elite civil service corps, like Landelino Lavilla (state advocates) and Marcelino Oreja (the diplomatic corps). The 'Tacitus' group was really a club formed for like-minded persons.

Only eight associations formed under the Arias law. The most significant was the Spanish People's Union (UDPE), whose lineage was clearly linked to the Movimiento. Its principal promoter was the minister of the Movimiento, Fernando Herrero Tejedor, who placed his protegé Adolfo Suarez in charge. Although Herrero Tejedor was killed in a car accident before the UDPE could develop into a political party, it was groomed to occupy the ground of the Movimiento once Franco died and the rules of the game changed. Suarez's position running UDPE permitted him to begin moulding elements of the Movimiento into a new role and it was to become one of the components in UCD.

In June 1976, one month before being sacked by King Juan Carlos, Arias managed to pass a limited law legalizing political parties through the still Francoist Cortes. The law excluded reform of the penal code, essential to permit legalization of the Communist Party and radical regionalist groups. But this law gave the centre and right the long-awaited chance to form parties. Parties mushroomed often with near identical aims and labels. From Liberals and Social Democrats through to Christian Democrats and Catholic Conservatives, the process of fragmentation was total, with parties usually formed round one or a limited number of individuals. The parties also went through a bewilderingly speedy metamorphosis in nomenclature as allies came and went. For instance, among the Social Democrats were the following: Fernandez Ordoñez's Partido Social Democrata (originally Izquierda Social-democrata); the economist Juan Ramon Lasuen's Federacion Socialdemocrata and the disillusioned Falangist turned Franco critic, Dionisio Ridruejo's Union Socialdemocrata Española.

The proliferation among Christian Democrats was even greater. Joaquim Ruiz-Jimenez, the former Franco Education Minister who had distanced himself sharply from Francoism and who fomented a christian democrat movement among intellectuals, formed Izquierda Democratica. Another

Christian Democrat of long standing, Jose Maria Gil Robles (son of the thirties politician), formed the Federacion Popular Democratica and a colleague Fernando Alvarez de Miranda, Izquierda Democrata Cristiana. Among the liberals there were at least four parties, the most prominent being Joaquin Garriguez Walker's Federacion de Partidos Democratas y Liberales.

These new parties hoisted themselves onto the democratic bandwagon. But none had any traditions, only the track record of their promoters under the previous regime. Since the nineteenth century, the centre and right were the parties of government (when parties were tolerated). They had been labelled Conservative and Liberal — the Liberals having coined their name after the progressive, but short-lived, Cortes of Cadiz in 1810. The Liberals moulded their credo on the idea that sovereignty stemmed from the people. But by the 1870s this ideology had been all but buried by opportunism. The Liberals connived in a power-sharing pact, the brainchild of the wily politician Antonio Canovas del Castillo. The Conservatives and Liberals alternated in power with near total disregard for the electorate, whose limited suffrage was grossly manipulated by the ministry of the Interior to ensure that any radical voice was excluded from power. This system of controlling the electorate from above, with a sort of gentleman's agreement between the ruling groups of the centre and the right, lasted up to the second Republic.

This was scarcely an edifying tradition to follow. There was no popular base, and votes cast were either bought or procured on the basis of paternalistic allegiance. Furthermore, the experience of the Republic was not a happy one for the centre and right. The main right wing party to emerge had been the Confederacion Española de Derechas Autonomas (CEDA), an amalgam of small Catholic and monarchist parties that constituted itself in 1933, quickly boasting 730,000 members.

The CEDA lasted less than four years. Led by a young barrister, Jose Maria Gil Robles, the CEDA owed its appeal to its overtly confessional status. Gil Robles obtained the backing of the Church, which gave CEDA respectability and provided organization and resources of a kind which none of the other parties in Spain had at the time. It attracted support because of the increasingly polarized atmosphere of the time, and capitalized on the anti-clericalism of the Republic.

Its disappearance, almost without a whimper, cannot be wholly attributed to the Nationalists' banning of political parties in 1936, permitting only movements — the Movimiento and the Carlists. The CEDA was never a party but, like UCD, a coalition, and its supporters were bound to it for self-preservation. Once they could embrace the broader nationalist cause, the CEDA lost significance and when the Church decided to throw its weight behind the Nationalists, CEDA was no longer necessary as a weapon of Catholic crusade.

UCD had elements of these traditions — it was a coalition imposed from above. But the most important difference was that it did not become a confessional party: the head of the Episcopal Conference, Cardinal Tarancon, firmly resisted pressure for the Church to support a christian democratic party. Suarez was equally determined to ensure that UCD was independent from the Church.

The first attempt to forge unity among the groups in the centre and right was Pio Cabanillas' Partido Popular. Christian democrat in inspiration, it sought to bridge the gap between Liberals, Social Democrats and those in the Francoist administration who until then had showed no interest in any political grouping or association. In early 1977, with the prospect of general elections, the Partido Popular went into a coalition with Alvarez Miranda's Partido Democrata Cristiano. The coalition called itself Centro Democratico, and soon attracted other groups into its fold including Liberals and some Conservative regional parties. Even so, this coalition was nothing more than a group of prominent personalities devoid of a popular base or organization. The sole hope of electoral success lay in an alliance with Suarez and his colleagues in the administration. In return for broader political appeal, Suarez provided the machinery of government. This was the 'union' of Centro Democratico.[1]

From then onwards, the struggle to balance the demands of the original groupings that had agreed to form the coalition was continuous. The number of deputies and cabinet posts within UCD was more or less determined by the individual strength of these groups. This, in turn, led to the emergence of the so called party 'barons' — those whose power bases lay in groups such as the 'Blue Shirts', Fernandez Ordoñez with the Social Democrats, Garrigues Walker and Ignacio Camunas the Liberals, Alvarez de Miranda, Cabanillas and Lavilla the Christian Democrats. Suarez maintains he was conscious from the start that UCD was nothing but a coalition of separate interests.[2] But his attempt to mould it round himself in a more homogeneous form failed.

FRAGA AND THE RIGHT

Pressure was exerted on Lavilla to fight the October 1982 elections in alliance with Fraga and Alianza Popular. The conservative Christian Democrats, backed by the Employers Federation (CEOE), canvassed hard for this option. Fraga favoured the idea, calling for the creation of 'the natural majority': the centre and right in a broad coalition. The alliance provided a reasonable alternative to the predicted socialist victory. At the same time UCD would be saved from extinction and given an umbrella under which it could regroup.

The public reason for failure to consume the alliance sounded high-minded. UCD's image as a centre party would disappear and Spanish politics would be polarized between left and right. But the real impediment was not the right-wing label or the image of Fraga as a former Franco minister — rather it was the latter's personality. AP was Fraga's party. The UCD leadership saw nothing but difficulty in dealing with his abrasive, authoritarian temperament.

Starting from a brilliant academic career, Fraga's first job in the administration had been with the Ministry of Education. He quickly moved up the ladder via membership of the Falange to become Minister of Information and Tourism in 1962, aged forty. Exceptionally ambitious, he had, to his credit, introduced some of the first substantive liberalizing measures of the Franco regime with his easing of censorship. He had imbued himself with the workings of democracy, and held an especial admiration for the British parliamentary system. Yet he was liable to intolerant bursts of temper, was belligerently nationalistic (a trademark was to wear braces in the Spanish colours) and displayed an uncompromising conservatism on matters of the family. He had fancied his chances of becoming prime minister after Franco died and hardly concealed his disappointment when the King chose Suarez, ten years his junior. It was pride and generational difference that made him avoid joining up with UCD in 1977. His own party was the best means to realize his ambition for the premiership.

AP began with a federal structure as a device to define the personal differences between the main figures — former Foreign Minister Laureano Lopez Rodo, and the two ex-Ministers of Public Works, Gonzalo Fernandez de la Mora and Federico Silva Muñoz. Having played prominent roles in the later Franco era, they did not, with the exception of Fraga, really understand parliament but assumed they should continue to direct the affairs of the nation. They were encouraged to do so by the composition of the first government of the monarchy under Arias which contained several of their ilk. AP started out with one foot firmly in the Francoist camp, holding the paternalistic view that the nation was ready for only the most gradual and carefully guided transition to democracy.

Fraga and his colleagues hopelessly misread the mood of the electorate in 1977. They were not alone: a number of western embassies expected Fraga to do well too. Instead, AP gained only fourth place behind the Communists with under 9% of the vote. By the 1979 elections this had fallen to below 6%, when AP teamed up with other right wing personalities like Areilza to form a coalition, Coalicion Democratica.

AP's subsequent revival owed much to the determination and sheer staying power of Fraga, who was convinced that the centre vote was a product of the transitional nature of the infant democracy. Sooner or later this vote would swing towards the right and embrace the philosophy of AP. However, Fraga was wise enough to read the electoral signals and dropped AP's image as a party of Francoist notables. He brought in a youthful secretary-general, Jorge Verstrynge, and concentrated on building up a better organization. But

169

the revival of AP would not have been possible without the disintegration of UCD. AP was there to pick up the disillusioned vote, first in Galicia's autonomous parliamentary elections, then in Andalusia, before reaping its full benefits in October 1982.

In 1982, AP quadrupled its number of votes, obtaining just short of 5·5 million. Put another way, UCD lost just short of 5 million votes and AP gained over 4 million on the 1979 results. Most of the switched UCD vote went to AP and its christian democrat partners, PDP. AP picked up the rest on the right and extreme right.

AP has now evolved into a much more heterogeneous grouping, containing Christian Democrats like Oscar Alzaga and Herrero de Miñon, stray Liberals like the economist Pedro Schwartz, reconstructed Francoists like Fraga, and some who verge on being fascists. Fraga remains controversial and almost certainly has a ceiling of support among the electorate. This ceiling was probably reached in the general elections of 1982 and the municipal elections of May 1983.

THE SOCIALIST TRADITION

In sharp contrast to the centre and right, the principal parties of the left — the Socialists and Communists — had a tradition. In the case of the Socialists this dated back to the late nineteenth century; the Communist Party was formed from two splinter groups that broke with the PSOE. Throughout the Franco era, these two parties possessed an organization and a recognized leadership. (The Socialists held thirteen congresses in exile.) These parties survived exile and repression, weakened, but ready to operate the moment they were legalized.

UCD and AP had set out in search of a 'sociological' vote, trimming their appeal to an imagined voter. The Socialists and Communists could appeal successfully to the historic loyalties of the left, whose tradition survived the long forty year break.[7] While UCD and AP were *sui generis* phenomena of the situation following Franco's death, the two main parties of the left had recognizable similarities with, and followed the tradition of, their European namesakes, which helped to define them more clearly. This was of particular advantage to the Socialists since they were linked to the style of modern social democratic socialism found, for instance, in West Germany. This helped to remove part of the initial stigma of their radicalism under the Republic. For the Communists it was a disadvantage because they were seen as too close to Moscow.

The Socialist Party evolved alongside the trades union, UGT, as part of a drive to secure a voice for the working class. The party was founded nine years before UGT in May 1879. First it was called the Partido Democratico

Socialista Obrero and later Partido Socialista Obrero Español. Until 1881 it was obliged to operate as a clandestine party. The leading light in the party's creation, and in its companion trades union, was a Madrid printer with piercing eyes and a distinctive beard, Pablo Iglesias. Initial membership relied heavily on Iglesias' circle of friends and companions at work. At the time of the party's founding, Iglesias had already been a member of the International for nine years. Via colleagues in France he was strongly influenced by marxist orthodoxy, and marxist ideas were the essence of early Spanish socialism. This was evident in the anti-bourgeois tone of the party's newspaper, *El Socialista*, which first appeared in 1886.

Iglesias saw the strike as the most effective means of making an impact on the authorities, and among the people he sought to recruit. Having created an impact, he was confronted with the difficulty of promoting a political party which had little prospect of power. He chose a path which never bore fruit in his lifetime (he died in 1925) but laid the foundations of the dominant role of the Socialists and the UGT under the Republic, and later after 1976. He insisted on discipline, an uncompromising acceptance of socialist ideals, and a tremendous inner confidence in the inevitability of socialism.

Brenan saw something almost Calvinist in Iglesias.[8] He certainly earned universal respect for his incorruptibility and his strong moral stand on the clean-up of the administration. Moral cleanliness, and a pledge to clean up public life were two of the most winning aspects of Felipe Gonzalez in the 1982 elections.

Socialist influence spread via the establishment of the *casas del pueblo*, which served as meeting places, education centres, and lending libraries. The *casas* were first brought to Barcelona in 1905 by Alejandro Lerroux's Radicals and were copied from Belgium. However, the Socialists in a sense patented the introduction and established them throughout Spain in both large and small towns in conjunction with the UGT. They became a fundamental influence in providing a form of political education to the working class. (At the turn of the century no more than five cities had free lending libraries.) Until the Republic, the strength of the Party lay in the support it could count on from the UGT. Its chief rival was the anarchist movement. The Socialists' appeal, however, was to a different group of people, the better educated members of the working class and some members of the liberal professions.

IDEOLOGICAL DIFFERENCES

The socialist leadership had to decide whether the party was strictly working class and antagonistic to other bourgeois parties or whether it should make tactical compromises. It was a question of both ideological definition and strategy, profoundly influenced as always in Spanish politics by the personalities of the leading protagonists. The first and most serious ideological split occurred in the wake of the Russian Revolution. Until this time Iglesias had favoured a parliamentary approach to change and indeed spoke more of reform than revolution; he himself had been elected to parliament. But the efforts of the monarchy, backed by the Church and the military, to prevent socialist reform, encouraged a group within the party to identify closely with the Russian Revolution.

In 1920 some members of the socialist youth movement came out in open support for the Soviet Union and announced the formation of the Partido Communista Español. The PSOE was now torn in opposing directions over whether or not to support the Third International. Finally, after three special congresses, a sixty/forty majority voted against joining the Third International on the urgings of Iglesias, by now an ailing man. Those who disagreed broke away to form the Partido Comunista Obrero de España (amongst them, Dolores Ibarruri, who was to become famous as the fiery *La Pasionaria* in the Civil War). These two splinter Communist Parties, at the behest of the Comintern the following year, became the nucleus of the Spanish Communist Party (PCE).

The Communist Party remained small until the outbreak of the Civil War when it rapidly increased its standing as a result of its more disciplined organization and the powerful backing of Moscow. The Communists also took advantage of divisions within the Socialists to poach new recruits. In early 1934 the communist and socialist youth movements merged. The secretary-general was Santiago Carrillo, aged nineteen. He was still a Socialist, as were most of the leaders of the movement; but they leant closer and closer to communism.

By 1936, Carrillo had joined the PCE and the whole youth movement came under communist domination. Carrillo had left his father behind in the Socialist Party, a stalwart member of the Cortes. Also in 1936, the Catalan Socialists decided to found their own party which was communist in all but name — Partit Socialista Unificat de Catalunya (PSUC). Subsequently, the PSUC was federated to — but remained separate from — the PCE. This erosion of the Socialists' influence was also felt in the Cortes even though in the 1936 elections they obtained the most seats (20%).

The conflicting strands within the PSOE at this stage tended to revolve round two larger-than-life figures — Francisco Largo Caballero and Indalecio Prieto. Largo Caballero, a Madrid plasterer who taught himself to read

172

at the age of twenty-four, was Iglesias' chief lieutenant and heir in the UGT. Hard working and impulsive he impressed himself on others by his sheer energy. He was baptised the 'Spanish Lenin'. He played heavily on his working class origins and was probably the most popular trades union figure Spain has ever known. More instinctive than calculating, he strongly supported the revolutionary uprising in Asturias in 1934. As Prime Minister in 1936, he made some serious errors as a result of not knowing how to handle power; but his appeal as an historic figure holds in the PSOE, underlined by a multitudinous reception for his remains when they were brought back for burial from France in 1979.

'Caballerismo' has come to mean a form of working class popularism. But his period as Prime Minister has also been associated with ill-considered maximalism. The lesson of his actions as premier has been one of the moderating influences on the present day PSOE. Prieto, on the other hand, represented the voice of moderation. Though starting his working life as a newsboy, he managed to gain the patronage of one of the wealthiest members of the Basque industrial oligarchy, Horacio Echevarrieta, and became relatively rich. He saw the PSOE as more than the preserve of the working class and a party of grievance and class struggle; he also wanted it to act as the social conscience of the middle class. His voice, however, carried less weight in the polarized climate of the Republic and the Civil War.

In various ways, these conflicting interests were played out in the post-Civil War period. The party leadership went into exile in France. Inside Spain, the party structure vanished and only the now banned UGT managed to retain a residual presence in former strongholds like Asturias. From the start it was decided not to collaborate with the Franco regime and this policy remained unaltered almost until 1975. The leadership tended to shut itself away in exile maintaining limited contact with the interior yet insisting that it was still in control. The congresses were filled with nostalgic rhetoric, awaiting the day when Franco would fall. Anti-communism was the keynote. The PCE's determined attempts to exert hegemony, both during the Popular Front government and then with the government-in-exile, put them on the defensive and were never forgiven. (This was another reason why the PSOE spurned the PCE's tactic of infiltrating the regime from within.) Desultory contact was retained with the Anarchists, but in general mistrust prevented the creation of a united front to oppose the regime.

Inside Spain, the Communists established a stronger presence, especially among the students and industrial workforce — their support growing on the back of the unofficial but highly effective Workers Commissions (see Chapter Five). The Communists, first headed by *La Pasionaria* and then by Carrillo, were more politically aggressive and internationally active. But the PSOE had not dirtied its hands in the same way during the Civil War. The Communists had indulged in cold-blooded sectarian killing, often in concert with Moscow, such as the shameful murder of Trotsky's one-time secretary, Andres Nin. No matter how much Carrillo sought to refurbish the party's image, this and other unpleasant memories stuck. With the insignificant presence of the Anarchists and the virtual disappearance of all the other republican parties, this allowed the Socialists to be, in public eyes, the principal inheritors of the positive traditions of the republican left.

YOUTH AT THE HELM

The PSOE was able to claim this inheritance largely thanks to the efforts of a small group of activists who took the initiative inside Spain in the late sixties, ignoring the moribund exiled leadership. These activists were concentrated in the south in Andalusia and in the north in Asturias and the Basque country. The Andalusian group was headed by two young labour lawyers, Alfonso Guerra and Felipe Gonzalez, and included others who were to become prominent in the PSOE—Guillermo Galeote, Rafael Escuredo and Luis Yañez. In the north the main figures were Nicolas Redondo, a seasoned trades unionist preparing to take over the illegal UGT, and a former communist student leader, Enrique Mugica. Of all these, Redondo was the most experienced.

Together they embarked on the dual task of rebuilding the party and reactivating UGT. For a while they were able to do things their own way, so scant was the contact and weak the hold of the exiled leadership of Rudolfo Llopis. A huge generational gap was further widened by the ideological dogmatism of the exiles. Llopis, for instance, could not forget that he had been nominated head of the republican government-in-exile in 1947. He was fighting another battle.

The activists were generally products of the universities, drawn from the generation that had been born after the Civil War. They did not share the same prejudices about this traumatic event as their seniors and had fresh energy to combat Francoism. Their support, strongly rooted in the universities, was given an added boost by the shock waves of France's May 1968 riots. Working class support mainly came from those areas where UGT had a long tradition. Their efforts were slowly rewarded.

In 1970 the PSOE's XXIV congress in Toulouse agreed to clip some of Llopis' powers. Then, in 1974 at the XXVI congress near Paris at Suresnes, the activists outmanoeuvred the old guard of the party and installed Felipe Gonzalez as secretary-general. Only thirty-two years old, since ending his law studies at Seville University he had devoted most of his waking hours to the party under the clandestine pseudonym 'Isidoro'; he was inseparable from Guerra, two years his senior. Son of a small tenant dairy farmer who came from Santander and settled outside Seville, Gonzalez's social background was not so dissimilar to that of Adolfo Suarez. Their careers under Franco represented, in some respects, opposite sides of the same coin. Suarez reached the top by working with the system, Gonzalez by working against it.[9]

This dedicated group, which triumphed in Suresnes, went on to gain the all important endorsement of the International Socialist movement. The latter was also being lobbied by a rival group of socialist activists formed round the distinguished academic, Professor Enrique Tierno Galvan. Tierno Galvan had formed the Partido Socialista del Interior (PSI) in 1968, later transforming it into the Partido Socialista Popular (PSP), claiming to be the true inheritors of Pablo Iglesias. Tierno Galvan — nicknamed 'the old professor' because of his bespectacled professorial face — had a commendable record of opposition, fighting for greater academic freedom and suffering as a result. But his PSP appealed more to intellectuals and an older generation. He also erred in allying himself too closely with Llopis. However, he was more flexible than other members of the left in seeking co-operation with the monarchists and Don Juan.

As a further sign of the PSP's distance from the PSOE, Tierno Galvan decided to join the opposition coalition Junta Democratica. This was formed in July 1974 to organize a common front in anticipation of Franco's imminent disappearance. The Junta was the first serious attempt by the exiled opposition to co-ordinate, regardless of ideology. It included such independents as Antonio Garcia Trevijano and the Opus Dei newspaper proprietor, Rafael Calvo Serrer, who had become a disillusioned Francoist and had had his daily, *Madrid*, closed down. The main component of the Junta was the Communist Party and its trades union arm, the CCOO. The PSOE suspected the Junta to be a communist manoeuvre to bring the opposition together and then dominate it. Accordingly they stayed clear of the Junta despite the urgent need for the opposition to co-ordinate at this stage.

Instead the PSOE promoted its own version — Plataforma de Convergencia Democratica — which attracted Ruiz-Jiminez and his left-wing Christian Democrats and the small christian marxist group, ORT. UGT also threw its weight behind the Plataforma. Even after Franco's death the two groups found it hard to go beyond mere verbal acceptance of their common interest in uniting to provide a common front in negotiations on the future nature of Spain.

Eventually the PSOE overcame its reluctance and the two groups agreed to merge, forming Coordinacion Democratica on 26 March 1976. This gave Spaniards the first concrete evidence that the Francoist opposition, both internal and external, was capable of being moderate, so undermining the monstrous image painted by the dictatorship's propaganda. Coordinacion Democratica called for a 'democratic' break with the former regime. In practice, this alliance acted as an umbrella to back increasingly open political activity on the part of the still banned political parties, rather than a united voice of the new democratic order. The parties were too preoccupied with building their own positions.

The PSP insisted on fighting the first elections alone. Tierno Galvan was one of the known 'personalities' in the electoral contest. Confronting the young, untested Felipe, the PSP drew away potential votes and confused some socialist supporters. The PSP obtained 4·5% of the vote and four seats in the Cortes. Combined with that of the PSOE this would have raised the total socialist vote to 33·9% — only 1% lower than UCD. Confronted with a limited future as a minority party the PSP agreed to merge with the PSOE, which itself had every interest in presenting a united socialist front. Tierno Galvan became the PSOE mayor of Madrid in 1979 in the first municipal elections.

The absorption of the PSP left the PSOE leadership unchanged. Indeed the leadership which took control after the Suresnes Congress was the same that led the party to victory eight years later in October 1982. The dominant element has been the 'Seville mafia' — the group consisting of Gonzalez and his colleagues that made contact in Andalusia in the late sixties. Their public positions in 1983 speak for themselves. Gonzalez remained the party leader but his duties as Prime Minister made this a nominal role compared to the level of activity expected of him when he was heading the opposition. Guerra, deputy Prime Minister and number two in the party, acted as the co-ordinator between the cabinet and the party apparatus, regarding himself as the PSOE's conscience inside government. Rafael Escuredo was head of the autonomous government of Andalusia, while Luis Yañez was head of the Instituto de Cooperacion Ibero-Americano and the Prime Minister's personal liaison with Latin America.

Despite the longevity of this group's control over the party, the average age in 1983 of the twenty-five-person Executive Commission was just under forty-one. The oldest member of the first socialist cabinet was the Foreign Minister, Fernando Moran, aged fifty-eight. He was originally a member of the PSP. Significantly, only two of the Executive Commission members had worker backgrounds, one being Redondo of the UGT; 36% of members were academics, 16% lawyers, and 12% economists.[10]

THE TRIUMPH OF SOCIAL DEMOCRACY

A major step in the PSOE's advance to power was the elimination of all reference to marxism and class struggle in the party manifesto. This was the work of Gonzalez and Guerra who were convinced that, so long as a marxist label could be stuck to the party, it would never break into the middle ground of the electorate. As early as 1973, Guerra had established his own unit to study electoral tactics and the PSOE was the first party to take psephology seriously. The first book dealing with electoral attitudes was by Jose Maria Maravall, the Oxford educated first socialist Minister of Education.[11]

While Guerra and Gonzalez were preparing to convert the PSOE into a party ready to govern, the first legal congress in 1976 had reaffirmed the heritage of the grandfather of socialism, Pablo Iglesias. One resolution reasserted that the PSOE was a party that believed in the class struggle and drew its inspiration from marxism. Many approved this on traditional grounds but at least 25% believed that the PSOE, as its name proclaimed, was a workers' party. The latter group's views were imperiously ignored the following year when the PSOE fought its first elections. The party's electoral propaganda concentrated on presenting a competent but moderate party, loyal to its boyish looking leader. (Felipe Gonzalez then wore an open necked shirt on the posters — by 1982 he was wearing a tie.)

The PSOE's relative success in the elections revealed many closet Socialists. A study in 1982 showed that 49% of PSOE members had joined the party *after* the 1977 elections; a further 32% had joined between the death of Franco and the elections.[12] More than two thirds of the party membership had joined as a result of the change in regime and the legalization of political parties. In the main it was a middle class affiliation, conscious of the need to create greater social justice in society, but fearful of radical change. The emphasis was on realism rather than idealism. When asked whether socialist measures should be introduced gradually or rapidly, 76% of members favoured a gradual approach. Only 19% wanted rapid change and these were predominantly of an older generation with experience of the Republic. The new members reflected the moderation and caution produced by the improvement in living standards during the sixties and early seventies which had given the working class and the expanded middle class a vested interest in not rocking the boat too hard.

In May 1978, Gonzalez first hinted that he would drop marxism from the PSOE programme. Backstage, Guerra began systematically weeding out left-wing dissidents from the party's national and regional organization. Guerra showed he could be every bit as ruthless as the much-criticised Communists. By the time of the party's XXVIII congress in Madrid in May 1979, Gonzalez was ready to do battle to convert the PSOE into a north-European-style social democratic party. Strong opposition remained to the dilution of the party's left wing ideology. Party stalwarts disliked Guerra's hatchet work with dissidents and objected to the way Gonzalez was talking behind the scenes with the government. Some were nostalgic for the Republic and had yet to accept the ease with which the PSOE had embraced the nationalist flag and the monarchy.[13]

The congress was a clash between the old and the new PSOE, between the wild echoes of Largo Caballero and a hard-headed, technocratic leadership. Gonzalez's critics were impatient, convinced that his strategy of moderation had weakened the party at the expense of the PCE. There was circumstantial justification for this view. The combined vote of the PSOE and PSP in the 1979 general elections dropped slightly to only 30%. Faced with critics who refused to endorse the party's political report, Gonzalez resigned. He called his critics' bluff, calculating boldly, but correctly, that they merely wanted to bring him to order. He knew that no-one else had the charisma to lead the party. From the moment of his resignation, it was clear his move had paid off. At a special congress in September, Gonzalez was re-elected on his own terms. He expunged the word marxism from the party's manifesto and had a free hand to shape the party in his own image. Without this fundamental shift in the party, the PSOE would never have enjoyed power.

This, combined with his own personality, was the key to the PSOE's electoral success in 1982. The collapse of UCD was a contributory factor, not a determining one. His own image of integrity and credibility and his capacity to communicate with a crowd or a television audience were vital assets. The PSOE electoral programme was carefully tailored to avoid doctrinaire policies. Nationalization was only mentioned in relation to the high tension grid network: the rest boiled down to a promise to reform the administration and introduce greater morality in public life. It could have been the programme of any moderate European centre party. The result was a massive 10 million votes for the Socialists.

Less than half these were true 'socialist' votes. Indeed Spain now has the Socialist Party with the lowest ratio of members to votes — 1:100 compared to 6:100 in West Germany and 5:70 in Britain.[14] The same phenomenon was evident in the 1983 municipal and autonomous parliament elections where the PSOE attracted a sufficiently wide vote to control two thirds of the provincial capitals and eleven of the thirteen autonomous parliaments.

The party still refers to itself as the Socialist Workers Party, yet it has succeeded precisely because it is no longer a workers party, but one that reflects the middle class aspirations of decency and social justice of the majority of Spaniards. The 'socialist' core remains, however, and will trouble the party's conscience for some time.[15]

CARRILLO AND EUROCOMMUNISM

While Gonzalez and his colleagues accurately assessed the mood of the electorate, Carrillo misjudged it. Fernando Claudin, the most coherent ideologue ever produced by the party (and expelled for being such), has pointed out how Carrillo believed the main enemy in 1977 was Fraga and AP. This was the gut reaction of a man geared to think of Spain in terms of Franco and Francoism. Claudin comments icily that Carrillo's assessment was odd coming from a man who for years had talked of the imminence of a national uprising to overthrow Franco: Carrillo was now saying, in essence, that the danger to Spain was popular endorsement of Fraga and right wing conservatism!

Carrillo was careful not to attack Suarez but was scathing about the

PSOE — Gonzalez was just a *chico* (kid). He trumpeted the virtues of Eurocommunism, explaining how the PCE was liberated from the guiding hands of Moscow. Stalinism had been locked in the cupboard of history. Carrillo was convinced that this line, combined with his and the party's record of opposition to Franco, would prove irresistible to the electorate.[16] Having hoped to pick up at least 20% of the vote, the PCE in 1977 got just below 10%, with 1·7 million votes. Over 500,000 of these came from the PSUC in Catalonia.

Inside Spain, the Communist Party had always been small. Primo de Rivera considered it so insignificant that he did not even bother to ban its newspaper when he set up his dictatorship. Its size at the time of the Civil War was out of all proportion to its influence and the impact it made both in the domestic media (on both sides) and internationally. In the aftermath of the Civil War, the Francoist press devoted exaggerated attention to its antics because the regime had a paranoid fear of Moscow's destabilizing influence.

Because the party was small and less visible, the heavy hand of repression fell on other groups like the Socialists and Anarchists. Without in any way denigrating the courage and perseverance of communist members in struggling against the regime, it is probably true to say that the party itself was deluded about its own importance.

The PCE leadership was given a grandiose sense of its own position in the world. They were courted by Moscow, anxious to retain a firm foothold in Spain when Franco disappeared; and in most socialist countries they were treated as government representatives would have been. They were a privileged elite. Meanwhile, continual politicking and the PCE's role in the international communist community provided a great deal of activity and considerable experience. All of this tended to flatter Carrillo and make him believe that one day he would return, like Lenin to the Finland station.[17]

There were a number of problems with this scenario. The bulk of the leadership had gone into exile in the Soviet Union, including Dolores Ibarruri, *La Pasionaria*, and therefore regarded the Soviet Union as the bulwark against the onslaught of fascism, the sole true friend of Spain. Stalin was so revered as a godfather figure, that it took a long time for even the more enlightened members to see his errors. Some never did. The PCE leadership-in-exile also got caught up in its own sectarian world and began to ignore what was really happening inside Spain. Due notice was not taken that armed struggle had failed and that the natural contradictions of the fascist dictatorship had not, as according to marxist logic it should have, provoked its downfall.

The first to question blind allegiance to the Soviet Communist Party, Stalinism, and the PCE's ignorance of socio-economic change inside Spain, were expelled in 1964. These were Claudin and Jorge Semprun, one of the party's best activists inside Spain. Not until 1968, with the Soviet invasion of Czechoslovakia, did Carrillo take stock and distance the PCE from the

179

dictates of the Soviet Party — this was eight years after he had succeeded *La Pasionaria* as secretary-general. He then began to apply some of the once heretical arguments of Claudin and Semprun, which marked the beginning of the PCE's Eurocommunism. The idea of revolutionary struggle was played down and the PCE envisaged co-operation with other progressive parties in a pluralistic system as a justifiable step towards the establishment of true socialism.

The principal strength of the PCE still lay in its control of the Workers Commissions which were the main trades union force in Spain at the time of Franco's death. The Party had also been active in penetrating *asociaciones de vecinos* which had grown up, semi-tolerated, as neighbourhood pressure groups, especially in the working class districts of the big cities. At the same time, the PCE had successfully recruited among the student community. But the leadership failed to realize the extent of the socio-economic changes that were taking place.

At the time of the 1977 elections, the thirty-five strong party executive had an average age of fifty-five. Carrillo was sixty-two, *La Pasionaria* eighty-two (both having returned after just under forty years outside the country). The secretary-general of the PSUC, Gregorio Lopez Raimundo, was sixty-four, the head of the Basque section of the party, Ramon Ormazabal, sixty-six, and Marcelino Camacho, the much-imprisoned trades union leader, fifty-nine.

There was a highly 'presentable' younger generation like the economist and academic Ramon Tamames (who had surprised the Madrid establishment with the revelation of his PCE membership) and Nicolas Sartorius, an aristocrat turned trades unionist. But they were kept on the sidelines while Carrillo continued to exercise absolute control, as if the party were still operating in secret. Out of touch, and badly affected by the impact of events in both Chile and Portugal, the PCE had serious problems of image. While the PSOE recognized the need to make a party of the left acceptable to the electorate, the PCE was more presumptuous. Carrillo swore to support the monarchy, accepted the nationalist flag, surrendered all thought of revolutionary change, and fascinated people as a political animal, but the communist option which he personified was unattractive.

If Carrillo's eurocommunist colleagues, especially the PCI in Italy, had fared better during this time, then his credibility might have increased. Indeed the Eurocommunist option appeared increasingly less possible. Worse, Carrillo found himself supporting a centre right government for the privilege of being the Communist Party in Spanish democracy. Marxist-leninism was dropped from the party's ideology. The contradictions increased between a supposedly revolutionary party co-operating with a bourgeois state, while the party was run on Stalinist lines of personal control by Carrillo. His unwillingness to modernize and make the party more democratic led to the steady exodus of its most enlightened cadres.

The major break came in November 1981 when the main reforming elements in the party, who believed in Eurocommunism, were expelled. Carrillo used the excuse of their support for a breakaway alliance between reforming elements in the Basque Communist Party and Euskadiko Euskerra.[18] Similar tensions occurred with the PSUC which itself was torn between those faithful to Carrillo, to the Moscow of old, Catalan nationalism and Eurocommunism. In these internal disputes, Carrillo demonstrated that he preferred a small loyal party to a large 'free' one. As a result of this attitude, the party was in a shambles for the 1982 elections. The vote fell to just over 800,000, 4%, half that of 1977. This residual communist vote either stood for a nostalgic view of the past or a simple rejection of the Socialists as being too middle-of-the-road.

Unrepentant, Carrillo resigned from the position of secretary-general in November 1982, forty-six years after joining the PCE. He handed over to an energetic but unimpressive young Asturian, Gerardo Iglesias, carefully selected to follow in his own mould. Despite the tremendous personal protagonism of Carrillo — 'the old fox' as he liked to be known — and his many errors, it is doubtful whther the PCE has appeal in modern Spain; the attention it receives still far exceeds its importance. In western Europe a communist party with pretensions to size is a media event because of the fear cum fascination of communism — the PCE has been viewed in this light. The sole national strength of the party lies in its control of the CCOO, though in Catalonia, the PSUC gives it limited parliamentary importance. The PSOE will never ally with the Communists unless absolutely necessary, as after the 1979 municipal elections. At best this was an uneasy pact, and was not formally renewed in 1983.

Claudin goes so far as to suggest that the label 'communist' has been irredeemably sold out by the behaviour of communist parties in power. 'With such a label, it seems highly unlikely that any relevant role can be played in the struggle to introduce socialism in advanced capitalist societies.'[19]. To the party faithful this may sound like jaded judgement from one who feels betrayed; but in the case of Spain, Claudin seems close to the mark. The lost communist vote has not been going further to the left, but to the PSOE.

RADICALS AND EXTREMISTS

So long as the PCE is incapable of adapting and the PSOE continues to occupy the centre in Spanish politics, there is a gap for a democratic party of the left. The plethora of small but active left wing parties that blossomed in the twilight of Francoism have burned up their energy and are unlikely to help fill this gap. The Anarchists too, once so strong, have all but vanished.

These small left wing groups were a direct product of youthful frustration

181

over the permanence of the Franco regime and the ineffectiveness of the recognized opposition. They resulted from the lack of attention given youth by the former regime and the process of alienation caused by the accelerating industrialization and urbanization. The ill-digested texts of Trotsky, and selective precepts of marxist-leninism and Maoism became easy slogans of discontent. One of the better organized groups was the Partido de Trabajo Español (PTE), which acquired a sizeable following in neighbourhood associations and in some rural parts of Andalusia.

The advent of democracy with the consequent opening up of society removed much of the raison d'être of this extremism on the left. The leaders of these groups mellowed as they were co-opted into democracy. The PTE, which made a determined showing in the 1979 municipal elections, did not even offer itself as a party in 1983. Many former PTE militants moved to the PSOE. Indeed, the PSOE rather than the PCE has absorbed many of these people.

Extreme left wing groups have ceased to have any political significance other than those who have spawned terrorist movements. The shadowy terrorist group, GRAPO, was founded primarily by former members of the Ligua Comunista (Revolucionaria).

The exception to the rule, is at the regional level in the Basque country, Catalonia, and to a lesser extent Galicia. The Basque country has produced an authentic non-communist party of the left — Euskadiko Euskerra — and a radical nationalist coalition, marxist inspired, Herri Batasuna. These are specific phenomena of the Basque country and have grown up as a result of the fierce repression of the Basques by the former regime, fuelled by long-standing nationalist feelings. Herri Batasuna, advocating separatism and acting as the political front for the hardline military wing of ETA, was still banned at the time of the 1977 general elections. But it was able to contest seats in 1979 gaining three and 173,000 votes in the provinces of Alava, Guipuzcoa, Navarra, and Vizcaya. This solid vote was a reflection of Basque separatist sentiment and frustration over the central government's unwillingness to accept or understand Basque demands. It also picked up a 'green' vote. Herri Batasuna has repeatedly refused to take its seats in the Cortes. Although the number of their votes rose to 210,000 in 1982, its share of seats dropped to two (again not used). However, in Guipuzcoa province the coalition still accounted for 19% of the total vote.

Euskadiko Euskerra (EE) was founded in the belief that a parliamentary party of the left could articulate radical nationalist sentiment and offer an alternative to violent separatism. In all three elections EE has managed to return one deputy, Juan Maria Bandres, who has been vociferous in his denunciation of torture, police excess, and in his advocacy of human rights. In 1981, EE sought to merge with the Basque Communist Party. Faced with Carrillo's refusal to endorse this alliance, the more progressive members followed their local secretary-general, Roberto Lerchundi, in forming a breakaway alliance with EE. In the 1982 general election, this alliance gained 100,000 votes, polling 9% in Guipuzcoa, its main stronghold.

In Catalonia the equivalent of EE is Esquerra Republicana — the sole party to achieve parliamentary representation with a republican label. This was a coalition of the Catalan left formed in the mid thirties, headed by a dashing former army Colonel and outright nationalist, Francisco Macia. After the 1930 municipal elections which ushered in the Republic, and in which Esquerra triumphed, Macia declared an independent Catalan Republic. The party believed in the socialization of wealth and only the Catalan slant prevented Esquerra from being openly marxist. Persecuted after the Civil War (Luis Companys, its Civil War leader, was shot) Esquerra lost ground to the PSUC which was more active in recruiting the younger generation. Once legalized, its appeal proved a shadow of its former self. It managed one deputy in all three general elections, mustering in 1982, 138,000 votes. Esquerra has a small offshoot in Valencia.

Together the non-communist left vote in the Basque country and Catalonia amounts to 450,000 — 2% of the total votes cast in 1982. This is not insignificant. To this can be added the two left-of-centre nationalist parties in Galicia — Bloque PSG and Exquerra Gallega — which between them won 60,000 votes.

The remarkable feature of parties to the right of Fraga and AP is their insignificance as theoretical heirs of Franco and the nationalist victory. The Falange and the Carlists were the sole tolerated movements and yet with the advent of democracy they have dwindled almost to extinction. They account for less than 1% of the vote. The tradition of the Falange and its fascist and neo-fascist splinter movements is drawn from their Civil War martyr Jose Antonio's semi-romantic, semi-violent view of national socialism. Social justice is to be achieved through the corporatist, centralized, Catholic state. The Falange were numerically small at the outbreak of the Civil War but its para-military gangs and vague fascist ideology made it the most aggressive and serviceable grouping on the nationalist side. The execution of Jose Antonio by the Republicans added a ready-made hero.

Franco kept a careful hold on the Falange after the Civil War. Social and economic change gradually diluted its fascism and weakened its support base. On Franco's death the fascists were slow to react, unable to understand or unwilling to contemplate the direction in which Spain was moving. They congregated round two main figures — the lawyer, Blas Pinar, and the long time Franco Minister of Labour, Jose Antonio Giron de Velasco. The latter had helped form the Juntas de Ofensiva Nacional-Sindicalista (JONS) in the thirties which merged with the Falange. In 1979, Blas Pinar managed to stand on a coalition ticket, Union Nacional, with his own Fuerza Nueva as one of the principal groupings. He won the coalition's sole seat in Madrid and Union Nacional obtained 378,000 votes throughout Spain. The coalition's platform appealed blatantly to nostalgia for the former regime, without explaining the virtues of national socialism and the corporatist state. By 1982, internal divisions obliged Fuerza Nueva to go to the polls alone and their vote was cut by a third; Pinar lost his seat.

In 1982 these fascist and neo-fascist groups were divided on the issue of whether to continue on the fringes of parliamentary activity. Some argued more could be achieved by voting for AP than acting in isolation on the basis of what was essentially a negative and protest vote. Others believed that groups like Fuerza Nueva had a future and should retain their identity. A third lot insisted that parliamentary activity in the current shape of Spanish democracy was meaningless. The most suitable action was outside parliament, using violence if necessary. As a result of these disagreements, Fuerza Nueva disbanded in 1982.

The main significance of the extreme right has been its links with unreconstructed Francoists and Falangists inside the armed forces. The tentative plot uncovered in September 1982 envisaged co-operation between rebel officers and groups of para-military civilians.

However, if voting is an indication, the party formed round the former Guardia Civil officer, Antonio Tejero, revealed the paucity of support in 1982. Solidaridad Española was a deliberate snub to the democratic system. All those who felt like Tejero had a chance to show their feelings. Only 28,000 did. At the same time, three Falange parties got less than 10,000 votes between them.

The extreme right is not a countrywide phenomenon but tends to survive off a few secure bases — especially in Madrid, Seville, Valencia and Valladolid (a fascist stronghold where in 1936 the Falange rose one day early). Spain, nevertheless, has probably the largest number of fascist and neo-fascist sympathizers in western Europe — even if their number is on the decline.

REGIONALISM AND POLITICS

There are no regional parties of the extreme right because of the latter's belief in the unity and centralized nature of Spain. The phenomenon of strong regional parties does, however, extend to cover conservative nationalists. These parties exist to defend regional interests against the demands of the central government, and in this sense they are defensive and inward looking. They are rooted in those regions where the sense of historical identity is strongest and where the central government is viewed with the greatest reserve — the Basque Country and Catalonia. In the case of the Basques and Catalans, the tradition dates back to the late nineteenth century. These two regions also happened to possess the broadest middle class at the time. Though primarily bourgeois, their nationalism made them, to an extent, classless. Having flourished under the Republic, these parties owe their present following to Franco's suppression of Basque and Catalan culture, accompanied by a residual mistrust of Madrid's centralist mentality. Their prime function has been as vehicles to recover historic cultural identities. In the Cortes they tend to be ideological mavericks willing to trade votes on issues which, by inclination, they would oppose in order to gain support for specific Basque and Catalan gains.

The oldest surviving regional party is the PNV, founded in 1894 by the Basque nationalist Sabino de Arana. The PNV attracted the support of some wealthy Bilbao industrialists like Ramon de la Sota (see Chapter Four) who helped to bankroll it. But for the most part the PNV relied on lesser merchants, teachers and small holders who mixed strong nationalism with a deep sense of catholicism. The PNV deliberately sought to set Basques apart from their fellow Spaniards and in this its credo was quasi-racist, extolling Basque superiority and ethnic difference. It also set up its own trades union, ELA/STV, which began more as a social welfare organisation for the Basque working class.

For purely tactical reasons, the PNV supported the Republic and was drawn into the Civil War on the republican side to ensure their autonomy statute. During this time, the PNV was the dominant force in the region. Its superior organization and the loyalty of its members ensured that it survived the dictatorship better than any of the other banned 'national' parties in the region. The *aberzale* (radical) element of Basque nationalism that was to produce first ETA and then Herri Batasuna was spawned from within the PNV ranks. This schism did not lose PNV its grass roots support. At its founding, the PNV had built many community centres and special halls for the teaching of Basque. The PNV was, in a sense, a club offering the benefits of mutual support to its members.

It is an interesting reflection on Spanish political parties that the only two of long standing that survived through to 1975 with grass roots support were those that established links with the community — the PSOE with its *casas del pueblo* and the PNV with its *Bazokis*.

A feature of the PNV is the internal democracy of its organization, and the separation of powers between its executive and the National Assembly which lays down policy. The Assembly contains representatives from local associations who have considerable administrative autonomy. It also has stricter rules on the rotation of office than any other party. The proof of the success of the PNV policy is in its pull at the poles. In elections to the Basque parliament in 1980, it picked up 38% of the vote with twenty-five seats, while the 'national' parties won only nineteen seats between them. Little can be done in the Basque country without PNV co-operation. In the 1982 general elections, the PNV averaged 32% of the vote; this performance improved in the 1983 municipal elections, indicating the allegiance of a solid 30% of the Basque electorate. The nationalist parties polled approximately half the electorate, and this proportion would probably be higher but for the high number of immigrants that have come to the Basque country.

In Catalonia the first modern nationalist party was founded by Prat de la Riba in 1902. Interestingly it did not invoke Catalonia in its title, Lliga Regionalista, which sought to underline the less fanatical Catalan approach to regionalism. The Lliga also differed from the PNV in the greater looseness of its organization, its more overtly middle class tone, and the lesser importance of catholicism. It was eagerly embraced by Catalan businessmen, and it acquired the financier and politician, Francisco Cambo, as its leader. Under Cambo's leadership the Lliga developed a more outward looking approach, the party seeking to make an impact on the wider Spanish stage and influence national policy. The Lliga, unlike the PNV, had to compete with other Catalan nationalist parties and, under the Republic, was constantly in danger of being outflanked by more radical policies.

It did not survive the Civil War. Its nearest heir today is Convergencia i Unio (CiU). This party is a coalition forged by Jordi Pujol founder of the Catalana bank group and a man with a consistent record of promoting Catalan separatism under the former regime. In 1974, Pujol founded Convergencia Democratica de Catalunya (CDC) which soon attracted other Catalan groupings of a liberal or conservative bent. The coalition process broadened in 1979 when CDC merged with Unio Democratic per Catalunya.

CiU is less of an inter-class party than the PNV. It has little penetration in the trades unions and its heartland is not so much Barcelona as Gerona. The size of CiU's vote reflects the extent of the Catalan middle class. In 1982 CiU polled 700,000 votes, only 100,000 less than the PCE nationwide. In the 1980 elections for the Catalan parliament, CiU obtained the largest share of the vote, 27% against 22% for the Socialists. The party has been active in the Cortes, especially Miguel Roca Junyent, who has championed the idea of an enlightened conservative grouping that would embrace nationalist parties.

In general, the Catalan Nationalists have shown more interest in influencing national policy in Madrid; but the power of the PNV and CiU in Madrid depends upon the working majority of the ruling party in parliament. Under Suarez and Calvo Sotelo, when UCD was always in search of a good working majority, these parties could use their support to obtain concessions for their own regions. The sweeping socialist majority has removed this influence, albeit temporarily.

Nationalist parties cannot be ignored, if only because they are latent vehicles of local discontent. The 'national' parties have been obliged to pay more than lip service to regionalism by either creating regional associations as federations, or by giving the association a clear regional name. Even AP, so totally committed to the centralist ethos, has baptized its regional associations. Except in the Basque country and Catalonia, no regional party now has sufficient support to elect a deputy to the Cortes, but they are in evidence in municipal and regional parliamentary elections.

The most remarkable party has been the Partido Socialista de Andalucia (PSA) which enjoyed a brief period of prominence from 1977 to 1981. Promoted by Fernando Abril as a weapon to steal socialist votes in their heartland of Andalusia, the PSA articulated an appealing brand of nationalism via its leader, Alejandro Rojas Marcos. He concentrated on Andalusia's poverty and the way the state had ignored Andalusian culture and economic development. Rojas Marcos not only managed to get elected to the Cortes, but, in the Catalan parliament elections, PSA candidates managed to win seats representing Andalusian emigrants — the 'Andelans'. By 1982, the PSOE in Andalusia had got the full measure of the PSA. In the Andalusian parliamentary elections the PSA only got three of the 109 seats compared to the Socialists' sixty-six. In the general elections, the PSA ceased to be a serious force.

The strong showing of the PSOE countrywide appeared to halt the rise in support for regional or nationalist parties — suggesting that a party offering greater understanding of national problems removed potential support. Small regional parties exist in Aragon, the Baleares, the Canaries, Extremadura, Galicia, Leon, Navarra and Valencia. Of the fifty-seven parties contesting the 1982 elections thirty-three were regional. If the national parties neglect these regions, there is always room for a resurgence of a local party — especially if there is a strong local personality. Until now most of the strong local personalities have seen more political mileage in bigger 'national' parties.

9 The Military: Nostalgia and Reform

The strongest opposition to any form of decentralization, and indeed to democracy, has always come from the armed forces. They were a central pillar of the Franco regime, which placed such emphasis on national unity, being extensively involved in government and ensuring order. Confused by the advent of democracy and reluctant to see their privileges eroded, the military adapted slowly and with difficulty to the post-Franco era. They remain a separate caste, unintegrated with society and upholding the values of the army that was victorious in the Civil War. The military have been considerably disturbed by terrorist violence and threats from Basque nationalism, and their discontent expressed itself in the serious coup attempt of February 1981.

How does one define being a hostage? Were the members of parliament hostages when held at gunpoint for eighteen hours on 23 and 24 February 1981? This seemingly innocent semantic quibble provoked the most serious incident in the court martial of the thirty-two officers and one civilian charged for the attempted coup.

When General Jose Saenz de Santa Maria, head of the police at the time of the coup, was called to give evidence, he likened the seizure of parliament to a hijacked aircraft in which the passengers were held hostage. One of the defence council, angered by such an infamous imputation to the accused, asked him to repeat this. He did. Tension quickly mounted as several of the accused officers got up from their seats and left the courtroom without bothering to ask permission. The most senior officer on trial, General Milans del Bosch, pulled himself erect bristling with anger, and began shouting; but his voice was lost without a microphone. The Court Martial's presiding judge, General Alvarez Rodriguez, ordered him to sit down in a flustered voice. With a disrespectful gesture of the hand Milans del Bosch resumed his seat. Immediately some of the families of the accused and the military observers left the courtroom, purposely banging the doors. Several lawyers also began packing their papers ostentatiously and leaving. Only one deigned to inform the president of his intention to leave. Saenz de Santa Maria stood expectantly, then said in a low loud voice that he would withdraw the metaphor of the hostage.

At this point, Milans del Bosch walked stiffly towards one of the microphones and in an excited voice announced: 'I wish to leave; I don't feel well.

188

This whole performance gives me nausea. It makes me sick. I'm off!' And he walked out, totally ignoring the presiding judge's orders. No one dared stop this rebel general, whose service record early on in the trial had taken over an hour to read. Several of the the remaining lawyers asked for the session to be suspended. Alvarez Rodriguez had little option since attendance had degenerated to something close to a mockery.

When the session resumed the next day, Alvarez Rodriguez issued a firm call to order, but he sanctioned no-one. Furthermore, for the sake of peace, Saenz de Santa Maria agreed to retract his hijack and hostage metaphor, admitting that it had unfortunate connotations.

The Court Martial, which lasted from 19 February to 24 May 1982, highlighted two completely different concepts of society. For the upholders of democracy, the army officers had behaved no better than terrorists seeking to hold the state to ransom, and they deserved to be punished accordingly. For a section of the military establishment and civilian right wing extremists, these were honourable soldiers bravely performing their patriotic duty to save Spain from terrorism, immorality, separatism and the grip of communism. It was a clear divide between the two Spains, between that part of society that had evolved and modernized, and the other which refused to understand change. The walkout on Saenz de Santa Maria, an open insult by one of the most decorated officers in the Armed Forces, underscored the divide. Saenz de Santa Maria had been unequivocal in his loyalty to the democratic order on 23 February, ensuring that the National Police were immediately at the disposal of the government.

The court martial revealed the limited extent to which the military, as an institution, had been incorporated into the democratic process. This was the first major military trial since the Sanjurjo uprising in 1932. Still there was no separation of powers, and military judges presided over their fellow officers. At times it was hard to tell who was in control, who on trial. From their plush velvet chairs the accused were allowed to fling hearsay accusations at the King without interruption. Democracy was blamed for forcing them to take action. They were always addressed with deference, and their families were permitted to cheer and barrack. On one occasion, the accused took offence at an article published in *Diario 16* and refused to attend the session until the paper's editor was ejected from court. The court was unwilling to force the accused to attend but agreed to expel the journalist from the courtroom (to loud cheers from the relatives).

The military judges, all senior generals or admirals, had, in their youth, rebelled against the established order and rallied to the nationalist cause. It was not easy to judge such men when they claimed to have acted for patriotic motives. Lopez Montero, the defence lawyer for Tejero, poignantly raised the issue of Alfonso XIII and General Primo de Rivera in 1923. Montero argued that it only required one word from the King, and Primo de Rivera and his supporters would have been considered rebels. But faced with an impotent government, Alfonzo XIII went against the constitution and backed Primo de Rivera. Rebels had become patriots. As if to remind the court of this, Milans del Bosch's ninety-two-year-old father attended the trial from time to time. Himself a general, he had supported both Primo de Rivera and Sanjurjo and was now in honourable retirement.

It was not surprising that the sentences imposed by the court martial were considered light by the politicians. Only two officers, Milans del Bosch and Tejero received the maximum sentence demanded by the prosecution — thirty years each. Of the rest, eleven were acquitted, mostly on the grounds of obeying superior orders; some sentences were reduced on consideration being given to officers acting for patriotic motives.

Totally different criteria emerged in 1983 when the civilian Supreme Court delivered judgement on the prosecution's appeal against the sentence. The Supreme Court in April rejected the concept of obeying superior orders when such obedience went against the constitution. The Court also found Armada fully responsible as the political head of the plot, and raised his sentence from six years to thirty accordingly. Overall, twenty-two of the thirty-three sentences were increased and eight of the eleven acquittals were overturned. Milans, Tejero, and Armada lost their ranks and were expelled from the service. This was the first time that a civilian court had heard an appeal from a court martial, and also the first time that civil courts overturned and reinterpreted military justice.[1]

THE 'PRONUNCIAMIENTO'

Tejero was not the first Spanish officer to threaten parliament. It first occurred in 1843 and on a more famous occasion in 1874 when General Pavia used army units to dislodge parliament. Then, riding on horseback to the Cortes, he forced the formation of a new (and very brief) government. From 1814 to 1936, Spain witnessed no less than fifty-four attempts by the military or groups of officers to alter or overthrow existing governments. Only twelve were successful.[2]

Such intervention has a ready explanation. In the nineteenth century the military were the only effective arm of the central government. Indeed, the military almost monopolised the state, absorbing in the 1850s over 60% of the budget and accounting for 90% of all its employees. The military had also inherited a tradition whereby they regarded themselves as both the ultimate repository and guarantor of national values and national sovereignty. Confronted by weak monarchies, dynastic squabbles and corrupt politicians, the military could not remain idle spectators for long. Those that intervened were by no means all reactionaries. Liberal ideas had filtered in from northern Europe, and the War of Independence had resulted in a shake-up in the composition of the army. Many of the figures to emerge from this were essentially popular, even untrained and non-professional soldiers who had been 'guerilla' leaders harassing the extended lines of the occupying French army.

In the nineteenth century those that intervened were reluctant to accept the consequences of their actions. Instead of using intervention as a direct attempt to assume political power, it was conceived much more as a corrective to the steering wheel of state. A group of officers would rebel and 'pronounce' (hence the *pronunciamiento*) what they wanted the politicians to do. Even Pavia had no intention of governing himself; at one stage during his occupation of parliament he *threatened* to govern when exasperated at the politicians' inability to agree among themselves. The success of the *pronunciamiento* depended on the power of the rebels to intimidate and the capacity of the politicians to implement what they demanded. Since the military were rarely prepared to move from their watch-dog role, the failure rate was high. But equally, each failure encouraged another attempt without the reasons for the previous failure being fully studied. By the end of the nineteenth century a tradition of intervention had been imbued in the military which was hard to discard. The military's contempt for politicians had, if anything, increased after the loss of Cuba. At the same time, the officer class had lost its social mobility.

The Primo de Rivera rebellion in 1923 and the nationalist uprising in 1936 followed this tradition but with significant differences. In both instances senior officers rebelled to push the politicians aside and exercise power themselves. The rebels argued that civilian authority had ceased to function in the interests of Spain and had therefore lost its legitimacy. The rebels were arrogating the right to judge who best served Spain's interests. In both instances an important conflict arose within the military establishment over the legitimacy of the rebel actions. The military after all were bound by their royal regulations to support the established order. This division was of particular significance in 1936. Contrary to the nationalist propaganda, the armed forces were profoundly divided. The division was not so much on ideology, since their overall complexion was conservative, but over whether or not to obey the legitimate government — which meant obeying the republicans. This division was partly responsible for the drawn out nature of the Civil War.

In February 1981 the rebels were acting in the same tradition. There was no attempt at *pronunciamiento*. The rebels wanted to push the politicians aside. Significantly, in order to persuade the military commanders to support him, Milans del Bosch sought to invoke legitimacy. He argued that the seizure of parliament by Tejero had created a vacuum of power.

STAMP OF VICTORY

The Nationalists had expected their uprising to result in a quick rallying of the military to their cause. Since this failed to happen and the conflict spread throughout Spain, they were obliged to cobble together an ideology. It was crude, simplistic and virulent — a crusade of Catholic Spain to restore traditional values against the foreign-inspired conspiracy of communists, masons and libertarians. This ideology of the crusade, forged in the heat of battle, was converted into the faith of the new regime in peace. As the military led the crusade and had been responsible for victory, they became the natural guarantors of the fruits of victory. The military therefore retained this partisan and reactionary ideology.

In the wake of the Civil War a new type of officer emerged. During the conflict the ranks of the officer corps had been swelled by over 29,000 civilians on provisional commissions. Of these, some 4,000 were killed and nearly 10,000 were demoted after the fighting. However, 10,700 opted to stay on as regular officers. This was equivalent to forty-three graduations from the academy at Zaragoza.[4] There was no need for such a large officer intake once the armed forces were off a war footing; but the authorities took the political view that these people were worth humouring, a central element in their support. Frequently, those who opted to stay on and become regular officers were the most closely identified with the ideology of the regime, and became an important component within the officer corps. A study in 1969 revealed that only 241 senior officers had joined before the Civil War, while 3,710 had joined via temporary commissions and 6,848 came from military academies.[5]

The intake of new and, by origin, non-military blood was accompanied by a purge of the republican professional officers. Under laws passed in 1940, the Varela Laws, military tribunals were given a free hand to get rid of any officer or non-commissioned officer associated with the republican cause. Regardless of conduct or professional capacity, some 5,000 officers and NCOs were purged. This further ensured that the armed forces were a faithful mirror of the regime. The purge also extended into the ranks of the para-military Guardia Civil. For the most part, the Guardia Civil had remained loyal to the Republic, so Franco insisted on the appointment of the most nationalist army officers to run the corps and its vital nationwide distribution of barracks.

Homogeneity was ensured by blocking promotion or through dismissal from the service. The main challenge came from Franco's own peers — the men who had experienced the Republic, served under Alfonso XIII, and witnessed the defects of the Primo de Rivera dictatorship. Between 1939 and 1943, four leading nationalist generals were sanctioned or silenced, including the commander of the air force during the Civil War, General Alfredo Kindelan, who, in 1943, held a meeting with seven generals to propose a restoration of the monarchy.

Zaragoza was the first of the military academies to open after the Civil War. The academy, founded by Franco in 1927, had been given a stern decalogue of precepts. In the forefront was love of the motherland and sacrifice.[6] To this was now added the ethos of the victorious army, and the military vocabulary was thus permanently distorted. Companionship excluded republican comrades; discipline was in the face of the enemy (the Reds); honour became the clothing of nationalist dignity; loyalty was to Franco and the Movimiento. The further the Civil War was distanced from individual experience, the more this ethos was imbued, distinguishing 'good' Spaniards from 'bad'.

THE CIVILIAN/MILITARY DIVIDE

This military ethos would have mattered much less if the armed forces under Franco had become integrated into society. But as Spain began to feel the effects of liberalization in the sixties and seventies, the military remained 'uncontaminated', and consciously sought to remain so. In one notorious case as late as 1973, four cadets were expelled from Zaragoza for among other things fraternizing with soldiers (using the familiar first person), for experiencing a religious crisis and rejecting catholicism, for making friends with university students and discussing the reform of society, and for reading a series of modern books and magazines all legally published in Spain.[7]

From the fifties onwards the gap in terms of wealth and social habits between civilians and the military widened. Conscription provided only a partial counter-balance. Almost 80% of the entire strength of the armed forces was, and still is, composed of conscripts doing their national service. The continuous influx of young men from all social classes and backgrounds should have helped make the military more open. But there was nothing to suggest this happened. Fraternization between officers and men was discouraged, and the only political views tolerated were those in favour of the regime. Trouble-makers, especially students, were garrisoned in special areas. As long as Spain possessed the Sahara, this was a favourite centre of punishment.

Another consequence of economic development was the increased regional imbalance of career officers. The wealthier regions, like the two coastal Basque provinces and Catalonia, supplied fewer recruits. This trend became more pronounced so that the bulk of recruitment came from the impoverished regions like Castile, Extremadura and Galicia. In turn, the wealthier regions have become much less tolerant of militarism.

Regiments are not formed on a regional basis and lack any regional identity of the kind traditionally seen in the British Army. They are centrally organized to ensure that the army embraces a centralist spirit. Franco went so far as to prevent conscripts serving in their own regions wherever possible.

This principle was applied with particular rigour to Basque conscripts. The deliberate suppression of regional identities among regiments, coupled with the low profile of Basque and Catalan officers in the armed forces, also helps to explain the incomprehension among the military of demands for regional autonomy — especially of these two historic regions.

By civilian standards the military are poorly paid, and this has only been partially improved by fringe benefits. Like the bureaucracy as a whole, the armed forces have been overmanned and underpaid, anxious for high levels of remuneration but reluctant to shed surplus manpower. They have simply been too large, especially the officer corps, and the treasury too poor to support decent pay scales.

From the fifties, civilian salaries increasingly outstripped military ones. On average a middle-ranking officer received, and still receives, less than half the salary of a civilian executive with a similar responsibility over personnel and equipment. The general in charge of the Brunete Division, Spain's main front-line armoured corps, was getting a total remuneration of 169,000 pesetas a month in 1983, and this was after an important adjustment in pay scales made in 1978. An executive in an equivalent position would earn triple that amount.

The bureaucratic mentality which conditioned pay also affected work hours. Until 1978, the military nearly all finished work at lunchtime and could take a second job in the afternoon. In 1964 almost 65% of all staff officers had a second job, mainly in the civilian sector.[8] This percentage has dropped since 1978 when new regulations were introduced, but one of the more public examples of military *pluriempleo* as late as 1982 was Colonel Manuel Monzon, one time Defence Ministry spokesman, who was on the board of the air charter company, Spantax, and also ran his own public relations consultancy. Theoretically, such extra work should have incorporated the military more into civilian society but it seems to have merely made them more schizophrenic.

The system of double-jobs was possible because the armed forces had ceased to play a fighting role except against internal subversion and, on a very limited scale, in the enclave of Ifni on the Atlantic coast of Africa and the colony of Spanish Sahara. In 1945, the Spanish armed forces possessed some of the most experienced officers in Europe. Twenty years later the bulk of the officer corps were armchair fighters living in big cities. Patriotism, under these circumstances, tended to be exaggerated. The less they performed their functions as soldiers, the more they became patriotic and attached themselves to such symbols as the flag.

Most garrisons were in large cities or their suburbs, but the military were obliged to live in military compounds to take advantage of cheap housing. They shopped in special military discount stores, had military hospitals, military pharmacies, and military holiday camps. In addition, since military families were on the move, they took advantage of the free education offered in military schools where the most reactionary and fanatical form of pro-regime indoctrination was available. As a result of this community living,

194

there was a good deal of inter-marriage among service families, and a high degree of auto-recruitment within the services. In a study of the years 1964-68 the indices proved as high as 79% in the case of the army, 65% with the navy, and 56% with the air force.[9]

Since this study was made, the level of recruitment among people with service backgrounds has remained similar. The social composition of the 'officer class', however, has altered. The economic boom created unparalleled job opportunities in the civilian economy and attracted many potential recruits from military backgrounds. Poor pay, a restricted life, the increased social prestige of civilian jobs, and declining prospects for real soldiering, all combined to reduce the influx of those from traditional military families. Instead, a new element in officer recruitment emerged: sons of NCOs. Military careers for such persons were encouraged by the availability of free military education and the fact that an officer's career presented the best prospects of social advancement. In any society this segment of the population is normally reactionary and these officer recruits are now considered the most nostalgic, and potentially the most dangerous to democracy.[10] Such people were prominent in the 'Manifesto of the 100' issued in December 1981. This was a statement signed by 100 junior officers and NCOs timed to coincide with the third anniversary of the approval of the constitution. The manifesto complained about media treatment of the armed forces and defended the honour of those charged with the abortive coup of 23 February.

Under Franco the divide with civilian society never bothered the military. As the essential pillar of Franco's authoritarianism and the ultimate guardian of the fruits of the victory, they had no reason to complain, and even they saw themselves as a privileged set. Superficially this was the case; but their privileges were rich in form and often empty of real content. They kept control of public order and their own military establishment right through the Franco era, yet were bypassed in all important economic decisions that were to alter fundamentally the shape of Spain. They were given lots of medals and parades; but very little new equipment to perform the proper functions of defence. They were seduced into supporting the regime at the cost of their own independence and professional capacity.

Of the 114 ministers that served under Franco, forty were either professional soldiers or involved with the military establishment, such as military lawyers. This is a high proportion but needs some qualification. Until 1965 a rough balance of numbers between civilians and military was retained; but as the process of government became more technical and Spain developed economically and socially, the balance switched sharply in favour of civilian ministers.

The sheer numbers of the military in the cabinet were also deceptive. Franco never considered appointing a civilian to any of the defence portfolios, and thus, since there was a separate minister for each of the service arms, three military men were always automatically in the cabinet. The most important portfolio which remained in military hands until 1973 was that of Home Affairs which covered internal security. Other ministries in which the military held portfolios were Industry, the Movimiento, Public Works and Justice. None of the military ministers showed particular talent in their jobs and their choice frequently owed much more to their loyalty and the need to balance out the various factions supporting the regime.

Franco's faithful administrator and right-hand man since the early forties, Carrero Blanco, was a naval officer. Although he climbed the ranks of the navy to become a full admiral in 1966, he had been involved full time in political administrative work since 1945. He possessed a rigid military mentality, but he was not a representative of the military establishment, any more than Franco was in governing Spain. Carrero Blanco always did what was best for Franco. On the whole the military were spectators in the government once the regime felt itself properly established. The same applied to the important military presence in the Francoist Cortes where they were mostly symbolic representatives, with especial attention given to former members of the Blue Division. Similarly, the jobs handed out to the military in the public sector, mostly INI companies and defence related, were more often sinecures than professional appointments. Had those appointed taken their work seriously, the military establishments might have shown more interest in developing modern military industries. Franco himself was little interested in such things, his military experience having stopped at the Civil War. He never, for instance, really appreciated the very expensive investments required by the Air Force.[11]

The real power of the military under Franco lay in their control of public order tribunals, that covered such matters as public morality, the manning of the intelligence services and the militarization of the police and security forces. This identification with the repressive aspects of the regime did not affect the civilian members of the administration to nearly the same degree and helped set the military apart in the public eye.

DEMOCRATIC OFFICERS

At the end of August 1972 a group of twelve officers formed a secret society, the Democratic Military Union (UMD). The aim of the group was to work within the armed forces to establish a democratic regime. The UMD officers maintained that the armed forces had lost their legitimacy by serving the interests of the regime and not those of the people. The UMD was composed of officers, most of whose fathers had served with the nationalist forces. They themselves had joined the services well after the conflict. For instance, Major Luis Otero's father was shot by the Republicans, Major Guillermo Relien's father was prominent with the Nationalists in Catalonia while Captain

Restituto Valero Ramos was actually born inside the El Alcazar during the famous seige and was known as the 'baby of Alcazar'. They insisted on their loyalty to the armed forces and on their desire for change from within. This was no group of Nasserite officers. Although they themselves had no intention of being subversive, nevertheless their very aims and existence were a direct challenge to the system.

Ten of the UMD founders were from Barcelona, the remaining two came from Madrid. It was no accident that such a democratic movement should have been principally inspired by Catalans, the most socially advanced region with the closest links with Europe. Interestingly, UMD's roots go back to a Catholic organization promoting christian fellowship among the military academies. The organization, Forja (forge, the idea being to mould young men), was founded in 1948 by a devout army officer, Luis Pinella. Forja members began a magazine at Zaragoza and established a college at Campamento on the outskirts of Madrid. In 1958, following a meeting at Campamento attended by four captains, fifty-nine lieutenants and sixty cadets, Forja was dissolved by the authorities on the grounds that it was potentially subversive. In 1979, Pinella became the first head of the Zaragoza Military Academy to reform its teaching.[12]

Although Forja dissolved, individual contacts were maintained and three UMD founder members came originally from that organization. The Burgos Trials in 1970 were a catalyst in persuading these young officers of the need for change. The international publicity attracted by the military tribunals, which condemned five members of ETA to death, and the wave of political protest inside Spain highlighted the manner in which the military were still at the complete service of the regime.

UMD grew quickly, garnering support from captains in the army. It was most numerous in Catalonia, followed by Madrid, Galicia, and then Ceuta. The organization numbered about 300; but it was unheard of until July 1975, when the government suddenly announced the detention of first seven and then two more officers for belonging to UMD. The detentions were a rude shock to many within the military hierarchy who reacted as if their own sons had turned against them.

The arrested officers were imprisoned after a campaign of vilification within the military. Their trial via court martial went ahead in 1976, four months after Franco's death. Seven received sentences ranging from four to eight years in prison, coupled with expulsion from the armed forces. The heaviest sentence was handed out to the most senior officer, Major Otero — all were subsequently amnestied, but attempts to have them reinstated failed. The military establishment regarded them as traitors — and still refuses to change its mind. The UMD have no place in the armed forces of the crusade.

197

REFORMS AND DEMOCRACY

The UMD officers were the sacrificial lambs given by the infant democracy to propitiate the military. Their proposals for reform have been closely followed even though they themselves have been reduced to the role of spectators. (Some have become journalists commenting on the military, and provide the only real source of inside knowledge.) One of the principal proposals of the UMD was the unification of the three service arms under one ministry, the Defence Ministry. They laid great stress on improving the lot and responsibility of the NCOs, and demanded a sharp reduction in the scope of military jurisdiction and the elimination of Honour Tribunals and disciplinary tribunals in the military academies. They sought a reduction in the length of military service and an end to the politically orientated intelligence organisation in the armed forces (SIBE). They further demanded the creation of a unified intelligence service with specifically military and national defence aims. Another important reform was to confine the role of the captain-generals of the nine military regions to purely military matters.[13]

The UMD officers were not the first to try and reform the armed forces. The Minister of War in the Republic, Manuel Azana, realised that a thorough reform of the army was essential for the republican experiment. He set about making the officer corps more professional, made officers swear allegiance to the Republic and dismissed the captain-generals who could wield power like feudal barons. The length of military service was cut, the army based in Africa was slimmed down and the officer corps was reduced. He offered golden handshakes to anyone wishing to leave the services, and as a result eighty-four generals and 8,650 officers took advantage of the generous terms offered. These reforms were well-intentioned and undoubtedly correct in their general approach. Nevertheless, against a background of political polarization and breakdown of public order, the military felt threatened and saw Azaña as their enemy. This sense of being victimized influenced many officers to support the nationalist uprising.

Franco must have known that his armed forces were overmanned and inefficiently organized. He did nothing, partly out of inertia, partly as a deliberate policy. The experience of Azana had not been forgotten; and besides, it suited the Caudillo that the armed forces were cumbrous, because it would be difficult for them to be turned against him. The situation was typified by the deployment of the armed forces. The army was mostly deployed in or around Spain's big cities, which could easily be intepreted as a deliberate move to protect the regime by ensuring that such cities could always be controlled. While obviously a factor, it was no less important that the officers preferred living in the cities and would have protested vigorously if moved to a less agreeable environment.

The only person to attempt reform under Franco was General Diez

Alegria. When he took over the High Command in 1970 he wanted to limit the power of the captain-generals to control recruitment and logistics, to make military service more selective, and to rationalize troop deployment throughout Spain. He also sought to tackle the whole question of promotion and introduce the concept of selectivity in the senior ranks. Promotion was rigidly defined by seniority, and reaching the top depended on a combination of good health and age. Good field officers did not necessarily make good staff officers, but under this system they had automatic promotion. In fact, the more prominent the person's performance in the field, especially in the Blue Division, the greater his chances of being noticed.

Diez Alegria's ideas of reform came to virtually nothing, and he himself quickly became unpopular for what were considered to be his liberal views. He fell foul of right wing generals like Lopez Angel Campano, who sought to influence Franco via the Caudillo's wife, and of Iniesta Cano, who was in charge of the Guardia Civil. The Guardia Civil leadership never forgave Diez Alegria for persuading Fernandez Miranda, acting as temporary premier after Carrero Blanco's assassination in 1973, to order the force to stand down from their state of alert — a decision taken on the initiative of the Guardia Civil.

Diez Alegria was removed from his job in 1974 on the trumped-up pretext that he had met President Ceaucescu of Roumania without prior authorization. In fact the mission was carried out with the knowledge of the Prime Minister Arias Navarro.

Diez Alegria was a victim of circumstance. He conformed little to the image of the typical Spanish officer — slight, self-effacing, and with enormous intellectual curiosity. Precisely because of this he was seen by the more progressive junior officers and some civilians as a hopeful symbol of evolution within the system. Although his reforms were blocked, this did not diminish his stature and, following events in Portugal, he came to be seen as a potential version of General Spinola: a father figure ushering in the transition. Diez Alegria shied away from political protagonism and was embarrassed when stories began circulating in Madrid that he had been sent monocles in the style of those worn by Spinola. The rumour was untrue, but it was symptomatic of the climate of opinion that it existed at all.[14]

Given these abortive efforts at reform and the reaction of the armed forces to any idea of change, the record of the UCD governments should not be judged too harshly. UCD, and more recently the Socialists, have treated the military with kid gloves, and at times with exaggerated deference. The pace of reform has been slow, compared to that of other changes in Spanish society. Nevertheless, reforms have been introduced as far reaching as any proposed by Azaña, and despite the expected opposition, these reforms stand more chance of permanent acceptance. Suarez had to take the problems up exactly where Azaña had started, but with two additional difficulties: firstly, the military still identified with and admired the former regime;[15] secondly,

Franco had bequeathed a series of worsening technical problems including a military hierarchy topped by almost 1,400 generals and admirals — most well beyond the normal age of retirement.

The politicians and the military regarded each other with mutual suspicion. The Suarez government, for instance, considered it a major triumph to change something as simple as the name of the annual Victory Parade to Armed Forces Day. But for the military, such a change was symbolic of a new attitude that denigrated the nationalist victory they had fought for. In this atmosphere it was difficult enough to persuade the armed forces to accept political, let alone military, reform.

The bitterest pill for the armed forces to swallow with the advent of democracy was the legalization of the Communist Party in April 1977. Suarez carefully timed the announcement for the Easter holiday, when all the barracks were closed and any concerted reaction would have to wait. The Navy Minister, Admiral Pita de Vega, resigned in protest and the Army Minister, General Felix Alvarez Arenas, issued a pained statement in the name of the army saying that the decision was accepted with discipline, but reminding the government of its concern for such basic principles as 'the unity of the motherland, honour and respect for the flag, the solidity and permanence of the Crown, and the dignity and prestige of the armed forces'.[16]

Many had expected a far more virulent response. The reaction on this occasion suggests that when faced with a firm decision the military will accept it, albeit grudgingly. Buoyed up by this apparent submissiveness, Suarez mistakenly believed that he had the measure of the military. He underestimated the antagonism he had caused, which perhaps could only have been limited if he had quickly followed up the legalization statute with military reforms. But he lost the advantage of surprise, and by the time military reforms were ready the armed forces had begun to organize their defences.

Reforms have been introduced gradually, beginning at the organizational level. The military High Command was replaced by the Joint Chiefs of Staff (JUJEM), the main executive body of the three services which were brought under a single Defence Ministry, formed in 1977. In 1978 the first civilian Defence Minister since 1936 was appointed, Augustin Roderiguez Sahagun. General Manuel Gutierrez Mellado remained deputy premier with responsibility for defence and until he left the cabinet in 1981, effective decisions on the military remained in the hands of a soldier. The more controversial changes, such as reducing the scope of military justice, and overhauling the system of promotion and retirement, came later.

Reform of military justice, for instance, figures prominently in the Moncloa Agreements of 1977. The new law first appeared in the Cortes the following year, but was not approved until 1981. During this time some notable conflicts occurred: the military prosecuted one of Spain's best known theatre groups, *Els Joglars*, and imprisoned its director, Alberto Boadella, for performing a play which insulted the armed forces; the film, *Crimen de Cuenca* by Pilar Miro, was banned because it was alleged to show the Guardia Civil in an adverse light; Miguel Angel Aguilar, editor of *Diario 16*, was prosecuted for publishing reports of subversive plotting by dissident officers. All these prosecutions concerned the representation or publication of true incidents, and were a serious embarrassment to Spain's democratic image.[17] When the Military Justice Law was finally approved, the main innovation was to permit appeal from a court martial to the civilian Supreme Court. A wide area of jurisdiction was left, however, under military control, including the prosecution of offenders against democracy; the doctrine of separation of powers was largely ignored. The inconvenience of this timed reform was underlined by the court martial for the 23 February coup attempt and the subsequent stiffening of the sentences by the Supreme Court.

Legislation on lowering the retirement age and permitting more flexibility in appointments finally appeared in May 1981. The retirement age for senior generals was cut from sixty-six to sixty-four, and under certain circumstances the government was allowed to retire officers prematurely. The generals still retained most of their perks and in effect retired on full pay. The day after this law was published one of the generals most closely involved in drafting it, Marcelo Aramendi, was found shot in his office with his pistol beside him. Suicide was never proved, but he was widely believed to have taken his life after being vilified by his comrades for his part in the law.

The first important changes as a result of this law occurred in January 1982 when the heads of the three services were replaced, along with the head of the JUJEM, General Ignacio Alfaro Arregui. The latter was succeeded by General Alvaro Lacalle Leloup, a former Blue Division volunteer. This reshuffle meant that the government had a military team who would remain the same for two years. Previously, because of automatic retirement and promotion through seniority, changes were unco-ordinated and the military administration lacked continuity. With this new team, first the UCD Defence Minister, Alberto Oliart, and then the Socialist, Narcis Serra, began discussing the basic issue of turning the armed forces into a modern, professional fighting force. Serious analysis was urgently needed of defence strategy and procurement needs for the eighties, manning levels and the geographical distribution of key service units, the organisation of national service, and the number and role of the captain-generals. The strategic context for this reassessment was a new bi-lateral defence treaty with the USA negotiated in 1982 and approved in April 1983, as well as membership of the North Atlantic Treaty Organisation. For instance, it made no sense to station the country's main armoured unit, the Brunete Division, in Madrid when it was over 500 kilometres from any potential zone of conflict — the Pyrenean borders or the North African enclaves of Ceuta and Melilla.

The presence of the Brunete Division garrisoned around Madrid has hung like a sword of Damocles over the capital since the death of Franco and has caused frequent rumours of mysterious troop movements. Two of the former commanders of the Brunete Division were on trial for the 23 February coup attempt — Milans del Bosch and General Luis Torres Rojas. The conduct of the Division's commander, General Jose Juste, on the night of 23 February left much to be desired. Even though he knew the Cortes had been seized and Torres Rojas had appeared in the Brunete officers' mess to take part in the coup, Juste failed to stop a column of thirteen military jeeps leaving for parliament.[18]

During 1982 a military modernization programme was drawn up — the first serious attempt to analyze and project procurement needs and manning levels. It was agreed in principle to reduce the strength of the services, fundamentally the army, by over one third during the eighties, and to toughen promotion exams. These plans were to be carried into practice by the socialist government. Parallel to this, expenditure will switch from being heavily orientated towards personnel and running costs to investment in materiel. The length of military service will also be cut from eighteen months to one year and permitted in regions where people live. National service was written into the constitution as a national duty and will therefore be difficult to abolish entirely. The left enthusiastically supported the principle of national service on the grounds that it provided a guarantee of plurality of opinion in the military and inhibited wide-scale support for any coup.

The constitution recognized the special status of the armed forces, laying down their mission to 'guarantee the sovereignty and independence of Spain and to defend her territorial integrity and the Constitutional order.'[19] This definition is quite similar to Franco's Basic Law of the State of 1967, in which the armed forces 'guarantee the unity and independence of the country, the integrity of her territory, national security and the defence of the institutional system.'[20] The principal difference is the specific reference to 'constitutional order' as opposed to the 'institutional system'. Also, the constitution excludes from this mission any overt reference to the security forces even though both the Guardia Civil and the National Police are para-military. This deliberately paves the way for their eventual demilitarisation.

By according the armed forces this exalted role, the spirit if not the letter of the constitution can be interpreted as justifying military intervention *in extremis*. As already mentioned, Milans del Bosch justified the imposition of martial law in the Valencia region on these grounds. Furthermore, guaranteeing Spain's 'unity' could be taken to permit military intervention in the Basque country to halt terrorism. Following a terrorist attack by ETA on General Joaquim Valenzuela, head of the King's military household, in May 1981, there was exceptionally strong pressure on the Calvo Sotelo Government to do this. Tempers were so fraught that the Defence Minister, Alberto Oliart, on leaving the Madrid hospital where Valenzuela was interned, was threatened by a national policeman with a pistol.

The constitutional framework of the Armed forces thus blurs the distinction between their political and professional roles. This unfortunately

202

opens the way for confusion because under the Franco regime no effort was ever made to distinguish between them. Confusion can only be reduced by increasing the emphasis on the professionalism of the armed forces.

PLOTS AND REACTION

Like a super tanker that can only alter course slowly and over a long distance, the military took time to react to the introduction of democracy. If the bulk of the officer corps had shown any real determination to intervene in the period after Franco's death up to the first elections in June 1977, it would have been easy to do so. But they neither knew their own strength nor understood the weakness of the government. They did not really believe that their position would suffer, and waited cautiously to see what would happen. They had no clear constructive demands: they only knew what they did not want — the kind of anarchy that led up to the Civil War.

It was almost two years after Franco's death before a group of senior generals gathered to voice their discontent. They met in Jativa near Valencia in September, and among those present were de Santiago y Diaz de Mendivil, who had resigned as deputy premier in late 1976 in protest against Suarez's liberalizing intentions, Pita de Vega, Alvarez-Arenas, and Milans del Bosch. They were united in their mistrust of Suarez, and had not forgiven him for betraying their confidence over legalization of the Communist Party. In September 1976, Suarez had promised before a special meeting of the military hierarchy not to legalize the Communist Party under its existing statutes. The military had not realised the subtlety of Suarez's position. He was merely promising that a Communist Party espousing revolution and rejecting the crown would never be legalized. The military showed even more dislike for the man who had succeeded de Santiago and was destined to carry out military reform, Gutierrez Mellado.

The sense of betrayal was even greater regarding Gutierrez Mellado because they believed he had turned against them. Originally a pupil under Franco at Zaragoza, he had once been a close friend of de Santiago's. Gutierrez Mellado became a *bête noire*. After the Jativa meeting, the hardline right wing did their best to discredit him by raising a particularly sensitive issue — Gutierrez Mellado's Civil War record. As an artillery officer, Gutierrez Mellado rose with the Nationalists in Madrid but found no support. He was forced underground and organized nationalist intelligence in the capital. His record for bravery was outstanding — he had been one of the few agents pulled out of the republican zone and then sent back at great risk. His enemies now claimed that he was, in fact, a republican spy and double agent. There could be no greater calumny.[21]

The Jativa meeting was in no sense a conspiracy; disgruntled generals were merely considering what could be done to stop the rot. The authorities got wind of this discontent and moved Milans del Bosch from the command of the Brunete Division to become captain-general of the Valencia military region. General Jose Gabeiras was brought in to be army Chief of Staff, and General Quintana Lacaci became head of the Madrid military region. In retrospect the Gabeiras appointment was an error. He was promoted over the heads of several generals and then behaved as a puppet of Gutierrez Mellado, which went down badly with those already against him.

On 17 November 1978 the first serious plot was uncovered and aborted. The plan was to use police cadets and a limited number of troops to surround the Prime Minister's office and seize the cabinet while in weekly session. The action was timed to coincide with the King's absence on a visit to Mexico. It was dubbed the 'Galaxy Plot' after the Madrid cafe where the conspirators met.

Only two arrests were made, a Guardia Civil officer, Colonel Antonio Tejero, whose bushy moustache and three-cornered hat were subsequently to become the symbol of the military threat to Spanish democracy, and a captain in what was still the armed police, Ricardo Saenz de Ynestrillas. Charged with conspiracy and intent to rebel, Tejero claimed that their plans were nothing more than cafe talk. One year later, a court martial appeared to accept this version and ignored the prosecution's demand for six years in prison, giving seven months to Tejero and six months and a day to his companion. They were allowed to retain their ranks. The government made the error of minimizing the incident and was therefore left with little recourse but to accept these mild sentences.[22] Although the planning was incomplete and support limited, subsequent events showed that Tejero was utterly serious. In a sense it was a dress rehearsal.

On the same day as the 'Galaxy Plot' was uncovered, an incident occurred involving Gutierrez Mellado that underscored the discontent among certain officers over the approaching endorsement of the new constitution. Gutierrez Mellado was addressing senior officers in Cartagena and a Guardia Civil regional commander, General Juan Atares Pena, shouted: *'La Constitucion es la mayor mentira! Arriba España! Viva Franco!'* (The Constitution is a big lie!) Some applauded. Gutierrez Mellado ordered him to leave which he did. But at the exit to the hall, he shouted: 'Traitor!' Gutierrez Mellado then called everyone to attention and said if anyone agreed with Atares then they too should leave the room. Most of those present applauded. One of those who left the room with Atares was Milans del Bosch. In May 1979, a court martial absolved Atares of misconduct. The general in charge was Luis Caruana who, on the night of 23 February, failed to arrest Milans del Bosch.[23]

The introduction of democracy and the reform of the military therefore came to be seen in extremely personal terms as the evil designs of Suarez and the 'traitor' Gutierrez Mellado. In this atmosphere, the apparent inability of the state to curb mounting terrorism, of which the armed forces were the prime target, only added to the sense of grievance. Serious indiscipline was evident at the funeral of General Ortin Gil, the military governor of Madrid assassinated in June 1979. The terrorist groups ETA and GRAPO, incidentally, selected democratic officers where possible, believing that it ultimately suited their strategy to have as reactionary a military as possible.

A number of right wing officers began seeking transfers to the Brunete Division and in June 1979 Torres Rojas was given command, further encouraging those who wanted to overthrow the government. Aware that Torres Rojas was up to no good, the government dismissed him in January 1980 and sent him to cool his heels in La Coruña as military governor. This bought only breathing space. By the end of the year, Madrid was once again immersed in talk of military gatherings. Out of this discontent grew the 23 February coup.

The most disturbing feature of the coup was the apparent failure of intelligence to forestall it altogether. The principal protagonists were people whom any half-vigilant intelligence service should have been watching. Even before the 'Galaxy Plot', Tejero had been identified as an 'ultra' for his zealous handling of a demonstration in Malaga and for writing an impertinent letter to the King, for which he was relegated to a desk job. Several of those involved in the 23 February coup visited Tejero while in prison for his part in the 'Galaxy Plot' — including Torres Rojas. Milans del Bosch made no secret of his views and was passed over in promotion. In 1979 he declared that the balance of democracy had not been positive: 'We, the military, in general have watched the transition expectantly and serenely but with profound concern.'[24] He had a reputation for hot headedness and his views on the role of the military in society were strongly influenced by his experience as military attache in Buenos Aires in the sixties. Armada's political ambitions were well known, and had caused Suarez to force him from the royal household as far back as 1977.

Three people with intelligence connections were among those brought to trial for the coup, including Major Luis Cortina, alleged to be the link between Armada and Tejero. Cortina was aquitted for lack of evidence, though it has been suggested that he was a double-agent. Cortina was a full-time intelligence officer and in theory should have known what was going on. Were the authorities really so ignorant? One theory is that the plot was discovered late in the day and deliberately accelerated so that it would fail.[25] It is hard to believe that the entire government was ignorant; equally hard to accept that a huge risk would be taken in letting the coup go ahead. Milans del Bosch put almost 3,500 troops on full alert in Valencia. It is more likely that since intelligence-gathering lay in the hands of people with ambiguous feelings towards democracy, the government was only partially informed. Considerable mental gymnastics are necessary to switch from monitoring subversion among people trying to introduce democracy, to those trying to overthrow it. Members of the intelligence community could well have hedged their bets.

The coup cast a dim light on the conduct of the Guardia Civil, no matter how much this para-military force sought to disassociate itself from what happened. The ranks of the Guardia Civil were recruited to seize parliament under false pretences. They volunteered to do a 'service for Spain', thinking it was some anti-terrorist action. None desisted when the nature of what they were doing became clear. Nor did they desist when the King had broadcast to the nation and made it unmistakably plain that anyone under arms had no right to be so. The existence of Guardia Civil regulations that demand blind obedience to orders made prosecution difficult, and over 230 Guardia Civil ranks were never charged. Of the eleven officers aquitted by the court martial, ten came from the Guardia Civil; most defended themselves on the grounds of obedience to superior orders. This argument, as we have seen, was roundly rejected by the Supreme Court on appeal.

POWER TO INFLUENCE

The Army Museum in Madrid has made only the most minimal concession to democracy — busts of King Juan Carlos, Queen Sofia and Crown Prince Felipe (which face one of Franco). The Army, more than any other service, is still rooted in the idea of the Crusade, and its language remains that of its Civil War victory. The officer corps has been imbued at all levels with a spirit that is out of tune with the democratic ideal. Franco is still admired both as a military commander and as a leader. Many a general retains a signed portrait of the Caudillo in his office, even if pride of place is now given to the King.

Nevertheless, there is a clear divide between those who have accepted — albeit with considerable reserve — the democratic system as the legally constituted order, and those who regard democracy as a betrayal of all that the Civil War victory represented. Within the latter group there is a division between those who reject democracy and those who are actively willing to overthrow it. The distinction is important because the military are naturally conservative and bound to resort to grumbling armchair talk about the need for drastic medicine. Yet probably no more than 5% of the officers corps and NCOs are still willing to contemplate force. 'We have always been convinced that the nucleus of plotters was a limited minority within the Armed Forces, and that the vast majority of the military, and of course those in key positions, respected constitutional legality unreservedly, as has been shown by the facts,' Felipe Gonzalez declares.[26]

This minority is encouraged by its own blind self-righteousness, by a residual mistrust of democracy among the bulk of the armed forces, and by a vociferous fascist fringe among the civilian population. The discovery of a plan by a group of colonels to seize power on the eve of the October 1982 general elections underlined this. The colonels planned to seize key strategic military and para-military units. Among the plans was a provision to place the Zarzuela Palace and the Prime Minister's office within range of heavy artillery. The plan was serious but abandoned at a very early stage.[27] It had similarities to the 'Galaxy Plot' and 23 February, but the conspirators had learned from mistakes made in both attempts. If necessary, the King would have been eliminated. Those involved were already under surveillance because of their contacts with the 23 February plotters.

In this atmosphere it is easy for the politicians to exaggerate the real threat posed to democracy by the armed forces, so giving them unnecessary influence. The military will obey a strong government, even if they do not like its policies; conversely, they will exploit a weak government. There were several uneasy confrontations (never leaked to the press) in the early days of the socialist government, but in the end the military were forced to show respect for clear authority. The greatest danger arises from mutual misunderstanding.

The military are uncertain of their role and constantly behave like the rejected child in search of parental affection. They need assurance that their role is essential and that they are appreciated. As a result, both the King and ministers are obliged to spend an inordinate amount of time attending often quite mundane ceremonies. The tremendous official propaganda each year for Armed Forces Day is designed to convey the impression that civilian and military society exist in noble symbiosis. Though heavily overplayed, it goes down well with the military.

As a collective body, the armed forces are unused to the idea that they too can be represented in parliament. The natural channel is through the ranks of the officers to the King. In parliament no group really speaks for the Armed Forces. The officer corps is wary of Fraga and Alianza Popular although the latter seeks to be their champion. The idea of a military candidate was launched in 1979 in the person of General Manuel Prieto, former head of the Guardia Civil. Prieto stood for the right-wing coalition headed by Fraga, Coalicion Democratica, but failed to get elected in Granada. Deprived of parliamentary representation the JUJEM, as the main operative body of the military hierarchy, becomes its point of contact with the government, creating the impression that behind-the-scenes pressure can be brought to bear. At the same time, the most vociferous group within the armed forces gains the most attention and is publicly seen as representative.

This honour goes to the extreme right. It has its own newspaper, *El Alcazar*, which unashamedly panders to nostalgia and the most primitive forms of patriotism. The whole tone of the paper is designed to convey a sense of outrage at democracy. Typical is their weekly page-long catalogue of offences against the Spain which Franco and the Nationalists sought to expropriate as their own: it is a list of attacks against the military and security forces, and examples of delinquency and offences against the national flag. This extreme element in the armed forces is also highly public because of its links with civilian fascist organizations. *El Alcazar* distinguished itself on 23 February by printing a front page photograph of parliament with a large arrow saying: 'Todo dispueso para la session de lunes' ('Everything ready for the Monday session').

The democratic press has also confused the military by the amount of attention it devotes to them. Woefully incompetent at handling their own public relations, the military are tied up with a mass of red tape and operate on the basis that all information is secret and potentially harmful. News is never transmitted properly or quickly, and the press inevitably reacts negatively and operates on the basis of conspiracy theories. The military are written about in the way that western Kremlinologists treat the Soviet leadership. In no other European country do the military occupy so much space in print — even appointments and changes in personnel are examined in detail. In September 1982, three newspapers, *El Pais, ABC,* and *Diario 16* between them managed to publish stories about appointments on nineteen days, and in October similar stories were published on sixteen days.[28] So much attention when there are so many barriers to the truth is a recipe for distortion. Other facts, for instance that the garrison enclaves of Ceuta and Melilla voted 45% and 49% respectively for the Socialist Party, tend to be less well reported.

Because the military have yet to establish an institutional framework to express themselves, the government tends to interpret their feelings. So far such interpretations have been based on a fundamental fear of military reaction to policy. Far more concessions have been made, for instance, to the military than to trades unions. The investigation into the 23 February coup exemplified this fear. It was strictly limited and only the minimum number of people was brought to trial.

Fear of antagonizing the military has influenced a range of domestic and foreign policies. Take foreign policy: the fate of the enclaves of Ceuta and Melilla is intimately connected with the military's refusal to contemplate any negotiation with Morocco over their future status. Equally, strong military feeling over British possession of Gibraltar obliged the government to adopt a severely nationalistic stance in negotiating the Rock's sovereignty. In domestic issues the military have had a profound influence on regional policy. Spain could well have moved towards theoretical, if not actual, federalism, had not this been contrary to one of the fundamental tenets of military ideology — the sacred unity of Spain. The rationalization in 1981 of regional autonomy laws, scaling down that previously promised to the Basques and Catalans and reducing the content of that offered to the rest, was a direct result of 23 February. The threat to the unity of Spain had been one of the principal grievances of the conspirators.

The mood of the military after 23 February was also a significant cause of the agreement reached between government and opposition on all-embracing state of emergency laws which came close to violating the constitution's guarantee of basic human rights. Army staffing of the security forces continues to give them enormous weight in matters of law and order. The military have also indirectly affected the behaviour of trades unions. The number of strikes fell sharply in 1981 and 1982, in part reflecting the fear that social disorder might provide an excuse for military intervention. The politicians have taken the military into special account in policies affecting national sovereignty, social order, the unity of Spain, and the military institution itself — an unacceptably broad zone of influence that the socialist government intends to reduce.

10 Church and State

Along with the armed forces, the Church was an essential prop for the Franco regime. The Republic's moves to secularize the state were overturned by Franco, who restored the Church to the position of privileged arbiter of national morals and education. After the Vatican Council II, the Church hierarchy began to distance itself from the regime. In particular the primate of Spain, Cardinal Tarancon, played a key part in removing the Church from an active role in politics and paving the way for a return of democracy. While Church influence has been eroded, catholicism and its practice remain a powerful force in national life.

On 31 October 1982, three days after Spaniards had overwhelmingly voted for a socialist government, Pope John Paul II arrived in Madrid. Humbly kissing the tarmac of Barajas airport, he began the first visit by a pontif to Europe's most Catholic country. Twice the visit had been postponed: first as a result of the assassination attempt on the Pope in 1981; then at the last minute because of the Calvo Sotelo government's decision to call a snap election — the Pope would have found himself in the middle of an election campaign, and this was judged too political.

Throughout his ten-day visit, the Pope was accorded a multitudinous welcome. The mixture of popular enthusiasm, curiosity and religious fervour was as potent as that of his native Poland. The Vatican, and the Pope himself, were careful to insist on the pastoral nature of the visit, yet his presence in Spain had an unavoidable political dimension. The organizers were determined to remind the incoming socialist administration of Spain's catholic heritage and its continuing presence as a moral force in the nation.

The reminder was so impressive as to be almost baffling in the light of the election result. Almost 40% of the total electorate had voted socialist. The record of the left in relation to the Church had been one of suspicion, intolerance and anti-clericalism. The sole explanation for this apparent contradiction was a new maturity in relations between Church and state, and between the individual and the Church. Spaniards showed that they were quite capable of differentiating between a political vote and an act of faith, while the institutions of Church and state demonstrated their capacity to maintain a respectful distance from each other. This situation was underlined by the huge open air mass celebrated in the centre of Madrid attended by

210

almost one million people. From an altar overlooked by skyscrapers owned by banks, and amidst mushrooming discotheques and bingo halls, the Pope pronounced a homily extolling the indissolubility of the family and the right to life. Among his audience there were many who had voted for the socialist party, whose programme included the liberalization of abortion.

The traditional context in which catholicism has been rooted in Spain has altered irreversibly. An isolated inward-looking agrarian society permitted the Church to exert a formidable influence over Spaniards. The Church's implacable insistence on the exclusivity of the Catholic faith and the persecution of heretics reflected the political need to forge unity in a divided nation, once dominated by Islam. Catholicism still helps define the nature of Spain. But the unity of the nation is based on a complex inter-play of regional interests, economic and social factors, and international relations; they depend little on religion.

Moreover, greater prosperity since the mid-fifties has steadily made society more materialistic and less religious, and this has combined with the major shift in population to the big urban centres to weaken the power of the Church in society. Thus, while the population may still be 95% nominally Catholic, the way in which such catholicism is expressed has altered. Being Catholic is defined less by regular observance of mass and more by a rudimentary religious instruction coupled with observance of the rituals associated with birth, marriage and death. In the big cities like Madrid, no more than 20% of the population regularly attend mass. This change has been accompanied by a gradual separation of the Church from the structure of state so that it performs a purely religious and moral function.

Under the Franco regime, the Church was an inseparable part of the establishment and enjoyed a highly privileged status. Such a symbiotic relationship was unacceptable for the democratic state. It was also explicitly rejected by the doctrine of Vatican Council II. The political power of the Church has therefore been reduced, and, just as important, so has its capacity to incite antagonism. Church burning and anti-clericalism, often described as the national sport, have lost their original context: the anger and frustration of a repressed population turning against the most readily indentifiable (and nearest) institution of the establishment.

The changing role of the Church has therefore been the result of two distinct, but at times, convergent, movements. One has been the sheer force of social and economic change since the late fifties backed by the doctrine of Vatican Council II; the other has been purely political — the advent of democracy.

A CARDINAL ROLE

Observing the Pope's visit with almost boyish pleasure was seventy-five-year-old Cardinal Vicente Enrique y Tarancon, former president of the Episcopal Conference and Archbishop of Madrid.[1] Though he took a back-seat role in the actual event, Cardinal Tarancon laid the essential groundwork for the success of the Pope's visit and for the tranquil acceptance by the Church of the socialist victory. As the capital's Archbishop and head of the Episcopal Conference from 1971 to 1982, he presided over a crucial period in Church history with moderation and consummate diplomatic skill. In the twilight of the Franco era, backed fully by the Vatican, Cardinal Tarancon deliberately distanced the Church from Francoism and supported the restoration of democracy.

This change of position brought him into serious confrontation both with the regime and the traditional elements among the clergy; but it removed the stigma of open identification with Franco and his Civil War victory that had characterized the Church until then. It therefore gave the Church considerable moral authority at Franco's death, and at the same time aided the prospects for a democratic solution. The moral authority endowed by Cardinal Tarancon was enhanced by his careful refusal to let the Church identify openly with any one political party in the emergent democratic process. This was the first time in the history of the Spanish Church that it had deliberately held back from political involvement.[2] If Cardinal Tarancon had not backed a renovation of the Church and it had persisted in its reactionary stance, its image would have suffered seriously and its social effect would have been divisive. As it was the Church emerged from the Franco era surprisingly unscathed, given its original endorsement of the 'Crusade'.

Although Cardinal Tarancon prided himself on his knowledge and ability to deal with fellow Spaniards, his achievement would have been impossible without the whole-hearted support of the Vatican. His appointment to the archbishopric of Madrid in May 1971 was a clear move by Pope Paul VI to promote a liberal figure as a counterweight to the conservative hierarchy. Pope Paul had made known his distaste for the Franco regime as early as 1963 when, as Archbishop of Milan, he interceded on behalf of the communist, Julian Grimau, condemned to death for his Civil War activities. The Pope was also a close friend of Cardinal Tarancon.

Tarancon's own rise to the top of the Spanish Church hierarchy was by no means smooth. Ordained in 1929 (he had wanted to take orders from the age of eight), he became Spain's youngest bishop when appointed Bishop of Solsona in 1946. But he was kept there until 1964 as a form of reprisal. A pastoral letter entitled 'Our Daily Bread', written in the forties, earned him the displeasure of the Falangists, who suspected him of being a communist. He was eventually moved to the bishopric of Oviedo where his human and intellectual qualities were fully recognized, and he subsequently became the

Archbishop of Toledo and Primate of Spain in 1969. Not only was Tarancon more liberal than the existing hierarchy, his approach was different — he made a point of listening to his priests and touring the parishes. This was entirely in the spirit of the new teaching approved by Vatican Council II and was the guiding spirit behind the renovation of the Spanish Church.

The antagonism between the regime and the liberal approach personified by Cardinal Tarancon came into full public view in 1973 during the funeral of Carrero Blanco. Members of the extreme right and supporters of the late Prime Minister jostled Cardinal Tarancon insulting him with cries and placards *'Tarancon al paredon!'* (Tarancon for the firing squad), and *'Fuera Obispos rojos!'* (Red bishops out). There had even been moves to prevent him taking the funeral service. The Chaplain-General of the armed forces, Jose Lopez Ortiz, was approached behind Tarancon's back. Ortiz refused.

A showdown with the regime followed shortly after Carrero's funeral. In March 1974, a row over a homily preached by the Bishop of Bilbao, Monsignor Antonio Anoveros, nearly resulted in Franco's excommunication. The homily, widely read throughout the Basque country, fully endorsed Basque culture and implicitly challenged the regime to alter its repressive policy towards the Basques. Without consulting the ecclesiastical authorities, the Franco Government prepared to fly Monsignor Anoveros out of Spain to Rome. Cardinal Tarancon sought to intervene while Monsignor Anoveros was placed under effective house arrest in Bilbao. As a sign of the regime's displeasure the government proposed he leave Spain temporarily: initially they suggested he stay away for a few days, but this was quickly extended to two or three years. At this stage, Cardinal Tarancon informed the government that the sanction of excommunication would be imposed under canon law against those who 'directly or indirectly interfere with ecclesiastical jurisdiction'. The cabinet, conscious of the threat, prepared to break diplomatic relations with the Vatican. Temperatures only cooled when Franco, who had probably been kept ill-informed, stepped in and a face-saving formula was agreed whereby Monsignor Anoveros publicly travelled to Madrid to explain himself to his fellow bishops.[3]

The way the incident nearly got out of hand reflected the increased lack of co-ordination in government decision-making at this time. Franco had never faced the church head-on. Yet the incident was also symptomatic of a move within the Episcopal Conference to assert the Church's independence from the regime in its own internal affairs. The Church could not afford to be seen to accept the dictates of the regime when political change was so close and the Caudillo's authority rapidly declining.

When Franco died, Cardinal Tarancon successfully resisted pressure for a gigantic religious commemoration for the Caudillo attended by every bishop in the country and staged in the Plaza de Oriente, scene of popular rallies supporting the regime. But as a gesture to the Caudillo's die-hard supporters, Cardinal Tarancon did not say the public funeral mass. This was left to the conservative Archbishop of Toledo, Monsignor Marcelo Gonzalez. Instead, far more importantly, Cardinal Tarancon pronounced the homily in the church of San Jeronimo for King Juan Carlos as he ascended the throne. This speech set the tone for the restoration of democracy and clearly defined the Church's role. Commenting subsequently on the sermon, he said: 'The Church could neither be expected to give moral support or backing nor should it be asked to do so. The Church is ready to work with everyone, but in its own way; the Church can even criticize certain things in its desire to co-operate, but on its own terms because it wants to be involved [politically] with nobody and nothing.'[4] This tone of co-operation and non-interventionism persisted throughout Cardinal Tarancon's thrice-renewed three-year presidency of the Episcopal Conference.

CIVIL WAR LEGACY

Cardinal Tarancon's stance can only be considered liberal in relation to the overall conservatism of the Church in Spain and the part played by the latter during the Civil War, which in turn was heavily conditioned by the experiences of the Republic.

The Republic disestablished the Church so clumsily that good intentions disappeared beneath measures which were seen as overtly anti-clerical. Too much was done too quickly, antagonizing the Church and confusing many a Spaniard. Unfortunately, when the Church and its supporters protested, the Socialists and Anarchists saw this as justification for the Republic's action and a sign that the Church was the real enemy of progress. The 1931 constitution declared that priests' stipends would be stopped within two years, breaking an agreement that stretched back to 1837 when Church lands had been confiscated. The state acquired the right to dissolve religious orders (with Jesuits particularly in mind). Religious education was ended and official approval was required for such public manifestations of religion as processions and public holidays to celebrate religious events like Holy Week. Even cemeteries were secularized. The Church's hold over the family was cut and only civil marriage recognized. Not surprisingly, the Church felt threatened and was prepared to throw its weight behind any catholic party or movement that might counterbalance the republican left. In this way the need to overhaul antiquated Church-state relations was forgotten behind a barrage of hostile propaganda and mutual mistrust.

When the nationalist uprising occurred the bulk of the Church, despite the fratricidal nature of the conflict, was ready to take sides. The atrocities committed by the Republicans on priests and religious orders in the first weeks of the uprising swayed many uncommitted people to the nationalist side, and it was easy for their propaganda to portray the Republicans as anti-Church butchers. Nearly 7,000 priests and persons in religious orders were killed including twelve bishops; while stories of priests having their ears cut off, or crucifixes being forced down their mouths were appallingly commonplace.[5]

The Spanish bishops, forty-one out of fifty-five of whom were in the nationalist zone, dithered between open support and a compromise — so did the Vatican. The Catalan and Basque Clergy, susceptible to regional feelings and conscious that they were in the republican zone, were reluctant to speak out against the Republic. Indeed, the Archbishop of Tarragona, Dr Vidal y Barraquer, declined to endorse the nationalist cause, and eventually escaped abroad to die in exile in Zurich; while the Bishop of Vitoria, Dr Mateo Mugica, refused to give open support. The Archbishop of Seville, Cardinal Pedro Segura, also kept his distance. However, in July 1937 the primate of Spain, Cardinal Isidro Goma y Tomas, Archbishop of Toledo, published a letter addressed to the 'Bishops of the World' in which the Church formally took sides in the Civil War. With the notable exception of the previously mentioned bishops, the letter was signed by the Church hierarchy. Arguing that the Civil War was not of the Church's making, the letter claimed that the Republic had sought to do things contrary to the spirit of Spanish history. Many christians, it said, had taken up arms to defend religion. The murdered priests were referred to as martyrs. The letter gave moral backing to the Nationalists, confirming the propaganda of a crusade of Good versus Evil. It fell just short of a full theological justification for the Nationalists.

Franco put a good deal of pressure on Cardinal Goma to produce such a document. If the Republicans had won the war (and at this stage the outcome was by no means clear), then the Church was without privilege and influence. On the other hand if the Nationalists won, then the position held before the Republic could be restored. Though tactically justifiable, the document made the Church a party to the bloodiest of civil conflicts and the totally unchristian reprisals in its aftermath. If the hierarchy had any doubts about such a negative image, none were shown until the sixties. The Church had identified itself with Franco and the two clung to each other out of mutual need. The reward for Church loyalty was re-incorporation into the apparatus of the state.

All the legislation under the Republic deemed anti-religious was repealed. The Church returned to control education and act as arbiter of the nation's family life and moral health; a censorious puritanism reigned. Divorce was once again banned, and the clergy had their state stipends restored. Franco pressed the Vatican to concede to him control over the appointment of bishops, and largely obtained it. He further acquired a right of veto over the appointment of parish priests on general political grounds. Despite these trade-offs, which underlined the Church and the Franco regime's desire to coexist harmoniously, the Vatican at first avoided signing any agreement which formalized the new relationship. Given his international isolation, Franco regarded a Concordat as a vital seal of diplomatic approval. The

Vatican was under pressure to resist conceding such international respectability but eventually gave way, again on tactical grounds — to preserve its influence in Spain.

This was a serious error on the part of the Vatican. Holding back the Concordat risked alienating an important sector of the Spanish Church hierarchy, but Franco needed the agreement far more than the Vatican. Given the regime's use of religion in its propaganda and the stake already established by the Church in national life, it is almost inconceivable that Franco would have significantly reduced the role of catholicism. The Virgin of Pilar was even, technically, commander-in-chief of the armed forces. Franco himself was a conscientious Catholic.

The Concordat was signed on 27 August 1953. The Catholic Church was recognized as *the* Church of Spain — incidentally permitting discrimination against other religious sects. Tax concessions were offered on Church property; priests were officially put on the state payroll; Church marriages were made binding in civil law; freedom of assembly (otherwise banned) was allowed for religious purposes; religious courts were allowed to try ecclesiastical offenders. Meanwhile, the head of state obtained almost medieval rights over the appointment of bishops but in return the Vatican was allowed unrestricted access to its bishops.

The 1953 Concordat remained the basis of relations between Church and state throughout the rest of the Franco era and only expired in 1980. Undoubtedly Franco was the chief beneficiary of this arrangement. Once he was covered by the respectability of Vatican acceptance, the Church was more beholden to him than vice versa. As for the Church, it could claim to have recouped a position of privilege unparalleled in 200 years but at the cost of a damaging identification with the regime. It was not until 1971 that the Church made any serious attempt to reconcile the two sides in the Civil War.

OPPOSITION WITHIN THE RANKS

While the Church as a whole had a sorry record in opposing the dictatorship, nevertheless, it was not a monolithic grouping. The hierarchy, certainly until the mid-sixties, was predominantly aged and reactionary, espousing a nostalgic form of catholicism that pandered to national chauvinism — 'national-catholicism'. Yet among the 23,000 parish priests, the picture was different. Living close to the realities of their flock they could see the tensions in society, the level of worker exploitation, the frustrations felt by students, and the crisis of conscience among honest catholics rejecting a corrupt authoritarian regime blessed by their own bishops.[6]

From the ranks of these priests and their parishioners the first internal noncommunist opposition emerged. It was able to survive and expand precisely

216

because of the close identification of Church and state. Church institutions and the Catholic faith provided the only respectable umbrella for dissent. The regime was reluctant to inhibit Catholic groups because it did not wish to risk confrontation with one of its main pillars of support.

This opposition from within was seen by the Church leadership as a challenge to its own authority. In part this was true, for it reflected the crisis inside the Spanish Church over its identity and direction. As seen in Chapter Five, Catholic worker groups were the first to dispute the role of the officially organized vertical syndicates. Militants from HOAC, including worker priests, helped to form the illegal Workers Commissions (CCOO), which were founded on a basis of christian-marxist ideology. Members of the Catholic workers youth movement, JOC, were behind the first independent trades union, USO, when it formed in 1960. Catholic militants also played a prominent part in the more radical illegal union, ORT. The Church failed to take sufficient notice of this grass-roots disaffection and, unwilling to offer real protection or support, lost any ability to control or influence trades unionism. Despite a certain amount of verbal acrobatics, the Church supported the official vertical syndicates, and the Communist Party came to dominate the most powerful clandestine union, CCOO.

Through Catholic action groups, the Church also offered protective backing to student protest, and to a number of intellectuals such as former Education Minister, Joaquin Ruiz-Jimenez, Jose Luis Aranguren and Julian Marias. Ruiz-Jimenez, by founding the magazine *Cuadernos para el Dialogo* in 1963, developed the first officially tolerated medium for 'free' thinking along christian-democrat lines. Church buildings were openly and secretly used as meeting places, one of the most publicized incidents being the holding of a constituent congress of the illegal Democratic Students Union (Sindicato Democratico de Estudiantes) in the Capuchine Convent of Barcelona — the police were kept outside for two days. The first dissent within the military also came from a Catholic organisation, Forja (see chapter nine).

A major new initiative came from the Vatican of the ebullient and socially conscious Pope John XXIII, formalized in Vatican Council II from 1962-63. The Council endorsed the need to separate Church from state and supported pluralism. More direct contact between the clergy and the people was encouraged. Pope John XXIII's successor, Paul VI, gave his full backing to the Council and in so doing was directly inviting the hierarchy of the Spanish Church to change. To chivvy them along he sent as papal nuncio, Cardinal Luigi Dadaglio, a close confidant.

By 1966, the bishops had already begun to react. In February the organization of the Church was completely overhauled. The main organizing and representative body, the Conference of Metropolitans, disappeared. This had been composed solely of Archbishops and Cardinals. The new organization, the Episcopal Conference, was given younger blood with a wider representative base. It was composed of four cardinals, twelve archbishops, sixty resident bishops, and fourteen auxiliary bishops, backed by a twenty-man permanent commission and an executive secretariat of seven. The latter was the new operational core of the Church hierarchy.

A new organization backed by the Vatican Council's teaching now enabled the Spanish Church to reassess its role, in the form of an Ecclesiastical Congress in 1971, painstakingly prepared over the two previous years. Part of the preparation entailed an exhaustive questionnaire sent to over 18,000 priests, seeking their views on a wide range of religious, social and political issues. The priests were, for instance, asked to say whether they approved of liberty of expression, freedom of association, conscientious objection, the defence of ethnic minorities and so on. The tenor of the replies provided sufficient ammunition for those like Cardinal Tarancon who wanted to steer the Church along the path of Vatican Council II and distance the Church from the regime.

The Congress also provided a platform for the first agonizing reassessment of the Church's role in openly supporting the nationalist side during the Civil War and afterwards. The reformers realized that the Church had to adopt a conciliatory stance to retain the faith of the growing number of students, intellectuals and workers in dissent with the regime. One motion at the Congress asked that the Church be forgiven for not realising sooner that it should have acted as true minister of reconciliation among a people split by civil strife. Thirty-four years after the bishop's 'open letter' backing the nationalist crusade, this was a tardy admission. Even then it was not unanimously approved — 138 voted in favour and 78 against.

The official press treated the Congress with barely-concealed hostility. The authorities regarded the renovative movement as inspired by the opposition and did their best to discredit the Congress. However, it would be wrong to see the Congress as an initiative against the regime, even if it had effects that ran counter to Francoism. The Congress was, above all else, an attempt by the Church to come to terms with and revitalize itself. With some Basque priests openly identifying with the separatist violence of ETA, with a strong movement in favour of worker priests in the fast burgeoning shanty towns of the big cities, with urgent new social problems created by urban life, the Church had to readjust and take a position. It also needed to salvage its reputation with the regime: the condemnation of five Basque priests in 1969 to prison terms of twelve to fifteen years had caused a tremendous stir among the clergy; in 1970 a worker priest and two more Basque priests were convicted by a court martial. The authorities even set aside a special prison in Zamora for dissident clergy. Here some 150 priests were kept. Other punishments included stiff fines for preaching 'political' sermons.

The Church had to decide, therefore, whether its members were acting within the bounds of their calling. Though the answer was sibylline, the direction was clear: the Franco regime lacked popular legitimacy and basic human freedoms were not being respected. The Church, if it was honest with

218

itself, had to be in opposition to, or, at the very least, distanced from the regime. From 1971 onwards, the distance became pronounced as Cardinal Tarancon and the papal Nuncio, Cardinal Dadaglio, began to work closely together. To sidestep Franco's right to vet bishops, the Vatican used its authority under the Concordat to create auxiliary bishops. It was not surprising, therefore, that relations between Church and state in the twilight of the Franco era came close to a serious rupture over the Bishop of Bilbao.

SEPARATION OF POWERS

Both the content and consequences of the Vatican Council II radically altered the basis of the 1953 Concordat between Spain and the Vatican. The Vatican would have liked an early renegotiation of the agreement to make it consistent with the Council doctrine. However, Franco was determined not to relinquish his rights, especially that of nominating bishops. One of the reasons why Pope Paul VI never came to Spain, although he wished to, was Franco's fear that he would be asked to forego some of his privileges regarding the Church. Equally, the hardline right regarded Pope Paul VI as an enemy of Spain who encouraged the trouble-making 'red' bishops. Thus a constructive dialogue with the Vatican was impossible.

After Franco's death, under Arias' premiership, the situation only marginally improved. He mistrusted the Vatican's intentions and was reluctant to forego the powers of visitation vested in the head of state. As a result, throughout his term of office under the monarchy, Arias blocked any deal with the Vatican, even though negotiations had reached an advanced stage under the aegis of the Foreign Minister, Jose Maria de Areilza.[7]

One of the first acts of the Suarez Government in July 1976 was to approve a revision of the Concordat. This was made possible when the King renounced his rights of visitation, a major sticking point with the Vatican. The revisions were signed on 29 July 1976. This then paved the way for negotiation of a series of new bilateral agreements which laid down the relationship between the Holy See and the new democratic state, partially effective as of 1981.

The framework for this new relationship was laid by the constitution, which clearly separated the Church from the state. Catholicism lost its status as the state religion — 'there shall be no state religion'. However, Spain's catholicism was recognized by the following commitment: 'the public authorities shall take the religious beliefs of Spanish society into account and shall in consequence maintain appropriate cooperation with the Catholic Church and the other confessions'.[8] This formula pledged co-operation and implicitly guaranteed Spain's Catholic traditions, yet fell short of creating a confessional state as before. An important element of the Constitution was the respect accorded to freedom of belief. Ministers, for instance, no longer felt obliged to swear on the bible before a crucifix on taking office. (Under Franco the religious oath of ministers was taken on bended knees.) The constitution also permitted private education, which, by the same token, safeguarded Church interests in education.

Spain did not need to have a new concordat with the Vatican. The existence of the Concordat implied very special links between the Holy See and Spain, which was inconvenient to both parties. Although the bilateral agreements give the Episcopal Conference less political muscle on all issues, whether moral, political or ecclesiastical, this is compensated for by the removal of an air of confessionalism which does not wholly accord with the reality of modern Spain. In the field of education — the single most important area of Church influence — the agreements favour the Church and inevitably tie the hand of any government.

The majority of private educational establishments are Catholic, and over 25% of all kindergartens are run by private Catholic organizations. In primary education, church schools account for 23% of the total. This percentage drops only slightly to 21% for secondary education.[9] Approximately 1.2 million students attend Catholic primary schools and a further 236,000 are in Catholic secondary school. In addition, the Church controls 110,000 people attending Catholic professional training colleges, and there are four church-run universities — Comillas, Deusto, Navarre and Salamanca. The total number of students in church-run universities, theological colleges and institutes of higher education is over 51,000.[10] This is a formidable presence.

The main practical difference in the new agreements centres round the principle that the Church should be self-financing. This overturns the concept that the state is under an obligation to subsidize the Church in view of its social and moral function. The handing over of a lump sum each year to the Church, latterly the Episcopal Conference, has been criticized even within the Church as unnecessary dependence. On the other hand, the state itself got good value for money. Apart from paying the stipends of the 23,000 priests, the subsidy covers 29,000 in male religious orders and 63,000 in female religious orders. Almost 13,000 in female religious orders work in the health field (mainly hospitals) while a further 14,750 teach in schools; male orders provide 9,000 teachers.[11] These are all paid a minimum wage — in 1983 the basic priest's wage was 32,160 pesetas per month with 1,402 pesetas deducted for social security. The clergy and religious orders only joined the social security in 1982. Additional work with the aged and in, for instance, psychiatric care is often done on a voluntary basis. This sizeable workforce has provided the state with a number of essential services at low cost.

Against these advantages, the state has been transferring money to the Episcopal Conference which the latter was not obliged to account for. More importantly, the persistence of the Catholic Church's financial dependence on the state while other religious faiths were excluded, explicitly recognized confessionalism.

The new agreement envisaged a gradual move towards financial independence over a three year transitional period. During this time, the state would maintain the subsidy, funded by a specific 'religious' tax of 1% per contributor. The contributor need not pay the 1% to the Catholic Church and has the right to say so on the tax form, in which case the funds go towards good works. The government is pledged to make good any shortfall in the subsidy which for 1983 was calculated at 9·3 billion pesetas. This was the year in which this tax system was due to be introduced, but the complexities of its introduction resulted in a postponement. The three-year transition period can be continued for another three years at government discretion. Thus the Church has considerable time to adapt.[13]

The Church, lacking pension funds, and sophisticated investment activity, claims to be poor. Its income has never been fully revealed but is certainly small and poorly managed. Yet Church assets, despite expropriation of land in the nineteenth century, are still significant. Proper reassessment of its assets in buildings, land, and art treasures, along with judicious sale and re-arrangement could provide much more capital than the Church hierarchy is willing to admit. At the same time, very little effort has been made to encourage the idea of Church support through donations and voluntary contributions. The one organization within the Church that stands notably apart in this respect is Opus Dei.

THE INFLUENCE OF OPUS DEI

Founded in 1928 by an Aragonese priest, Jose Maria Escriva de Balaguer, Opus Dei ('The Work of God') has acquired considerable influence within the Catholic Church and especially in Spain. In 1982, after an intense period of lobbying, it was accorded the status of personal prelature by the Vatican. The mix of missionary zeal, piety and clannish secrecy surrounding Opus Dei has made it a polemical and much-misunderstood organization. Within the Church in Spain it has appeared the most political of organizations even though it denies any political aims. Its members played a major role in the liberalization of the Franco regime and in the development of a modern economy. At the same time the name of Opus Dei has figured in the two major financial scandals of the past twenty-five years — Matesa and Rumasa.

Father Escriva conceived Opus Dei as a group of people, both lay and clergy, who should spread the Catholic christian word through their daily working life. He wanted his devotees to win over converts like missionaries, through example — demonstrating humility, charity, and hard work. The difference from any previous order was the emphasis on lay men and women and on the fact that people should continue in their chosen jobs. Indeed, they could best serve Opus Dei by being in these jobs and setting an example. The code of conduct for Opus devotees was laid down in a book published by its founder — *El Camino,* (The Way) — in Burgos in 1939. The book is a curious melange of homely aphorisms, common sense, puritan zeal and exhortations to success. The appeal of Opus Dei is towards elitism and its impact has been greatest among the bourgeoisie.

Parts of *El Camino* have been likened to a Spanish version of the puritan capitalist ethic.[13] Certainly it offers a religious and ethical framework for Spaniards in which to come to terms with a modern capitalist economy — something which the traditional face of Spanish catholicism was ill-equipped to do. But this does not wholly explain the remarkable success of Opus Dei. It now has 72,000 members worldwide and 1,400 priests. Members are divided into three categories: numeraries, all of whom are unmarried, take vows of personal conduct and live in hostels devoting their leisure exclusively to Opus; supernumeraries, who do not take vows and live in their own homes but devote themselves to Opus; and co-operants or assistants who follow the teachings of Opus, do good works, and provide financial assistance.

The success of Opus in Spain cannot be separated from the religious persecution of the thirties and the reinstatement of the Church by Franco at the expense of all progressive and liberal thought. Opus provided a refuge for thoughtful Catholics, and offered some way out of the moral dilemma of accepting the partisan nature of the Church and its open identification with an authoritarian regime.

Father Escriva formed Opus among a circle of friends at Madrid University, whence its main impetus came. Its growth was fostered by the regime since the first Education Minister, Jose Ibañez Martin, was a close friend of one of Father Escriva's first disciples — Jose Maria Albareda. The latter became head of a newly formed Council for Scientific Research (Consejo Superior de Investigaciones Cientificas) in 1939. This job, which Albareda held until his death in 1966, gave him very substantial academic patronage. Opus pursued a conscious policy of penetrating the universities and, in this way, sought to influence society as a whole with its philosophy. Since everyone who applied for a university chair was screened for political acceptability, it was comparitively simple for Opus members to establish themselves. Opus was extremely successful in this and thus obtained an important hold on the elite of Franco's Spain.[14]

Opus made a point of recruiting among the most gifted students. This encouraged a sense of elitism, which was reinforced by the mutual self-help promised by members. Questions over the political nature of Opus came to the fore in 1957 with the introduction of two members in key cabinet posts — Alberto Ullastres was made Minister of Commerce and Mariano Navarro Rubio, Minister of Finance. The impression of Opus as a political force was emphasized by the incorporation of another member into this team running the economy, Laureano Lopez Rodo, who took charge of planning. This strong Opus presence in government drew odium from the Falangists who fomented suspicion within the bureaucracy and the public at large over the true intentions of the order. It was not difficult to spread the idea of an Opus conspiracy to usurp power.

Members of Opus have consistently denied this and there is no conclusive proof that it seeks crude political power.[15] Opus does, however, seek power indirectly because it aims to influence the direction of society. That the principal technocrats to emerge at the time of economic take-off were Opus members is not mere chance. Opus technocrats were willing to enter government, and, in a field restricted by the exclusion of liberals and anyone to their left, they were the best talent available. But the emphasis of Opus is on the individual, not the group. In the absence of political parties this permitted individual Opus members to exercise influence within the Franco administration.

Whether individually or as an organization, Opus and its members deserve some credit for being the liberalizing element within the Franco regime. But this was liberalization with a very small 'l' and no prominent Opus member opposed the regime or sought to accelerate the pace of change towards democracy. Instead Opus hid behind solid support for a monarchist solution, and with the advent of democracy the organization and its members had only limited political credibility. Its influence therefore declined. Some Opus members argue that with the advent of democracy there is no need even to consider political influence.

The presence of Pope John Paul II in the Holy See and his confirmation of the status of personal prelature has given new importance to Opus. The Pope's candidature was backed by Opus-inclined cardinals and he is seen to support Opus as a force to reinstall conservative orthodoxy in catholicism, to the detriment of the Jesuits. Papal support for Opus was seen in the choice in 1981 of the new Nuncio, Archbishop Innocenti. The Opus line in the Vatican was reinforced by the choice of replacement for Cardinal Tarancon as Archbishop of Madrid — the Archbishop of Santiago de Compostela, Angel Suquia, close to Opus. This revived ascendancy of Opus could help push the Church towards a more conservative ecclesiastical view of society.

The most important direct influence Opus has is in education and certain sectors of the financial community. Opus controls the university of Navarre, which, among other things, runs an important school of journalism. It also controls, via the University of Navarre, Spain's main graduate business school, IES, based in Barcelona.

The head of Banco Popular, Luis Valls is a member, and this seventh largest private bank is regarded as an Opus bank. Several other leading Opus members hold important positions in banking: Gregorio Lopez Bravo (former Franco Foreign Minister), is on the board of the largest private bank, Banesto; Enrique Sendagorta is vice-president of Banco de Vizcaya;[16] Rafael

Termes is head of the bankers association. For those who subscribe to conspiracy theories, this array of names and their activities in collecting money for Opus are sufficient to inspire any manner of rumour and comment over the real aims and power of this organization. Yet at this level, Opus operates as a form of mutual aid but never as a concerted political and financial pressure group. Pressure, if applied, is exercised individually so that the organization is never directly implicated.

It also has to be said that Opus has been particularly unfortunate in its financial history. Navarro Rubio's legislation in 1962 permitting the formation of new banks was seen as an attempt to break the monopoly of the large banks, and allow more Opus financiers a share of the action. The majority of the banks given licence under this legislation have collapsed or been taken over. One bank that set out to be an important Opus centre, the industrial bank, Bankunion, collapsed in 1981 and was subsequently taken over by Hispano-Americano. This bank had made a series of investments, including in publishing, whose main logic appeared to be their connections with Opus.

Bankunion was originally the industrial arm of Barcelona-based commercial bank, Atlantico; this too had Vatican and Opus connections. It became the flagship of the Rumasa group of banks under Ruiz-Mateos in 1979. Ruiz-Mateos himself never admitted Opus membership although many of his personal ideas were very close to those of the organization, and it is suspected that Opus supported him in the early stages of his career. He denies this.[17] Following the expropriation of Rumasa in February 1983 it emerged that the group had pledged credit facilities of 1·5 billion pesetas to an educational institute, Insituto de Educacion e Investigacion, S.A., intended to provide educational grants. This institute, which had yet to function, was headed by Gregorio Lopez Bravo and Enrique Sendagorta, both known for their Opus membership. Only part of the funds had been used, according to Lopez Bravo, who denied that the institution had any connection with Opus. Whatever the Opus-Rumasa connection, the image of Opus as a shadowy organization operating in the world of finance to promote undisclosed ends has been given another airing. This can only discredit Opus and make it harder for the organization to establish a political and financial power in Spain — if indeed this is its real objective.

TEMPORAL POWERS

Cardinal Tarancon's policy of disassociating the Church from direct political action was deliberately limiting. It was pursued at the same time as the Church reserved its capacity to influence events behind the scenes, especially where its own interests were directly concerned. The most important form of this self-limitation concerned Church support for political parties when they were legalized in 1976. Cardinal Tarancon, directly and indirectly, told those who wished to form a christian democrat party that the project did not have his approval. He was against a confessional label being attached to a party for which the Church itself was not responsible. As a result, the overtures by politicians like Joaquin Ruiz-Jimenez, Jose Maria Gil Robles, Alfonso Osorio and Jose Luis Alvarez, came to nothing. This refusal helped the loose grouping of centre and right wing forces to coalesce in UCD.[18] When Ruiz-Jimenez and Gil Robles offered their Christian Democrat Party to the electorate in the first democratic elections of June 1977, they got only 1·4% of the vote. There is little doubt that if the Church had swung behind this party it would have done better. As it was, the Episcopal Conference in its cautious public statements clearly supported Suarez and UCD — understandable enough since UCD then offered the best chance of stability and the greatest respect for Church interests.

The issue of a christian democrat party is far from resolved. The christian democrat element within UCD was a principal force behind the latter's disintegration. The Popular Democratic Party (PDP), of Oscar Alzaga, formed from UCD in September 1982, is a thinly disguised christian democrat party.

With the departure of Cardinal Tarancon, elements of the hierarchy believe that Church interests need to be more vigorously defended in the political arena, and that support for a christian democrat party is beneficial. The debate is liable to be divisive and long-running. Supporters of Cardinal Tarancon argue that the strength of the Church in relation to society should stem from the role of the priest among his parishioners. 'Just imagine in Madrid alone every Sunday there are 700 priests preaching to 300,000 people — no political party can mobilize that,' says Father Jose Maria Martin Patino, frequently used by Cardinal Tarancon as a go-between with the politicians.[19] Often this power is slow to materialize, but once formed it is far more long-lasting than a demonstration. Under UCD, the Church and its friends in parliament successfully blocked any major reforms of educational syllabuses, finance and university reorganization, out of fear that Church influence in this vital area might be reduced. The Church also mobilized opinion to make divorce and abortion into polemical moral issues.

Yet despite this power to mobilize opinion, the Church cannot go against the trend of modern society. It was obliged to accept the introduction of a divorce law in 1980. The law was given a more liberal touch by the Justice Minister, Francisco Fernandez Ordoñez, contrary to what Spanish bishops regarded as previous assurances. The Episcopal Conference did not like the law but their protests were muted since they knew a law permitting divorce was inevitable. The Church has been more combative and overtly political on the abortion issue. But here again there are limits to which the Church can convincingly go against trends in a modern society. For instance, abortion in Spain is still penalized in the most primitive way, but nothing stops

Spaniards travelling to London where some 20,000 a year have abortions. The socialist government will eliminate such anomalies and establish a law which permits abortion where the life or health of the mother is at risk. It is an issue which has produced the most serious conflict between the government and the Church hierarchy since Franco's death. However, the Catholic Church had already lost the abortion battle in other European countries and this was a rearguard action. Indeed, what concerns thinking priests most is that the abortion issue could reawaken anti-clericalism. The socialist government cannot ignore the catholicism of its own militants, who act as a balance to any anti-clericalism. A study of party members conducted in 1980 revealed that 39% of all questioned held religious beliefs; of these 71% professed to be Catholics. The study showed a direct link between religious belief, age, and level of education. In general, the degree of religiousness was greater among those with secondary and higher education. The least religious members affiliated to the party during the Republic, while those who joined the party after 1976 were the most religious.[20]

The strength and influence of the church in contemporary Spain essentially depends upon two factors: the politicians' perception of its powers, and the Church's acceptance by society. Like the army, the Church is an institution that is not directly represented in parliament. As such, it is seen as a de facto power — an institution that can manipulate from behind without direct interference. Both UCD and now the socialists have been wary of antagonizing the Church. There has been a good deal of behind-the-scenes skirmishing, but this has not stopped infringements on traditional Church ground, such as the indissolubility of marriage, being ignored by the divorce law. The politicians also realise that the Church is a cumbrous organization, yet to achieve a real degree of internal cohesion.

The Church today embraces die-hard conservative reactionaries alongside progressive christian-marxists. This lack of homogeneity permits it to shepherd a wide flock. But it also creates confusion and genuine doubts about the real nature of the Church's mission. Should the Church, for instance, spend more energy denouncing torture in police custody and corruption in local government (issues assiduously ignored by the hierarchy), and give a moral lead in this way? Or should all energy be directed to preventing the liberalization of abortion — even though widely practised in secret? This sense of confusion has been translated into a steady decline in the number of people applying for the priesthood from 1963 onwards. The intake for seminaries reached its lowest point in 1979 with only 1,500; the figure rose to 1,728 in 1982, but it is not clear whether this indicates a genuine upwards trend. The average age of Spain's clergy in 1982 was forty-nine years old — only 20% were under forty.[21] The Church has lost its attraction as a calling, and this in turn has been translated into lower mass attendance and fewer faithful. One poll in 1980 showed that 82% of all Spaniards were Catholic believers, but few considered themselves very good Catholics. In the case of the young, the level of belief and practice is far lower. A 1976 study among university students revealed that only 2·3% considered themselves to be very good Catholics, and 20% to be practising Catholics.[22]

Even in the important field of education, Church influence is being eroded. The Church can no longer count on having its friends in the two ministries with which it has traditionally been most associated — Education and Justice. This is especially the case with the socialist government which is pledged to reform education and make the law more socially acceptable.[23]

11 The Media and Public Opinion

The media under Franco faithfully reflected the views of the government. Where the press and radio were Church-controlled or Catholic in orientation, some freedom was permitted. But in the twilight of the regime, newspapers and magazines began to appear, bravely exploiting the relaxation in censorship and challenging the old order. These played a key role in forming public opinion and in setting the pace of reform.

Not long after taking office, Felipe Gonzalez sent a circular to all the ministries insisting that no one read *El Pais* before midday. The Prime Minister was concerned that his ministers and senior civil servants might allow the newspaper to make up their minds on policy decisions rather than using their own judgement. The story is told with relish at *El Pais* and dismissed airily in the Prime Minister's office. Apocryphal or not, it underlines the influence acquired by *El Pais*. Though founded only in 1976, it is one of the few well established institutions of democratic Spain.

From the start *El Pais* has been obligatory reading. As the media broke free from the censorious shackles of the Franco era, the paper became the most authoritative voice of progressive change and cultural renewal. *El Pais* caught the mood of a changing nation and successfully articulated its hopes and fears — helping to an important degree in shaping the nature of democracy. Proof of its appeal is in its circulation and profitability: circulation has doubled to almost 300,000 making it by far the biggest selling newspaper in Spain. Its older rivals have meanwhile witnessed a steady decline, and have only staved off bankruptcy with the help of state subsidy and the generosity of the banks.

Three factors determined *El Pais*' rapid success and acquisition of institutional status: the timing of its launch, the composition of its shareholders, and the editorial team. The application to publish an independent newspaper was made as far back as 1972, by a group of investors who formed a company specifically for this purpose, Promotora de Informaciones (PRISA). It was impossible to publish a paper without inscription in the official Newspaper Register (Registro de Empresas Periodisticas). Despite continued hesitancy on the part of the administration, PRISA went ahead and bought premises and machinery. Only in March 1975 did the Ministry of Information finally give the green light. Originally it had been hoped to name the paper *El Sol*, linking it to the newspaper of the Republic and the illustrious pen of Ortega; but this idea was overruled, and *El Pais* was named after a nineteenth-century liberal paper.

The paper's backers had varying motives for the venture. For some, like PRISA's chief executive, Jesus de Polanco, who already had experience in publishing, it was a mixture of business risk and a desire to influence events behind the scenes. Other shareholders were more overtly political, such as the conservative Manuel Fraga and the communist economist, Ramon Tamames. Yet another group of persons, such as leading shareholder Antonio Garcia Trevijano, had professed independent political views. (Trevijano had, nevertheless, already thrown in his lot with the Junta Democratica.) The smaller shareholders were basically investing money they could afford to lose. Yet all the backers were convinced of the ready made market for a new quality daily. The state-run media was dull and uninformative. The private media lacked credibility because they had survived under the Franco regime by submissive, even servile, acceptance of the status quo.

El Pais was launched at a felicitous moment. Politically untainted by Francoism, it came onto the news stands at a moment of political vacuum. Arias had promised political change and liberalization but had done little of substance to make good his promises. Political parties were still illegal more than six months after the Caudillo's death. The independent media were thus the sole public platform for new political ideas and views. The relatively broad base of political ideology, from conservative through to communist, among the shareholders provided *El Pais* with the essential credibility of an independent platform. They were supported by the establishment, even if they did not agree with it, and this reassured the authorities of the paper's respectability. *El Pais'* tone was set by the first editorial on 4 May 1976: a sharp attack on the dithering Arias and a call for the quick introduction of political reforms.

A further advantage was the strength of the editorial team under Juan Luis Cebrian, who was only thirty-one when chosen to be editor. He personified a new generation of Spaniards who had grown up in the later Franco years, enjoying the privileges of economic development yet conscious of the defects of the Franco regime. He was educated at Madrid's select Colegio del Pilar, which has produced many of the ruling elite in Spain of the eighties. (One of his classmates was Javier Solana, first Socialist Minister of Culture.) His father was a prominent journalist working within the state media and it was through him he got his first job—as news editor of the Movimiento's creaking news agency, Pyresa. After working with the French news agency, Agence France Presse, and the US Associated Press, he did spells in *Pueblo* and *Informaciones* before being made head of the first channel news on television (RTVE). He resigned in 1974 over political disagreements and returned to *Informaciones* from where he was recruited to start up and edit *El Pais*.

Before deciding on the style and layout, Cebrian and his team made an extensive study of the international papers they most admired. They aimed to achieve the influential status of *Le Monde* — authoritative with a liberal and progressive philosophy at home and internationally sympathetic to the aspirations of the Third World and wary of great power rivalry. In terms of layout the closest model was the recently established *Republica* in Italy. The product, using the latest print technology, was a revolution in Spain. For once a newspaper was produced with a clean, fresh 'read-me' look. The Francoist press had been so dismally laid out that it conveyed the impression of being deliberately obscure.[1]

THE PRESS AND DEMOCRACY

El Pais was the most prominent of the publications that grew up in the twilight of the Franco regime and its immediate aftermath. It overshadowed the achievements of the weekly magazine, *Cambio-16*, founded in 1972 as the first real journalistic challenge to the system. The magazine's very name proclaimed this — sixteen people staking their claim in a 'change'. These publications were of vital importance and their role in helping the establishment of democracy has been greatly underestimated.

Trades union protest and ETA's political violence tended to scare the authorities. The new press, battling within the frontiers of censorship, caused the authorities to take note of their demands and opinions. They defined the limits of change and, on occasion, forced its pace. For instance, one of the most controversial topics was the torture of political suspects by the security forces. In May 1976 *Cambio-16* took the lead by publishing an extensive reportage, with photographs, on torture in Spain. The Ministry of Information could have seized the issue, but held back, uncertain of the consequences. Soon afterwards, however, it declared that all reference to torture in the media was *materia reservada*, and under this power removed another reportage on torture which appeared in the magazine *Cuadernos Para el Dialogo*. *Cuadernos...* was able, nevertheless, to publish a statement that told readers 'obstacles beyond our control' prevented publication of an article on torture. This skirmish with the Arias government helped highlight the contradictions in a system pledged to create liberties yet unwilling to put the pledge into practice. It also emphasized the disagreements inside the administration on the nature and pace of reform, and alerted the public to an explosive issue.

Strident criticism of the Arias government by *El Pais* and public exposure of its incompetence undoubtedly hardened the view that he had to be dismissed. Indeed, if there had not been such public pressure on King Juan Carlos to remove Arias, it is questionable whether the vital switch to Suarez would have been made in time.

The nascent liberal press took advantage of the divisions within the Arias government to become ever bolder. Every attempt at stifling criticism made the journalists more determined to find ways of making their views known. The cause of the independent liberal press was inadvertently boosted by the officially controlled media, whose bias and selectivity became increasingly obvious.

The departure of Arias and the advent of Suarez in July 1976 further emboldened the press, although the former secretary general of the Movimiento initially inspired little confidence. In October, another new independent daily was born, *Diario-16*, from the same stable as Juan Tomas de Salas', *Cambio-16*. Unlike *El Pais*, it was Madrid orientated. *El Pais* set itself out to be a national daily from the start.

Diario-16 nailed its colours firmly to the democratic mast by calling in its first issue for the abolition of the Ministry of Information, which Suarez had inherited and chosen to retain. By late 1976, *El Pais* and *Diario-16*, accompanied by the magazines *Cambio-16, Cuadernos...* and *Triunfo*, enjoyed influence out of all proportion to their readership in the educated elite of the big urban centres, especially the capital. 'They were an "alternative government" constantly calling for amnesty, democratic reforms and, most important of all, a general election.'[2] They highlighted the anomaly of the Cortes permitting the establishment of political parties in June, while leaving the penal code untouched. The Communists were specifically excluded while moderate parties enjoyed an ambiguous semi-legality.

The existence of a well organized, clandestine Communist Party was common knowledge but declarations by its leaders were not tolerated by the Ministry of Information. Once the Suarez government had allowed *El Pais* to publish an interview with *La Pasionaria*, the Party's veteran president, it became clear that the Communists were tolerated, if not officially. Press conferences given by the leaders of opposition parties became the main platform for airing political discontent, and were held when the parties were still illegal. Their impact was reinforced by the occasional arrests that ensued, and by the appearance of the international press in Spain. Sometimes articles from the international press were reproduced on the journalistic principle of 'export, re-import'. Spanish journalists fed foreign colleagues sensitive stories, and once these had been written up in authoritative international publications, the information was public. The Spanish press was thus able to pick up and elaborate on a government denial to make it look ridiculous, or reproduce the foreign stories wholesale. In this atmosphere, the Suarez government could either clamp down on the press, or reform existing laws to make their new freedom official. Since the first was incompatible with the whole raison d'être of the government, Suarez opted for the latter — with a number of provisos that gave particular protection to the monarchy and the armed forces.

In April 1977, just two months before the elections, the Suarez Government removed the all-embracing curbs on press freedom.[4] These curbs could not have been retained much longer without reducing the election campaign to a farce. The new legislation was not comprehensive and revealed the sensitivities of the government. The decree contained, for instance, powers to control obscene and pornographic publications, reflecting the anxiety of the Church hierarchy and the right over the upsurge in 'soft porn'. More important, the legislation contained some restrictive conditions on libel, geared to tone down investigative reports on the activities of persons connected with the former regime. This was abundantly clear in the specific reference to infringements of the libel provisions committed during an election campaign, which were subject to tough extra penalties.

This measure ensured that the campaign focussed on the future and avoided a slanging match about the past. But the benefits of democracy could not be fully explained if the defects of Francoism could not be truly exposed. Under this veil of silence, many figures with Francoist pasts changed unchallenged into democratic clothing.

Since the liberal press itself favoured gradual reform not revolutionary change, a dialogue was established with the Suarez administration based on a mixture of personal contacts and mutual interest. Once the elections had passed off smoothly there was an unwritten pact that the liberal media would not 'rock the boat'. Friction only occurred when editors and administration differed on the terms of this pact. The government made its view known via 'telephone pressure' rather than the battery of laws still at its disposal.

IN THE SERVICE OF THE MOVIMIENTO

The vigorous but responsible role of the liberal independent press at the end of the Franco regime was possible because theoretically tight regulations were interpreted with growing laxity. Journalists also became adept at getting round restrictions and the attentive reader had become used to interpreting metaphors. Stories about de Gaulle were a favourite short-hand for describing how dictators hung on to the reins of power.

Freedom of expression under Franco was defined with breathtaking simplicity. Under the 1938 Statute of the Spanish People (Fuero de los Españoles), every Spaniard had the right to express his ideas freely 'provided they did not attack the fundamental principles of the state'.[5] The media was, of necessity, loyal to the regime, and its views conformed with it. As a result of the Civil War, the State seized or expropriated republican newspapers and radio stations. Only those newspapers whose proprietors had shown loyalty to the Nationalist cause, such as the Luca de Tena family of *ABC*, and the Godo family of Barcelona's *La Vanguardia Española*, escaped seizure. The media thus acquired were incorporated into the Movimiento and entitled the

Press and Radio of the Movimiento. It contained thirty-five newspapers, forty-five radio stations, and the news agency, Pyresa, in addition to the Movimiento's official mouthpiece, the daily *Arriba* and, subsequently, the Madrid evening paper of the vertical syndicates, *Pueblo*.

The majority of these were small provincial newspapers. The most important were *Alerta* in Santander, *Informacion* in Alicante, *Levante* in Valencia, *La Nueva España* in Oviedo, and *Sur* in Malaga. Though generally small in circulation they were frequently the main and sometimes the sole source of written news. In eleven provinces the Movimiento press was the sole paper. The press was unimaginative and rarely aimed at the 'popular' reader — crime and scandal, the lifeblood of popular newspapers, were avoided almost entirely for fear of reflecting ill on the regime. Readers were thus deterred rather than encouraged, and this was one of the principal reasons why Spain failed to raise its newspaper readership level significantly during the Franco era. Statistics vary, but Spain has on average 80 papers read per 1,000 inhabitants, compared to 118 in Italy, a country not noted for its newspaper reading habits.[6] A by-product of the stifling boredom of the official press was the success of social magazines such as *Hola* that portrayed the glamour of the rich and famous.[7]

The Movimiento news network was fed by Pyresa and more importantly by the national news agency, EFE, established in 1939. EFE was the principal source of news for state and private newspapers and radios. A semblance of impartiality was given by the state allowing one third of the shares to be distributed among the private newspapers who subscribed to the service. But since the private newspapers had to tow the official line, this was no more than a cynical means for the private proprietors to get the state to subsidize a cheap source of news supply.

Pueblo was outside the direct control of the Movimiento. Owned by the vertical syndicates, it was run as a trades union paper. At its high point, *Pueblo* had a circulation of over 200,000 — the largest of any state-controlled newspaper. It attracted a better staff in its latter days and had as editor, for a time, Emilio Romero, the most gifted journalist of the Franco era.

The state-run press did not really compete with the private newspaper groups. Only two independent papers had pretensions to being quality nationals — *ABC* and *YA*. *ABC* relied for almost a third of sales on its Seville edition. The paper's editorial line could only be considered critical of the regime in that the Luca de Tena family were firm monarchists and basically disapproved of Franco's refusal to hand over to Don Juan. But *ABC* never challenged the nature of Franco's authoritarianism.

YA, owned by Editorial Catolica, was the independent voice of the Catholic Church, fully backed by the ecclesiastical hierarchy. Having made its peace with the regime, the church was not ready to let journalistic integrity interfere with the privileges acquired from Franco. As for *La Vanguardia*, though it retained a network of its own foreign correspondents, it was essentially a Catalan paper supportive, like *ABC*, of the monarchy.

In 1966 there was an important change in official handling of the media, signalling a more sophisticated approach to control. Under the guidance of Fraga in the Information Ministry, a new press law was approved which abolished prior censorship. Instead, discretion was put in the hands of the editor who was free to publish what he chose provided it did not contravene the principles of the Movimiento or the interests of the state. It was a lengthier version of the 1938 Fuero, the principle of 'you are free, but...'. The difference lay in the more liberal interpretation and a new form of censorship.

Copies of newspapers had to be placed in the hands of the Ministry of Information no later than half an hour before publication. Magazines were subjected to similar scrutiny. The authorities therefore knew what was going to be published and could give advice, warnings, and threats to influence the final content. By placing the burden on editors rather than censors, everything depended on their caution and courage, and the willingness of the management to tangle with the regime. Rather than fight, most editors opted for self-censorship, far more invidious than outright censorship. Furthermore, the penal legislation against publication of material harmful to state interests or public morals remained in force.

As a result of the loosening of censorship, Ruiz-Jimenez, the former Education Minister, decided to found a christian democrat magazine, *Cuadernos Para el Dialogo. Cuadernos ...* was instrumental in bringing together a group of christian democrat writers who, first timidly then more openly, distanced themselves from the regime. The Madrid daily *Informaciones* emerged as the most innovative and most effective of the private newspapers alongside the evening paper, *Madrid.*

Madrid was closed down by cabinet order in November 1971, after a long-running skirmish with the authorities. The paper was run by Rafael Calvo Serrer who had begun life close to the Franco regime, became an ideologist of Opus Dei, and then launched a personal crusade to get Franco to step down in favour of Don Juan. *Madrid* suffered a series of fines including one of 250,000 pesetas in 1968 for a serious attack on state security. The offending article was about Franco, but referred to him as de Gaulle. As a result of this, the paper was closed for four months. Calvo Serrer followed this up with a sharp critique of the regime published in *Le Monde* in November 1971. The authorities reacted by closing *Madrid* and seeking to imprison Calvo Serrer, who went into exile. His shares were expropriated and the *Madrid* building was taken over and subsequently dynamited. Calvo Serrer successfully challenged this action and was awarded unspecified damages by a Madrid court in 1976.[8]

Calvo Serrer showed that the regime could no longer rely on the docility of journalists and editors — even if journalists still had to be the products of state-approved journalism courses. But the seizure of the paper and its assets was a stern warning to newspaper proprietors, who lived in constant fear of such actions. It was this fear, coupled with the authorities' determination to prevent the accumulation of large press chains under single ownership, that prevented the rise of press barons. The largest empire was that of the Godo family. Apart from *La Vanguardia*, the Godo family owned, under Franco, *Gaceta Ilustrada, Tele-Expres, Historia y Vida,* and *El Papus.* Those who in other countries might have owned newspapers for political motives shied off in Spain. The shrewder operated on the principle, 'cheaper to buy a journalist than the newspaper he is producing'.

THE CONTROL OF TELEVISION

State control of the media had its greatest effect on television. Television was introduced as a State monopoly in 1956 when major social and economic changes were beginning in Spain. In a country unused to popular newspapers, but with a population curious about their environment and conscious of their status, television was irresistible.

Television lured many a potential newspaper reader quickly and permanently away from the written word. If the programmes had been any good this would not have mattered so much. They were not. The nature of television production, with nearly everything pre-recorded, made control easy. Television became *the* propaganda tool of the administration. The Caudillo's public appearances would now be viewed by millions.

The first channel was launched on 28 October at 6.00 pm with viewers having fifteen minutes to adjust their sets before a solemn mass, followed by pompous opening speeches led by the Information Minister, Gabriel Arias-Salgado. The first programme was folk dancing and singing. The three items of the first evening — Church moral influence, the paternalistic voice of officialdom, and a fare of safe folklore — came to typify television broadcasts in Spain. Arias-Salgado is reported to have convinced Franco of the value of television not only as a means of political control but also of sending more Spanish souls to heaven.[9]

The first head of RTVE, Jose Maria Revuelta, a State Advocate, had earned the distinction of quarrelling with the Falangist Minister of Labour, Jose Antonio Giron, while his subordinate. Revuelta knew nothing about television. However, he was a friend of Arias-Salgado who was anxious to ensure that television come under the patronage and control of the Ministry of Information. Television was given its own set of censors who operated inside the RTVE; but they were merely a fall-back mechanism to ensure that both the RTVE administration and the Minister himself were not caught unawares by any errors of judgement. From the start it was a question of 'jobs-for-the-boys' in the organization with loyalty and friendship put above technical competence.

Television conveyed the image of a country serenely governed by a distant but all-caring and all-comprehending Caudillo. The viewers were never alarmed by strikes, terrorist actions or international disrespect for the regime. Such incidents did not happen, since they were never reported. At a superficial level television created a reassuring sense of calm which served the regime well, but it did not stop the opposition. If anything it divorced the educated elite from the mass of Spaniards, making the latter unwilling to mix in politics and therefore difficult to politicize with the advent of democracy. On the other hand, the profoundly moral tone of television, strongly influenced by the Church (dubbed Hollywood films were special victims), failed to prevent a gradual loosening of traditional morals in the country, or sustain attendance at Church. Franco's television failed to attract Spain's youth. Pop music was cautiously staged since the management feared its decadent influence. Television emphasized the new middle-class values the nation was acquiring — happy christian families enjoying increased prosperity.

One side effect of this type of programming was the boost given to the popularity of sport, particularly football. The opposition claimed the RTVE management operated on the basis that nothing distracted the nation's mind further from politics than a good football match. Certainly the victories of the national team satisfied the regime's need to stimulate national pride. The same sense of nationalism could not be provoked in a bullfight! The popularity of football, incidentally, was given an added impetus through sheer political frustration. Clubs like Barcelona, Atletico/Bilbao and Real Sociedad of San Sebastian became aggressive projections of regional identity. Their victories were Catalan or Basque.

A more fortunate effect of the development of television was to divert the authorities' censorious attention away from films. Bolder uncensored criticism of the state of Spain at this time was made in the cinema than in any other medium. Juan Bardem with his *Muerte de un Ciclista* (1955) and *Calle Mayor* (1956) showed a neo-realist touch every bit as good as the earlier Italian films of the genre. His colleague, Luis Garcia Berlanga preferred parody and satire but was just as telling. These films caught the mood of protest just beginning in the universities. Other directors followed, like Carlos Saura and Jose Luis Borau, who were more overtly political. (Their works were incidentally only shown on television after 1977.) Borau got past the censors the harshest parable of Francoist authoritarianism — *Los Furtivos* (1975). This film subsequently became one of the top five Spanish box office hits. The censors seemed better able to cope with the printed word.

Television was treated as a political stepping stone for the ambitious members of the administration. The alumni of RTVE included Adolfo Suarez who headed it from 1969 to 1973 — a period during which he seemed more concerned with cultivating political influence than the quality of the product offered to the public. Typical of the distorting acts of censorship under his rule was the cutting in the first television showing of *Casablanca*. When the French police chief, Renaud, admits to Bogart, 'I am just a corrupt official' the word 'corrupt' was excised![10] Juan Jose Roson, a future UCD Interior Minister, and Jesus Sanchez Rof, future UCD Labour Minister, both followed in Suarez's footsteps.

When Suarez became Prime Minister he ensured that control of RTVE moved from the Ministry of Information to the Prime Minister's office. He appointed Rafael Anson, a public relations specialist with whom he had already worked, and whose brother was head of the national news agency EFE, to take charge. Anson gave way to Fernando Arias-Salgado, son of RTVE's inaugurator, Gabriel, and brother of Rafael, who was appointed by Suarez as UCD's link-man with the Cortes, and later became party secretary-general.

At Franco's death and during the ensuing two years, television continued to be controlled and heavily manipulated. On 20 November, the day Franco died, viewers had been scheduled to see *Satan Nunca Duerme*, (Satan Never Sleeps). According to the synopsis in *Tele-Radio*, 'The Heavenly Empire is in the hands of the army of the people who have gradually conquered the country...'. It was substituted for *Franco, Ese Hombre*.[11]

The first substantial change occured with the 1977 elections. The main contestants in the election impressed on Suarez the need for an electoral committee to determine the amount and type of electoral coverage. Television coverage was enormously important since it offered the best exposure to previously unknown figures — and in the case of the left it put faces and personalities to names. An electoral committee was agreed upon, and operated fairly. But by its very nature it treated television as a vehicle for the parties. They controlled coverage, not the television management, and the interests of the viewers were a secondary consideration. Coverage was restrained and, by agreement, live recordings of meetings were avoided. UCD, however, held the trump card. Suarez reserved the right as Prime Minister to make a television address to the nation on the eve of polling. This address was instrumental in swaying the electorate behind him. He repeated the performance in March 1979 when he warned in a tough speech of the dangers of not voting UCD. Again, this was crucial in persuading the undecided. As many as 10% of the electorate only decided on the day whom they would vote for.[12]

After the 1977 election, there was a move to control RTVE via a joint parliamentary committee. In October 1977, RTVE acquired a new charter which established an inter-party committee as a governing body. The charter did not pretend to guarantee RTVE managerial independence within its status as a state-run monopoly. Instead the new charter formalized the situation whereby RTVE was a political football over which the parties fought for influence; and since the charter gave the government more committee representatives than the opposition, this raised the danger of permanent conflict between the other parties and the government over political bias. The governors were turned into stooges of the political parties, protecting sectarian interests rather than controlling the quality of output. Under these circumstances efforts to provide a better professional service were invariably submerged.

In the last three years under UCD there were three changes in the top management of television — each one the result of a different balance of forces within the party and among its allies. The last UCD appointment to the post of director-general was Carlos Robles Piquer, senior diplomat and brother-in-law of Fraga, who subsequently joined AP. The Robles Piquer appointment was the most blatant of political moves, designed to head off criticism from a powerful sector of UCD that television had become too liberal. In theory, the director-general of television cannot be removed providing he is acting competently. However, the Calvo Sotelo government 'persuaded' Fernando Castedo to resign in favour of Robles Piquer. Regardless of Robles Piquer's capacity, the manner of his appointment seriously undermined the neutral image of RTVE management and, in the process, damaged improvements in programme quality which had occurred.

The advent of the socialist government did not put an end to this process of politicization. Robles Piquer resigned to be replaced by a socialist appointee, Jose Maria Calvino. This established the precedent that a change of government is accompanied by a change in the top hierarchy of RTVE. Calvino, though an independent lawyer, was originally the PSOE representative on the board of governors. He would never have got the job without the complete trust of the government.[13] With this system of appointments it remains difficult, if not impossible, for the government of the day to resist the temptation to manipulate television for its own ends.

The political control of RTVE has given added incentive to the promoters of private commercial channels. In particular the centre and right have favoured commercial television knowing full well that the backers would hold similar political views to their own, and that therefore they would possess a powerful means of attacking the government when out of office. Had UCD survived another year, commercial television would probably have been introduced.

Finding an acceptable method of licence awards and establishing an adequate system of controls will be a formidable obstacle to commercial television in an over-charged political atmosphere. Problems inherent in the process are sufficient to make the socialist government shy away from introducing the necessary legislation. Lobbying will continue but attention instead will focus on the impact of a third channel for regional television — first in the Basque country and Catalonia — run by the autonomous governments. This third state channel is 'political' in that its raison d'etre is to stimulate a sense of regional identity. Basque television, in particular, will be used as a platform for Euskerra, while Catalan television will reinforce their own sense of identity.

Given that over 90% of Spaniards have access to television, those running it have a tremendous responsibility for forming opinion.[14] Until now, the demands of professionalism have been affected on one side by clumsy political control and on the other by cynical abuse of RTVE as a constant source of bounty. This has meant that professionals inside the organization have never been able to perform their jobs adequately. The programmes broadcast have made abysmally little effort to inform Spaniards about their own country. For instance, RTVE, in over twenty-five years of existence, has made not one serious programme about the Basque country and ETA — precisely because it is one of the most sensitive issues facing Spain. The only balanced portrait of the King shown on television was a programme made by the BBC in 1980. (It was originally a co-production, with RTVE providing some financial and technical assistance but RTVE got cold feet and dissociated itself in the credits.)

Television remains the biggest repository of the Francoist fear and mistrust of information. So much attention has been devoted to controlling the political content of what is broadcast that such basic issues as the level to which children should be exposed to violence and standards of advertizing have been ignored.

In addition, RTVE was so poorly managed until the advent of Calvino that there was no proper control over expenditure. The possibility of making original programmes was scotched by absurdly high wage bills for unnecessarily large numbers of staff. Calvino revealed that in 1982 RTVE had paid 442 million pesetas in car hire alone, and that one Madrid company had eighty-two cars with chauffeurs on permanent rent to RTVE.[15]

RADIO – A LESS HEAVY HAND

Radio has been a different story: it has adapted more quickly to change, and enjoys looser censorship and the advantages of competition betwen state and private stations. The most popular station is the privately controlled SER with 8·6 million listeners as opposed to the 5·9 million of the state-run national radio, Radio Nacional (RNE) in 1982. Perhaps this audience reflects what would happen if viewers were offered state or private commercial television in Spain.

RNE was established in 1939 as the principal national radio network, providing light entertainment, sports coverage and propaganda. Gradually, the same sort of separation of the various arms of the state that occurred with the press was repeated with radio. RNE was *the* national radio service, but the Movimiento had its own set of radio stations and the vertical syndicates had theirs. Together, the Movimiento and the syndicates controlled nearly seventy radio stations. These are grouped under one chain, Radio Cadena (RCE). The Ministry of Information had a centralized hold on the distribution of news, which came exclusively from RNE, and applied also to the private stations. There was no independent source of news on the radio until the law was changed in October 1977.

As part of the formalization of relations with the Vatican, the Catholic Church was allowed to establish its own radio stations. These were set up in 1961 under the chain, Cadena de Ondas Populares Españolas, (COPE). The Church established fifty-four such stations around the country on a diocesan basis. The basic purpose behind this move was religious and moral, but the chain also sought to provide some educational programmes. The stations took advertisements to cover running costs but COPE was non-profit making. The most important station of the chain continues to be Radio Popular in Madrid, which has the third largest number of listeners in Spain. Following the Vatican Council II, when the Spanish bishops under Cardinal Tarancon began to distance the Church from the regime, the COPE chain was able to separate itself clearly from RNE.

The most dynamic private chain was SER, founded principally with capital from the Garrigues Walker family and the Fontan family, who retain just under a third share each. Both families were considered liberals within the system — Antonio Garrigues Walker, son of the founding shareholder, is now head of the Liberal Party.[16] The motive for the investment was financial rather than political. From the outset, SER was far more lively than the state-run radio, and remained so despite the state forcibly taking a 25% stake in SER in 1975. Since 1977, SER has demonstrated that it can transmit news quickly and independently, further establishing its popularity over RNE.

Since the lifting of censorship, radio in general has covered stories far more rapidly than television — and this is not just because television is more cumbrous and complicated to take around the country. Radio has used initiative where television has hesitated. It was radio that alerted the public to the events of 23 February and maintained a continuous commentary. In the early morning of 24 February, when Tejero was close to surrender, SER drafted in their best-known sports commentator, which involved the public even more.

In 1982, a new round of radio licences were granted in response to developments in FM. Among the purchasers were newspaper groups like *Diario-16* (Antena 3) and *El Pais*. The latter regarded the investment as a means of promoting the newspaper and maximizing its own news network, but most sought licences on a purely commercial basis. By 1983, the flurry of interest in FM stations waned as the hoped-for profits failed to materialize.

POLITICAL INTERFERENCE

The UCD government did remarkably little to reorganize the media it inherited, and information policy was tackled piecemeal. The Ministry of Information, the most austere and imposing of the 'New Ministries' built by Franco, was rechristened the Ministry of Culture. However, the new ministry was split between trying to promote culture and regenerate the arts and at the same time monitoring and funding the state media. Government information was handled out of the Prime Minister's office with an official spokesman of secretary-of-state rank; his office had the last say on dealings with television, the state network of newspapers, and on matters concerning the private press. But information was too important to leave in the hands of a ministry. Suarez, an arch anti-intellectual whose pleasure outside politiking was the card game *mous*, had scant respect for the Ministry of Culture, and as a result it was poorly funded. Its entire budget was less than that of France's Pompidou Centre, and half went to RTVE.

In 1977, all the state-owned press were grouped in a new body, Medios de Comunicacion Social del Estado (MCE). Total circulation was just over 450,000 and falling sharply. The government did not really want these papers, yet was reluctant to part with them. All but five were losing money, some heavily: 85% of the papers in the chain were loss-makers, and to close them down would remove two thirds of the MCE's circulation. However, the state could scarcely justify pumping in funds to revive them, either to compete unfairly with the private press or not to be read at all.

The employees complicated the situation still further since as state employees they were nearly impossible to fire. Yet there were limits to the employment opportunities within the state apparatus for printers and journalists. Between June 1979 and February 1980 the near defunct news agency, Pyresa, was closed down along with eight newspapers. Among these was *Arriba*, whose case was the most anomalous. Suarez inherited *Arriba* as the official government nespaper, founded by Jose Antonio and the Falange. That there should be an official newspaper, other than the official state bulletin (for laws, decrees and appointments), contradicted the elementary principles of democracy. The situation was all the more absurd because *Arriba* had virtually no readers and was devoid of influence. By the end, its sales had fallen to around 4,000 copies a day, most of which were bought by official bodies using state funds.

The advent of the socialist government saw the number of MCE newspapers reduced from twenty-seven to twenty-two. Some of the autonomous governments showed an interest in buying or controlling the defunct newspapers in their own region.

One big change in early 1983 was an end to the Ministry of Culture's practice of writing the editorials which were distributed throughout the MCE

241

chain. This practice had continued without comment since the Franco days until raised in parliament in May 1983! The most independent of the papers was the Madrid based, *Pueblo*. However, *Pueblo's* existence was much criticized, since this loss-making evening paper needed a state subsidy to survive while its private rival, *Informaciones*, which had performed valiant service to the cause of democracy, collapsed because of debts.

The importance of the national news agency, EFE, in forming opinion and controlling the distribution of news, remained unaltered throughout UCD's term of power, and continues today. The political nature of EFE was underlined by the resignation of Luis Anson from the presidency following the election of the socialist government — he was too closely identified with the outgoing government regime. The Socialists insisted that their appointment of Ricardo Utrilla was based purely on his professional qualifications. He had worked for Agence France Presse and came from *Cambio-16*. However, the appointment was made direct from the Prime Minister's office and he clearly had the latter's confidence.

EFE competes domestically with the privately-run Europa Press, but the competition is unequal and the media uses EFE much more. Apart from being used for official leaks, EFE's importance lies in its monopoly on the distribution of foreign news and photographs inside Spain. It has held this since 1966, as part of the Fraga law. No publication can have an individual contract with the main international news agencies. EFE thus selects what it chooses to distribute in both news and photographs. This is of particular significance for the provincial newspapers who have no foreign sources of their own. The foreign news agencies have long fought to break this monopoly and it is not expected to last.

The tensions inherent in this monopoly were graphically illustrated over a photograph of an after-dinner fall by Felipe Gonzalez's wife, Carmen Romero, whilst accompanying her husband to Mexico in June 1983. EFE withheld the photograph on the grounds that it offended the dignity of the Prime Minister's wife. The American news agency, UPI, acquired a copy in Mexico and distributed it. *El Pais* wanted the picture and EFE, under pressure, released a cut and less embarrassing version. *El Pais* then obtained the picture independently and published it. The incident, small in itself, reveals the difference in view over EFE's role. *El Pais* regards EFE as a news agency at the service of its clients, who exercise their own discretion depending on their own readership. The agency believes it should decide matters of taste. EFE's independence, or potential independence, vis-a-vis the government is also compromised by its dependence on substantial state funding. Furthermore, EFE is treated as the mouthpiece of Spain abroad. In Latin America this has real political overtones, since the agency is treated as one of the more overt manifestations of 'hispanidad'. This makes EFE's presence and actions almost part of Spanish foreign policy in Latin America.

SUBSIDY, INDEPENDENCE AND INFLUENCE

The financial plight of the majority of the press is so parlous that without subsidies they could not survive. Newspapers are obliged to buy Spanish newsprint, which is more expensive than imports, but such purchases are underwritten by a subsidy. This aid is justified as assisting both the newspapers and the Spanish pulp and paper industry.

For each copy sold, newspapers receive one peseta from the State under the 1977 Moncloa Agreements. Since newspaper prices are officially controlled, this assistance is linked to the readership. Price control and a block on the use of foreign newsprint considerably reduce the commercial freedom of the newspapers and the system is by no means ideal. Nor is it entirely transparent. For instance, in addition to these subsidies, newspapers can obtain funds for new technology and modernizing plant. The use of these funds has never been monitored and they have tended to be used by the financially weaker publishing companies to cover current expenses rather than for genuine investment. Thus the stronger newspapers have grown financially healthier (by making proper use of these funds) and solutions to the problems of the weaker newspapers have been delayed.

Apart from these direct subsidies, newspapers are bound to the state and government by advertising. Official advertisements (especially from the Ministry of Finance) and those from state companies account for, on average, a third of all advertising revenue in the press.

The morality and value of state subsidies to loss-making publications is not an issue that has been squarely faced. While in power UCD, and especially the Suarez administration, was not unduly troubled. A financially weak press going cap-in-hand to the government paved the way for manipulations and discreet pressures. Under Suarez, an under-the-table fund — dubbed 'the reptiles fund' — existed to aid friendly publications. Perhaps out of a visceral reaction to the Franco days of paternalism, newspapers looked first to the government for aid. However, the change in the political complexion of the government in late 1982 forced the centre and right-wing press to rely for salvation more on private funding.

The financial health of the newspapers is an important issue, because it has repercussions on both quality and independence. The basic flaw in the system since Franco's death is that too much money has been handed out regardless of the quality and appeal of the newspaper. During this time there has been a clear decline in the weight and readership of the main independent newspapers that existed under the previous regime: *ABC, La Vanguardia* and *YA* have all lost ground. *ABC* has lost almost a third of its pre-1975 readership, *YA* slightly more. These newspapers stuck to their conservative formulas in editorial comment and presentation. The hiring by *YA* of well-known columnists like Emilio Romero and Ricardo de la Cierva, and a more sensationalist and polemical approach by *ABC* under Luis Maria Anson in 1983 failed to regenerate the interest of readers. These two national newspapers retain their faithful following but their loss of readership has reduced their prestige and political influence. *ABC*, because of its strong monarchist stance and readership among the conservative establishment, retains the most influence, and indeed claims to speak for the conservative establishment, having swung behind Alianza Popular and its allies. *La Vanguardia* is important in forming opinion in Catalonia among the centre and right.

The influence of these newspapers has been surrendered to *El Pais* at a national level. *El Pais* has also picked up a new class of reader, starved under Franco of critical comment and comprehensive information. With its liberal, centre-left stance, and with the support of the Spanish intellectual establishment, it has become the conscience and mouthpiece of thinking Spaniards under the age of fifty. Its impact covers not merely the political arena but also the business world and the Spanish cultural scene. Its extensive coverage of the arts has done much to stimulate a post-Franco cultural renaissance. Meanwhile, its profitability reinforces its editorial independence.

Success in Spain has made it a model for many (unfulfilled) journalistic aspirations in Latin America and it has begun to acquire weight as a voice there, especially since the launching of a weekly airmail edition in May 1983. By opening its pages to Latin American writers and journalists the paper has done much to encourage a genuine appreciation of common cultural links, and let stifled Latin American political voices be heard.

The rapid rise of *El Pais* to a position of such influence has nevertheless created its own problems. *El Pais* risks developing an exaggerated political role and an enlarged sense of its own importance. It now has the power to make and break ministers and prime ministers, which places great responsibility with the editor and gives added importance to the share base of the controlling company, PRISA. The shares were distributed and arranged so as to prevent one group gaining dominant control. However, there have been several behind-the-scenes battles over shares, with clear political overtones, including an abortive takeover attempt by Fraga and his friends.[17]

Diario-16, after a rocky start, has successfully found a different market and formula from that of the more sober *El Pais*, and its readership has topped the 120,000 mark. Its sensational presentation of news and comment has captured a younger urban readership, mainly in Madrid. Its editorial line has been less consistent than *El Pais*, and oscillates between moderate conservatism and liberalism, as does its senior stable companion, *Cambio-16*. *Diario-16*'s political influence is limited, its sensational presentation of stories having merely 'nuisance' value for the government. The paper's main impact has been on military issues and in treating the cultural interests and problems of urban youth — drugs, sex, and pop music. These subjects have been poorly treated by the press as a whole, which has fumbled between doubts over the bounds of taste, and a general ignorance of youth readership.

What *Diario-16* has done in Madrid, *El Periodico* has achieved in a nearly similar way in Barcelona. Starting up in 1978, *El Periodico* was selling nearly 107,000 copies four years later. In 1982, the combined circulation of these three main, post-Franco papers exceeded by almost a quarter that of the three main independents who existed under the dictatorship.

Both the influence and circulation of *El Pais* is likely to be extended by its plans for regional publication. Poor distribution makes it difficult for a paper to be national. Madrid papers often arrive more than a day late and therefore the local press has an artificial advantage. However, print technology now makes it possible to set up local production centres which are fed the core of the paper from head office. In October 1982, *El Pais* began publishing an edition for Catalonia and the Baleares in Barcelona. Initial circulation was 46,000 but readership targets are even more ambitious.

Apart from Catalonia, the Basque country is the sole region where the local press is important in forming opinion. Here two papers, *Deia* and *Egin* play different but significant roles. Both support Basque nationalism and are products of the post-Franco era. *Deia*, with a circulation of 51,000 acts as the mouthpiece of the conservative Basque Nationalist Party (PNV) which controls the autonomous government. *Egin*, with a circulation of 47,000 is the mouthpiece of the radical coalition, Herri Batasuna, the political front for the military wing of ETA. The authorities, whether UCD or PSOE, have on several occasions been on the point of closing down *Egin* under pressure from the military. The Ministry of the Interior regards *Egin* as part of the support apparatus of ETA (it carries all ETA communiques) and there have been frequent fines for infractions of various aspects of the law. Sweeping curbs on press dealings with terrorists in the anti-terrorist laws of 1981 were primarily aimed at preventing *Egin* giving publicity to ETA.

These two newspapers are the most identified with political parties and movements. Party newspapers or magazines have had a chequered history, and carry no weight outside the parties themselves. The biggest failure was the collapse of the communist *Mundo Obrero* in 1980 due to a disastrous editorial policy and profound ideological disagreements within the party. This was the sole left wing daily geared to the working class. But it lacked funds and bored its readers by using ideologues and party hacks instead of journalists. The hope of transforming *Mundo Obrero* into a French *Humanité* or an Italian *Unita* never materialized, even though *Mundo Obrero* earned considerable prestige while operating in secret. It continued as a weekly with fewer pretensions and less impact.

By contrast, the extreme right has managed to keep alive its mouthpiece, *El Alcazar*, as a daily. Between 1977 and 1982 its circulation nearly doubled to over 90,000. Its financial health has been parlous but always underpinned by sympathizers anxious that the Falange and supporters of the former regime should have a voice. The authorities have considered closing down *El Alcazar* as a result of its incendiary and seditious tone. The paper would have carried the proclamation of the 23 February rebels had they been successful. It organized a collection to help Tejero pay a fine for damaging parliament when he and other members of the Guardia Civil seized it. The paper is most read among the military upon whose seditious fringe it has most influence.

TRIALS AND TRIBULATIONS

The press, like the political parties, having opted for a gradual introduction of democracy has been obliged to work within certain constraints. Only *Egin* and *El Alcazar* have ignored the general guideline that no journalistic enterprise should undermine the establishment of democracy. The press saw it as in the national interest to avoid mention of specific topics or to do so in a cautious and oblique way. On occasions this has led to collaboration between the government and the media, both independent and state-run, on the presentation of issues. On others, it has been an intelligent relationship of give and take, based round the common good of establishing democracy.

In this way, for instance, the media and political leaders have been instrumental in building up the King's reputation and projecting the Royal Family as a national institution within the democratic framework. The Church has been treated with almost exaggerated respect for fear of arousing anti-clericalism. When the divorce laws were passed through parliament in 1980, the process was accompanied by the minimum of journalistic noise. Even the more polemical issue of abortion has been kept low key by papers like *El Pais*, which are naturally sympathetic to the legalisation. Reporting on the military has been circumspect and deferential, conditioned by the constant fear that criticism and exposé could goad them into action.

The constraint of ensuring political stability at the expense of information has been reinforced by the legal vacuum in which editors and their newspapers operate. The 1966 Press Law was altered only in parts in 1977. The rest remained in force, with such issues as professional secrecy and the status of the editor unresolved. In theory the law still defines who is fit to hold the editor's job. The Church and more especially the military still have a battery of laws, some of dubious democratic credentials, with which to threaten the press.

The system of justice itself is stacked against press freedom. It is difficult for a newspaper or a magazine to attack judicial decisions or expose the workings of the courts without fear of the latter invoking protective laws that punish what the judges themselves interpret as attacks on their own honour. The most remarkable legal judgement concerned the Vinader case in 1982. Javier Vinader was a reporter for *Interviu* magazine who wrote a story based on an interview with a policeman uncovering extreme right wing activities directed against ETA in the Basque country. Not long after the article was published, ETA assassinated two of the persons named. He was found guilty of aiding the assassinations through his article and sentenced to two years in prison; but he jumped bail to live in London in the hope of an amnesty.

In 1976, several journalists were threatened by the extreme right for what they were writing. Jose Antonio Martinez Soler, editor of a short-lived weekly, *Doblon*, was kidnapped in February 1976 and tortured near Madrid following an article he had written about the Guardia Civil. His kidnappers, never brought to justice, were believed to be members of the Guardia Civil; he had to have police protection for three months. On public occasions such as demonstrations, members of the security forces have frequently been violent, especially with photographers.

In general the pressures are more subtle, sometimes transmitted through the management. Cebrian says that the greatest pressure he faced while an editor has not been from the military but from members of the Church and its supporters. He also conceded that since 23 February the level of self-censorship in the press has grown. This is the most worrying phenomenon.

Self-censorship arises primarily when dealing with sensitive topics like the military and the security forces, the Royal Family, and the private lives of prominent persons. Though the specific topics are limited, the effect tends to be all-pervading. This permits the continuation in freer and more fluid form of the old Francoist two-tier system of news and information. On one tier news circulates as a mixture of gossip, rumour and fact among a privileged group composed of the government, political parties, senior civil servants, bankers, businessmen, and journalists. At another, news is disseminated to the general public on the basis of what the first group sees fit to give them, with the determining judgement of the journalists, or the government, or both. In the first instance, gossip and rumour interfere too much with fact in forming opinions. In the second, the public is too often treated condescendingly and left without explanation, like airline passengers delayed at the airport.

The persistence of self-censorship also makes the media frustrated and more liable to attack easy targets that can take — or they think can take — criticism. Unfortunately very few persons or institutions in Spain can take criticism without feeling victimized, and this is where the real power of the press lies. Suarez now says failure to cultivate the press was one of his major errors.[18] True, he failed to exploit his public image and from 1979 onwards shut himself away in the Moncloa, antagonized by hostile press articles. But he was also a victim of press frustration with being unable to attack other targets, principally the military. In this respect, Felipe Gonzalez has learnt from Suarez's mistake. He employed as Secretary-General in the Prime Minister's office, Julio Feo, a sociologist by training and public relations consultant by profession. Feo has managed all Gonzalez's election campaigns and has studied American political media management. A professional journalist, Eduardo Sotillos, was employed as government spokesman. Sotillos, former head of the state radio network was, until joining the government, editor of a new Basque paper, *Tribuna Vasca*. Neither Suarez nor Calvo Sotelo had such professional image builders, but this does not mean that in time the inherent frustrations of self-censorship will not be vented on Felipe Gonzalez.

The election of the socialist government has emboldened the press to touch some sensitive areas. For instance, the government's drive to clean up the administration has been a catalyst in encouraging journalistic exposure of corruption. However, the press has found the socialist government more prickly than UCD, and it has been put on the defensive by the political colour of the press. Only *El Pais* could be considered, in principle, sympathetic to the Socialists. But *El Pais*, having basically supported the PSOE to gain power, could not refrain from criticising it in the exercise of power. Equally, socialist ministers found it hard to accept that journalists whom they had regarded as friends in opposition should be writing critical things about them. Old attitudes die hard.

Despite these inevitable frictions there is now a healthier distance between the press and the government. Unfortunately, the same is unlikely to happen for the foreseeable future with television, the medium which most affects the opinions and general culture of Spaniards.

Part Four

DEMOCRACY AT WORK

12 Democracy at Work

The unique feature of Spain's return to democracy has been the way in which there has been no automatic break with the past. Those institutions most identified with the Franco regime — the armed forces and the Church — have been relegated to lesser roles but their reform has been gradual and deferential. The new institutions — an elected parliament, trades unions, and a free press — have been grafted on to the old order. This has caused frictions and resulted in a democratic system that is not yet complete.

Police on a routine patrol in central Madrid came across four suspicious persons in a parked car. As they approached to question them, the four broke from the car firing guns. In the confusion two escaped, one was hit in the shoulder by police gunfire falling close to the car. The fourth tried to hold off the police with steady gun fire, but emptied his magazine quickly and was cornered. He fought wildly with his captors before being subdued and driven off for interrogation at the security headquarters in Puerta del Sol. Jose Arregui was a powerfully built thirty-year-old truck driver from the Basque country. He was taken into custody on 4 February 1981. Nine days later he was dead.

Arregui, suspected of being a veteran ETA commando, died while being transferred from Carabanchel prison hospital for emergency treatment in a civil hospital. The autopsy attributed death to lung failure as a result of bronchial pneumonia. That he had been tortured was beyond doubt. His body bore extensive bruises and the soles of his feet had burn marks. Lawyers for Arregui's family claimed that the police had caused his death using the interrogation technique of dipping the head in a bucket of fouled water and holding it there until the victim is forced to imbibe. The germs thus drunk, they claimed, caused the pneumonia.

News of Arregui's death was released by the Ministry of Justice, in charge of prisons and appalled at what had happened. Arregui had been admitted to Carabanchel after being in the hands of police interrogators for the statutory nine days. There the prison doctors immediately recognized that they had been handed a virtual corpse. To them it looked as though the police and the Ministry of the Interior were palming off the embarrassment of a corpse onto the prison hospital, to make the death seem more natural.

This was not the first time since the introduction of democracy that

251

someone had died as a result of interrogation. It had happened the previous September. The outcry over this incident was greater because of the political atmosphere at the time and the emotive involvement of ETA. The week before ETA had committed a serious error in assassinating Jose Maria Ryan, the chief engineer of a controversial nuclear power plant at Lemoniz near Bilbao. ETA had kidnapped the unfortunate Ryan, offering his life in return for the shut-down of the Lemoniz plant. Unable to climb down, ETA shot Ryan and dumped his huddled body in the boot of a car. This cold-blooded killing led to the biggest ever demonstration against ETA in the Basque country; a general strike on 11 February culminated in a march through the centre of Bilbao three kilometres long, attended by 150,000 people. The death of Arregui so soon after this, undermined the wave of condemnation against ETA in the Basque country. Arregui was seen as a hero among the extremists, while moderate Basques were confirmed in their belief that democracy had not altered the old anti-Basque prejudice of the security forces.

The Ministry of the Interior initially sought to justify what had happened by releasing Arregui's record. He was suspected of having carried out a string of terrorist actions including the blowing up of a Guardia Civil convoy in which two of the Guardia were killed. But this move merely revealed that the Francoist philosophy prevailed: a man was guilty until proved innocent.

The liberal press and the left clamoured for details in parliament and were loud in their condemnation of police behaviour. Behind this lay an agonized reappraisal of the anti-terrorist laws passed in December 1980. The legislation bore the scarcely democratic name of the Law Suspending Fundamental Rights (Ley de Suspension de Derechos Fundamentales). Instead of holding terrorist suspects for seventy-two hours incommunicado, the police could keep a person without access to a lawyer for nine days. Only one deputy had voted against the law, the radical Basque Juan Maria Bandres, even though there was a deep fear that it went against the spirit of the Constitution. That the law might be an invitation to use torture had been borne out by Arregui's death.

As a result of the outcry, five plain clothes policemen concerned with the interrogation were suspended and put under the orders of an examining magistrate — so too was the regional police intelligence officer and the medical officer of the plain clothes police responsible for monitoring Arregui. This was the first time the government had taken such firm action to sanction the behaviour of its security forces. Within twenty-four hours of the suspensions, the three most senior officers concerned with combatting terrorism had handed in their resignations in protest, with the backing of a good many of their subordinates. The police were directly challenging the government by saying in effect: 'You let us run the fight against terrorism our way, or else you have no one to do it for you ... '

The extreme right and the armed forces threw their weight behind the police protest. They were incensed that the government should blame the police in their fight against terrorism, when the fault lay with ETA and its friends who were trying to destroy Spain. The military had been the chief victims of ETA's gunmen. They found the idea that a state should be 'fair' with terrorists hard to stomach.

The passionate debate provoked by Arregui's death polarized right wing opinion to such an extent that it was a contributory element in triggering the coup attempt of 23 February. The incident itself touched a central nerve of the democratic system. The government had to be assured both of the loyalty and the behaviour of its police force. In fact, it could not entirely do so, although in the case of Arregui, the issue was submerged in the events of 23 February. As a result, the resignations were quietly ignored and the five policemen involved in the interrogation were released from custody. Rather than face a revolt, the government acquiesced.[1]

TODO POR LA PATRIA

Democracy demanded a fundamental change in the role of the security forces. Instead of being geared to control political offences in the service of the regime, they had to protect civil liberties and be responsible to society as a whole. Their role had to be social not political. They had to win the respect of the public, not rely on fear. Yet while the function of the security forces changed, their institutional framework evolved more slowly.

On Franco's death the security forces comprised the Guardia Civil and the Policia Armada (Armed Police); both were para-military. The Guardia Civil had responsibility for policing rural areas and towns of less than 20,000 inhabitants, but they also had certain urban functions, such as the protection of key government buildings. They had an independent communications network and intelligence service — the most comprehensive of the eleven intelligence operations bequeathed by the former regime. Their equipment included helicopters and armoured personnel carriers. With just over 60,000 men in 1975, the Guardia Civil had nearly one third more personnel than the Policia Armada.

The Policia Armada were created by Franco as an urban force to show the flag of authority in large towns. A key function was the monitoring and control of political activity, which also involved providing riot squads for the regime. The students dubbed them 'the greys' (grises) from their grey uniforms.

Independent but working with them were a corps of plain clothes police (Cuerpo Superior de la Policia), whose role was mainly to investigate serious crime and political offences. Subordinate to all these were the municipal police, Policia Municipal, who did the minor policing jobs — petty crime, neighbourhood relations, and traffic control. These were jobs that the

253

Guardia Civil and Policia Armada were too grand to dirty their hands with. The lesser function of the municipal police was emphasised by their non-military status.

The Guardia Civil and the Policia Armada were commanded by army officers and had a military hierarchy. However their traditions differed enormously. The Guardia Civil had been founded in 1844 in order to take over control of public order from the army, and was conceived as a highly disciplined volunteer force that would act as the extension of civil power in the countryside, relieving the army of internal security duties. The Guardia Civil's code of conduct cited honour as the principal badge of the force: they had to impress Spaniards both by their conduct, self-sacrifice, dress, and cleanliness. (The original regulations specified that they had to shave at least three times a week and ensure that their nails were clean when going outside barracks.)[2]

They lived with their families in isolated barracks, which often looked like stockades designed to repel a hostile population. Everything was done in the service of the motherland, and '*Todo por la patria*' was written above every barracks. This tough, disciplined credo was well suited to pre-industrial Spain. It enabled recruits, generally from impoverished regions of Spain, to exercise their duties in isolated areas with poor communications and little ready access to the law courts. This gave the Guardia Civil great power to assert their authority over the countryside, and little could be done without their active support.

The Guardia Civil was extensively reorganized after the Civil War because in the republican zone units had remained loyal. During the Franco era, its commanding officers were carefully selected for their unwavering loyalty and were ultra right-wing. They saw the Guardia Civil as the repository of all the finest Spanish military traditions and made no effort to adapt the force to a fast-changing society. Nor was there much effort to stamp out age-old abuses of authority: since they were badly paid, the temptation to use authority for financial gain often proved irresistible, especially along the coasts where smuggling was commonplace.

Arias left the security forces untouched and their reform was one of Suarez's severest headaches. There were moments in early 1977 when the government seriously doubted its ability to control its own police forces. One of these occasions was the huge demonstration to protest against the killing of five left-wing labour lawyers in January. Yet to have disbanded either the Policia Armada or the Guardia Civil, or both, would have presented tremendous practical problems to say nothing of the political consequences. The authorities were therefore obliged to act discreetly and employ the very same people used by the former regime to watch for and punish opposition to Franco.

The Policia Armada was the simpler force to change, and was also the most urgently in need of adaptation. The easing of political tension and a greater sense of liberty encouraged an upsurge in crime. The Suarez government hesitated as to how to act, and one of its more clumsy moves in 1978 was to send the Policia Armada on foot patrols in the main cities. The aim was to demonstrate their authority on the streets; but a patrol of four men in the familiar uniform of repression, guns at the ready, did as much harm as good.

Eventually the Suarez government made the all-important decision to rename the Policia Armada and give them a new uniform. As of 1979 they became the Policia Nacional, trading their grey uniforms for brown. Initially the change was purely formal; but it created a great psychological impact on both the public and the police themselves. It distanced the past and laid the groundwork for a modern urban police force. Under the guidance of General Saenz de Santa Maria, the Policia Nacional adopted new training methods and within the space of three years had acquired a positive image. This was helped by a new democratic movement inside the force, which energetically claimed union recognition and severance from the military. The next step was the gradual integration of the plain clothes police corps into the Policia Nacional. Discussions on this began in 1983. In the long term, the Policia Nacional aimed to have an officer corps drawn from the ranks of civilians. The first conscious effort to demonstrate the distance between the Policia Nacional and the armed forces occurred with the 1983 Armed Forces Day parade in which, for the first time, they did not take part.

The Guardia Civil were far more reactionary. While the authorities consciously sought to give the Policia Nacional a civilian image, the military character of the Guardia Civil remained unaltered. Unions, tolerated among the Policia Nacional, were rejected by both the UCD and socialist governments inside the Guardia Civil. The left talked half-heartedly about disbanding them, but the issue was never pressed, even when incidents occurred which cast serious doubt on their methods.[3]

The basic issue of two para-military units existing side by side, often apparently duplicating functions or competing for the same task, has never been faced. For instance, there is no apparent logic in having the Guardia Civil protect the Prime Minister's particular part of the Moncloa Palace complex and the Policia Nacional the remainder. Rivalries between the two corps and their separate structures has complicated concerted action against terrorism.

Police methods were slow to alter, with a disturbing incidence of torture continuing in the first four years after Franco's death.[4] However, the fact that in 1983 instances were still being denounced did not necessarily mean that the level was as high under the socialist government. Rather, it could be argued that people who previously preferred not to report torture were now less afraid to do so. The socialist government made the first systematic effort to weed out corruption within the security forces, devoting attention to the Guardia Civil covering coastal areas. In May 1983 an entire barracks of twelve Guardia Civil was dismissed and a further fifteen arrested in connection with the protection of tobacco smuggling in Galicia.

Perhaps the democratic state was lucky to inherit a divided police force, which facilitated the build up of the Policia Nacional. Without this, the security forces, so essential to the functioning of the state, could have risked permanently tarnishing the government's democratic image. The transformation of the Policia Armada into the Policia Nacional was one of the most significant successes of the new democracy — offsetting the inability to update and alter the image of the Guardia Civil.[5]

JUSTICE IN A VACUUM

The judicial system inherited by the first elected government needed drastic overhaul. Its moral framework was the conservative Catholic reaction to the republican experience, and the laws governing social, criminal and political behaviour were designed to protect an authoritarian regime. Although the conditions in which justice operated could be altered, the persons interpreting and administering the law remained the same, and the government was further restricted by the need to respect the principle of judicial independence. No democratic government could be seen to be interfering in judicial appointments, so it was obliged to work with the personnel it inherited. By no means all were closely identified with the former regime, but a substantial number had administered laws which were completely undemocratic, especially those relating to public order, even if armed violence against the regime and acts affecting state security were usually tried in military courts.

Judicial reform could not be carried out in earnest until the constitution defined the role of the judiciary, and for three years the judiciary operated in a vacuum. Some laws were new and definitive, like the December 1976 law of political reform, legalizing political parties. Others were provisional; the bulk were inherited from the former regime, such as those relating to freedom of expression and social habits. Since society had advanced well beyond these laws, anomalies abounded.

The immediate reforms involved the abolition of the Public Order Tribunals and a limited reorganization of the courts. For instance, a Madrid-based Central Court (Audiencia Nacional) was established in January 1977 with two divisions — one for criminal offences and the other for dealing with administrative conflicts. The criminal courts thus established overcame the problems concerning offences committed in various, or indeterminate, parts of the country, the normal courts being strictly territorial in scope. This was of particular importance for dealing with terrorist offences; other reforms of institutions such as labour courts were not seriously tackled until after 1980. The latter had been set up by Franco to regulate problems between workers and management in the context of the vertical syndycates. Their basic

256

philosophy was to ensure that labour did not organize itself freely and remained subservient to employers.

The constitution recognized that 'justice emanates from the people'. This justice was to be administered by a judiciary 'who shall be independent, irremoveable, and liable and subject only to the rule of law'.[6] The constitution specifically excluded the possibility of special tribunals and postulated the principle of judicial unity under civilian control. This was highly important given the wide domain covered by military jurisdiction. The constitution also created a new governing body, the General Council of the Judiciary (Consejo General del Poder Judicial), set up in 1980, which was a vital step in ensuring the impartiality of the legal system. It was composed half of professional judges and magistrates elected from within their ranks, half of members designated by both houses of parliament. The constitution also approved the principle of trial by jury, abolished by the Nationalists in 1936, and the formation of a constitutional tribunal.

The constitution stipulated that military justice was subordinate to civilian justice but left the delineation of military justice vague. The first reforms in this field were not to come for three years after the approval of the constitution, as the politicians felt their way through a minefield of military sensitivities. The 1981 law on military justice reduced the competence of martial courts and made their judgements subject to appeal in the civilian Supreme Court. This procedure was tested for the first time in the prosecution appeals against the court martial sentencing of those involved in the 23 February coup. The Supreme Court sharply increased the sentences and in effect rebuked the military tribunal for failing to properly interpret the crime of rebellion. However, the fact that an offence so serious as rebellion should be tried first in a military court underlined the timidity of the curb on the scope of military jurisdiction. This said, anomolies such as the military's ability to censure and ban films, books, theatre, and newspaper articles were remedied.

The difficulty of any judicial reform was underlined by the delay in re-introducing trial by jury. Initially introduced in Spain in 1812, primarily to assess cases of electoral fraud, the use of juries was formalized in 1888, suspended under the Primo de Rivera dictatorship, and restored again under the Republic before being abolished by Franco. With the judges self-elected and self-monitoring, the system was an essential check on their subjective judgements in moral matters like the interpretation of obscenity and public scandal, and was just as important in cases of contempt of court. Introduction of the jury figured prominently on the PSOE 1983 electoral programme, but resistance by the judiciary to the precise function of the jury delayed its introduction.

The socialist government, to its credit, adopted a much more comprehensive approach to legal reform than UCD. Both Suarez and Calvo Sotelo avoided controversial issues and therefore only select changes were made.

The PSOE set about reforming the penal code, particularly to end anomalies by which, for instance, patriotism was a mitigating motive in criminal offences.

For the public the legal system remained an expensive tangle of bureaucracy and unfamiliar terminology: justice a remote and abstract ideal. Perhaps early introduction of the jury system would have initiated a greater sense of popular participation, but years of accumulated fatalism about the system being loaded against the individual still had to be overcome. Bringing cases to trial took sometimes two and three years, during which time suspects in criminal cases all too often had to stay in jail. In 1982, half the prison population in Spain were awaiting trial. This in turn led to overcrowding in prisons and serious prison riots, which produced a criminality of their own. During the first six months of 1983, twenty-five persons died in prison violence. The socialist government tackled the problem by speeding up trial hearings and releasing more suspects on bail. But speeding up trials was hampered by ancient restrictions on the number of judges and magistrates — there were simply far too few to deal with the available work.

ADMINISTRATIVE REFORM

The position of the Civil Service inherited from the Francoist system was fundamentally different from that of the judiciary. The civil servants had powerful job protection but they were responsible to their ministers, who in turn were answerable to an elected parliament.

The Civil Service was dominated by the system of *cuerpos*. These were separate corps of people such as engineers, economists, lawyers etc. These corps were entered by competitive examination, judged by existing members. The exams could be repeated and once passed the person was admitted to the corps for life, with the added benefit of being able to leave temporarily and always return. Within the corps, enormous differences of academic ability existed and those with the highest standards were distinguished by the denomination of *cuerpo superior*. Some corps dated back to the early nineteenth century, such as the civil engineers' corps, founded in 1835; others were founded as recently as the sixties, such as the post office and treasury executives' corps.

The emphasis was on specialization rather than producing civil servants who could easily be switched between departments and ministries. Indeed, the system was so specialized that people with, for instance, an economics degree could end up in one of ten different corps, and still carry out broadly similar responsibilities. There were even three separate corps for architects. With time the corps had become narrow-minded professional associations protecting specific civil servants' interests. Individual ministries tended to become strongholds of particular corps, so increasing inter-ministerial rivalry.

The corps lacked any sense of owing service to the public or state. They had a genuine espirit de corps; nothing else. The fragmentation of the corps hardly helped: throughout Spain in 1980 there were 220 different corps with 1300 grades of job. An elite, consisting of civil servants well up in the hierarchy, such as the Abogados de Estado (state advocates), tended to abuse the prestige attached to membership by acquiring extra jobs which left them little time to do their official work. The practice of holding down more than one job was also encouraged by low rates of pay (there were special incentive payments for civil servants to work a full day!). Low salaries fostered corruption and a numbing idleness, since once inside the civil service it was virtually impossible to be fired.

This state of affairs was aggravated by a huge number of unnecessary appointments made by the Franco regime as political favours to former nationalist Civil War veterans and members of the Movimiento. After Franco's death these people were retained as part of the Civil Service, including the 32,000 members of the disbanded Movimiento.

UCD began to draw up a law reforming the administration in 1978 but this was largely rewritten the following year and never actually saw the light of day. In 1980 a leading expert on administrative practice, Professor Alejandro Nieto commented:

> The Administration is a tangle of self-destructive vicious circles. The Treasury is not willing to pay more for worthless civil servants; and the civil servants are not willing to work for the salaries they receive. The overall wage bill is exorbitant but individual salaries are inadequate. There is an excess of function-aries yet at the same time services are wanting. Never has it cost so much to maintain so many badly paid people. Never has corruption thrived with such impunity; never have the grotesque efforts to denounce this corruption sounded so phoney ... The Administration is a lawless zone where the citizens are persecuted and where amidst the ruins of public services a few civil servants and political parties successfully cultivate their own backyards with the fertiliser of corruption. The light of discipline and ethical behaviour has been switched off, only propaganda and demagogy shines.[7]

The UCD failed to make headway because it was unwilling to tackle vested interests in its own party, especially those of doctors and lawyers. The broad lines of the proposals were valid. For instance the law would have abolished the unhealthy practice among certain corps of monopolizing certain adminis-trative posts; it would have limited the number of non-civil servants brought in by ministers to run the departments, and introduced a more rational system of grading. However, it was excessively vague on such vital aspects as conflict of interest and the holding of more than one job in the administration.

Felipe Gonzalez came to office regarding reform and democratization of the administration as an historic challenge. He claims this was one of UCD's most serious failings while in power. 'Without reform of the administration it will be difficult to implement other aspects of the socialist electoral platform.'[8] The broad outlines of the socialist reforms go back to proposals in the censure motion against Suarez in May 1980. During this debate, Gonzalez committed his party to the creation of a professional full-time civil service, with no second jobs, and less than half the number of corps. Without losing the advantages of specialization the Socialists aimed to create more flexibility in job transfers, rationalize pay structures, reduce the number of grades, and tighten up on recruitment. When the Socialists took over they discovered 58,000 non-career personnel in the administration!

As a demonstration of their seriousness, the socialist government insisted, in early 1983, that all civil servants clock in at the appointed hour. The traditional work hours of 8.00 am to 2.30 pm had rarely been observed, and finishing at lunch-time made it easy to contract second jobs in the afternoon. This pattern of work conditioned the working hours of all non-industrial operations in Spain. The socialist aim was little short of revolutionary — to move the civil service over to a 'nine-to-five' schedule as in northern Europe.

A serious problem in policy-making, both under Franco and UCD, was ministerial rivalry. Certain ministries, through the prestige of their corps, had been historically dominant. The Treasury was the most powerful of the civilian ministries because it controlled the purse strings. It was constantly warring with the Ministry of Commerce and Economy for hegemony not merely over financial but also over economic decisions. Industry, a new ministry covering a vital area of the economy, had little political muscle which meant that industrial policy was too often at the mercy of the decisions of the other ministries involved. The Foreign Ministry jealously guarded its diplomatic preserve, causing considerable confusion over international economic relations. Similar conflicts arose in most bureaucracies. But the specific Spanish characteristic of the corps exacerbated them. Under UCD this interministerial rivalry was also fomented by the factional nature of the party. Rivalries lessened under the socialist government because the cabinet was a more homogeneous group which did not need to cater to individual power bases within the party.

Even without new legislation, a motive for change was created by the concession of regional autonomy and the consequent devolution of power by the central government. This caused a transfer of personnel to the direct control of autonomous governments, and by 1983 200,000 of the 1 million civil servants were employed by the regional governments. These consisted mostly of teachers and health staff.[9]

DEVOLUTION TO THE REGIONS

The concession of regional autonomy has been one of the most significant and far reaching developments in the working of democracy. Pressures and precedents existed for devolution but Spain has embarked on an enterprise which could fundamentally alter the historic nature of government. The principle has been conceded not just to those regions which historically have enjoyed certain privileges from the central government, but also to seventeen regions embracing the whole of Spain.[10]

Recognition of the historic claims to autonomy by the Basques and Catalans was implicit in the process of national reconciliation which began after Franco's death. Although these claims were recognized, nearly four years elapsed before they began to be satisfied. Precious time was lost while first Arias and then Suarez hesistated over how far to go in meeting them. Offers of amnesty and the promise of autonomy, made late in 1977, were too long in coming and too ambiguous to end the armed violence of ETA. The Basques as a whole were frustrated by the apparent lack of priority given to their grievances.

The Catalans were calmer but not less frustrated. On 11 September 1977, Catalonia's national day, almost one million people demonstrated in Barcelona — a demonstration only rivalled in size in democratic Spain by that on 27 February 1981, after the abortive coup. A year later the veteran Catalan leader in exile, Josep Taradellas returned to greet an ecstatic crowd with the words 'Ja soc aqui' (I'm here at last).

Taradellas proved to be a consummate politician who quickly took control of the strings of power in Catalonia and thus became an effective negotiator with Madrid. Even so, the Catalans had to wait until 1979 for their autonomy statute to be approved, pending the outcome of negotiations with the Basques.

Tensions and frustrations between these regions and Madrid were inevitable. The suppression of Basque and Catalan identity under Franco made them impatient for redress. But before the Constitution was approved, Suarez could only make concessions with great difficulty. He had to take particular account of the feelings of the armed forces — even over such apparently minor issues as the flying of the Basque flag alongside the Spanish one.

When the Constitution was put to referendum in December 1978 both the conservative Basque Nationalist Party and the radical groupings that backed ETA campaigned for a negative vote on the grounds that the provisions on autonomy did not go far enough. Perhaps they did not, but in relation to the rest of Spain it was a radical departure to talk of the 'right to autonomy of the nationalities and regions'.[11] The reference to 'nationalities', proposed by the Catalans, was a clear sop to the Basques and Catalans; but it left the question of the exact nature of these nationalities completely in the air. Were the people

261

of Extremadura a nationality? And if they were not previously a nationality, could they become one now?

The bench-mark for the Basque and Catalan autonomy statutes was vague and the government sought to avoid tying itself to those negotiated under the Republic. In psychological and political terms, the Basque statute proved the toughest to frame because negotiations took place against the backdrop of mounting ETA violence. The Basques also demanded the greatest degree of mollification to offset the repression suffered under the former regime. In the end it was ETA that pushed the government into action. (In 1977, twelve people were killed by ETA, the following year sixty-four, and in 1979, seventy-eight.) The Basque leader, Carlos Garaicoetxea, insisted that a document that fell short of the 1936 Statute of Guernica would never be accepted. This was a key bargaining point since, among the militant separatists, the 1936 statute was considered a basic point of departure for negotiating autonomy.

The statute negotiated at the end of July 1979 went further than the Suarez government had planned. But its wording was ambiguous, suiting the final spirit of understanding and personal compromise that emerged from the marathon sessions with Garaicoetxea. The tone of the new arrangement was laid down in the first article of the new Statute of Guernica: 'The Basque People or Euskal-Herria, as expression of their nationality and in order to accede to self government, establishes itself as an autonomous community within the Spanish State, known as the Basque country or Euskadi, in accordance with the Constitution.' One reading might suggest that the Basques had achieved semi-federal status within Spain; another that this was mere window dressing, the central government conceding nothing of substance because the terms of the Constitution could always be invoked.

The Statute recognised Basque as an official language inside the region, acceptable in all educational institutions. The Basques were given their own parliament and government with eventual authority over the promotion of regional economic development, control of the local savings banks, and administration of the local social security system. The Basques also managed to have the right to form their own internal police force included. The Statute applied to the three Basques provinces of Alava, Guipuzcoa and Vizcaya. The fourth province, Navarre, was excluded because of the special status it had acquired under the Franco regime; but the possibility of its subsequent inclusion was left open.

The Catalan statute was tied up in August 1979, after the break-through with the Basques. The terms obtained were broadly similar, but there was an important difference over financial arrangements. The Basques arranged that each year a total sum of what the Basque country was due to pay in taxes was negotiated with Madrid. It was then up to the Basque government to collect this and be responsible for handing it over. They also sought a lump sum from the government to cover those areas which it was to administer. The Catalans, on the other hand, agreed to negotiate the transfer of specific sums for the areas concerned — the same system in reverse. The Catalans also pressed harder on control of education and the universities. Initially they ignored the issue of their own police force, but subsequently followed the Basque example.

The constant constraint on negotiations over devolution was the hostile attitude of the military towards concessions by the central government. The regions believed they had won concessions that paved the way for genuine autonomy; the military were told that no more was being done than a rationalization of government and a decentralization of the administration. To further confuse matters, Suarez offered autonomy not just to those regions with historic identities, but to every region. The military could then see that the Basques and Catalans were not receiving special treatment.

The offer of autonomy to all was a serious error. Made without careful study, it was a crude political manoeuvre to lessen the content of Basque and Catalan demands. The only real concession made by Suarez was to accept that the Basque country, Catalonia, and Galicia had historic identities and should be treated first. However, once the offer of autonomy had been made to all regions, sentiments of regional identity began to stir in areas which previously had shown little or none, such as Andalusia, the Canaries, Extremadura, and Valencia. Instead of containing the autonomy issue, Suarez's policy exacerbated it, dragging Spain towards de facto federalism. The pandora's box of demands quickly obliged Suarez to back-track. In early 1980 he was forced to introduce technical measures to slow the pace of regional autonomy demands.

The process might have continued unchecked but for the events of 23 February. The loss of national unity was one of the chief fears and complaints of the disgruntled military, and an implicit condition for the uneasy peace between the politicians and the military in the wake of the abortive coup was the adoption of a restrictive approach towards granting autonomy.

In June 1981 the main political parties approved a half-turn in regional policy. Clumsily titled the Law for the Harmonization and Ordering of the Autonomy Process, LOAPA, it introduced a restrictive interpretation of the Basque, Catalan, and Galician statutes and sharply clipped the powers of the regional parliaments, obliging them to seek the approval of the Cortes in Madrid of all legislation. The law went against the spirit, if not the letter, of existing agreements. The Basques, in particular, claimed that the LOAPA indirectly altered the constitution because it appeared to downgrade the idea of 'nationalities'. In the Basque country, the LOAPA was dubbed "the law of the three-cornered hat' in reference to the Guardia Civil who had held parliament to hostage.

It was an unfortunate law in many respects. The main political parties sooner or later had to clarify the ambiguous structure of the state envisaged in the constitution, but the LOAPA took far too little account of what had already happened in the Basque country and Catalonia and so undermined

263

most of the goodwill that had been generated between Madrid and these two regions. It also underestimated the existing mechanisms of control available to the central government. By the end of 1982, the Constitutional Tribunal had heard nineteen disputes between Madrid and the regional governments. In all but one the court had ruled in favour of Madrid. In the first three years of the Catalan parliament, ten of its forty-one laws were challenged in the Constitutional Tribunal by Madrid.

The LOAPA did, however, have the positive effect of smoothing the mechanics of granting autonomy. Absurdly complex methods of referendum and staggered timetables for elections were removed. This, for instance, ended the practice of all regional parliaments holding elections at different times, so that elections for thirteen regional parliaments could be held in May 1983, simultaneously with the municipal elections.

Even with these restrictions, important trends were established, especially in the fields of education and bi-lingualism. Autonomy provided a powerful impetus for the spread of Basque, Catalan, and to a lesser extent Galician. Road signs and street names have now appeared alongside public advertising in these languages. Internal documents of the local administration are either exclusively in Basque or Catalan, or appear jointly with Castilian. Catalan is the most widely used in schools, but by 1983 over 40% of all primary schools in Guipuzcoa were teaching Euskerra. Films are being dubbed in Catalan and publishing rights of the better-known authors are negotiated in Catalan, Basque, and Castilian. This, in turn, has stimulated a cultural revival which initially has made the regions much more inward-looking.

The brief experience of autonomous governments suggests that local administration improved and greater care was being taken in matters such as road maintenance, health services, and schooling. However, an enormous amount of duplication has occurred. The state is often represented in the regions by officials with no other function than to monitor whether the new regional powers are being properly used. In a federal system such an arrangement is understandable, but the government representative serves virtually no useful role in the present instance. If anything he is an impediment. Meanwhile, the parliaments risk duplicating the work of the municipalities and county councils. It is hard to see why the deputies representing the regions in the Madrid Cortes are not capable of defending these regions' interests without the addition of a regional parliament. Certainly the votes of regional parliaments are no more likely to influence Madrid than pressures from the Cortes deputies themselves.

The most serious criticism of both UCD and socialist policy towards the regions has been their failure to establish a continuous dialogue with the Basques. The Basques themselves have by no means been blameless and have at times been prickly and self-important. However, the PNV has been given insufficient room to manoeuvre and outflank the radical separatists. As a result, the destabilizing violence of ETA continues. The LOAPA played right into ETA's hands. It confirmed the militant separatist organization's thesis that Madrid was never serious in conceding autonomy via negotiation: only the barrel of the gun was understood.

Since its foundation at the end of the fifties, ETA has become the largest and most effective guerilla organization in Europe. None can boast such a complete support apparatus after twenty-five years of intensive police action. ETA has a political front, Herri Batasuna; a trades union organization sympathetic to its aims, LAB; a youth organization openly backing it, Jarrai, and a daily newspaper, *Egin*, in basic agreement. ETA's public support has declined since the approval of the Basque autonomy statute, but if one takes as a measure of support the votes obtained in the 1983 municipal elections by candidates in favour of ETA's radicalism, it has over 155,000 sympathizers. Of this, some 100,000 could be considered a hard core. Experts calculated that, in 1982, ETA could rely on 500 persons at any one time to aid or carry out terrorist acts, of which 200 were armed commandos.[12] The leadership lived in relative safety on the French side of the border. The organization financed itself through bank robberies, kidnaps, and extortion of 'revolutionary' taxes on businessmen and other individuals.

Part of the organization abandoned the armed struggle in return for amnesty. Others quietly agreed to take up new lives in Latin America, mainly Venezuela and Mexico, assisted by funds from the PNV. Meanwhile, ETA's claim that it was fighting against a dictatorship for a socialist democracy became increasingly hard to sustain, especially after the 1982 elections, and the organization itself faced tremendous internal difficulties in arguing over whether to abandon armed struggle. The leadership consisted of people now in or approaching their forties who had spent a lifetime underground fighting an armed struggle. They would have to admit failure. Their reintegration into society, even with amnesty, posed great difficulties both for them and the legal system.

Thus terrorism has acquired its own impetus, which continues despite the attractions of negotiation. Various unofficial government contacts with ETA have failed because of the latter's insistence on full publicity in all dealings, and the difficulty of establishing who actually speaks for the organization. Between 1959 and 1982, the ETA suffered nine major splits.

PERSONALITIES AND POWER

The dominant feature of the new parliamentary system has been the importance of the party leaders, who have proved more influential than organizations or ideologies. Parties, in the initial stages of democracy, have become instruments of personal power. The parties have promoted themselves on the image of their leaders rather than on policies, as in the case of UCD under

Suarez. When UCD ceased to be his party and failed to establish a new leader, its voter appeal diminished. CDS, the new centre party formed by Suarez, was established solely on the image of the former Prime Minister. AP was the party of Manuel Fraga and if he were to go, then a huge vacuum would be created. The PCE, despite the heresy of the cult of personality among the Communists, was Carillo's party until his resignation in 1982, and he treated it as such. In the case of the PSOE, its broad electoral appeal rested almost exclusively on Gonzalez's successful projection of his own integrity, and the attractiveness of his person. In the 1982 election campaign, posters devoted more attention to the personality of party leaders than electoral offers. Even in the subsequent municipal elections, where national politics were theoretically of secondary importance, votes were sought on the basis of the confidence generated by national party leaders.

The importance of individuals over institutions has tended to personalize decision-making and favour a presidential style of government. Perhaps psychologically this tendency has been increased by the insistence of the media and the Prime Minister's staff on referring to the premier as *El Presidente*, as if he were head of state, which gives rise to some confusion when, for instance, President Gonzalez meets President Reagan, who really is both head of government and state. If Suarez had been able to control his own party better a presidential style would have been more pronounced. Gonzalez's ascendancy over his own party automatically puts him in a position to be presidential.

If the policies of government are identified largely, if not exclusively, with that of the Prime Minister, there can be no ministerial scapegoats, and the opportunity for quick political wear and tear is great. Both Suarez and Gonzalez sought to offset this by having close personal aides to act as deputy premiers. Suarez had Fernando Abril Martorell, and Gonzalez, Alfonso Guerra. Significantly, Suarez began to be more vulnerable once he was forced to dismiss Abril Martorell in September 1980. Calvo Sotelo, who never had such a collaborator, probably suffered because the public, his own party, and ministers, were all too ready to land him with the blame instead of establishing collective cabinet responsibility.

Gonzalez is enormously fortunate in his close relationship with Guerra who, from the early sixties, has almost been his alter ego. Guerra once described his role thus: 'I am the chef preparing the dishes in the kitchen and Felipe is the one who serves them.'[13] Without such a partner the daily pressures on the Prime Minister's time in a system where all decisions are referred to the highest level would be unbearable. Abril Martorell and Guerra, negotiating in private, were responsible for many of the formulas for legislation in the first parliament, including the Moncloa Agreements of October 1977.

In addition to this emphasis on the leader, the parties have been run — or attempts have been made to run them — on a tight rein from the centre. The

PNV has been the only party not to govern itself along undemocratic, centralist lines. Generally the leaders have imposed their will on the rank and file, rather than vice versa. This system is encouraged by the practice of the party executives, or a limited group within them, choosing parliamentary candidates. Local party committees rarely select their own candidate; instead, the people whom the party headquarters or leadership wishes to be candidates are chosen and farmed out to constituencies, often quite foreign to them. The candidates are loyal to whoever selected them — a homogeneous parliamentary group is ensured, which is good for discipline but does not necessarily enrich parliamentary life or the quality of legislation.

The selection committee also decides the order in which a candidate stands, so that a popular candidate placed low on the list can attract votes for the party but not win a seat. Whether he or she is elected depends on how many votes the party gets and where they are in the party's pecking order. The electorate therefore is encouraged to feel represented by a party, not an individual. Deputies from constituencies outside the capital are constantly torn between being at the centre of power, and staying with those they represent. The usual option has been to go to the capital, and in consequence local representation is insufficient. This almost certainly helps to explain the popularity of regional parties who, in the Basque country and Catalonia, are considered by the electorate to be much more attentive. Indeed, the inability of a central system of government to appreciate local grievances is the core of the Nationalists' success.

An indirect effect of this control from above has been the political experience of the candidates. In established democracies, the career of an aspiring politician starts in local politics and moves on to national politics. In Spain, the experience of the initial legislators was the reverse. Candidates to the Cortes and Senate were suddenly propelled into a representative role. Lack of local experience, combined with the system by which candidates are selected centrally, made the Cortes seem, in the first two parliaments, an essentially remote institution. Televised debates did little to alter this since there was virtually no debate — merely set piece party speeches read from notes with the speaker never sure whether his main task was to address the Cortes or the television audience. Parliament only acquired a different image as a result of its seizure on 23 February. Then, in brutal fashion, the public was made to understand that it was the sovereign body of the nation.

As a result of the 1982 elections, 202 of the 350 seats were occupied by new deputies. This parliament was strikingly young — the average age of AP members being forty-five and of PSOE members, forty-two. Those elected tended to come from the professions, with a strong emphasis on civil servants — either those working in the administration or as part of it, such as teachers. Of the 202 Socialist deputies, 27% were university, secondary, or primary school teachers, and almost 15% were administrative civil servants.

Civil servants were encouraged to stand because they, of all professions, could easiest obtain leave of absence to campaign. The social complexion of the socialist-dominated parliament in 1983 was middle class, with less than 10% of all deputies being considered working class.[14]

Despite the size of Spain's working class, it has been poorly represented in parliament, worse than in any other western democracy. The two main unions, financially weak and linked to political parties, lacked the muscle to establish a group of deputies to champion their interests. Both the leaders of UGT and CCOO have, however, held parliamentary seats and through their own political weight were probably as influential as any group of trades union deputies. Marcelino Camacho renounced his seat before the end of the second legislature to devote himself full time to the CCOO, but as a deliberate decision on the part of the UGT, Nicolas Redondo remained in parliament.[15] This placed him, at times, in an awkward position, caught between supporting the government and backing the interests of his union members. Indeed, the advent of the socialist government produced an area of potential conflict with the UGT. Members instinctively expected the government to lend a sympathetic ear and were at times dismayed to discover that interests of state prevailed. In 1983, there were a number of one-day regional strikes to protest against the lack of employment or, in the most notorious instance, the closure of part of the steel-works at Sagunto near Valencia. The protests emphasized that workers felt excluded from the decision making process, and revealed a potentially dangerous gap between working-class aspirations and the government's ability to satisfy them.

The main change in parliament after the first two legislatures was the move away from consensus politics. With the PSOE and AP so clearly parties of government and opposition respectively, Spain began to experience two-party politics. The bulk of the Cortes was filled with people anxious to be full-time politicians. The large Socialist majority has, however, led to an unfortunate practice whereby the opposition, refusing to accept defeat in parliament, refers controversial issues to the Constitutional Tribunal for arbitration.

The role of the opposition will continue to be conditioned by the small and essentially incestuous nature of the political class. The decision-makers of the government and the business world are familiar with one another and can be found in fewer than ten restaurants in Madrid on any one day. This automatically leads to backroom horse-trading and personal rather than official relations. In the past, this situation has produced a good deal of corruption and abuse of authority because the people taking the decisions were often the beneficiaries. UCD avoided tackling the delicate issue of conflict of interest, and ignored the need to force deputies to declare their interests, and to lay down rules for public office. To their credit, the PSOE tackled this immediately, and arguably the healthiest development has been at municipal level. Here democratic elections, though delayed until four years after Franco's death, have resulted in a major improvement in dealing with local problems. The incestuous mould of local cliques has been broken, or at least the power structure is now more evenly distributed.

The municipalities had been run via the local civil governor as an extension of the central government. The mayor was a direct government appointment who was under the authority of the civil governor (a mayor theoretically needed the civil governor's permission if he was to be away for longer than fifteen days). The mayor was answerable to no local body and was free to promote the interests of himself and his friends, which was invariably what happened. Pressure to control local expenditure was limited and larger corporations, like Barcelona and Madrid, were run as though the state would always bail them out. They piled up huge, uncontrolled debts even though their level of expenditure was low. In the late seventies, local government spending in Spain was one third that of the European norm, equivalent to only 3·2% of GNP.

The 1979 municipal elections, the first to be held in forty-six years, produced a shake-up of major proportions. Over 80% of all municipalities chose to be run either by left-wing or by nationalist parties. In the small towns and villages, the political changes were often no more than cosmetic, and the local power structure remained unaltered, with the *cacique* still pulling strings. In the larger cities, the change was significant even if it was slow to be noticed. For the first time, town councils took a rational look at planning needs. Emphasis was placed on improving facilities like transport and curbing pollution; people were encouraged to treat cities as though they belonged to them. Madrid, under the guidance of the socialist mayor, Tierno Galvan, acquired a vibrancy and soul lacking throughout the Franco era. The success of the PSOE in the May 1983 municipal elections could not be attributed wholly to the reflected effects of their general election victory six months earlier: there was a clear popular endorsement of socialist-run municipalities. The PSOE in 1983 had mayors in thirty-five of Spain's fifty-two provincial capitals.

MANAGING RECESSION

The 1977 Moncloa Agreements laid down with confident authority the broad lines of economic policy and reform for the UCD government. Even for the Socialists, in office six years later, they served as a point of reference. The leaders of the political parties deserve credit for reaching the agreement but the pressures to do so were very strong. Drastic measures were needed to curb inflation, control wages and reduce Spain's dependence on imported energy. In the last quarter of 1977, inflation was running at an annual level of 37%. Uncontrolled inflation and a failure to finance imports risked provoking social disorder and so undermining democracy. Behind this was a broader consideration: the economy had to be adapted to accommodate a new model of society — fairer distribution of wealth, improved social services, a mixed private and public sector economy committed to the removal of protectionism. All parties had backed the formal application for EEC membership in July 1977, and these were the conditions laid down. The majority had done so for essentially political reasons: joining the Community bound Spain to the mainstream of European political life and was a form of insurance against military adventurism.

The Moncloa Agreements were based on a series of trade-offs. The Communists and Socialists, in return for selling wage restraint to their supporters, were promised fiscal reform to redistribute wealth, improvements in the social security system, and legislation to permit the unions to operate. Wage restraint gave the Suarez government an all-important framework in which to plan economic policy. Meanwhile the employers and business community, in return for accepting tighter credit and more taxes, were promised liberalization, reform of the financial system, and a co-operative trades union movement.

Undoubtedly the broad aim of the agreements was achieved. At a vital moment, Spain's social cohesion was retained and the most serious immediate economic problem, galloping inflation, was brought within manageable bounds. The agreements permitted a radical overhaul of the tax system with comparatively little pain. For the first time, the majority of wage and salary earners were contributing to the treasury — compared to the end of the Franco era the number of taxpayers rose sevenfold. This enabled the government to provide more social services, especially improved unemployment benefits and pensions. At the same time, the trades unions acquired legislation that enabled them to establish a dialogue with employers on an independent footing. The importance of the Moncloa Agreements, therefore, cannot be over-emphasised.

Nevertheless, the price of consensus was a series of half-measures. The economy demanded draconian action with major sacrifices from the working population. Yet politically it was extremely difficult to sell a policy of 'blood, sweat and tears' when democracy was being introduced. Unpopular policies might be identified with the introduction of democracy. Take the issue of wages. Ideally wage rises should have been held below the level of inflation with people suffering a drop in real earnings. Between 1973 and 1978, Spain's industrial wages increased by 47% while the average for the industrial countries was only 11·5%.[16] Spain has ceased to be a cheap labour economy. The Moncloa Agreements established the principle that purchasing power would not merely be retained, but kept slightly ahead of inflation. This principle was to hold good until 1981, with the consequence that inflation never fell below 15%, double the European average. Even in 1983, the government was struggling to reduce inflation to below 13%, largely because wages were kept high. It was politically comprehensible but economically unacceptable.

In fairness to UCD and the signatories of the Moncloa Agreements, the economy was inherited in an unenviable state. Economic decisions, whether conjunctural or structural, were the ones most affected by the sense of drift that overtook the final Franco years. There had been a near total failure to understand the nature of the 1973 oil price rises. Spain, of all the European nations, could least afford to ignore the consequences of a tripling of its energy import bill. She was over 70% dependent upon imported energy and, by 1974, oil accounted for a quarter of all imports. The recessionary effects on Spain's main trading partners were ignored; so too were the consequences on domestic production costs and domestic demand. When the rest of Europe began to tighten its belt both the public and private sector in Spain embarked on new investment.

By 1977, Spain had not only ceased to be cheap labour country, but also her production costs in many base industries like steel and chemicals, were nearly on a par with the rest of Europe. The era of cheap credit — so important for the industrial boom — was closing. Surplus labour was no longer being absorbed by northern Europe and a sizeable reverse flow had begun. Suddenly Spain was saddled with costly base industries that were working to over-capacity. For instance Spain, which had become one of the five biggest shipbuilders in the world, was working to 40% overcapacity in this industry. The textile industry, which employed over 400,000 people, faced EEC restrictions as well as tough competition from developing countries in traditional export markets. Demand for such items as steel and domestic appliances fell to its late-sixties level. Growth, which on Franco's death was only 3·5%, moved close to negative rates. It was only a matter of time before unemployment became substantial, since any growth under 3% per year would fail to keep pace with the influx of new job seekers.

The fault of UCD policies lay less in their content (the options were limited), more in the lack of speed and the inevitable order of priorities. The economy came second to politics, and reactions to the economic situation were slow and confused. An energy plan did not materialize until 1979, though once introduced it was successful in cutting back Spain's dependence on imported energy by over 20%. At least four imperfect schemes to restructure the steel industry were adopted and left incomplete under UCD.

Consensus politics imposed an important additional constraint in re-structuring industry. To placate the unions and lessen the impact of growing unemployment a benign approach was adopted to surplus labour. The brutal rationalization of jobs carried out in northern Europe to combat recession was not carried out. Between 1974 and 1979, the European steel industry shed almost 120,000 jobs; in Spain the number was no more than 1,000. Through-out Europe, labour in the textile industry was slashed by between 30 and 40% yet in Spain a plan finally approved in 1981 envisaged no more than a 20%

cut. It was left to the first socialist Minister of Industry, Carlos Solchaga, to sound a note of realism in early 1983. His warnings were greeted with dismay within the PSOE rank and file, since the party electoral platform had optimistically pledged to create 800,000 jobs in four years. Solchaga suggested that for industry to become competitive some 200,000 jobs would first have to be lost. The need for this kind of surgery emphasized the point that Spain's unemployment was even more serious than the figures suggested. From constituting only 1% of the active population in the early seventies, it had reached almost 17% by 1983, with 2·2 million jobless.

While the unions were placated with the kid-glove approach over redundancy, employers and the business community were similarly treated over economic liberalization. Even though the application for EEC membership demanded a major reduction in Spanish protectionism, no serious effort was made in the first six years of democracy to cut tariff barriers. If anything, the deep recession and the financial plight of many companies obliged the government to resist early moves towards free trade. The most successful area of reform was that of the financial system, where liberalization led to the admission of foreign banks and the beginnings of genuine competition. But here the government was dealing with a small community, sufficient of whose number were aware of the benefits of competition. For the most part, Spanish private capital preferred the safety of protectionism.

The difficulties of introducing greater liberalization in industry affected the pace of negotiations with the European Community over membership. Spain and the EEC found themselves with almost diametrically opposite arguments. Spain sought to have a long period of accession during which industrial protectionism would be slowly dismantled. At the same time it sought a quick integration of its competitive agriculture. The EEC wanted quick access to Spanish markets and a lowering of industrial tariffs, which were often three times higher than those imposed by the community on Spanish products; but with agriculture, the EEC sought to delay the period of accession for as long as possible to offset the harm to French and Italian production of wine, olive oil, and citrus fruits. This said, the goal of EEC membership provided both the motive and the framework for economic and fiscal reforms.

EDUCATION AND NEW LIBERTIES

The economy was not alone in playing second fiddle to politics in the infant democracy. Such a fundamental issue as reform of the educational system was another casualty. UCD lacked the cohesion and will to tackle this. Reform would have to touch on the heavy subsidies paid by the state to private schools, and since the Church was deeply involved in private education, any change would immediately call into question broader aspects of Catholic influence on society's mores.

UCD inherited a system that guaranteed free primary education — the so-called Educacion General Basica (EGB) — for children between the ages of six and fourteen years.[17] The system of subsidies only dated from 1972, and was justified on the grounds that it was a cheaper means of expanding the education system. With 30% of all primary schools and 50% of secondary schools run privately, the subsidies were presented as an efficient means of making education available to lower income groups. The move, however, was not so entirely disinterested. Lower income groups were brought into the system of private — and Church — schooling, which kept the cost of private education down for the middle classes. The real disadvantage of the system was the amount of money channelled to private education and the corresponding lack of interest in state schooling. The 20% failure rate of pupils in the EGB largely reflected poor results in state schools. The subsidy, which in 1982 reached 70 billion pesetas, was paid out without any control over how it was spent. While this money was being spent on private education, a promise by UCD to provide 400,000 places in the state system failed to materialize. The Socialists promised to respect the principle of private education and set two immediate priorities — establish accountability for the private education subsidy, and focus attention on improving the level of state education.[18]

A more specific problem was the plight of the country's thirty-one state and four private universities. Most were of recent creation whose numbers had been swelled by a new consciousness of the advantages of university education. From being only 105,000 in 1966 the university population had reached 600,000 by the late seventies. This gave Spain the second highest ratio of students in Europe, with 180 students per 10,000 of population, but this figure was unfortunately not reflected in the resources devoted to university education. Spain's spending per student was one third of the European average; there were insufficient teachers and facilities were poor. The Franco regime attached more importance to getting people to university than the quality of education once there. It was a conspiracy of mediocrity — the regime preferred to award easy degrees rather than risk the wrath of the middle-class parents aspiring to university status for their children.

Dedication among the staff was low, since the brightest often used university appointments as platforms from which to launch careers elsewhere. The university system bore little relation to the country's needs. For instance, far too many students were admitted to read for medicinal degrees, even though entry was more selective. In 1980, there were no less than 74,000 people studying medicine in twenty-one universities. There was no inter-connection between the universities and business and a general lack of interest in encouraging scientific investigation — Spain's miniscule spending on research and development was a direct reflection of this situation. Not only was she well behind the rest of Europe in this field, Spain was slow to catch up, and spent no more than 0·3% of GDP compared to 2·07% in the UK.[19]

Three UCD ministers promised but failed to draw up a statute for the universities. However, in less than six months of office the socialist Minister of Education, Jose Maria Maravall, prepared a law which, for the first time since the Republic, sought to give universities greater autonomy in controlling programme studies, administration, and finance. It also sought to resolve the vexed issue of the large number of contract staff, drafted in to aid the permanent staff. The inter-relationship between business, the administration, and the universities was encouraged.

Initially the socialist government ducked the question of selectivity. They were caught between believing in the universal right of access to university education yet knowing that the state lacked the resources to provide good standards for those admitted. Selectivity threatened controversy since, on one moderate estimate, admissions would be reduced by as much as 60%. As it was, no more than 20% of all university graduates were reckoned to reach the standards prevailing in northern Europe.[20] Along with the need to improve academic standards professional training was inadequate. This acquired particular importance with the rise in unemployment.

Diminishing job prospects for graduates has cast a sombre shadow over the universities. The politicization of the sixties and early seventies has given way to a sense of apathy. As Spain entered the eighties political clubs were abandoned in favour of sex and drugs. There is also little doubt that the establishment of democracy removed the raison d'etre of most student protest.

Democracy inevitably lifted the lid on the gradual liberalization of society that had been in motion since the late fifties, and the student community was just one manifestation of this. Emigration to northern Europe stimulated contact with new cultures and split families. Internal migration broke the historic isolation of the regions and swelled the urban centres. The spread of basic education established new standards and fomented secularization of the people. The tensions inherent in these changes, repressed or less visible under the dictatorship, rose to the surface under democracy. Between 1975 and 1979, the number of crimes against property brought before magistrates rose by one third. In the five years to 1981, the prison population doubled. Drug use increased dramatically — in 1982, police detained over 11,000 people in connection with drug offences, 2,000 more than in 1980, and during this time drug seizures doubled.[21] Yet another sign of the lifting of the lid was the upsurge in pornography. Flesh magazines and sex films flourished as censorship was lifted.

However, the complaints of the right that democratic Spain was becoming a decadent, libertarian society were wide of the mark. Much of what happened was a natural reaction to years of accumulated repression. The introduction of divorce did not lead to long queues in the courts.[22] Pressures to legalize abortion were no more than a reflection of a social reality already faced in other European countries. Democracy at work, in fact, showed most Spaniards to be conservative. This could, in part, be attributed to the wide-ranging effects of recession, which made people worried about jobs and anxious to preserve living standards above all else. Indeed, it could be argued that the great drawback of introducing democracy during a severe recession was offset by the conservatism created by the recession itself.

Conclusion

No European country has experienced such a rapid period of industrialization and social change as Spain. Between 1955 and 1975, accelerated economic growth irreversibly altered the face of the country. In these twenty years Spain ceased to be Europe's backward rural cousin. It emerged as the west's tenth industrial nation, making up for much of the lost ground caused by the brutal interruption of the Civil War. A massive flow of population from the countryside laid the seeds for a society which, by the 1990s, will be overwhelmingly urban, with the major concentrations in a few large cities like Barcelona and Madrid. Unprecedented prosperity established a middle class whose existence on a broad base for the first time in Spain's history provided a new element of stability. At the same time, the traditionally impoverished working class and rural peasantry tasted the first real opportunity of material choice. These economic and social changes were well in advance of political developments, which were artificially held back by Franco's authoritarianism. Nevertheless, the Franco regime, in its later years, was obliged to respond to these economic and social realities with political concessions, beginning a process of liberalization which was frequently checked but never fully halted.

On Franco's death in 1975, a military government was unacceptable to the mood of the country and to international opinion. To have continued as before was only a pipe dream of the right, for even though King Juan Carlos had sworn to uphold the principles of the Movimiento, only a more liberal system could satisfy the accumulated economic, political, and social pressures. If Spain were to come to terms with itself, the divisions created by the Civil War had to disappear. Thus, while democracy was not inevitable, this was the direction in which Spain was evolving.

It is a curious irony that the two persons most influential in guiding Spain towards democracy — King Juan Carlos and Adolfo Suarez — should have possessed wholly undemocratic credentials. Juan Carlos had been groomed in the footsteps of Franco and seemed his faithful puppet; Suarez had been schooled in the fascist blue shirt of the Movimiento. Yet in retrospect their credentials were no less valid for the task. They were not much different from the bulk of the population who tolerated Franco while alive yet knew that once he was dead, things had to change. The opposition had remained divided for forty years and failed to unseat Franco. They could therefore lay no special claim to direct the nation's affairs. This said, the communist and socialist leadership deserve considerable credit for their moderation and willingness to collaborate in the establishment of democracy. Without their co-operation, nothing would have been achieved so peacefully. But the unifying force was the monarchy. The monarchy could claim to be the one institution relatively untainted by the Civil War. The fact that the King's father, Don Juan, sought to enlist with the Nationalists and showed persistent mistrust towards the Republicans who ousted Alfonso XIII might have weighed against them. Instead it proved the added spur for Juan Carlos to act as King of all Spaniards. Only as such could the crown be universally accepted. Spain had never before seen the crown act as impartial umpire. This was, and remains, the lynchpin of democracy.

The metamorphosis of Francoism to democracy was slow. It was like a new branch grafted onto an old and withering tree that gradually acquired the life of the trunk. The new institutions of democracy — the monarchy, parliament, the trades unions, and a free press — were established alongside an unchanged judiciary, the civil service, the armed forces and security forces. The Church, traditionally such an influential institution, awkwardly straddled the two. The Church hierarchy under the leadership of Cardinal Tarancon distanced itself from the Franco regime in time and refused to be drawn into supporting any particular political party. This acted as a vital moderating influence.

On a psychological level, the haunting spectre of the fratricidal Civil War also acted as a force of moderation. Franco's supporters and the protagonists of democracy eyed each other warily. The former were slow to realize that their privileged status was ending, the latter were afraid to do anything that might provoke their wrath. The pace of reform was therefore gradual. Indeed it took three years from Franco's death to approve the Constitution. During this time, government was exercised in a dangerous legal vacuum, and the main actors were by no means sure of themselves.

The King's initial moves were profoundly cautious. He continued to employ Franco's last Prime Minister, Carlos Arias, and this decision nearly proved disastrous. Nine precious months were wasted, frustrating the opposition and doing nothing to satisfy the general level of expectation. Don Juan showed his own misgivings, which did little to help the crown, by withholding the renunciation of his rights to the throne until eighteen months after his son's accession. In the end, the vital reforms to pave the way for democracy passed off with less antagonism than expected. The most significant were the Law of Political Reform in December 1976, which abolished the Francoist Cortes, and the legalization of the Communist Party in April 1977.

Democracy was basically imposed from above and the slowness of its implementation tended to remove popular enthusiasm, so that the majority of the population took democracy for granted. It took the traumatic events of 23 February to make Spaniards aware of the value of what they had achieved. In an odd way, Spaniards can be grateful to former-General Milans del Bosch and ex-Colonel Tejero for exposing the anachronism of military adventurism and the hollowness of the extreme right's nostalgic patriotism. The trial of these rebel officers revealed just how out of touch they were with the reality of modern Spain and how incapable they would have been of governing the country. The high turn-out in the 1982 general elections and the resounding victory of the Socialist Party must be interpreted in the light of the abortive coup. It was a firm endorsement of the democratic process and showed the military that the spectre of an irrresponsible 'Red' government — standard propaganda of the Nationalists — was no longer taken seriously by the electorate. The divisive image of the Republic had been buried for good and Spain had largely come to terms with its past.

Elements within the armed forces remain viscerally opposed to democracy and will continue to plot. The sole comfort is that they are a minority and should be easily monitored by the intelligence services. The danger lies in the lessons they should have learned from previous failures. They may be tempted to attack the King's person since he was the principal obstacle on the night of 23 February. Yet even though the monarchy has been intensely personalized, the institution of the crown has acquired increasingly strong roots. The King himself has consciously promoted his teenage son, Crown Prince Felipe, against precisely such an eventuality. The public, meanwhile, as a result of the coup attempt, have been given tangible evidence of the monarchy's value and the Royal Family are genuinely popular.

Of all the institutions inherited from Franco, the military remain the least reformed. It was a mistake to write into the constitution a role which could be interpreted as sanctioning intervention if the sovereignty of the nation is threatened. This sustains the military's belief that they have a special concern in matters of public order, terrorism, and the unity of Spain. Military views of these matters have affected policy — less through direct pressure and much more out of governmental deference. The military establishment has been essentially timid and confused, and their influence has rested on an exaggerated view by the politicians of their potential power. The military retain a destabilizing influence, but this has been enormously weakened by the popular vote entrusted to the Socialists in 1982, which gave the government great moral authority in dealing with them.

Felipe Gonzalez has acquired, through his election victory, a position of unprecedented authority. In 1983, he was heading a party that not only had an ample parliamentary majority but also controlled the municipal councils in the majority of Spain's large cities, most of the regional parliaments, and the largest trade union. An elected government of Spain has never been in such a position of complete control over the life of the nation. The strength of the PSOE is all the greater given the disarray among the other parties. To the left, the Communists have failed to make an impact and have been riven by internal differences. To the right, the centre party experiment of UCD collapsed with remarkable speed through personal differences. Alianza Popular struggles to define itself and incorporate the remains of UCD. The PSOE apart, the political map remains ill-defined.

Politics has yet to move from personalities to ideology and the PSOE itself bears the strong imprint of Gonzalez's own moderation. It contains a left wing, but as a party of government it is social democrat and pragmatic in inspiration, occupying the middle ground of politics. Such moderation demonstrates a hitherto unseen maturity in Spanish politics. Gonzalez would have to squander his electoral goodwill disastrously not to enjoy a second term in office and remain in power for a minimum of eight years. He should be Spain's longest-ever serving Prime Minister.

UCD performed a very necessary function but it deserves little credit for allowing itself to be torn apart by internal differences when a sizeable chunk of the electorate had voted it into office. Internal differences slowed the pace of reform and many of the most controversial issues were handed over to the Socialists. UCD would have achieved much more had there not been such a game of musical chairs in the ministries. For instance, in five years there were four different Ministers of Industry. This was a moment when vital industrial decisions had to be taken, yet with each change valuable time was lost as new ministers brought in their own teams and rewrote existing plans. UCD lacked the courage to tackle corruption and clean up the civil service, top priorities of the Socialists. Many abuses, such as cheating on social security or the conflict of interest in holding office, were public knowledge but left untouched.

Perhaps the most serious criticism of UCD, and more particularly of Suarez, was the way municipal elections were delayed for fear of the left. The democratic running of local councils, which affected citizens more directly than parliament, was delayed for four years. This was unnecessary, and represented a curious reversal of the republican experience. After Franco, it was the general elections of June 1977 that established the popular will for a democratic system. In 1930, it was the municipal election results that brought in the Republic.

All the main political parties must take a share in the blame for the shambles in dealing with Spain's long-standing problems of regionalism. Federalism has been expressly avoided at the expense of a clumsy system that falls uneasily between genuine devolution and disguised centralism. The autonomous regions have been given the appearance of mini-states complete with parliament, head of government, and the right to control a sizeable area of administration that includes health, education, and regional planning. But none of these powers can be used outside the provisions of the constitution which stipulates the primordial need to preserve the unity of Spain. As a result, regional policy has only exaggerated the importance of some regions like Madrid, which had no previous pretensions to autonomy, and demeaned the aspirations of others with historic claims, like the Basque country and Catalonia.

Decisions have been made on regionalism with wholly inadequate study of their consequences. For instance, one of the areas of greatest freedom permitted to the regions is control of their cultural affairs. This has led to an almost exaggerated emphasis on culture in regions like Catalonia: a form of regional narcissism. Bilingualism has been conceded but in a wholly different climate to when it previously existed in Spain. Previously there was little conflict because the bulk of the population were illiterate. Now bilingualism among a literate population threatens serious conflicts in people's daily lives, and to pit regional governments in the Basque country and Catalonia permanently against Madrid. As it is, devolution looks likely to produce a huge extra duplication in the administrative process, as the central government zealously watches every move of the regions.

If regionalism is to work, a basis of trust must be established between Madrid and those regions with historic identities. Madrid has so far made concessions only because it has been forced to do so. This grudging attitude has merely stimulated the Basques and Catalans to demand more, and they live in permanent fear of restrictive and niggling interpretations of what has already been agreed. In the case of the Basque country, this situation prolongs the destabilizing influence of ETA, whose policy of the gun retains its hard core of supporters.

Even with the restrictive nature of devolution applied by both UCD and the socialist governments, the Basques and Catalans are making their regions distinctive, and they are certainly run more efficiently than the rest of Spain. There is a serious risk that the existing regional imbalance of wealth which favours the north over the south will be increased. Already the two most economically and socially advanced regions are the Basque country and Catalonia (to this one could add Valencia and Madrid) which happen to be closest to Europe. They enjoy the best communications and are now linked up through Aragon. The main pole of economic development in Spain is the Bilbao-Zaragoza-Barcelona axis, which has been reinforced by the decision of General Motors to establish itself in this northern triangle. If, and when, Spain joins the Common Market, geographical proximity and the weight of existing industry are bound to make the north the main beneficiary.

Such a consequence of EEC membership has been little studied, and the emphasis has been much more on the political virtues of joining this club of western nations. It has been seen as a political insurance for democracy and a badge of modernity. Within Spain, being European is synonymous with being 'modern'. Membership should eliminate the stigma of Spain's exclusion from the European decision-making process caused by the unacceptability of the Franco regime. This is important psychologically because Spain possesses an historic inferiority complex regarding Europe. The other manifestation of this inferiority complex is a woolly neutralism, encouraged by the links of 'hispanidad' with Latin America.

A number of Franco legacies will take time to disappear. He accustomed

Spaniards to a strong paternalism which created a general reluctance to take decisions or initiatives. Decisions were always referred to the top whether in private enterprise, government, or the civil service. Thus a few people at the top work very hard and underneath a mass are working inefficiently and without responsibility. At all levels, Spaniards became accustomed to a cocoon-like state protection and this has been extended into democracy. State funds subsidize the political parties, the trades unions, the press, television, the Church, and private education. The subsidies themselves need not be harmful: rather, it is the belief that they should be automatically forthcoming which inhibits people and institutions from being independent. Too many are dependent on the state in a passive way. Even in the case of businessmen, the free market economy to which Spain is aspiring fills most with apprehension rather than excitement at the challenge and opportunity.

The reverse side of paternalism is a fear of authority, whoever or whatever it represents. There is a fear of challenging authority because authority is automatically assumed to be more powerful than the individual. This is the residue of a police state — people are still, for instance, afraid of talking over the telephone. The whole area of information is surrounded by self-censorship, and exaggerated deference to authority. Criticism is frequently misunderstood and poorly taken. The Francoist view, that you are either for us or against us, tends to prevail. This inhibits constructive debate and increases the danger of people, especially in authority, hearing what they want to believe. Failure to accept criticism is also a reflection of the mediocrity of the educational system inherited from the Franco era. Rightfully, the Socialists have given educational reform priority treatment.

The political class has inherited a residual condescension towards the electorate who tend to be treated as not mature enough to understand. There is a reluctance to stimulate popular participation out of fear of losing control. This encourages apathy which is punctuated by sudden bursts of protest, suggesting that a residue of feeling still affects the populace. The electorate has rarely been taken into the government's confidence and little attempt has been made to form public opinion intelligently. An elite opinion is formed by one newspaper, El Pais, while the bulk of the electorate are left in the limbo of low quality television which does shamefully little to inform Spaniards about their own country.

Yet on the positive side, a new civic education has begun. For the first time, Spaniards have been encouraged to believe in the partnership of citizen and state. A breakthrough here has been the introduction of a more progressive tax system, stimulating the concept of both giving to and receiving from the state. In the past there was little reason to believe in the state, hence people took refuge in self and family. The grandiloquent language of patriotism of the Franco era appealed solely to the emotional but abstract notion of motherland, not state, so disguising the essential selfishness of society. Gonzalez has been successful in combining the notion of state with patriotism.

At the same time, he has broken the monopoly of patriotism arrogated to themselves by the Nationalists after the Civil War.

Spain's principal challenge now lies in the economic sphere. Having hoisted itself up into the top rank of the industrialized nations in the seventies, the country sat back complacently as though this achievement were self-sustaining. Failure to understand quickly the significance of increased energy prices has cost Spain dear. This, coupled with the inability to generate its own technology and hold down production costs, has once again widened the gap with the advanced nations of Europe. As a result, unless Spain restructures its economy and improves economic performance, it risks being relegated to second class status in Europe, hovering awkwardly close to the most developed nations of the Third World.

Since 1975, Spain has been engulfed in an ever-deepening recession — the worst and longest in recent European history. Understandably, political priorities dominated the early years after Franco's death, compounding the vacuum of economic indecision before he died. However, Spain has to adjust to the brutal fact that its prosperity was based on premises which are no longer valid. The fast-expanding market has contracted, and growth has slowed to near negative rates. Credit, labour and energy are no longer cheap. The production costs in industries dependent on largely imported inter-mediate technology are far too high, and a major rationalization will be needed if they are to stay afloat. Joining the EEC — no matter how long the period of transition — entails a sharp cut in the level of protection previously enjoyed. It is doubtful whether much of Spanish industry can survive increased competition; any that does may do so only at the cost of being dominated even more by foreign capital. Solutions are complex. Stimulating renewed growth, of which there is great potential in a still undeveloped market, risks fuelling inflation which has been double that of Spain's main trading partners since 1975. If growth is not stimulated then no dent can be made in the 17% of the active population out of work. This is the highest in Europe. Any economic growth that averages less than 2·5% a year will fail to absorb the number of people seeking jobs for the first time.

Beyond this are two further considerations concerning the basis of Spain's prosperity. Firstly, Spain has relied on short-term views of profit rather than the broader quality of life. The thriving tourist industry evolved at the expense of a cavalier rape of Spain's coastline. Industry developed with scant respect for polluting the environment or investment in industrial safety. Products have been marketed with limited quality control. As a result, much of the country's priceless coastline has been irretrievably ruined; Spain has an appalling industrial safety record; many large cities like Barcelona, Bilbao, and Madrid have serious and costly pollution problems; and there is the permanent risk of such incidents as the 400 deaths caused by the illegal distribution of adulterated rape-seed oil. The general absence of controls has permitted individuals to take liberties with society which sooner or later have to be paid for. This means a more regulated society. Spaniards have rejected such regulation until now largely, one suspects, because such liberties have offset the burden of political conformity.

Secondly, the nation's prosperity has grown at the expense of the rural community. The 20% of the population living in rural areas have notably inferior facilities of all sorts — whether housing, roads, electricity, water, or schooling. This segment of the population has, in a sense, subsidized an artificially high standard of living for the rest. Despite limited resources and dependence on imported energy, this imbalance of wealth will need to be rectified. In particular the rich, who have contributed so little in comparison to what they have syphoned off in the past thirty years, are likely to be asked to lose some of their privileges. This may not happen immediately, especially as the rural communities have no coherent voice, but democracy has raised the level of aspiration for a better life and it is hard not to see the trades unions becoming increasingly frustrated over continued unemployment and diminishing real earnings. The deeply conservative mood which has over-taken the country as a result of recession could convey an air of deceptive calm about social stability. In the end, the ability to sustain social stability with economic progress will influence Spain's future far more than any perceived threat from the nostalgic military.

NOTES

SELECT BIBLIOGRAPHY

APPENDICES

INDEX

Notes

CHAPTER 1
1. Cifra Press. The assassination of Carrero Blanco coincided with the opening of a trial of ten labour leaders for illegal organization, the biggest such trial of the Franco era.
2. Gregorio Moran, *Los Españoles que Dejaron de Serlo* (p. 350), Planeta, Barcelona, 1982. Moran maintains that ETA was obsessed with the idea of executing a major act of violence like the Irgun's blowing-up of the Hotel King David in Jerusalem to force the British to end their mandate in Palestine. A film was subsequently made of the Carrero Blanco assassination by Gilles Pontecorvo called *Operacion Ogro* (the codename given to the operation). Carrero's Dodge is now on display in the Army Museum, Madrid.
3. Victor Salmador, *Las Dos Españas y El Rey* (p. 43), Planeta, Barcelona, 1981.
4. The communist leader, Santiago Carrillo, commented, 'The assassination of Carrero Blanco ... had great political importance, because he was the man who was to have ensured the transition from Franco to Juan Carlos. He was the regime's strong man — the man who was to have ensured continuity.' Santiago Carrillo, *Dialogue on Spain* (p. 8), Lawrence & Wishart, London, 1976.
5. See Pablo Lizcano, *La Generacion del 56*, Grijalbo, Barcelona, 1981. Among the first organizers of student activity were Enrique Mugica, subsequently a leading figure in the Socialist Party, and Ramon Tamames, for a while the Communist Party's chief economic spokesman. Later activists included Miguel Boyer, first Socialist Minister of Economy.
6. Luis Nuñez, *La Sociedad Vasca Actual* (p. 121), Editorial Thertoa, San Sebastian, 1979.
7. For an account of Franco's final eighteen months, see Vicente Pozuelo Escudero, *Los Ultimos 476 dias de Franco*, Planeta, Barcelona, 1980. Escudero was Franco's personal doctor and involved in all major decisions concerning the Caudillo's health.
8. By far the best account of Franco's upbringing in Galicia is given in George Hill's *Franco*, Macmillan, New York, 1967. The film script depicts a woman left to bring up four children while the husband goes off to Cuba. Franco's mother was left with the elder brother, Nicolas (later to be an adviser to Franco and ambassador to Portugal), Franco himself, Ramon (who started off as an anarchist and ended up as an aviation ace) and his sister Pilar.
9. Heleno Sana, *El Franquismo Sin Mitos* (p. 190), Grijalbo, Barcelona, 1982. Of all the persons closely associated with Franco, Serrano Suner has been the most garrulous in commenting on the man, in part to set his own historical record straight.
10. Quoted by Franco's Labour Minister, Jose Antonio Giron, in *Franco Visto por sus Ministros* (p. 46), Planeta, Barcelona, 1981.

11. Hill, *Franco* (pp. 61-2). On one occasion, Franco became so infuriated by torments that he hit a cadet officer with a candlestick.

12. Escudero, *Los Ultimos 476 Dias de Franco* (pp. 38-46). The first tune he played was '*Soy Valiente y Leal Legionario*'. Escudero claims this therapy was repeated daily with marching to two or three military marches!

13. Sana, *Franquismo Sin Mitos* (p. 49).

14. Many accounts exist of the Civil War fighting, e.g., Hugh Thomas, *The Spanish Civil War*, Pelican (revised edition), London, 1968. But Hill's *Franco* has the most space devoted purely to Franco and is based on conversations with him and consultation of his archives.

15. Max Gallo, *Spain under Franco* (p. 58), Allen & Unwin, London, 1969. Jose Antonio came to be called 'the absent one', which led his followers to scribble graffiti saying 'still present'. The Church was also prepared to take part in the mythologizing of Jose Antonio.

16. Gallo, *Spain under Franco* (p. 28). Franco's apparent early lack of political ambition perhaps helps to explain his detachment in power. He did not allow success to turn his head.

17. Gallo, *Spain under Franco* (p. 28).

18. Giron, *Franco Visto por sus Ministros* (p. 49).

19. Sir Samuel Hoare, *Ambassador on a Special Mission*, Collins, London, 1946.

20. Jose Maria Maravall, *Dictadura y Disentimiento Politico* (pp. 16-28), Alfguara, Madrid, 1978. See also, C. J. Friedrich & Z. K. Brzezinski, *Totalitarian Dictatorship and Autocracy*, Harvard, 1956, for a theoretical definition of totalitarianism; and essay by Juan Linz, *Una Teoria del Regimen Autoritario – El Caso de España*, Akal, Madrid, 1978.

21. Franco's habits and his dealings with ministers are well documented in Giron, *Franco Visto por sus Ministros*.

22. Francisco Franco Salgado-Araujo, *Mis Conversaciones Privadas con Franco*, Planeta, Barcelona, 1976. As Franco's cousin, he acted as confidant, but the critical comments on the amount of time wasted by the Caudillo in shooting and fishing made in his diary were probably not conveyed to the man directly concerned. On one occasion, Franco was in a shooting party that killed 5000 partridges in one day.

23. The country house was in theory donated by the grateful inhabitants of Franco's native El Ferrol and La Coruña, but Sir Samuel Hoare, *Ambassador on a Special Mission*, Collins, London, 1946, has some scathing comments on this; see p. 220.

24. Carrillo, *Dialogue on Spain* (pp. 93-96). Carrillo also claimed that the guerilla struggle in Spain after the Civil War caused the loss of some 15,000 comrades.

25. Nuñez, *La Sociedad Vasca Actual* (p. 127).

26. Serrano Suner has tried to claim much of the credit for keeping Spain out of the War. See his account *Entre Hendaya y Gibraltar*, Madrid, 1947; and Sana, *El Franquismo Sin Mitos*.

CHAPTER 2

1. *La Guerra Civil Española*, Ministerio de Cultura, Madrid, 1980.

2. Ian Gibson, *Paracuellos: come fue* (p. 218), Argos Vergara, Barcelona, 1983.

3. Honoré de Balzac, A Murky Business, (*Une Tenebreuse Affaire*) (p. 21), translated by Herbert Hunt, Penguin, London, 1972.

4. Pilar Urbano, *Con la Venia... yo indague el 23F* (p. 130), Argos Vergara, Barcelona,

1982. General Milans del Bosch is quoted as saying, 'Take Mola's proclamation and adjust it...'

5. Pedro Sainz Rodriguez, *Un Reinado en la Sombra* (p. 55), Planeta, Barcelona, 1977.

6. Xavier Tussell, *La oposicion democratica al Franquismo* (431), Planeta, Barcelona, 1977.

7. Hugh Thomas, *The Spanish Civil War*, Eyre & Spottiswoode, London, 1961. In his preface to the third and revised edition (Pelican, London, 1977), Thomas comments, 'The recent past was as forbidden a subject as the immediate future. To probe too deep risked silence or enmity. Almost nobody in Spain was writing works on very modern history which could be in any way regarded as seriously historical. Not only the war but the Republic was taboo.'

8. I have used Thomas as a norm without pretending that his figures are definitive. See *The Spanish Civil War*, p. 926. Gallo, *Spain under Franco*, Allen & Unwin, London, 1969, gives the casualties as 560,000 (p. 70). George Hill in *Franco*, Macmillan, New York, 1967, agrees broadly with Thomas but believes the executions between 1940 and 1945 totalled only 40,000 to 50,000 (p. 360). Ricardo de la Cierva, *Historia Ilustrade de la Guerra Civil Espanola*, Barcelona, 1970, gives among the lowest figures for reprisals during the fighting and afterwards — as might be expected from a pro-Franco historian (vol. II., pp. 221-23).

9. Galeazzo Ciano, *Diplomatic Papers* (pp. 293-94), 1948.

10. Laurie Lee, *As I walked out one midsummer morning* (p. 159), Penguin, London, 1969.

11. Samuel Hynes, *The Auden Generation* (p. 242), Faber, London, 1979.

12. Heleno Sana, *El Franquismo Sin Mitos* (p. 252), Grijalbo, Barcelona, 1982. Serrano Suner quotes War Minister Varela saying: 'What's this! A division is going from the Spanish Army!' to which Serrano Suner replied: 'No, Sir. A division of the Spanish Army will not go because the Spanish State is not the one involved in the War.'

13. Sana, *El Franquismo Sin Mitos*. Serrano Suner, when asked about 10,000 Spaniards dying in Oranienburg and whether he was aware of the Holocaust, replies: 'In all honesty, we knew nothing. We heard about these things much later when they were in the public domain. I'm sure that Franco too knew nothing of this.' The same ignorance of atrocity in an entirely different context, that of Paracuellos, is expressed by Carillo in Gibson's *Paracuellos* (op. cit. pp. 192-222).

14. The Nationalists claimed Moscardo's son was killed as a result of this phone call; but apparently the killing occurred later. The relief of the Alcazar probably delayed the outcome of the war as it diverted nationalist troops from their march on Madrid. See Hill, *Franco* (op. cit. pp. 250-51).

15. See Gibson, *Paracuellos* (op. cit.) and Carlos Fernandez, *Paracuellos del Jarama: Carrillo culpable?* Argos Vergara, Barcelona, 1983. Fernandez has a totally contrasting view to Gibson. See also *El Alacazar*, 1 January 1977. This article claimed that up to 12,000 persons had been buried in Paracuellos, victims of the massacre. The basic confusion over numbers stems from differences over whether all killings by Republicans of Nationalists in Madrid are included since persons other than those taken from the prisons and shot were buried in mass graves at Paracuellos.

16. See Angel Vinas, *El Oro de Moscu*, Grijalbo, Barcelona, 1979. This definitive analysis of the fate of Spain's gold reserves was withdrawn from publication in November 1976 on government orders. The order was lifted without explanation in July 1977, following the renewal of diplomatic relations with the Soviet Union in February 1977.

CHAPTER 3

1. V.S. Pritchett, *The Spanish Temper*, Chatto & Windus, London, 1954. He asserts that no other race in Europe has such a consuming preoccupation with death. He knew the country well since the 1920s but makes no allowance for the backward state of development.

2. Gerald Brenan, *The Literature of the Spanish People* (p. xii), Cambridge University Press, 1953. Brenan considers the greatest glory of Spanish literature to be its resistance to foreign influence (p. 464).

3. An interesting exhibition on the impact of these hispanicists was organized in 1981 by the Ministry of Culture with an extensive two volume catalogue — *Imagen Romantic de España*. Also see *El Greco to Goya*, National Gallery, London, 1981, for a concise survey of English interest in Spain and Spanish art.

4. Miguel de Unamuno's most important work was *Del Sentimiento Tragico de la Vida en los Hombres y los Pueblos*, written in 1913. The most influential of Ortega's works was his essay *España Invertebrada*. The first to begin this soul-searching was Angel Ganivet with his *Idearum Español* in 1897.

5. The racist attitude of Francoist legislation towards gipsies could be also traced to the racialism of the old christians. Legislation discriminated against the large gipsy population, treating them as inferiors and refusing to accept them as proper Spaniards. Police records referred to people 'of gipsy race'.

6. Castro's main work is *La Realidad Historica de España*, Porrua, Mexico, 1966. Others include *Cervantes y los Casticismos Españoles*, Alianza, Madrid, 1974. For a useful summary of the debate surrounding Castro's historiography and the contribution of others like Claudio Sanchez Albornoz, see Gabriel Jackson, *Historian's Quest* (pp. 206-25), Alfred Knopf, New York, 1964.

7. Bernard Moses, *Spain Overseas* (p. 7), Hispanic Notes & Monographs, New York, 1928.

8. The fastest speed on any rail track is 103 kilometres per hour Madrid-Valencia. To save costs tunnelling was limited; but this meant that journey times were longer and rolling stock maintenance more costly.

9. Jose Ortega y Gasset, *España Invertebrada* (p. 106), Alianza, Madrid, 1981.

10. Article Two states: 'The Constitution is based on the indissoluble unity of the Spanish nation, the common and indivisible country of all Spaniards; it recognises and guarantees the right to autonomy of the nationalities and regions of which it is composed and solidarity amongst them all.'

11. Ortega's idea is that Spain is without a spinal vertebrae to hold the various units together — hence it is invertebrate.

12. Andalusia derives from Al Andalus, the domain of the Emirate of Cordoba which originally covered the area conquered and ruled by the Arabs.

13. An Andalusian is on average one centimetre smaller than a Basque and weighs nearly four kilos less. The average height for a Basque is 171·7 centimetres and weight 67·2 kilos against 170·3 for an Andalusian's height and 62·9 kilos for weight. See *España*, Anuario Estadistico, 1982 (pp. 519-20).

14. W.J. Entwistle, *The Spanish Language*, Faber, London, 1969. This contains an analysis of the impact of Arabic (pp. 125-34), and of the origins of Basque and its relationship with Iberian (p. 47).

15. *El Pais*, 6 April 1982. Entwistle (*op. cit.*), whose study was first published in 1936, estimated that 16·5 million Spaniards of the 24·2 million population spoke Castilian as their mother tongue, 5·4 million were Catalan speaking, 45,000 Basque speaking and the remainder Galician speaking.

16. The Seville monopoly of trade with the colonies lasted until 1717. Brenan speculates over what would have happened if the Catalans had been allowed a share earlier on. See *The Spanish Labyrinth* (p. 25), Cambridge University Press, Cambridge, 1980 edition. Preventing Catalans from an early share in the trade was another example of the crown and Castile preferring control to economic development.

17. The cult of St James of Santiago was seen by some as a counter to the success of the figure of Mohammed in Islam.

18. For the changing sociology of Spain, see Jose Felix Tezanos, *Sociologia del Socialismo Español* (pp. 23-46), Editorial Tecnos, Madrid, 1983.

19. The first year in which tax reforms became operational was 1979 — the number of tax payers rose from 1·8 million in 1977 to 5·3 million by 1979.

CHAPTER 4

1. Interview with Joaquin Saez Merino in June 1980. See also *Financial Times*, 15 August 1980. In 1977 the company, Saez Merino S.A., was split so that Saez Merino retained the domestic market and Canada, managed by Manuel Saez Merino, and a new company, Textiles y Confecciones Europas, controlled by Joaquin, covered the rest of the world. One of his sayings is 'I would rather burn my jeans than sell them cheap'.

2. El Corte Ingles annual reports 1977-81. See also *Financial Times*, 13 November 1978.

3. In November 1957, opening the Zaragoza Fair, Ullastres made what was then a bold speech: 'We have got to break models [economic] and create new ones.' He was the first economics minister to travel extensively within Europe and his efforts with the EEC led eventually to the 1970 preferential agreement.

4. The other mining finance and credit company formed was Sociedad Española Mercantil e Industrial, mainly financed by the Rothschild family. This built the Madrid-Zaragoza-Alicante railway. For Spain's early industrial history see Gabriel Tortella Casares, *Banking, Railroads and Industry in Spain* (pp. 113-18), Arno Press, New York, 1977. Also an essay by the same author in *Banco de Bilbao 125 Años de Historia*, Madrid, 1982. Also Sima Lieberman, *The Contemporary Spanish Economy* (pp. 121-27), George Allen & Unwin, London, 1982.

5. Tortella, *Banco de Bilbao 125 Años de Historia* (op. cit., p. 16).

6. Juan Antonio Cabezas, *Cien Años de Telefono en España* (p. 28), Espasa Calpe, Madrid, 1974. This was an official history of the telephone heavily biased against the Republic. The first Bell telephone was installed in 1880 by Sanchez Arjona in Fregenal de la Sierra near Badajoz.

7. *Banco de Bilbao 125 Años de Historia* (op. cit.) and conversations with executives of the bank.

8. The Catalana group was regarded by bankers as 'more than a bank'. In Catalonia a strong conviction remains that the group's difficulties were exaggerated and that there was a deliberate campaign mounted against Catalana to destroy public confidence — precisely because it was trying to be a powerful Catalan bank. All its internal memorandums were in Catalan and the bank went out of its way to sponsor Catalan culture and industry. Jordi Pujol himself was obliged to sever direct links when he became head of the *Generalitat* (Catalan government) in 1979. His links were also considered damaging and were exploited by the bank's rivals, according to comments made to the author by former chief executive Fransec Cabana. Other instances of

Catalan banks suffering are the temporary receivership of Banco de Cataluña in 1931, due to withdrawal of funds by Campsa (at the time when Catalonia was obtaining its autonomy statute); and the collapse of Credito Balear in 1935. The only strong Catalan bank remaining is Banco de Sabadell, founded in 1881.

9. *Banco Hispano Americano, El Primer Medio Siglo de su Historia*, Madrid, 1951. This is a poorly written and vainglorious official history with a few useful facts. I am also grateful to Hispano's president Alejandro Albert, and to Fernando Urbaneja for more information.

10. *Hidrolectrica Española, 1907-1957*, Madrid, 1958. A half-centenary history.

11. See Gregorio Moran, *Los Españoles que Dejaron de Serlo*, Planeta, Barcelona, 1982. This is the only attempt to analyse and understand the importance of Neguri (pp. 131-33). However, several Neguri families believe he overstates their importance.

12. Under Franco, Ramon de la Sota was a taboo subject and as a result he became a neglected figure outside the Basque country. I am grateful to his grandson, Ramon de la Sota, for checking facts and information. See Moran, *Los Españoles que Dejaron de Serlo* (op. cit. pp. 174-76), also *Banco de Bilbao 125 Años de Historia*. In 1977, as a result of the Amnesty Law, the Sota family sought cancellation of the 1940 fines and various judicial acts confiscating goods. This was refused, even though the punishments were imposed posthumously. The heirs agreed to pay 62·3 million pesetas to recover some assets. The fate of the shipyard Euskalduna was a merger in 1979 as part of the restructuring of major shipyards. It is now part of the state owned complex, Astilleros Españoles.

13. Three biographies have appeared on Juan March — none of them very complete and all without the co-operation of the family. Ramon Garriga, *Juan March y Su Tiempo*, Planeta, Barcelona, 1976; Manuel Benavides, *El Ultimo Pirata del Mediterraneo*, Ediciones Roca, Mexico, 1975, a reprint of the 1934 reportage; Bernardo Diaz Nosty, *La Irresible Ascension de Don Juan March*, Ediciones Sedmay, Madrid, 1977. The March Foundation has made no effort to aid a study of its founder, and the major gap in his career is the period after 1940. By far the best investigative work appears in the *Barcelona Traction Case*, by John Brooks. *The Games Players, Tales of men and money*, Times Books, New York, 1980, has a section on him entitled 'The Spanish Privateer'. Carlos March, his grandson, claims that Juan March's greatest power was in the latter days of the Primo de Rivera dictatorship: 'contrary to what people think we did not obtain great advantages under Franco'. *El Pais*, 2 January 1983.

14. *Politica Commercial Exterior en España* (Vol II, pp. 804-820), Banco Exterior Servicio de Estudios Economico, Madrid, 1979. This two-volume study has access to reserved documents and is the most comprehensive to date on trade and foreign exchange policy. But even in this there is only one minor reference to the role of Andorra.

15. *INI Informe Annual*, 1977, '78, '79. I am also grateful for information on INI to Jose Miguel de la Rica and Carlos Bustelo, former presidents, and Enrique Badia, former chief press officer. See also *Financial Times* 18 May 1978 and 23 September 1980.

16. See the comments of his cousin Francisco Franco Salgado-Araujo, *Mis Conversaciones Privadas con Franco* (p. 178), Planeta, Barcelona, 1976.

17. The legal and financial complications of the case were finally tidied up in 1983 with a symbolic sale. Vila Reyes insists on his innocence.

18. OECD annual reports and also Lieberman (op. cit., p. 213).

19. This period is covered in detail by Alison Wright, *The Spanish Economy, 1959-1976*, Macmillan, London, 1977.
20. The average in Europe is reckoned to be 70% of families falling with the middle class; in Spain it is only 54%.
21. *Banco de Bilbao Informe Economico 1981*. This bank has the best series of independent and reliable statistics, largely the work of Julio Alcaide.
22. Half of the average spent by each person on types of gambling and lotteries goes on the Christmas lottery, the so-called *Gordo* (fat one). Ticket sales for the Gordo were 25 billion pesetas in 1970 and topped 165 billion pesetas by the end of the decade. By 1982 revenue to the treasury in taxes on gambling, bingo and lotteries was 60 billion pesetas compared to 13 billion pesetas in 1978.
23. ERT annual reports and conversations with Leahman Brothers, financial advisors, October 1982.
24. *El Pais*, 24-28 February 1983.
25. *Instituto Nacional de Estadistica, datos sobre suspensiones de pagos y declaraciones de quiebras, 1981. Suspension de Pagos* (temporary receivership) is a peculiarly Spanish device in which a company applies to a court to suspend all outstanding payments, including wages, pending a renegotiation with its creditors. The courts grant this on the basis of debts exceeding a certain proportion of assets.
26. This study was prepared by the Ministry of Commerce as the first attempt in 1980 to establish the level of foreign investment. See *La Internacionalizacion de la emprese Española, Secretaria General Tecnica Libros* (Ministerio de Economia y Comercio, Madrid, 1981). Also *Financial Times*, 1 August 1980.
27. *Crisis y Reforma de la Economia Española 1979/82, Secretaria General Tecnica Libros* (pp. 281-300), Ministerios de Economia y Comercio, Madrid, 1982.

CHAPTER 5
1. The last two independent industrial banks of size, Bankunion and Banco Urquijo, were taken over by Hispano-Americano in 1982 and 1983 respectively. Bankunion had already been intervened by the Deposit Guarantee Fund because of substantial losses that required over 40 billion pesetas of Fund finances to refloat. Urquijo was taken over directly by Hispano but with Fund assistance and other special aids. Since 1944 there had been a cross-share relationship between Hispano and Urquijo.
2. Banco Popular and the Barcelona-based savings bank, La Caixa, were the first financial institutions to be internationally audited. From 1977 onwards the bigger banks came under greater pressure to disclose details since they were involved in more international operations. Banesto was the last of the big seven banks to agree to an independent international audit.
3. This percentage is a conservative estimate since during the Franco era, INI, the state holding company, had the majority of its interests in mixed companies and these were very much under the sway of the private equity representatives. Also, individual bank stakes may have been small, but their possession of nominee shareholdings was very important. See Ramon Tamames, *La Oligarquia Financiera en España*, Planeta, Barcelona, 1977.
4. These estimations are based on conversations with Union Electrica Iberduero, Enher, Endesa and members of Banco de Bilbao, Vizcaya and Urquijo. Also, in 1974/75/76, the Bank of Spain intervened to support the electricity company shares and at one stage held approximately 12% of all utility stock. The bulk was sold off in 1981, the

biggest sale being 5% of Hidrola stock. In 1983 it still retained a similar percentage of Iberduero. See *Financial Times*, 30 October 1981.

5. The existence of the compensation fund was confirmed to the author by representatives of Iberduero, and Unesa, the utilities association; but details of its operation have never been disclosed. However, the Brussels Commission regards it as a form of non-competitive cartel.

6. Based on information supplied to the author by Iberduero.

7. *Anuario Estadistico de la Banca Privada, 1981* (p. 244-45), Asociacion Española de Banca Privada, Madrid. Central directly absorbed twenty-one banks, Bilbao fourteen, Banesto ten, Santander eight, Popular eight, Hispano-Americano four and Vizcaya four. Prior to the decree permitting foreign banks to operate in Spain four had been operating 'historically' — Bolsa, Credit Lyonnais, Societe Generale and Banco Nazionale de Lavoro. Bank of America meanwhile had enjoyed a relationship with Banco de Santander via Ameribank. The principal foreign bank for the Franco regime was Manufacturers Hanover Trust.

8. General Francisco Franco Salgardo-Araujo, *Mis Conversaciones Privadas con Franco* (p. 458), Planeta, Barcelona, 1976. In an entry in his diary of 25 November 1965, Franco's cousin described a conversation about the proposed Central-Hispano merger. Salgardo-Araujo himself comments: 'Spain can't put itself into the hands of four men because they will be masters of all the companies and everyone will be at their mercy'.

9. Comments to the author by Jose Ramon Alvarez Rendueles, governor of the Bank of Spain in June 1981.

10. The Spanish banks managed to limit to ten the initial number of foreign banks permitted to operate branches or establish local subsidiaries. By 1983 there were thirty — a number unlikely to increase substantially. As a reaction against the increased foreign presence, the banks also prevented the sale to Citibank of eleven finance and hire purchase companies in the Mapfre group.

11. Banco Exterior established the largest presence — a logical development in view of its involvement in export finance. Santander and Central were particularly aggressive in moving into Latin America and most of the big seven established a presence in Miami and New York. Presence in the London market was not such a new phenomenon. Quite often the purchase of banks in Chile and Argentina by Spanish banks was forced by the former's debts.

12. Information supplied to the author by Jaimie Carvajal, president of Urquijo October 1981. Half of Urquijo's divestiture occurred in 1981. But Urquijo was unable to divest fast enough to cover industrial losses. See also *Financial Times*, 30 November 1981.

13. Comments to the author by Carlos Solchaga, Minister of Industry, December 1982.

14. Prior to the expropriation of the Rumasa group of banks, the banking crisis had seen two banks struck off the register; eight banks taken over directly by other banks as preventive measures with official assistance; and nineteen banks intervened first by the authorities — either by the original Corporacion Bancaria (the bank hospital) or latterly directly by the Deposit Guarantee Fund. In addition at least fifteen savings banks and rural co-operative banks had to be intervened and aided. 90% of the banks affected were granted licences between 1963 and 1976.

15. Information based on a series of interviews with Jose Maria Ruiz-Mateos between 1977-82, answers to written questionnaires. Also see *El Pais*, 23 February-2 March 1983, *Financial Times*, 3 May 1980.

16. *El Pais*, 2 March 1983.

17. The annual average funding of the Deposit Guarantee Fund totalled around 25 billion pesetas. But outlays in 1981 totalled over 70 billion pesetas as a result of Bank of Spain anticipatory payments. In late 1982 the Bank of Spain issued a decree that obliged the banks to raise their contributions if its own advances exceeded a certain level. This effectively meant raising contributions to two per million deposits. However, this threatened to wipe out bank profits and the introduction of the decree was held back.

18. *Banco de Bilbao, Balance Social 1979/81* (p. 138). In the four years to 1981, the most labour shed among the big seven was by Hispano, cutting 7% of its staff. The big seven account directly for 57% of bank employment. The banks have pay levels well above the norm. Average annual pay in the Banco de Bilbao in 1981 was 1,341,000 pesetas. In addition, there are a wide series of fringe benefits which the banks can, with some difficulty, continue, including private education payments and special life insurance schemes. The Banco de Bilbao, which provides most information on such fringe benefits, showed that in 1981 special Christmas pay-outs totalled 65 million pesetas; presents for the Three Kings Festival *Reyes* totalled 19 million pesetas, and contributions to the Christmas *Gordo* lottery 2 million pesetas.

19. Comments to the author by former premier, Adolfo Suarez, April 1983.

20. See Pilar Urbano, *Con la venia . . . yo indague el 23-F* (pp. 26-33), Argos Vegara, Barcelona, 1982.

CHAPTER 6

1. Based on information provided to the author by CCOO and conversation with Marcelino Camacho in November 1982. Several times while in prison after the Civil War, Camacho was in bad health and in 1942 was in Carabanchel Military Hospital for forty-seven days with a fever of 39-40° C. He was married in Oran in 1948 to Josefa Samper Rosas, daughter of Spanish immigrants from Almeria — a reminder that Oran under French colonial rule was dominated by Spanish immigrants. See also Marcelino Camacho, *Charlas en la Prision*, Editorial Laia, Barcelona, 1976.

2. For the origins of CCOO see Nicolas Sartorius, *El Resurgir del Movimiento Obrero* (p. 50), Editorial Laia, Barcelona, 1976. Also, by the same author, *Que Son Los Comisiones Obreras?*, Editorial La Gaya, Barcelona, 1976. The latter was initially confiscated as part of a campaign during the transition to harass CCOO.

3. Most commentators have wondered how an Italian without a word of Spanish could have been able to communicate so successfully. But it is extraordinarily easy for Spaniards to understand Italian and in the case of Fanelli they were hanging on every word. See Brenan, *The Spanish Labyrinth* (op. cit. pp. 138-40).

4. F. Almendros Morcillo, E. Jimenez-Asenjo, F. Perez Amoros, E. Rojo Torrecilla, *El Sindicalismo de Clase en España (1939-1977)* (pp. 159 and 188), Ediciones Peninsular, Barcelona, 1978.

5. Ibid. pp. 218-25.

6. Jose Maria Maravall, *Dictadura y Disentimiento Politico, Obreros y Estudiantes Bajo el Franquismo* (p. 82), Ediciones Alfaguara, Madrid, 1978.

7. *El Mercado de Trabajo en España, Secretaria General Tecnica Libros, Serie: Economia Española No. 4*, Madrid, 1982. See study by Salvador Garcia Atance (p. 21).

8. *Franco Visto por sus Ministros* (op. cit. p. 37). Pedro Gonzalez Bueno, Minister for the Syndicates 1938-39 quotes Franco as saying: 'It offends the dignity of a worker to eat standing by a machine.'

9. Maravall, *Dictadura y Disentimiento...* (op. cit. p. 40).
10. *El Mercado...* (op. cit.). See study by Felipe Saez Fernandez (p. 98).
11. *El Mercado...* (op. cit. pp. 108-9).
12. Comment to the author by Nicolas Redondo, March 1983.
13. These rights are broadly established in Article 7, and then amplified in Articles 35-37.
14. *El Mercado...* (op. cit. pp. 123-25) contains a useful summary of the main points of these agreements.
15. Figures supplied by CEOE.
16. *El Pais*, 25 April 1978.
17. Written reply to a questionnaire submitted by the author, March 1983.
18. Based on comments to the author by Fernando Abril Martorell, February 1983, and by Nicolas Redondo, March 1983.
19. See Sagardoy, Bengoechea, Blanco, *El Poder Sindical en España* (p. 71), Planeta, Barcelona, 1982, for studies of union members' attitudes.
20. Sagardoy ... (op. cit. pp. 127-32).
21. Documents of II Congress of Federacion Estatal Minera de CCOO. This also ties in with Sagardoy (op. cit. p. 145).
22. This estimate came from Jose Solis Ruiz in a TV programme on union assets. Solis was in charge of the Movimiento and delegate for the syndicates for twelve years. See also Sagardoy (op. cit. p. 152).
23. This meant that the two main unions benefitted at the expense of the others since they took over 60% of the vote.
24. *El Mercado...* (op. cit. p. 372) study by Jose Ignacio Perez Infante.
25. In the EEC on average, companies cover only 38·5% of total social security costs and the state 36·7%. The Spanish state contribution is more than four times smaller than the EEC norm, but is likely to be raised.
26. *El Mercado...* (op. cit. pp. 403-18) study by Rafael Gomez Perezagua.
27. In 1975 pensions and unemployment payments represented only 3·8% of GDP but by 1981 it had risen to 8·7%.
28. One important reason for the deficit has been the rapid rise in the non-payment of contributions. In 1981 non-payment was equivalent to 7% of total contributions and by 1983 almost 10%.
29. Comments to the author by SOC leader, Paco Casero. See also *El Pais*, 14 November 1983.
30. See *Tierra y Libertad*, 3 September 1982.
31. *Extremadura Saqueada* (p. 381-87), a collective study. Ruedo Iberico, Barcelona, 1978.
32. For a good glimpse of a Galician agricultural family, see Jose Yglesias, *The Franco Years* (pp. 243-72), Bobbs-Merril, New York, 1977.
33. Information supplied by the CCOO representative for industrial safety and health, Angel Carcoba.
34. Over 20% of the workforce handling asbestos is believed by CCOO to have had their health impaired in one form or another.
35. This was a sample prepared by CCOO, the union most concerned by these matters, on a very representative group of companies — 122 small, 63 medium sized and 38 large.
36. Figures drawn from a symposium on female employment, Madrid, October 1982, prepared by the women's section of CCOO — main paper, *Medidas de Fomento del Empleo Femenino*.

CHAPTER 7

1. The King's speech, written by the historian Pablo Fussi, paid homage to the Basque people, the first time their historic rights had been recognized by a head of state in more than a century.

2. Laureano Lopez Rodo, *La Larga Marcha hacia La Monarquia* (pp. 362-71), Editorial Noguer, Barcelona, 1977. 'The Kingdom which we, with the approval of the nation, have established owes nothing to the past; it springs from that decisive action of July 18 ...' Lopez Rodo gives by far the most complete account of Franco's moves over the succession.

3. Ibid. (p. 529). See text of a note submitted by Carrero Blanco to Franco dated 1 December 1946. Carrero Blanco was mainly concerned with the problems of heredity producing a 'bad' king, and did not question the principle of a monarch ruling Spain.

4. Victor Salmador, *Las Dos Españas y El Rey* (p. 93), Editorial Edilibro, Madrid, 1981. See comments by Serrano Suner.

5. *Santiago Carrillo, Dialogue on Spain*, interviewed by Regis Debray and Max Gallo (p. 168), Lawrence & Wishart, London, 1976.

6. Swearing before the Cortes on 23 July 1969, the Crown Prince said: 'Yes, I swear loyalty to your Excellency the Head of State and fidelity to the principles of the National Movement and all other Fundamental Laws of the Realm.'

7. Don Juan spent two and a half years on the British cruiser *Enterprise*. He justified his request by saying that the Civil War had become internationalized. See Lopez Rodo, *La Larga Marcha* (op. cit. p. 501).

8. See *Cuenta y Razon, No. 1, 1981*. 'España; Una Reconquista de la Libertad'.

9. Article 1.3 of the constitution.

10. Alfonso XIII abdicated in favour of Don Juan on 15 January 1941 and died on 28 February. The British Ambassador, Sir Samuel Hoare, noted that the houses in the back streets of Madrid were covered in black flags of mourning. See *Ambassador on a Special Mission* (pp. 292-93), Collins, London, 1946. Franco's attempts to suppress the manifestations of grief had ended in complete failure.

11. Xavier Tusell, *La Oposicion Democratica al Franquismo* (p. 33), Planeta, Barcelona, 1977.

12. Francisco Franco Salgado-Araujo, *Mis Conversaciones Privadas con Franco*, Planeta, Barcelona, 1976. For a typical conversation about the succession see p. 277. 'Franco keeps talking about the monarchy which appears to obsess him and no day passes without his saying something.' (p. 359).

13. Hoare, *Mission* (op. cit. p. 292).

14. For text of the Lausanne Manifesto see Lopez Rodo, *La Larga Marcha* (op. cit. pp. 48-50).

15. Pedro Sainz Rodriguez, *Un Reinado en la Sombra* (pp. 220-22), Planeta, Barcelona, 1981. Don Juan was convinced that he got the better of Franco in the meeting. When asked why he did not send his son to be educated in Spain, Don Juan replied: 'How am I going to send my son to Spain so long as it is considered a crime to shout *Viva el Rey*, while all monarchist propaganda is prohibited and my supporters are persecuted?' Franco almost certainly got the better of Don Juan.

16. Rodriguez, *Un Reinado...* (op. cit. p. 80).

17. See Lopez Rodo, *La Larga Marcha* (op. cit. pp. 193, 353, 638). Juan Carlos confided that he feared his father was sometimes badly advised. The monarchist Joaquin Satrustegui refers to the news of the designation of Juan Carlos as Franco's successor as being the 'bitterest days' of Don Juan's life.

18. Heleno Sana, *El Franquismo Sin Mitos* (p.356), Grijalbo, Barcelona, 1982.
19. Based on a conversation with Gen. Diez Alegria, November 1982.
20. Sainz Rodriguez, *Un Reinado...* (op. cit. pp.23, 94).
21. See interview with Alfonso de Borbon, *semanal Diario 16*, 14 November 1982. A divorce was granted in May 1982, an ecclesiastical tribunal having previously declared the marriage null — Alfonso de Borbon appealed against the latter sentence. General Salgado-Araujo recounts how in 1963 Franco commented that Alfonso de Borbon 'could be a solution [to the succession] if it does not work out with Don Juan Carlos'. See Salgado-Araujo, *Mis Conversaciones...* (op. cit. p.369).
22. See Lopez Rodo, *La Larga Marcha* (op. cit. pp.414-23).
23. Lopez Rodo, *La Larga Marcha* (op. cit. p.354).
24. Recounted to the author by General Diez Alegria, November 1982.
25. Alfonso was almost fifteen years old; the accident happened on Thursday of Holy Week, 29 March 1956.
26. Arias' own account in a collection of recollections by Franco ministers: *Franco Visto por Sus Ministros* (p.310), Planeta, Barcelona, 1981.
27. Based on comments to the author by Adolfo Suarez, April 1983.
28. The military had been especially impressed by Suarez's handling of the situation that arose after the death of five workers in clashes with police in Vitoria on 5 March 1976. There was a massively supported general strike in the Basque country and protest demonstrations in other cities. Interior Minister, Manuel Fraga, was out of the country and Suarez had to deputize.
29. Article 56.1. of the constitution.
30. The message concluded: 'The crown, symbol of the permanence and unity of the motherland, cannot tolerate in any form actions or attitudes by persons who seek to use force to break the democratic process laid down by the constitution which the Spanish people have duly endorsed in a referendum.'
31. Written reply to a questionnaire submitted to the Prime Minister, Felipe Gonzalez, March 1983.
32. Based on conversations with close colleagues of Adolfo Suarez, including Josep Melia, September 1983. See also Pilar Urbano, *Con la venia ... yo indague el 23F* (pp.52-54), Argos Vergara, Barcelona, 1982.
33. Based on comments to the author by Suarez, April 1983.

CHAPTER 8
1. For a full breakdown of the parties involved in UCD, see Jorge de Esteban, Luis Lopez Guerra, *Los Partidos Politicos en la España Actual* (pp.88-92), Planeta/Instituto de Estudios Economicos, Barcelona, 1982.
2. Based on comments to the author by Adolfo Suarez, April 1983.
3. In the March 1979 elections UCD dropped only 18,319 votes. Another reason for Suarez calling general elections in March was to lessen the impact of an anticipated swing to the left in the long-delayed municipal elections.
4. The Basque country, Catalonia and Galicia were allowed to negotiate autonomy under Article 151 of the constitution. This was a shorter process conceeded to 'historic' regions. For Andalusia to obtain autonomy under this article there had to be a referendum in which an absolute majority in each province approved this route. If the required majority was not obtained then Andalusia had to follow Article 143, which contained a more restrictive interpretation of the powers to be devolved by

Madrid. The difference in approach to autonomy was introduced by Suarez in December 1979 to halt a progressive slide towards de facto federalism. This change of policy would not have mattered had not Andalusia been expecting to be considered an 'historic' region. This provoked protests in Andalusia and, when the region embarked on the referendum to be included under Article 151, the government was in the unusual position of urging voters to vote against the proposal! The real motive for Suarez treating Andalusia in this way was his fear of a strong socialist presence in the autonomous parliament. When these elections were finally held in May 1982, the PSOE got 66 of the 109 seats and UCD only 15.

5. Based on comments to the author by Adolfo Suarez, April 1983. See also Josep Melia, *Asi Cayo Adolfo Suarez*, Planeta, Barcelona, 1981, for an account by one of his advisers and chief spokesman. Melia was part of Suarez's inner cabinet, known derisively as the 'plumbers'. Also Jose Oneto, *Los Ultimos Dias de un Presidente*, Planeta, Barcelona, 1981, for a journalistic background. For a fuller biography of Suarez, see Gregorio Moran, *Adolfo Suarez, Historia de Una Ambicion*, Planeta, Barcelona, 1979.

6. The title chosen was Duque de Suarez.

7. Jose Maria Maravall, *La Politica de la Transicion* (pp. 40-2), Taurus, Madrid, 1982.

8. Gerald Brenan, *The Spanish Labyrinth* (p. 218), Cambridge University Press, Cambridge, paperback edition 1980.

9. Felipe Gonzalez's father was a supporter of the UGT. From Santander, he moved to Seville in 1929 following the International Fair where his elder brother had found a job. The family settled in Puebla del Rio some twelve kilometres from Seville. Felipe, one of four children, was born on 5 March 1942. See Felipe Gonzalez, *Un Estila Etico, conversaciones con Victor Marquez Reviriego*, Argos Vergara, Barcelona, 1982, also Eduardo Chamorro, *Felipe Gonzalez*, Planeta, Barcelona, 1980. The latter has some useful background on his early political activism.

10. Jose Felix Tezanos, *Sociologia de Socialismo Español* (p. 176), Tecnos, Madrid, 1983.

11. See Maravall, *La Politica...* (op. cit.)

12. Tezanos, *Sociologia...* (op. cit. p. 122).

13. Felipe Gonzalez points out: 'In the history of Spanish socialism there has been no constancy regarding the model for Head of State... with the Party only attaching itself to the Republican cause at the end of the twenties when various circumstances had closed the channels of participation in the [political] system for large sectors of society. As a result, and backed by a profoundly renovated party in tune with the times, there were no difficulties and full support for the Constitution that established the parliamentary monarchy which is our form of government.' Written reply in March 1983 to author's question on the debate inside the PSOE over acceptance of the monarchy.

14. Tezanos, *Sociologia...* (op. cit. p. 93).

15. A survey of PSOE voters in the 1979 elections showed that 30% considered they came from the middle class, a 5% increase on 1977. On the other hand, 33% considered themselves working class compared to 37% in 1977.

16. Fernando Claudin, *Santiago Carrillo* (p. 254), Planeta, Barcelona, 1983.

17. Santiago Carrillo, born in Gijon in 1915, has had one of the most adventurous lives of any political figure of his generation. He was in prison during the Republic with Largo Caballero. At the outbreak of the Civil War he was caught trying to reach republican lines and was lined up against a wall to be shot, before being rescued. After the war, in exile, he travelled first to Moscow and then Latin America, returning via Portugal and French North Africa to Europe. He settled in Paris, unlike many of the

PCE members who had opted for Moscow. For some lively incidents of Carrillo's career, see *Santiago Carrillo, Dialogue on Spain* (pp. 75-80), Lawrence & Wishart, London, 1976.

18. Among those expelled was Manuel Azcarate, the party's chief foreign affairs spokesman and editor of the PCE's theoretical magazine, *Nuestra Bandera*. Azcarate explains his position in a bitter personal account — *Crisis del Euro-communismo*, Argos Vergara, Barcelona, 1982. One of the most interesting features of the book is Azcarate's description of how as a 'bourgeois' (his family were prominent intellectuals) he was never fully accepted in the party — even though he had done good party service, including several miserable years in Moscow. Another bitter comment on the internal workings of the party was Jorge Semprun's *Autobiografia de Federico Sanchez*, Planeta, Barcelona, 1977.

19. Claudin, *Santiago Carrillo* (op. cit. p. 388).

CHAPTER 9

1. The trial, known as Case 2/81, was held in a converted warehouse belonging to the Army Ordinance Survey Department at Campamento on the outskirts of Madrid. Only one civilian, Juan Garcia Carres, a prominent figure in the Francoist vertical syndicates, was charged. He was kept in a civilian prison (though mostly hospitalized) but tried by military justice.

2. Julio Busquets, *Pronunciamientos y Golpes de Estado en España*, Planeta, Barcelona, 1981; what a sorry reflexion on military interventionism that a book should even be published with this title.

3. In 1950 the War Ministry employed 128,178 men, Home Affairs 4,387, a third of whom worked in the post and telegraph service. See Diego Lopez Garrido, *La Guardia Civil y Los Origines del Estado Centralista* (pp. 115-22), Grijalbo, Barcelona, 1982.

4. *Colectivo Democracia, Los Ejercitos Mas Alla del Golpe* (p. 47), Planeta, Barcelona, 1981.

5. Julio Busquets was the first person to conduct a serious sociological study of the armed forces and was only able to do this because he himself was a soldier. His book, *El Militar de Carrera en España*, Ariel, Barcelona, 1972, was initially seized. He was also a founder member of the UMD.

6. George Hills, *Franco* (p. 155), Macmillan, New York, 1967.

7. Busquets, *Pronunciamientos...* (op. cit. pp. 175-77).

8. Busquets, *El Militar...* (op. cit. p. 269). See also Jose Luis Pitarch, *Diario Abierto de un Militar Constitucionalista* (pp. 44-46), Fernando Torres, Valencia, 1981.

9. Busquets, *El Militar...* (op. cit. p. 200).

10. Comment to the author by former Defence Minister, Alberto Oliart, March 1983.

11. Comment to the author by General Manuel Diez Alegria, November 1982.

12. General Pinilla, after leaving Zaragoza Academy in 1981, began a christian youth centre in a poor district of Madrid. The conservatives felt that Zaragoza had become too liberal under his guidance.

13. *Colectivo...* (op. cit. pp. 434-36) for text of UMD aims.

14. Based on comments to the author by General Diez Alegria.

15. Of the fifty-eight who voted against the Political Reform Law in 1976, fifteen were military.

16. For the text of General Alvarez Arenas' statement, see Pilar Urbano, *Con la venia ... yo indague el 23F* (p. 357), Argos Vergara, Barcelona, 1982.

17. Boadella was imprisoned for a play, *La Torna*, about a stateless East European, Heinz Chez, condemned to death by court martial in 1974. Pilar Miro's film was eventually reinstated after considerable legal battles and government intervention.
18. General Juste also ordered the take-over of the main television studios at Prado del Rey. These studios were temporarily occupied. At the court martial when he gave evidence, several of the accused muttered that he should have been charged with them. He was relieved prematurely of his command.
19. See Article 8 of the constitution.
20. See Title VI, Article 37, The Organic Law of State.
21. In August 1981, Milans del Bosch took offence at comments by Gutierrez Mellado. This resulted in the publication of a letter by Milans del Bosch of unparalleled virulence, which said among other things: 'It is clear that neither I nor anyone else can receive lessons of military ethics from you, for the simple reason you don't know what they are ... The only time you fought, instead of being at the front of your troops and in the face of the enemy, it was done in the dirty manner of a spy, double-faced, the dagger in the back! Wasn't that how you fought in what I call the War of Liberation and now is known as the Civil War?' See *El Alcazar*, 28 August 1981.
22. General Quintana Lacaci, as captain-general of Madrid, appealed against the sentence but it remained unchanged. The new law on military jurisdiction, permitting appeal of sentence to a civilian court, had yet to be approved.
23. Prior to this incident, General Atares had already been publicly sanctioned by General Gutierrez Mellado. On 24 November 1977, Atares gave such a negative assessment of the transition that Gutierrez Mellado ordered him from the room.
24. Maria Merida, *Mis Conversaciones con los Generales* (p.198), Plaza y Janes, Barcelona, 1979. This book was the first attempt to get the leading military commanders to express their views about democracy.
25. See Pilar Urbano, *Con la venia...* (op. cit.). Of all the books on 23 February, this is the sole to try and explain Cortina's role and that of the intelligence services. But the explanation is not convincing. For an account of the court martial, see Martin Prieto, *Tecnica de un Golpe de Estado*, Grijalbo, Barcelona, 1981. This is a brilliantly written daily journal of the trial, originally produced in *El Pais*.
26. Written reply to author's questionnaire, March 1983.
27. Oliart maintains the plot was far from being operational but insists on the seriousness of the intent. Some doubt was cast on its seriousness, in view of the timing of the discovery — at the opening of the electoral campaign — and the limited arrests. Three colonels, two of them brothers, were arrested.
28. This was a random period selection by the author.

CHAPTER 10
1. Cardinal Tarancon retired from the presidency of the Episcopal Conference in 1981 and from the Archbishopric of Madrid in 1983. The primate of Spain is traditionally the Archbishop of Toledo. However, the political importance of the Archbishopric of Madrid was underlined by Pope Paul VI's switching of Cardinal Tarancon from Toledo to Madrid.
2. A eulogistic commentary on Cardinal Tarancon's role was given by *El Pais*, 13 April 1983: 'Without exaggeration, one can say that the contribution of the man who until yesterday was Archbishop of Madrid made the course of Spanish life, though

perhaps inevitable, towards agreement, peace and the establishment of liberties, much easier and less dramatic. Not only did ordinary citizens benefit from this but also the Cardinal's own co-religionists, who transformed in a few years — thanks to the efforts of the grass roots christian community and new pastoral teachings — the archaic and obsolete image of the Church...'

3. See *Cinco Dias en la Vida del Cardenal*, ABC, *semanal*, 22 February 1981. This interview gives the most detailed description of these events.

4. Ibid. See also Maria Merida, *Entrevista con la Iglesia* (pp. 63-91), Planeta, Barcelona, 1982 for an interview with Cardinal Tarancon.

5. The main source for researching the fate of the clergy and religious orders during the Civil War is Antonio Montero, *La Persecucion Religiosa en España, 1936-9*, Madrid, 1961. Twelve bishops, 283 nuns, 4,184 priests, and 2,365 monks were reported killed. The bishops killed were Almeria, Barcelona, Ciudad Real, Guadix, Jaen, Lerida, Segorbe, Tarragona (a suffragan) and Teruel, plus two others with the rank of bishop — the apostolic administrators of Barbastro and Orihuela.

6. At the beginning of 1982 there were 23,039 priests spread throughout 65 dioceses — an average of one per 1,898 inhabitants. In 1868 the proportion was one per 420 inhabitants. As a sign of the changing times 53% of all parishes contain 500 people or less.

7. For the background to the Vatican negotiations under the Arias Government see Jose Maria de Areilza, *Diario de un Ministro de la Monarquia* (pp. 71-73, 78-80, 134-39), Planeta, Barcelona, 1977.

8. Article 16.3 of the constitution.

9. *España Hoy* (p. 291), Secretaria de Estado para la Informacion, Madrid, 1982.

10. *Ecclesia*, 23 October 1982.

11. *Ecclesia*, 23 October 1982.

12. Based on information supplied by Gonzalo Suarez, director-general of Religious Affairs, March 1983.

13. See Jose Antonio Martinez Soler, *Los Empresarios Ante la Crisis Economica* (pp. 24-26), Grijalbo, Barcelona, 1982.

14. According to Max Gallo, between 1931-51, Opus Dei secured almost a quarter of all university chairs. *Spain under Franco* (p. 133), George Allen & Unwin, London, 1973.

15. Alberto Ullastres in a conversation with the author, March 1983, insisted that the presence of Opus Dei members in the cabinet carrying out economic policy was unconnected with any Opus plan to gain access to power. He did not, however, deny that the Opus members were also friends, which made co-ordination easier.

16. Enrique Sendagorta has been known to approach senior members of the banking community seeking donations for Opus. Another banker frequently linked to Opus, former Bank of Spain governor and currently president of Banco de Madrid, Jose Maria Lopez de Letona, denied to the author that he was a member of Opus.

17. Jose Maria Ruiz-Mateos in various conversations with the author has insisted that Opus never helped him. But he never disapproved of or disavowed the organization.

18. For a description of attempts to persuade Cardinal Tarancon to endorse a christian democrat party, see Alfonso Osorio, *Trayectoria Politica de un Ministro de la Corona* (pp. 194-95), Planeta, Barcelona, 1980.

19. Comments to the author by Father Jose Maria Martin Patino, March 1983.

20. Jose Felix Tezanos, *Sociologia del Socialismo Español* (pp. 115-17), Editorial Tecnos, Madrid, 1983.

21. *Ecclesia*, 23 October 1982.

22. *España Hoy* (op. cit. p. 290).
23. A study of the top administrative posts in the sixties revealed that 14% considered themselves very good Catholics and 54% practising Catholics. Only 3% admitted to be non-practising. The two leading ministries where the top civil servants considered themselves to be good or practising Catholics were Justice and Education — the two key ministries for the Church. See Miguel Beltram, *La Elite Burocratica Española* (pp. 221-33), Ariel, Madrid, 1977, in association with Fundacion March.

CHAPTER 11
1. Based on information supplied to the author by Juan Luis Cebrian.
2. William Chislett, *The Spanish Media since Franco* (p. 15), Writers and Scholars Educational Trust, London, 1979. This booklet contains a very useful analysis of the role of the press during this period.
3. The most sensational case was a press conference held in Madrid by Santiago Carrillo on 10 December 1976. Carrillo had not been formally allowed to enter Spain (although he had done so in February wearing a wig) nor had the Communist Party been legalized. To present the authorities with a fait accompli he staged the press conference, challenging them to arrest him. He was duly arrested for a few days before Christmas but then released and allowed to stay in Spain.
4. The main offending articles were Article 2 of the 1966 Press Law and Article 165(b) of the Penal Code. Article 2 defined the limits of freedom that included respect for truth and morality, obedience to the laws of the Movimiento, safeguarding personal privacy and good reputations of families, and respect for state institutions and state security. The Penal Code covered much the same ground. These two articles were catch-alls for fines, seizure and suspension of publication.
5. See Article 12, Fuero de los Españoles, 1938.
6. See Chislett (op. cit. p. 8). Also, *Libertad de Prensa* (pp. 166-67), AEDE, Madrid, 1982. This is based on a course at the summer university of Menendey Pelayo, Santander.
7. On a careful formula of glossy pictures, chat and discreet scandal involving Spanish and international celebrities, *Hola* has consistently improved its sales. It is the fourth biggest selling weekly with 467,000 copies sold in 1982, against 367,000 in 1977.
8. In June 1983, damages were finally fixed at 518 million pesetas. This excluded the expropriation of the building and its destruction, since this was done under a separate legal device relating to the nature of the shares registered.
9. *El Pais*, 28 July 1981.
10. Gregorio Moran, *Adolfo Suarez, Historia de una Ambicion* (p. 218), Planeta, Barcelona, 1979. For a devastating inside account of Suarez's time at RTVE, see pages 201-51.
11. *El Pais*, 18 October 1981, domenical.
12. Jose Feliz Tezanos, *Sociologia del Socialismo Español* (p. 79), Tecnos, Madrid, 1983.
13. The political nature of the RTVE board of governors was underlined in early 1983 when a prearranged pact on representatives between the PSOE and AP nearly broke down because these candidates' approval was linked to concessions sought by AP over nominations to the Supreme Court.
14. In 1982, a major effort was made to ensure that reception was possible country-wide by improving relay stations. However, parts of the country in 1983 could still

only receive the first channel and needed special aerials for the second channel if they could get it at all. Less effort was made with the signals of this, the slightly more 'highbrow' channel.
15. *El Pais*, 17 February 1983.
16. Antonio Guarrigues Walker (father) was Justice Minister in the Arias Government. One of the Fontan brothers, Antonio, was associated with Opus Dei.
17. The main shares have been held by Antonio Garcia Trevijano and Jesus de Polanco. The latter was considered the leading shareholder in 1983 with over 25%.
18. Based on comments by Adolfo Suarez to the author, March 1983.

CHAPTER 12
1. *El Pais*, 15-21 February 1981.
2. Diego Lopez Garrido, *La Guardia Civil y los Origines del Estado centralista* (pp. 192-93), Critica, Grijalbo, Barcelona, 1982. This book gives a useful background to the establishment and early operations of the Guardia Civil.
3. The most controversial incident has been the 'Almeria Case', which concerned the deaths of three youths from Santander in May 1981. They hired a car in Ciudad Real and drove it to Almeria for a family celebration. The youths were considered suspicious in a week that had seen two major terrorist actions in Madrid (including an ETA attempt on the life of General Valenzuela, head of the King's military household). They were detained in Almeria, interrogated and, according to the official version, were being driven in convoy to Madrid when they tried to escape. An escorting Guardia Civil vehicle fired at the back of their car, hitting the fuel tank. Trapped in the car, they were burned to death. There were many discrepancies in this version. The youths, for instance, were handcuffed in the back of the car; their escorts managed to escape; the bullet holes in the back near the fuel tank were neat; and it was most unusual for terrorist suspects to be driven in their own car. Eventually the Guardia Civil colonel in charge of the convoy was prosecuted along with three others for failure to carry out his duty, but the private manslaughter charges were never upheld. Lawyers for the family of the dead suspected they had been tortured and it was a deliberate killing.
4. See the reports of Amnesty International 1976-80. In the first six months of the socialist government, 160 instances of torture were reported. See *Tiempo*, 4 April 1983. Initially it was very difficult to bring police torturers to trial. One case concerning a Basque labour militant, finally brought before the courts in 1983, had been consistently obstructed by the Ministry of the Interior since 1979. (See *El Pais*, 24 March 1983.) The most difficult aspect was not to prove torture but to identify those responsible.
5. The Guardia Civil in 1983 accepted national servicemen in the force but there was no suggestion of changing its image. One of the most disturbing features of both the Guardia Civil and the Policia Nacional has been the high instance of persons killed while refusing to stop in front of patrols.
6. Article 117 of the constitution.
7. Alejandro Nieto, *La Noche oscura de la Funcion Publica* (p. 18), Quadernos Economicos de ICE, numero 13, Madrid, 1980. This issue is entirely devoted to the civil service and its reform. It was the first officially tolerated critique, the publication being run from the Ministry of Commerce.
8. Felipe Gonzalez, in written replies to author's questions, March 1983. 'I think one

of UCD's greatest failings in office was its incapacity to undertake a serious reform and democratization of the Administration — for this is an historic challenge facing Spanish society and is one of the priorities of the present Socialist government.'

9. In 1982, the central government employed 711,107 persons of which 380,916 were civilians and 251,478 were members of the armed forces and security forces. The remainder were on contract. In addition, the autonomous governments employed 76,876 as permanent civil servants and another 110,000 on contract.

10. The enclaves of Ceuta and Melilla were not included in the autonomy process and were run by military governors until 1980.

11. Article 2 of the constitution.

12. Andres Cassinello Perez, *Seminario sobre Terrorismo Internacional — ETA y el Problema Vasco*, Madrid, 10-12 June 1982. This paper is the most comprehensive analysis of ETA from a semi-official point of view with access to police files. Of the 239 ETA members arrested in 1980-81, only 58% had both parents Basque and 23% had no Basque antecedents. The social composition of those detained was 134 working class, 57 middle, and 48 upper class.

13. Comment by Guerra to a group of foreign correspondents in October 1982. Guerra has a more powerful intellect and a more acerbic tongue than Gonzalez. Though Guerra is two years Gonzalez' senior, the two have developed a remarkable intuitive relationship.

14. Jose Felix Tezanos, *Sociologia del Socialismo español* (p. 145), Tecnos, Madrid, 1983.

15. In the elections, UGT obtained thirteen deputies in the Cortes and nine senators. The CCOO under the PCE flag obtained no seats.

16. Italy was the country that came closest to Spain with an increase in industrial wages during this period of 26%. See Bank of Spain annual reports 1981, 1982, and 1983.

17. Free public education was established by the Mayano Law of 1857. This covered schooling from age six to twelve. This was expanded to six to fourteen in 1945.

18. Subsidies began in 1972. Initially they were very small. The main increase came after Franco's death, being only 9 billion pesetas in 1975.

19. Another reflection of the lack of indigenous technology is the limited use of domestic patents. Only 21% of patents are domestic compared with 40% in the UK and 50% in West Germany. At the same time Spain spends 3·6% of GDP on royalties and licences for imported technology, compared to 1·7% of GDP in the UK.

20. *El Pais*, June 1983. Also based on comments to the author by Francisco Bustelo, rector of Madrid University, November 1980.

21. In 1970, police detained 5,419 persons for drug offences — 54% were for trafficking and the rest for possession. By 1982, 78% of detentions were for trafficking. It was essentially an urban phenomenon, like attacks on pharmacies. Of the 716 pharmacies attacked in 1981, 533 were in Madrid, and 42 in Barcelona.

22. The divorce bill became law in June 1981. In 1981 there were 9,483 divorces and in 1982, 22,578.

Select Bibliography

Books referring to specific topics are mentioned in the Notes and are not necessarily included in this select list.

GENERAL

Brenan, Gerald	*The Spanish Labyrinth* (Cambridge, 1943)
	The Literature of the Spanish People (Cambridge, 1951)
Burrow, George	*The Bible in Spain* (London, 1842)
Carr, Raymond	*Spain 1808-1939* (Oxford, 1969)
	Modern Spain (Oxford, 1980)
Castro, Americo	*La Realidad Historica de España* (Mexico, 1966)
Cierva, Ricardo de la	*Historia basica de la España actual* (Madrid, 1974)
Entwistle, William	*The Spanish Language* (London, 1936)
Jackson, Gabriel	*Historian's Quest* (New York, 1969)
Madariaga, Salvador de	*Spain, a Modern History* (London, 1946)
Ortega y Gasset, Jose	*España Invertebrada* (Madrid, 1922)
Pritchett, V.S.	*The Spanish Temper* (London, 1954)
Vilar, Pierre	*Histoire d'Espagne* (Paris, 1965)
Vincens Vives, Jaimie	*Aproximacion a la historia de España* (Barcelona, 1952)

THE CIVIL WAR

Beevor, Anthony	*The Spanish Civil War* (London, 1982)
Carr, Raymond (ed.)	*The Republic and the Civil War in Spain* (London, 1971)
Cierva, Ricardo de la	*Historia de la Guerra Civil española* (Madrid, 1969)
	Historia illustrada de la Guerra Civil española (Barcelona, 1970)
Fraser, Ronald	*Blood of Spain* (London, 1979)
Jackson, Gabriel	*A concise history of the Spanish Civil War* (Princeton, 1969)
Payne, Stanley	*The Spanish Revolution* (New York, 1970)
Thomas, Hugh	*The Spanish Civil War* (London, 1971)

FRANCO AND FRANCOISM

Bayod, Angel (ed.)	*Franco visto por sus ministros* (Barcelona, 1981)
Cierva, Ridardo de la	*Historia del Franquismo* (Barcelona, 1975)
Crozier, Brian	*Franco* (London, 1967)
Escuredo, Vincente Pozuelo	*Los ultimos 476 dias de Franco* (Barcelona, 1980)
Gallo, Max	*Spain under Franco* (London, 1973)
Hill, George	*Franco* (London, 1971)
Medhurst, Kenneth	*Government in Spain* (Oxford, 1973)
Miguel, Amando de	*Sociologia del Franquismo* (Barcelona, 1975)
Preston, Paul (ed.)	*Spain in Crisis* (London, 1976)
Salgado-Araujo, Francisco	*Francisco Franco, Mis Conversaciones Privadas con Franco* (Barcelona, 1976)
Sana, Heleno	*Franquismo sin Mitos* (Barcelona, 1981)
Tamames, Ramon	*La Republica; la era de Franco* (Madrid, 1973)
Tunon de Lara, Manuel, & Biescas, Jose Antonio	*Espana bajo la Dictadura Franquista* (Barcelona, 1980)
Trythall, J.W.D.	*Franco: A Biography* (London, 1970)
Vilar, Sergio	*La naturaleza del franquismo* (Barcelona, 1977)
Yglesias, Jose	*The Franco Years* (New York, 1977)

TRANSITION AND THE MONARCHY

Areilza, Jose Maria de	*Diaro de un ministro de la Monarquia* (Barcelona, 1977)
Ben Ami, Shlomo	*La revolucion desde arriba: España 1936-79* (Barcelona, 1980)
Carr, Raymond and Fusi, Juan Pablo	*España, de la dictadura a la democracia* (Barcelona, 1979)
Lopez Rodo, Laureano	*La larga marcha hacia la Monarquia* (Barcelona, 1978)
Maravall, Jose Maria	*La politica de la transicion 1975-81* (Madrid, 1981)
Osorio, Alfonso	*Trayectoria politica de un ministro de la Corona (Barcelona, 1980)
Sainz Rodriguez, Pedro	*Un reinade en la sombra* (Barcelona, 1981)
Salmador, Victor	*Las dos Españas y El Rey* (Barcelona, 1981)
Tusell, Xavier	*La oposicion democratica al franquismo* (Barcelona, 1977)

CONTEMPORARY POLITICS

Azcarate, Manuel	*Crisis del Eurocomunismo* (Barcelona, 1982)
Chamorro, Eduardo	*Felipe Gonzalez* (Barcelona, 1980)
Claudin, Fernando	*Santiago Carillo* (Barcelona, 1983)
Estaban, Jorge de and Guerra, Luis Lopez	*Los partidos politicos en la España actual* (Barcelona, 1982)
Melia, Josep	*Asi cayo Adolfo Suarez* (Barcelona, 1981)

Moran, Gregorio	*Adolfo Suarez* (Barcelona, 1979)
	Los españoles que Dejaron de serlo (Barcelona, 1982)
Reviriego, Victor Marquez	*Felipe Gonzalez, un estilo etico* (Barcelona, 1982)

THE TRADES UNIONS

Bengoechea, J.A., Sagardoy, J.A. and Blanco, David Leon	*El poder sindical en España* (Barcelona, 1982)
Camacho, Marcelino	*Charlas en la prision* (Barcelona, 1976)
Maravall, Jose Maria	*Dictadura y Disentimiento politico, Obreros y Estudiantes Bajo el Franquismo* (Madrid, 1978)
Morcillo, Alejandro et al.	*El sindicalismo de clase en España 1939-77* (Barcelona, 1978)
Sartorius, Nicolas	*El Resurgir del Movimiento Obrero* (Barcelona, 1976)
	El sindicalismo del nuevo tipo (Barcelona, 1977)
Tunon de Lara, Manuel	*El movimiento obrero en la historia de España* (Madrid, 1972)

THE MILITARY

Busquets, Julio	*El militar de carrera en España* (Barcelona, 1972)
	Pronunciamientos y golpes de estado en España (Barcelona, 1982)
Colectivo Democracia	*Los Ejercitos mas all del golpe* (Barcelona, 1981)
Merida, Maria	*Mis conversaciones con los generales* (Barcelona, 1979)
Payne, Stanley	*Politics and the Military in modern Spain* (Stamford, 1967)
Prieto, Martin	*Tecnica de un golpe de Estado* (Barcelona, 1982)
Urbano, Pilar	*Con la venia ... yo indague el 23-F* (Barcelona, 1982)

THE ECONOMY

Banco de Bilbao	*Una historia de la banca privada en España* (Bilbao, 1982)
Banco Urquijo	*La Economia Española en la decada de los 80* (Madrid, 1980)
Lasuen, Jose Ramon	*La España Mediocratica* (Barcelona, 1979)
Leal, Jose Luis	*Una political economica para España* (Barcelona, 1982)
Liberman, Sima	*The Contemporary Spanish Economy* (London, 1982)
Malefakis, Edward	*Agrarian reform and Peasant Revolution in Spain* (Yale, 1970)
Ministerio del Commercio	*Crisis y reforma de la economia Española, 1979-82* (1982)
	El mercardo de trabajo en España (1982)
	La internacionalisacion de la empresa española: inversiones españolas en el exterior (1981)

308

Tamames, Ramon — *Introduction a la economia española* (Madrid, 1973)
La oligarquia financiera en España (Barcelona, 1977)

Tortella Casares, G. — *Banking, railroads, and industry in Spain 1824-1874* (New York, 1977)

Vinas, Angel et al. — *Politica commercial exterior en España 1931-1975* (Madrid, 1977)

Wright, Alison — *The Spanish Economy 1959-1976* (London, 1976)

Appendices

APPENDIX A

General election results 1977-82

	1977 votes	seats	1979 votes	seats	1982 votes	seats
PSOE	5,358,781	118	5,469,813	121	10,127,392	202
AP	1,524,758	16	1,067,732	9	5,478,533	106
UCD	6,337,288	166	6,268,890	168	1,494,667	12
PCE	1,718,026	20	1,911,217	23	865,267	4
CiU	—	—	483,353	8	772,726	12
CDS	—	—	—	—	604,309	2
PNV	314,409	8	275,292	7	395,656	8
HB	—	—	172,110	3	210,600	2
ERC	143,409	1	123,452	1	138,116	1
EE	60,312	1	85,677	1	100,326	1
Others	2,850,908	20	2,075,354	17	736,385	—
Eligible voters	23,616,546	—	26,852,885	—	26,517,393	—
Turnout %	77		67		78	

Source: Ministry of Interior

The increase in the size of the electorate in 1979 was due to the inclusion of eighteen-year-olds

The number of seats refers to the 350-seat Cortes and excludes the 208 members of the Senate

APPENDIX B

Growth in urban population (millions)

	1930	1950	1960	1970	1981
Madrid	1·08	1·62	2·26	3·15	3·19
Barcelona	1·08	1·28	1·56	1·74	1·75
Valencia	0·45	0·51	0·50	0·65	0·75
Seville	0·31	0·37	0·44	0·55	0·65
Zaragoza	0·24	0·26	0·35	0·48	0·59
Malaga	0·24	0·27	0·30	0·37	0·50
Bilbao	0·19	0·23	0·29	0·41	0·43
Rest of Spain	22·28	23·43	24·8	26·69	29·88
Total	25·87	27·97	30·52	34·04	37·74

Source: INE

All figures have been rounded off

APPENDIX C

Historic changes in active population (in percentages)

	Agriculture/ Fishing	Industry	Services
1897	73·7	21·4	4·9
1920	59·2	22·0	18·8
1960	41·7	31·8	26·5
1970	29·1	37·3	33·6
1979	20·4	34·4	45·2

Source: Banco de Bilbao

APPENDIX D

Changes in educational level of active population (in percentages)

	1964	1980
Illiterate/primary schooling	93·3	72·4
Secondary/technical education	5·2	24·2
Higher education	1·5	3·4
Total	100·0	100·0

Source: Survey of active population, INE.

311

APPENDIX E

Changes in structure of wage earners (in percentages)

	1963	1970	1976
Technicians with degrees	1·4	2·3	3·0
Technicians without degrees	3·1	3·8	5·0
Administrative staff	12·9	16·9	19·0
Skilled workers	36·5	37·6	39·8
Unskilled workers	46·1	39·4	33·2
Total	100·0	100·0	100·0

Source: Survey of active population, INE

APPENDIX F

Real hourly earnings (average annual percentage increase)

	74	75	76	77	78	79	*accumulated*
SPAIN	8·9	9·9	10·7	4·5	5·5	6·8	56·0
Italy	2·4	8·2	3·8	7·1	3·3	2·8	30·9
France	4·8	4·9	4·1	3·0	3·5	2·1	24·6
West Germany	2·4	2·6	2·4	3·6	0·1	3·1	15·0
UK	1·4	1·6	6·9	-10·4	5·1	2·0	5·9
US	-2·4	-0·4	2·1	2·6	0·8	-2·6	0·0

Source: OECD

APPENDIX G

Labour unrest by regions (as percentage of total hours lost)

	1970-74 average	1979	1980	1981	1982
Andalusia	4·3	11·5	32·9	20·5	15·2
Aragon	0·8	3·0	5·4	3·6	5·9
Asturias	23·2	5·3	13·0	10·0	18·1
Balearic Islands	—	0·4	0·5	0·3	0·7
Basque Country	28·4	24·0	**	**	**
Canaries	0·6	2·7	3·8	9·5	1·3
Cantabria	0·3	0·7	0·6	6·8	5·1
Castille-Leon	5·8	6·2	3·5	2·4	2·4
Castille-La Mancha	0·3	0·4	0·9	1·6	1·8
Catalonia	22·4	13·7	***	***	***
Extremadura	0·1	0·2	0·1	0·5	0·1
Galicia	4·6	2·9	7·6	5·8	6·4
Madrid	4·0	9·8	8·3	17·0	26·2
Murcia	—	1·0	2·5	1·8	2·9
Navarre	4·6	7·0	5·1	2·6	3·9
Rioja	—	1·2	—	0·4	—
Valencia	0·6	10·0	15·8	17·2	10·0
Total	100·0	100·0	100·0	100·0	100·0

Source: Ministry of Labour

** Basque Country figures unavailable for 1980-82
*** Catalonia figures unavailable for 1980-82
Figures supplied by the CEOE in both these regions for these periods suggest that the Basque Country accounted on average for 25% of all hours lost and Catalonia for 12%

Index